W9-DIS-683

A BAD NEIGHBORHOOD AT 3 A.M. . . .

Suddenly, two figures with drawn swords stood before Alaire and the drunken prince. Drawing his own weapon, Alaire rushed one assailant. The other assassin engaged Kai, who, a little slow in getting his own blade out, was being beaten back in a staggering semicircle. Meanwhile, almost as if it had been choreographed, Alaire's man recovered, forcefully parried, sidestepped, and lunged—at Kai, plunging his blade in the prince's unprotected side, and wrenching it out with a hideous sucking sound. Then the killers, apparently satisfied with their work, ran off.

Kai lay face up in the snow, staring blankly. A stain spread over his tunic and shirt. He opened his mouth to speak, but couldn't, though the wound in his side spoke for him. He was going to die. Unless— Alaire ripped open the pack protecting his harp. He fought the urge to weep. There wasn't time.

Don't think! Don't think of anything. Just feel the magic . . . the power. . . .

He took a deep breath, centered himself, and started to play. As he ran through the song once, twice, Kai remained still, even peaceful in the snow. Then, with one spastic motion, the boy gave a deep sigh. Then nothing. The Magic had failed.

Alaire stared emptily at his friend as snow that a moment before had melted as it touched began to lay a lacy shroud.

In the silence suddenly he could hear his Master's voice: *"The essence of Bardic Magic is the ability to make, and unmake."* To unmake Death—and make Life?

Again Alaire began to sing—but this time his mind and heart focused on the faint, fading tendrils of Kai's life source, followed them inward, imagined Kai's wound closing, the tiny folds of tissue reassembling, knitting, binding, the blood vessels sealing, cauterized with Light. Then he imagined new blood slowly filling Kai's veins, restoring what had been lost. At some point he stopped playing Naitachal's tune; a new one had taken form, and was playing *him.*

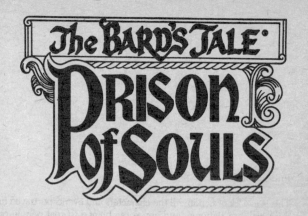

The Bard's Tale®
PRISON of SOULS

MERCEDES LACKEY
&
MARK SHEPHERD

BAEN

PRISON OF SOULS

This is a work of fiction. All the characters and events portrayed in this book are fictional, and any resemblance to real people or incidents is purely coincidental.

Copyright © 1993 by Mercedes Lackey and Mark Shepherd

All rights reserved, including the right to reproduce this book or portions thereof in any form.

A Baen Books Original

The Bard's Tale characters and descriptions are the sole property of Electronic Arts and are used by permission. *The Bard's Tale* is a registered trademark of Electronic Arts.

Baen Publishing Enterprises
P.O. Box 1403
Riverdale, NY 10471

ISBN: 0-671-72193-3

Cover art by Larry Elmore

First printing, November 1993

Distributed by Simon & Schuster
1230 Avenue of the Americas
New York, NY 10020

Printed in the United States of America

Chapter I

"Let's begin," Naitachal said, casting his black cloak to one side and raising his practice sword in salute. "And see if you can get through *this* drill without tripping over yourself." He smiled, softening the sarcasm just a little. Few ever saw a Dark Elf smile and survived to tell about it; but Naitachal's smile meant only what any human's would, and it warmed his cold blue eyes in a way that no other Dark Elf could match.

His apprentice Alaire returned the salute with his practice sword, and stifled a sardonic reply.

This time, Master Naitachal, you'd better watch out, Alaire thought as he checked his footing on the coarse gravel. *I've been practicing while you were away!*

They faced each other on the small practice field of the Dark Elf's modest estate. Alaire was a head taller than his mentor, but Naitachal had decades of experience. Both were slender, rather than heavily muscled. At high noon the sun shone directly from above, a disadvantage to neither swordsmen.

The contest began, a graceful dance of flesh and wood, their oak swords clacking away in the bright sun. Alaire lunged early, catching Naitachal by surprise. But the elf parried and thrust easily, slipping out of the trap the youth was setting up, trying to pin the elf against a tree. Alaire charged, using his blade like a broadsword, and using his greater reach to force his Master to the edge of the field. Naitachal tucked and rolled, becoming a blur of black motion that vanished behind Alaire before he turned, then reappeared at the periphery of Alaire's vision.

"I thought you said no magic!" Alaire protested, fielding a counterattack with difficulty.

"None used," Naitachal said smoothly. "Pay attention to the sword, lad."

Alaire yielded to Naitachal's powerful, but measured thrusts, hoping to gain control of the contest. The Dark Elf tripped and wavered momentarily as he lost his balance, but gained it back quickly.

"Good move," Naitachal said, as their weapons clacked; the contest fell into a mesmerizing rhythm as Alaire probed for a weakness in the Dark Elf's defense. "Ten more of those and we might come out even."

The bardling grinned; he liked how his teacher turned praise into a demand for more and better effort. It kept the game interesting.

Alaire sensed that the Dark Elf was intentionally ignoring his weaker left side. Only yesterday Naitachal had drilled him endlessly, attacking on his left, until that side ached. Now . . . nothing. Even as he considered this, Naitachal sidestepped off the field, ducked behind a tree and came out on the weaker left.

Alaire was ready. Instead of backpedaling he lunged again. The tip of the sword touched the edge of Naitachal's black tunic, but no more; the elf had sidestepped. Alaire cursed softly, catching a glint of amusement in Naitachal's dark blue eyes.

Anger surged briefly over him as the swords clashed, though Naitachal was only doing what any Master should. The pace of the combat increased. The two moved back towards the center of the practice field, kicking up dust in the process. Naitachal was not going to relinquish his control of the combat that easily. The

Dark Elf's breathing was a little more labored now. After first faking high to lure Alaire's point away from his intended target, the elf came in low with his sword. Alaire deflected it, knocking the elf's swordtip into the dirt. If he'd parried a little harder, he might have disarmed his Master, and that would have been a first.

Too easy. Far too easy, Alaire thought, wondering what distracted his mentor today. *Normally he would have landed me on my backside by now.* He knew he was an average swordsman; Naitachal was a master, with uncounted years of practice behind him. Was something wrong? Had the elf learned something on his last journey to cause him worry?

The bardling's thoughts wandered slightly, enough to give the Dark Elf an advantage.

"Look!" Naitachal shouted, pointing with his free hand. "A comet!"

Alaire looked without thinking, following Naitachal's gaze and pointing finger, to something above and behind him. As his attention wavered, Naitachal dropped his own blade to the side and shouldered into him. The next second, he was sitting in the dust in an undignified heap.

Naitachal regarded him calmly with disappointment and faint, elven amusement. "I can't believe you fell for that, bardling."

"Not fair!" Alaire protested weakly, somehow managing to laugh at himself. *Boy, was that stupid. Fell, or rather stepped, right into that one.* "I was winning and you cheated."

"If you were *really* winning you wouldn't be sitting there like that," Naitachal said. "We're getting to the point in your training when almost anything is fair. The real world is like that. Assassins," he added, his sword waving in the sunlight as if to punctuate the sentence, "will go to any lengths to kill their mark."

"What would an assassin want with me?" he replied, but only half seriously. *Someone might want me dead, if only to get at my father.* Being the eighth son of the King put him in an awkward position. Derek, the first born and oldest brother, would almost certainly become king one day. The other brothers were training for important government or military positions.

Yet, the King had never planned on having so many sons. As he once half-complained to the Queen, any other woman would have produced *at least* a few daughters along the way. Eventually he ran out of things to do with them.

Alaire, being the eighth and youngest son, enjoyed the rare luxury of choosing his life's work. He had been a very precocious child, and at six, he had decided to become a Bard. Fortunately, Naitachal was an old friend of the King as well as a loyal friend to many generations of the family. No one questioned who his Master would be.

This had not been a childish whim, but a real vocation. Naitachal had been able to assure the King that his son's talent was considerable, and that all would be well.

In many ways, his choice of lifework made him a less likely mark. The older brothers would certainly make better targets than he would. However, Alaire could not ignore the possibility that he could be singled out by young toughs looking for a fight. Naitachal had often pointed this out when he was sitting in the dust after a thorough trouncing.

For a year Alaire had trained under the King's Bard Laureate, Gawaine, and under his guidance convinced everyone that he had an exceptional degree of musical, and magical, talent. However, Gawaine was getting no younger; he had other students besides Alaire, as well as the enormous burden demanded by his office of Laureate. Gawaine eventually found it increasingly difficult to keep up with the workload. Since Alaire was hardly an ordinary, common student, Gawaine had known he ran the risk of favoring him over the other bardlings. It would have been a situation fraught with trouble for a younger man than Gawaine; for the Laureate, it was something he simply did not have the strength to deal with.

By this time Alaire was eight, and he had heard enough tales about Naitachal to be both excited and alarmed by having him as his Master. Though he had "always" assumed Naitachal would be his teacher, he certainly didn't know what to expect from the mysterious elf; the Necromancer's becoming a Bard was bizarre enough. He had never seen a Dark Elf before; he'd had no notion that his father had used the name "Dark Elf" so literally.

In the bright, airy colors of the court, Naitachal had stood out like a drop of ink on a white lace tablecloth. The black cloak he wore habitually flowed about him as if it were liquid, and the tunic, hose and boots seemed to absorb whatever light hit them, as if the Bard's body was a place that canceled daylight. Topping the darkness was his straight, silver hair that hung down his back, long as all elves wore it, and swept gracefully from side to side as he turned. His brilliant blue eyes, twin pools of color in the smooth black skin of that ageless face, burned right through Alaire when they first met. They distracted him, even now, during sword practice. Alaire soon found out Naitachal was no ordinary Dark Elf, if there *could* be such a thing. The somber darkness that seemed to follow him wherever he went was only deceptive camouflage; within lurked an absurdly cheerful Bard, a master of his trade, as well as a teacher of other, more practical skills.

Naitachal had often reminded him of his royal obligations and duties, and the possibility that one day he might be nearer the throne than he was now. However, this was the first time Naitachal had mentioned assassins.

It disturbed him at first, but after a moment of reflection, he shrugged it off. Sometimes the meaning of the elf's words didn't become clear for days or even weeks.

He's probably talking about years from now, when I join Father's court. Right now, the prospect of Alaire's ever having to deal with an assassin seemed vague. How would an assassin get out here near Fenrich, this remote village on the northeast coast? And once here, how could he ever be less than conspicuous?

Alaire loved this place, its peace and quiet, although he knew it would probably drive his brothers mad with boredom to stay here for more than a day. It seemed the ideal location to learn Bardic skills as well as magic; after all, there were few distractions here to speak of.

Naitachal had chosen this location to settle, in part because of the isolation, but also because the village folk readily accepted him as himself. His money was good, after all. In times of trouble Naitachal had generously given his time and magical expertise, winning considerable popularity among the townsfolk.

Alaire stood and brushed the dust off his breeches, nursing some pride back into his damaged ego.

"Living out here on the edge of the kingdom doesn't change your lineage," Naitachal reminded him. "There's always the chance some enemy of your father's may want to kidnap you and hold you for ransom. This is more likely to happen, though the same people often kidnap or kill with equal indifference."

"Perhaps," he said, acknowledging Naitachal's

warning, but not really believing he could ever be a target. At least, not while he was a mere bardling, and under Naitachal's supervision. First, so few people knew he even existed, and even fewer knew he was way out here, Next Door to Nowhere. He didn't like the sudden serious turn the conversation had taken, but then what could one expect from a Dark Elf? Despite Naitachal's cheer he sometimes lapsed into the gloom and doom of his own kind. The bardling had met only a few Dark Elves, who were far more morbid than his Master had ever been.

No, it was probably just that Naitachal was having one of those relapses into depression. Probably no one remembered his existence, outside his own family. Alaire could almost forget his royal blood out here on the outskirts of the kingdom.

It's a good thing I'm the eighth son. I know I could never handle being king. Lucky Derek, he has the throne and all its responsibilities to look forward to. By now he must feel like an actor in a play, with all his lines and actions written out for him.

Alaire struggled to his feet and answered Naitachal's salute with one of his own.

"We aren't finished *yet*," the Dark Elf said.

As if I was worried we might not be, Alaire thought, heeding the challenge nevertheless.

Naitachal struck with a vengeance, taking Alaire by surprise. *What's gotten into him?* The boy thought as he frantically defended himself. The elf *was* attacking his left side, just as he had the day before.

He did his best, but it became painfully evident that either Naitachal had been toying with him earlier, or else he *had* been distracted by something and was now leveling his full concentration on the bout. Within moments, Alaire was struggling just to keep from being scored on.

Within a few breaths, it was obvious that he was not going to manage even that.

"Hit," Naitachal declared; the swordpoint wavered just above his heart. "You're dead."

Alaire froze, then dropped his swordpoint to the ground.

They both bowed, formally, as the etiquette of Swordmaster and pupil demanded. Then both grinned, and Alaire wiped sweat from his forehead with his sleeve.

"Let's take a break," Naitachal said, "then back to work."

"I was about ready for a breather," Alaire admitted, omitting the real reason he wanted to stop: he wanted a drink to wash away the dust he'd eaten.

They set their wooden swords on a small rack near the practice field and went to the well beside the front door. Dipping a ladle into the bucket of ice-cold water, Alaire drank deeply, clearing his mouth of the dirt.

Naitachal drank too, though he didn't seem winded or even truly tired. *His folk have a constitution we humans can only dream of,* the bardling thought with envy, at the same time uttering a brief prayer to the gods that be that he would never have to fight an elf for real. *The practices are hell enough!*

Naitachal's age was as much an enigma now as it had been when Alaire first met him. From some of the old songs and tales, Alaire learned that he had been around in King Amber's time. Even then he was old by human standards.

Now's a good time to ask him again, Alaire thought. *He might even answer.* He'd met only with annoying silence every other time he'd inquired.

"You know, you seem to be holding up well for someone as, well, *old* as you," Alaire ventured, cautiously. Naitachal frowned; but then, he usually did when *that* question came up. The bardling's words still came out wrong, as if his mouth assumed a will of its own whenever he asked something personal about his Master. Inwardly, Alaire winced. He didn't want to annoy the elf, particularly when the swords were within reach. The next bout might be even harder! "How old *are* you, Master?"

The elf took his time answering. Alaire wondered if he had ignored what had become a rather rude question, or had chosen not to hear it.

"You're all of nineteen years old, young bardling," Naitachal began softly, after drinking from the ladle. His eyes softened, and Alaire sighed in relief. "A mere infant. A toddler. At best, a child." He smiled wistfully, as if considering a secret, amusing thought. "I am old by your standards."

Alaire waited, but the elf did not answer.

"Well?" Alaire asked.

"Older than you think," he said, "and not as old as the hills or the trees." That seemed to be the end of that.

The boy shrugged, deciding to drop that particular line of questioning, but his curiosity still burned. *Naitachal served King Amber. From what Father told me, he was quite the hero. He mentioned that he was involved with doing away with Carlotta.* He shivered whenever he thought of the evil princess who had tried to seize the throne by kidnapping the rightful heir, Prince Amber. The story had real meaning in his family. His descent from Amber gave it more impact than "just a tale." This particular bedtime story had places where Father would say, "And then Amber used to say . . ." or "Gawaine told me that Kevin . . ."

Carlotta failed, and then vanished. Years later she reappeared and hatched a plot involving Count Volmar and a book of Bardic spells. Gawaine's own teacher, Kevin, had searched for the book in Volmar's library, found it, and used it to defeat her.

That was all Alaire knew about the incident. The royal family seldom *discussed* it, even among relatives, and kept the details to themselves. Alaire knew there was some kind of scandal the royal family wanted to keep hushed up, but he didn't know the details.

Perhaps Naitachal knows.

"I feel more comfortable with the sword now, Master Naitachal," Alaire ventured. "It's becoming a part of me, as you said it would. I'm sorry I came to you with such holes in my education. My brother Grant promised me training, but he became so involved with his own he must have forgotten."

Naitachal ignored him. Alaire knew from experience, however, that he wasn't missing anything.

Alaire scratched his head a little; his hair was sweat-damp and his scalp itched. "Still, I never expected weapons training when Father sent me here. Is this the kind of fighting you used when you defeated Carlotta?"

At the mention of the evil princess, Naitachal turned slowly. The look he gave Alaire turned the boy's spine to ice. His skin crawled uncomfortably, as if it were trying to slither off his body. *Gods, I hope that wasn't the wrong thing to say,* he thought. *He could kill me with one look, if he dared.*

"Who said we defeated Carlotta?" Naitachal replied casually.

The words stunned Alaire. *What is he trying to say this time?* "Are you speaking in riddles to confuse me?" Alaire asked, finally. "Or are you just posing questions to make me think?"

Naitachal replaced the ladle and dropped the bucket back into the well, then gave Alaire an appraising look. "They never told you the entire story, did they?"

Alaire perked up at the prospect of hearing some secrets from his family's past. *They never went into much detail when I was around; all I ever got was the bedtime story, with the moral "be good, or Carlotta will carry you off."*

Sometimes when he walked into his father's study, and his mother and Grant and Drake were talking, he would overhear something about Carlotta. As soon as they saw him, everyone got really quiet.

He hadn't paid as much attention to his own family's past as he might have. There was all the scope of history to learn, a vast mine to delve in for gems that could become songs. It would have seemed presumptuous to use his family as a basis for balladry. Still, the mysterious story of Carlotta occasionally nagged at him. Even if he was not likely to become king, he still wondered what had happened back then, and why they were keeping it from him.

"No," he said quickly. "No one ever did. The whole family has been rather evasive about Carlotta."

"Then perhaps I should keep quiet as well," the Dark Elf replied slyly.

"Not that they were *intentionally* keeping it a secret from me," he quickly supplied. "I'm sure they just never, well, had the time. Or the chance, I mean, there are some things you just don't discuss with children. I've been here what, eight years now?"

"Nine," Naitachal said. "And you were never curious about it before."

"I'm nineteen now. I'm not a child." Alaire withered under Naitachal's answering *look*, which seemed to say, *oh, are you not, really?*

His Master shrugged. "The royal family never swore me to secrecy on everything. I insisted on a free rein in your upbringing, and got it. What would you like to know?"

"Details. Like, did you use this kind of swordsmanship," he said, pointing towards the rack of swords, practice and the lethal, metal kind. "Or something a little more esoteric?"

"I was not the hero," Naitachal said, "and I'm still not certain any victory was had on that day, by anyone."

His gaze turned brooding, as it always did when he was about to relate some story from the past. Naitachal's gift for tale-telling extended beyond songs and ballads, and Alaire settled back with a feeling of anticipation.

"It began before I became involved," Naitachal said, with a sideways glance at his apprentice. "A Bard named Aidan sent his apprentice, Kevin, to the libraries of Count Volmar to copy a manuscript called *The Study of Ancient Song*."

Alaire nodded, although he had known all this before.

"Thirty years before, Aidan had prevented Carlotta from stealing her brother's throne. At the time, he thought Carlotta had been disposed of, but he had recently learned that she was still alive. Although the situation had changed, Carlotta's ambition had not. Since you humans have such brief lives, Aidan was now an old man and didn't have the strength to deal with Carlotta. His apprentice, Kevin, was only seventeen then."

Naitachal shook his head, as if he could not believe the years had passed so quickly. "Kevin was young, eager, and dying to have an Adventure. What he lacked in brains and maturity he more than made up with enthusiasm. However, he was rather reluctant to go off to copy some old manuscript. Aidan didn't tell him how important it was."

"If Aidan was an old man, then wasn't Carlotta an *old woman*?" Alaire asked, puzzled.

"Yes, and no." Naitachal frowned. "Carlotta was half fairy and a shape-changer. Because of her fairy blood she lived as long as any halfling. As a shape-changer she could simply shift herself out of the ravages of old age. By that time, she had also mastered many of the Darker Arts. She was a fair match for anyone."

Alaire had never heard this before. Now he knew why. *A member of the royal family was a halfbreed, and she was practicing black magic? Good gods, no wonder they wanted to keep this secret.*

Naitachal took no notice of his shock. "Kevin was all alone in an unfriendly place, so it wasn't hard for Carlotta to learn what Aidan had sent him to do. She won Kevin's confidence by assuming the form of Volmar's pretty young niece, Charina. This was easy enough for a shape-changer, and the result was quite effective. I believe Kevin had even fallen in love with her."

Alaire closed his mouth and nodded wisely. "What happened to the real niece?" he asked. This was not part of the bedtime story, which usually never got past the tale of Amber and Aidan.

Naitachal sighed. "What you might expect. The Count, we later discovered, murdered her to get her out of the way. She apparently knew something was afoot." He shook his head. "Poor little thing. They killed her before she could enjoy her life."

He brooded on that for a moment, and Alaire gently prodded him back onto the story. "So Kevin came to copy the manuscript, and Carlotta found out what he was doing. Why didn't she simply take the manuscript?"

Naitachal chuckled. "Because the manuscript hid itself from anyone except Aidan or his deputy. When the manuscript disappeared, Carlotta and Volmar staged the disappearance of the fake 'niece' out of desperation. They blamed both Dark and White Elves for the 'kidnapping,' and that was how I became involved. I was visiting Volmar's court during some rather aimless travels. Count Volmar appointed Kevin to lead a search party. To clear my people's name I volunteered to help."

So that's where you came in, Alaire thought. *This is getting interesting.*

Naitachal squinted up at the sun for a moment. "None of us knew the book in question had a hidden spell in it, a spell that could 'unmake' Carlotta. Which is to say, to return her to her original fairy form."

Alaire nodded somberly. "Only full blood humans can sit on the throne of Althea." Inwardly, he was both excited and a little appalled. *A fairy? In the royal family? I would really like to know how that happened! If Carlotta is half fairy, my great-great-great-grandfather must have — ahem.* His ears burned as he wondered how a human and a diminutive fairy could have —

Stranger things have happened, I suppose.

Naitachal continued. "Our party would have failed if not for Kevin's leadership. He made us all work together in spite of our continuous bickering. Not surprising, since the Count intended us to fail, and chose us for that reason. We were an Amazon, a fairy, myself and a White Elven fighter. Anyone would have thought we would *never* stay together for more than a day. We became certain, in the course of some interesting adventures, that Count Volmar had sent us away so Carlotta could find the manuscript."

I would truly like to hear that in detail, Alaire thought, but Naitachal was obviously trying to make this a short tale.

"In time we returned to the castle, discovered that 'Charina's' captors had 'released' her. The Count treated us like heroes even though we had done nothing to rescue her." His expression became grim. "We were all highly suspicious, and as a precaution I spent an evening fortifying Kevin with magical protection. We were certain now that Carlotta was somewhere around in disguise, possibly as Charina, although we could not be sure. When Kevin finally found the manuscript, Carlotta was there beside him. She knew what it was, and she wanted it. If we hadn't fled Volmar's castle when we did, she would have seized it and destroyed us. She pursued us with her magics. Not all of us survived those magics . . ."

His voice trailed off, and Alaire saw something he had never seen before on his Master's face.

Grief.

He dared not interrupt, although he was burning to hear the end of it all.

Naitachal seemed to shake himself, and completed the tale. "When we returned to Volmar's castle it was with a band of some traveling musicians. Kevin thought they were his Master's human friends, but actually they were elves and allies of King Amber. Volmar was staging a grand event of some sort, inviting nobles from all over, and we suspected it had something to do with Carlotta. We knew we had to work quickly."

"And you were a hero," Alaire said.

Naitachal shook his head. "Hardly. It was Bard Kevin, for he was truly a Bard by then, who should get the credit for what happened. In a short time he mastered the spell, and delivered it flawlessly, once Volmar and Carlotta appeared. There, before everybody, she returned to her original, fairy form."

"I thought she died," Alaire said. "That's what Mother said. Gawaine thought so, too."

Naitachal laughed, but it had no humor in it. "That's what the Queen wants to believe, but alas, I'm afraid that simply isn't what happened. Carlotta escaped in the melee that followed. It was all we could do to keep Volmar's soldiers from executing us on the spot. His men followed him blindly, and it was only when they saw Charina's ghost, who openly accused the Count of her murder, that their loyalties turned. And I had *nothing* to do with that! By then I'd had my fill of Necromancy." He took a deep breath and his face cleared of the shadows of the past. "And that is the end of that tale. Where Carlotta went after that is anyone's guess. She didn't die. She only changed."

"Do you think Carlotta is still alive?" Alaire had to admit he didn't feel too comfortable with the chance that Carlotta still lived.

Naitachal seemed to consider this seriously for a moment, but Alaire suspected he already had an opinion formulated. "Simply put, yes, though I haven't the first clue where she would be, or when she might surface. It's not worth worrying about, at least not at the moment. You have more important tasks at hand, such as learning real swordsmanship." He laughed again, this time with real humor. "When I think how Kevin begged the Amazon and me to teach him the sword! And how horrified his Master was when he learned that we had!"

Alaire's thoughts, and gaze, had drifted during the brief history lesson. Perhaps this was why he didn't notice when Naitachal slipped over to the swordrack and retrieved his weapon. He even managed to hide it, until now.

"*I* hold a weapon," Naitachal said, smirking, and saluting him with the practice sword. "Why don't *you*?"

Alaire opened his mouth to say something, but nothing came out. *Damn him,* the boy thought. *He knows when I'm not paying attention! That's when he pulls these little stunts!*

The Dark Elf tossed Alaire the wooden sword, which he caught skillfully by the hilt, then took another from the rack.

"On your guard," Naitachal said. Alaire took the position, and tried to focus on the swords. Carlotta's story still haunted him.

Naitachal quickly tore into him, with more energy than he expected; once he started trying to avoid the elf instead of countering his blows, he knew it was all over.

Again Alaire lay sprawled in an exhausted heap. He did not even know what he had tripped over. *My own feet, probably.* During the fall, he lost track of his sword. It was now sticking upright out of the ground, quivering slightly.

"You have more lives than a cat," Naitachal said, holding out his hand. "You're dead again."

"Don't remind me," Alaire said, struggling to his feet. *At least I'll improve, even if he beats me like this every time.*

The sun was still high in the sky, reflected brightly in the white walls and the little fishpond in the yard of their home. The house was roomy, and by local standards was certainly a "mansion," but of course it was nothing like the opulence Alaire had grown up in. That made it all the better; he felt free here, and the simple pleasures of country life were a welcome relief from the court.

Rising from the center of the home was a watchtower, giving the house a templelike appearance. An odd conceit, but one that gave both of them pleasure in watching storms and stars. From the watchtower, one could see the distant coastline, and sometimes even the sail of a ship.

Up on the hillside above the house, in Alaire's line of sight with the watchtower, he caught movement.

Up there was the only road leading into the estate, and the moving figure on it might have been a man on a horse, or a carriage. It was too far away for the bardling to make out exactly what it was, much less who. Naitachal apparently noticed too, regarding the approaching visitor with interest.

"Messenger," Naitachal said simply. "From the court." Alaire squinted, but still couldn't make out the outline. Naitachal had demonstrated, repeatedly, that his eyesight was superior to any human's, so Alaire took his word for it.

"Messenger?" he asked. "Is he armed? Is he from Father's personal guard?"

"No," Naitachal replied, and Alaire sighed with relief. A messenger from the Royal Bodyguard would have been a certain sign that the news was bad. It would have meant, at the very least, a death in the family. Or an invasion from a foreign land, or some other earth-shattering calamity.

Naitachal frowned. "Odd. There must be some urgency to whatever he's delivering. His horse is exhausted. He's been riding hard for some time now."

Visitors were a rare treat, but Alaire awaited this one with mixed emotions. If he merely bore a friendly message from home, why would the messenger run his horse into the ground? *What could have happened?* he wondered. He tried not to let his imagination get the better of him.

The messenger and his horse drew closer, and slowed. The boy was sixteen at most, and was wearing the dark blue riding uniform and plain blue saddle of Reynard's livery. Perhaps he had simply ridden hard to impress his own Master with his diligence. Inwardly, Alaire groaned. *No! Not another fancy, gaudy, foofy, royal visit from some princess at the castle!*

"I come bearing a message for Master Bard

Naitachal from his Majesty King Reynard!" the young man announced even before coming to a stop. The horse, a beautiful gray palfrey Alaire recognized as one of the best in the messengers' stable, did a weary little dance as the boy pulled up next to them. The messenger, obviously winded and tired, waved a blue envelope aloft.

Alaire changed his mind again. *He would have had to ride straight through two days to get here looking like that. The horse doesn't look much better.* A visit from one of Derek's would-be brides would not justify this degree of urgency, and the Master of the Horse would take this youngster apart for exhausting his beast if he had only done it to impress. Naitachal reached up for message, an envelope sealed in wax with the family crest.

"Please, take your horse to the stables," Naitachal said, motioning toward the somewhat dilapidated barn behind the house. "There is a water pump with the trough. When you are done, you may go into the house to wash."

"Thank you, sir," the young man said, saying nothing to Alaire. He directed the palfrey toward the stables.

He apparently doesn't know I'm the King's son, Alaire thought. *All he sees is Naitachal's bardling.* It was rather refreshing, and he grinned to himself with a certain amount of relief. They really *had* forgotten all about him at court! He might even be able to sneak back some time and enjoy himself without having to put up with all the nonsense.

"Well, what is it?" Alaire said, unable to stand patiently any longer. *Is it about me?*

Naitachal flipped open the wax seal and read the message quickly, at a glance. Then he looked up.

"*Well?*"

Naitachal's expression was neither grim nor darkened, as it would be in response to bad news. It wasn't quite neutral, either. Alaire quivered with barely restrained excitement. *It's about me. It has to be!*

Naitachal raised an eyebrow, then folded the paper back up and returned it to the envelope. Then, as it lay flat on his palm, the envelope burst into flame.

Startled, Alaire stepped back. He wasn't expecting that.

Naitachal calmly brushed the ashes from his hands and fixed Alaire with a measuring and unreadable look.

"Tell me!" Alaire said, barely restraining himself. The Dark Elf never became melodramatic, and burning the message like that required an exercise of magics he seldom used.

"Your father," Naitachal said, after a lengthy and infuriating pause, "wants to send us on a little errand."

Without elaborating, Naitachal started back towards the house.

For a moment Alaire stared at his retreating back. Then, flustered, he hurried into the house after him.

Naitachal's study was usually a private place where he wouldn't allow anyone, not even a maid. Alaire had set foot in the study only six times in the years he lived there, and then only because Naitachal had invited him, when some royal crisis was a-brewing.

Now Naitachal stood at the door and beckoned Alaire to follow. He cautiously followed his Master into the mysterious den, shivering in its chill. The place gave him the creeps.

The study had no windows, no source of light besides a single black candle as big around as Alaire's forearm. In the darkness the candle flared to life, illuminating Naitachal's face. Standing behind him was a large shelf of ancient, dusty books, all in Elvish, which had been in Naitachal's family gods only knew how long. The Bard carefully pulled and examined the volumes, which had no titles on the spines.

"We are going to Suinomen," Naitachal said flatly, as he searched.

Suinomen, Alaire thought. *He can't be serious!*

The name conjured uneasy feelings. King Reynard discouraged all his subjects, and particularly the royal family, from traveling to Suinomen. His teachers never spoke about it in school, it never even appeared on maps, and it never had diplomatic relations with any country. After a while, one just forgot it existed. The only contact Althea had with Suinomen was a light, seasonal trade in animal hides. Alaire didn't even know who was ruling the country nowadays. *Suinomen. Why, in the seven hells, are we going there?*

Their home at Fenrich was near the northern boundary with Suinomen. This probably explained why King Reynard picked them, since the border was a day's travel away, the capital two; and since Naitachal had often run "little errands" that involved diplomatic maneuvering for the royal family. This still didn't explain *why* they were going.

"Found it," Naitachal said, selecting a thin leather book from the shelf and placing it on the desk. In the dim candlelight Alaire could make out vague Elvish script on the cover, but couldn't decipher its meaning.

"You still haven't said why we're going to this place," Alaire said, trying to sound nonchalant.

Since the Dark Elf had so few visitors to this room, it took the boy a moment to find something to sit on. He finally found an old stool, layered with dust. Since his backside was already dusty he didn't have any qualms about using it.

Naitachal was perusing the book. "The land is only

off limits to those who wield magic," he said, as if in an afterthought.

"So where does that leave *us*?" Alaire asked. "Did the King forget what you are, and what you are training *me* to be?" Even before all the facts were in, he found himself resisting the whole idea.

"No one in Suinomen knows we are Bards," Naitachal replied absently. "Let me explain, before you prejudge the entire mission. You know Suinomen has been an uncomfortable neighbor for centuries, but for the most part our two nations left each other alone. Now they are making vague, but disturbing war threats."

Alaire was about to say something else, but at the mention of war, he kept his silence.

Naitachal turned a page. "This was why I destroyed the letter. Our mages, through their own spells, have Seen an impressive military buildup. The Suinomese have stepped up their recruiting efforts despite a productive harvest. Why should they draft youngsters when the family farms need them the most? The war threats must be taken seriously."

Alaire shook his head; it made no sense. "We've lived in peace with them for so long. They want nothing we have. Do they?"

Naitachal looked up for a moment and shrugged. "The King thinks they're afraid of us. I must agree, only I believe the fear has gone back many centuries. For about a century now, Suinomen has strictly regulated magic. Althea, of course, never has. To practice magic or even the lowest level of *healing* is strictly illegal, unless the Crown issues a license. This is why your father discourages travel to their land. Too many times our people have never returned because they practiced a healing to mend a broken bone, or created a magelight to start wet firewood, and wound up imprisoned for life. Or so we assume."

Alaire had heard the rumors of people vanishing into the North, but he'd never heard one confirmed. It was one of the curses of living a sheltered life. Idle street talk seldom reached his ears, even now. Being of royal blood meant you just didn't hear common gossip, even if you wanted to.

Naitachal's attention had gone back to his book. "Magicians, even their healers, take tests in specific areas. Then, when they have paid their licensing fee, they may perform only the simplest of spells, and *then* only under the supervision of the Suinomen Magery Association."

"What about Bards?" Alaire asked. "You haven't mentioned them."

Naitachal's mouth twitched. "They permit simple musicians, but *never* Bards. However, they have no effective barriers to keep them out. Their mages are, in my humble opinion, amateurs. They probably wouldn't recognize a Bard unless one whacked them over the head with his harp."

Alaire stifled a chuckle, as Naitachal continued.

"But somehow they fumble about in their incompetence, and nab a magician or two for making a lopsided circle on the ground with onion flakes." He turned another page. "So, as I said, they permit only harmless, non-magical minstrels, even though no one over there knows how Bardic Magic really works. This is how we will present ourselves. We are *minstrels*, only. If anyone asks about our instruments, it is our hobby. The King chose us to be his temporary envoys."

Alaire shrugged. "Wonder why our ambassador can't handle this."

Naitachal gave him a withering look, as if he should

already have known the answer. "We don't _have_ one in Suinomen. _We're_ going to be the ambassadors. We'll have to be careful there. The reason Suinomen is making threats is because they feel endangered. Our unlicensed and unregulated magic is a threat to their security, or so they claim."

Alaire considered this, while Naitachal went through the leather-bound book. _It makes sense, in a distorted fashion_, he decided. _We make perfect envoys. We're practically at their doorstep already, and I'm high up on the royal lineage ladder._ However, something else nagged at him.

"Question," Alaire said, raising a hand. "If they don't permit magic, how can we be the ambassadors? I mean, you're an elf, and all elves are mages, right?"

Naitachal frowned, and gave Alaire that look he knew so well, which told him, _don't you see_ yet?

"Magic use is illegal," he said, with a look of bored patience. "They permit magicians _themselves_, but those mages cannot invoke any powers, internal or external."

Fine. But Naitachal had been a Necromancer, and in a country that feared mages, this could cause some . . . problems. "You're a Dark Elf. Isn't that likely to incite, well, hostilities?"

This time Naitachal just shrugged. "My people have never had an ambassador at the Suinomen court. That is probably why King Reynard wants to send us in that capacity. Chances are they haven't seen too many Dark Elves, and if they have, do you really think they would give _me_ any trouble? If the reputation of Dark Elves in _this_ kingdom is bad, what do you think it is over there?"

Alaire had to chuckle. _Well, I guess he has a point. No one's going to harass him, particularly when he can turn you to powder with a single muttered spell. And_ *it's not painless, either. Father knows he wouldn't do that, of course, but they don't.*

"Your role in all this is to be rather subdued," Naitachal said, almost apologetically.

Alaire raised an eyebrow. "What do you mean, *subdued*?"

"You are to be my . . . secretary, of sorts. We will keep your real identity secret."

For a moment Alaire was resentful, then he reconsidered; what better way to have fun with an otherwise serious assignment? *If I went as a prince this trip would bore me silly. Of course they can't know who I am, and I bet they won't even suspect, since so few people in our own kingdom know I'm Naitachal's bardling.*

"Ransom, you see," Naitachal said. "It's something your father would rather not contend with."

Alaire edged closer to the volume, which Naitachal held in his dark hands. "What is that book, anyway?"

"A very old travel log," Naitachal said. "Here's the map we'll need. This is the less traveled route, if my grandfather is right. He wrote this book centuries ago."

Alaire thought about the plan, and began to feel relieved, for other reasons. Visiting another country as the son of a king meant hours of boring, endless pomposity, formalities, uncomfortable formal dress, and *no* privacy. Going incognito meant none of this.

Well, at least not as much. He suspected that being an Envoy would include some of the royal trappings. *But not, thank the gods, the full course.*

"It's a rather difficult responsibility," Naitachal admitted. "I think we're up to it. We need to find out why they are suddenly acting so aggressive, and to stop them if we can. Do you agree, Alaire?"

"Of course I do," he said, without thinking. He had

another thought, which left him a little awed, a little excited, and a little afraid. *Responsibility.* Naitachal had described it exactly with that single word. *This is important work we can do for the kingdom. And we're the best ones for the job.*

"Remember, the fact that we are Bards is to be kept absolutely secret," Naitachal said. "The Association can regulate unlicensed magic, so we must assume they must have a way of detecting it. We don't know what the penalties are, after all."

He looked up from the book again, and his eyes glowed in a rather sinister fashion. "I'd rather not find out the hard way."

Chapter II

Early the next morning Naitachal rose to the noisy arrival of men on horses. He glanced through the shutters and saw the messenger greeting three older comrades, each wearing the same dark blue uniforms. They'd brought two additional horses, each loaded with goods, presumably for the journey to Suinomen. Though Naitachal and Alaire usually didn't rise till mid-morning, it looked as if their day had started without them.

That was enough to wake the dead, he thought, frowning at the noise. *Not very courteous. And they're not even trying to be quiet.*

The Dark Elf threw on a robe and, with a tiny amount of magic, heated a cup of khaffe. As he walked past Alaire's bedroom he saw through the open door that the boy was, as usual, sprawled like a monkey on a bed of twisted blankets.

Such a raw youth, Naitachal thought, suddenly aware how sheltered he really was. Watching him, he felt warm, paternal *human* feelings, which surprised him. Even the White Elves had been known to make unflattering comments about human emotions, not to mention his own dark and more serious brethren.

Asleep, Alaire looked especially vulnerable. *Are you ready for this journey, my boy?* Naitachal asked the slumbering bardling. Somehow he'd managed to keep his long blond hair from getting tangled in the covers.

Have I done enough to prepare you for this? Have I taught you enough to keep you safe and to be able to take care of yourself if need be?

Then he smiled. *And am I going to be able to wake you without building a fire under your bed?*

"Time to rise," Naitachal said, without much hope. "Our horses and supplies have arrived. We must be on our way."

Nothing.

He spoke louder. "Alaire? Will I have to cast a spell to raise the dead?"

The boy rolled over, and flung a pillow at Naitachal, who ducked expertly under it as it whizzed past. The burst of activity was brief; Alaire buried his head under a wad of blanket.

"Behavior like that is not very respectful," Naitachal scolded. "Water from the well should be particularly cold this morning." He paused, for effect. "If you catch my meaning. Get up now, or you will find out in the most direct way just *how* cold that water is."

Alaire reacted by sitting up slowly on the edge of the bed. "You'd do it, too," he complained, yawning. "Did you say more messengers are here?"

Naitachal laughed. "They're out front, where I expect to see you soon."

Satisfied that his apprentice was truly awake, Naitachal started for the front door. Mug in hand, he stepped outside to greet the new arrivals, trying to look more awake than he felt.

"Milord," one of the messengers said. Naitachal sensed fear, of his race rather than his title, a common reaction to any Dark Elf. "We have brought horses and supplies in the name of King Reynard. For your journey."

"To Suinomen," another said awkwardly, still mounted on his sweaty horse. The King's men just stood there, visibly afraid, as if waiting for lightning to strike them.

Naitachal sighed in resignation. *If only they knew how much I dislike Necromancy*, he thought, sadly. At times like these he wished humans would regard him with a little less terror.

Then again, this was partially his own fault. In the past, assuming the appearance and attitudes of a Necromancer had gained him more authority than he probably deserved. However, Naitachal had never bothered to correct those who feared him by saying that he no longer practiced the Black Arts.

The spells and powers of Necromancy never go away. I was a Black Sorcerer for many, many years. They are right to fear me.

He could still summon the forces to convert an enemy to dust. Or, at any moment, call up his Death Sword, or order the spirits of the dead to serve him. He could flay the skin from living flesh, and flesh from bones. Few humans ever guessed that he would rather put on a jester's outfit and juggle live rats than do any of that.

The two fine horses pleased him. At least they would ride in good ambassadorial style. The horses' tack was more elaborate than he would have preferred however, particularly since they would be riding in lands that might harbor bandits or robbers. *We might as well wave a banner*, Naitachal thought, with exasperation.

Alaire appeared in the doorway. He regarded the messengers calmly, with ice-blue eyes now wide awake with curiosity. The new arrivals hardly looked at him. Apparently they had no idea Alaire was the King's son, and knew only that Naitachal was a court Bard.

By wearing simple peasant clothing, Naitachal saw that Alaire had gone out of his way to affect unimportance.

They probably think he's my servant, Naitachal thought, admiring how well the royal inner circle had kept Alaire's apprenticeship a secret. *That's perfect. These messengers have no idea that this is a prince of the blood royal.*

Naitachal invited the messengers inside; they dismounted reluctantly, as if fearing even this show of hospitality. He showed them the guest quarters and invited them to stay a night or two in their absence, knowing it would have taken three days of hard riding to get here. Without waiting to hear their reply, he returned to his own quarters, and Alaire followed his lead. In earnest, they began packing for the trip.

The fancy costumes the messengers had presented them with would never do for traveling; they left those items securely packed away for when they arrived in Rozinki, Suinomen's capital. He inspected the impressive weapons the King had sent them, two new crossbows with an ample supply of arrows, swords from the royal blacksmith and jeweled daggers. *The cloaks would at least conceal most of these,* he decided. *We must leave the jeweled weapons packed. The daggers are too tempting a prize for bandits.*

If this was too early in the morning for Alaire, he no longer showed it. The lad had an extraordinary amount of frenetic energy for someone who had just awakened. Naitachal watched him discreetly, trying to determine from body language if the boy was trying to conceal uneasiness about the journey, or if he really thought this was going to be a grand adventure, without pitfalls.

My father could tell him some tales about Suinomen, thought Naitachal. The book his father had written was more than a traveler's diary; it was a warning. *Father never really said what was so frightening about the place. The only thing that could frighten a Necromancer would be something beyond, or worse, than death.*

Alaire brought out their two harps from the house. The boy's instrument was slightly smaller, and had the brighter, less mellow tone of newer wood. Naitachal's instrument had belonged to an old hermit who claimed it was a thousand years old; Naitachal guessed three hundred, but its tone, and the odd composition of the varnish, had intrigued him.

"How long will it take us to get there by horse-back?" Alaire asked, stowing the harps carefully away in their canvas sacks, which became a balanced pair of saddlebags. "Or maybe I should be asking, when are we *supposed* to be there?"

Included in their supplies was another sealed letter, which Naitachal opened. *Perhaps we do have an appointed arrival time,* he thought, glancing over the parchment. Included with this was a detailed map of their route, which took them around the marshes and bogs that made up the southern portion of the kingdom and led them along the fjord filled, rocky coast. Swamp flanked the route on the west, with ocean on the east.

The letter was from King Reynard to King Arche-nomen, stating his desire to establish diplomatic relations between their countries. Included in the packet was another letter, for Naitachal's eyes only, giving details of the King's thoughts on the whole matter, and a separate certificate that confirmed Naitachal's position as a royal envoy. There was nothing that would indicate Alaire was a prince; once they were in Suinomen, he *would* be an underling, or at least give the appearance of one.

"No particular day to be there," Naitachal said. "I would guess two, maybe three days at the most. The provisions should suffice us. If not, we can hunt, though I doubt much game lives on that narrow channel." *Oh well, he needs to get rid of some of that baby fat anyway.*

Since the girl who cleaned and cooked for them had not arrived from the village, Naitachal cooked a hearty breakfast for everyone, instructing Alaire to play as if he was Naitachal's assistant.

"I know you outrank them, but it will be good practice," he added.

Alaire's face became a distorted mask of humility, and he bowed humbly before the Dark Elf. "I am at your service, my gracious Master," he said, smirking.

"You should be able to do a more convincing job of posing as my secretary than that," Naitachal whispered. "They might figure out who you really are, and take you hostage. They are preparing for war, you know."

The smirk disappeared. "Aie yes, you're right. As usual. This is a serious matter, in need of your expert diplomacy. I will play the role to the best of my ability." Alaire grabbed the wooden tray of biscuits, gravy and boiled eggs.

"We will be leaving promptly after breakfast," the Dark Elf said, but Alaire had already vanished into the dining room.

Once they'd packed their belongings, Naitachal leaned over and gave parting directions to the messengers on how to close up the house. Their curiosity didn't concern him; any room they shouldn't be in, they couldn't *get* in. Certain spells wouldn't allow anything less than a mage, and a more powerful one than he, into the study or watchtower, which were both secret and dangerous spaces. Similar spells would not let common bandits near the house. For the most part Fenrich had a peaceful, law-abiding population, more likely to protect Naitachal's property than try to take advantage of his absence.

They mounted up. The Dark Elf rose in his stirrups

for a moment; from here he could see the village, deep in the hollow of a long valley. They took to the road, riding along a rocky ridge just above the village, the sort of terrain that would become all-too-familiar before the journey was over.

Alaire followed his gaze. "Should we stop and tell Mayor Woen we'll be gone?"

"I have already instructed one of the messengers to do so," Naitachal said. "The house defenses will take care of themselves, once the messengers are gone."

"Aye, they will," Alaire said gleefully. "Remember, I helped you lay a few of those magical traps myself, should you have to 'step out' for a little while."

Since Naitachal was the only mage of any ability who lived in the area, he had become the village protector. He had pointed out to the mayor that he was likely to come and go, and that if trouble ever came to the village he might not be around to get rid of it. With Alaire's help Naitachal had laid all kinds of tricks and traps to protect the village in their absence.

"Even 'ordinary' humans have outwitted magic users," Alaire pointed out. "In my great grandfather's time the court relied as much on the ordinary, non-magical folk as they did the magic users to fight Carlotta."

"Quite true. A respectful fear of the unknown, even unknown humans, is a healthy response," noted Naitachal as he glanced over at Alaire, who eyed his saddle, as if he felt it might be loose. "But until we get to Suinomen, I doubt there is much that will bother us, human or not. What we have to fear once we get to there is the breaking of our magical anonymity. *Remember*, we are mere ambassadors, with musical abilities. We are not Bards, or magicians. We don't even do card tricks."

Alaire made a noise Naitachal couldn't immediately interpret. "Strict, hmm?"

"Strict is not the word I would have chosen," Naitachal replied.

Soon the village receded out of sight; the ocean came into full view on their right, and mountains grew up on their left. Here the weather had cooled; where they were going, it would already be winter. Fortunately, the King had included two fine dieren coats with their wardrobe, in the traditional Suinomen cut.

They traveled the coastal road into Suinomen. Weeds now grew in the rutted tracks left by the carts and wagons that brought in dieren wool, the primary source of income for the Northerners. The dieren themselves were splay-footed, antlered beasts, the only visible asset of that kingdom, although Naitachal had never seen one alive. Every spring the herders carefully brushed out the wool, a warm, silky material which was in high demand throughout Althea.

Dieren meat was delicious, and the herders even made a very succulent cheese from the milk. Villagers from Fenrich often tried to bribe the Suinomen traders to bring down and sell a few of the beasts, preferably a mixture of male and female, but they just laughed, only to return with more processed dieren goods the next year. But no dieren. *They're not fools,* the Dark Elf thought. *Assuming the beasts could even live in our climate, why should they give us the means to breed them ourselves?*

As if reading Naitachal's mind, Alaire said, "I wonder what dieren look like."

"Well," Naitachal said, feeling mischievous. "I'll bet they have fur. And four feet. And antlers."

Alaire turned slowly, giving him a wry grin. "Your powers of deduction never cease to amaze even me," Alaire said in jest. "Seriously, do you think we'll see them before we get to Archenomen's castle?"

Naitachal considered this a moment. "I doubt it. All we'll see is coastline and marsh. They herd the beasts further north, on the prairies. Maybe. I've never been there myself, so I can't say."

"As long as you've lived, you've never visited Suinomen?" Alaire seemed genuinely surprised.

What, did he think I have been everywhere and seen everything?

"No. Not *there*. After my father returned from that land, he warned us never to go there, that something unspeakable awaited us all if we did." Naitachal shook his head. "Remember that it made a practiced Necromancer feel threatened. We were not likely to ignore his advice."

"And he never said what it was?"

Naitachal wished that he had. "Not once. He seemed particularly rattled by whatever he saw. His attitude concerning his children even once we were grown was, 'obey, and ask no questions,' so we didn't. And we do not have the time to seek him out, wherever he has cloistered himself, and ask him. If he would even *talk* to me, renegade that I am."

Alaire pulled up closer to him as the trail narrowed to an overgrown tunnel of trees. "Did he ever tell you anything else about Suinomen? I heard only giants live in the north, in enormous ice castles, and that Suinomen allowed some mages to cast spells that wreaked havoc with the weather."

Naitachal replied, "I've heard the stories too, but they are mostly rumor according to Father's journal. I doubt that anyone can control the weather, but as I told you, these folk do permit magic under tightly controlled circumstances. Their passion for regulation has frightened many visitors away. Not that I blame them. Who would want to live in a place where one cannot even cast a simple Healing spell without licenses and fees?"

"Then perhaps we could cast one last Bardic spell before we arrive?" Alaire asked coaxingly.

Naitachal considered this; the practice would be helpful to the young bardling. But he could think of no good reason to cast a spell just then, except something protective, and a protective spell would last for some time. *If we conjured something to protect us they may detect any lingering magic.*

"For what purpose?" he replied reasonably, as his horse shook its head until the bridle ornaments jangled. "We can't go tramping into Suinomen with magical residue dripping off us. I assume they have some means of detecting magic, if they are policing their kingdom of it. Which means they might even detect it from within our borders. Not a good idea."

Alaire nodded, apparently agreeing with his Master. "You were up most of the night reading that journal of your father's. What else did he have to say?"

"We can expect a rather subdued atmosphere wherever we go. According to Father, these people don't have much fun." *Not that Necromancers are known for having a good time.* "Even he remarked on that extensively; he thought it might be because of the long nights, or the difficult conditions that most of the people there must face. It is a strange land, dotted with thousands of lakes filled with islands. The people tend to be small, slender, and very blond. On a dark night some might even be mistaken for a White Elf."

Alaire shook his head. "I can't think of anything we have that they would be desperate enough to go to war over. It makes no sense. Unless something has happened to change things within the government; I mean something drastic, like the overthrow of the Royal House."

Naitachal gave him points for *that* notion. He guided his horse easily across a particularly bad stretch of road before making a reply. "This is one of the things we must find out. Who rules, and who follows. The land has no mines, no source of gold, silver or gems. For whatever they need they must trade heavily in dieren goods. They do have amber in large quantities, but that is all." A thought occurred to him. "I wonder if one of the reasons why they're making these threats is to gain access to our mines in the North? I would have thought that those mines were much too far south of their border to qualify as a target, but perhaps King Archenomen thinks he can conquer enough territory to take them."

"Makes sense," Alaire said ominously. He apparently hadn't considered the mines as the possible target either.

Naitachal had not even thought of the mines until this moment because they were technically "owned" by the dwarves who worked them. If the Suinomites felt they "belonged" to Althea, and desired them, that changed the complexion of things. *There is something in Althea that's worth fighting over.*

Naitachal sensed uneasiness in the boy, which carried over to his horse, which fretted at the bit. Alaire said, "I was excited about this trip, and all the good it will do for Althea. Now, though, I don't have a very good feeling about what might happen to us in Suinomen, even though this trip could accomplish much for Althea. Yesterday, before that messenger arrived, I wouldn't have thought twice about the place. Now it's all I *can* think about, but it's as if there's a dark blot where there should be light, or discord where there should be harmony, and it makes me nervous. Maybe mystery and the lack of information has colored my imagination."

Naitachal eased his horse up beside his bardling, and looked carefully into Alaire's eyes. Something lurked there besides the youngster's active imagination. "Maybe your magic is telling you things," he said slowly.

Alaire's eyes narrowed. "A warning?"

"Perhaps." Naitachal turned away himself, feeling a deeper sense of warning and foreboding than he had in many, many years.

What are we going to find in Suinomen?

They stopped for the night at a stay-station, a crude one-room stone cottage with wooden frames for their bedrolls, a fireplace, and a scanty supply of wood. Alaire and Naitachal spent the better part of an hour gathering enough wood in the forest to keep warm through the night.

Alaire suggested tentatively that he use magic to warm the place up; the temperature had dropped below freezing, and promised to plunge further.

"This is only a taste of what we're in for, up there," the Dark Elf commented as they met at the doorway, hefting a bundle of deadwood over his shoulders. "We won't be able to use any of our usual powers to warm a cottage, or whatever lodging we find between here and there, if indeed we find any at all. We'd better get used to it. Anyway, we'll be at the palace soon enough, where we won't have to worry about gathering wood for fires."

"Of course not; we'll be putting out political ones," Alaire said sardonically.

Naitachal nodded. *And I won't be able to use magic to deal with that, either. I suspect I am going to be very busy. And so will Alaire.*

Chapter III

Alaire thought he would fall asleep immediately after the long ride. Instead, his aching muscles and the hard, unfamiliar "bed" kept him turning and tossing all night. Long after the fire had burned down to coals, he dozed off, his dreams colored by the sounds of wild things prowling the night outside the shelter.

Curled up in a tight little ball in his snug bedroll, Alaire awoke to the sound of sloshing water. Naitachal was holding a leather bucket of water above him, tipping it ever so slightly over his stomach. Even from this position he saw that the water was just about to drench him.

"Ae-ye, you wouldn't!" Alaire shouted, scrambling into a defensive position — as well as he could, burdened with his bedroll. The bucket got his attention, as did the mischievous glint in Naitachal's blue eyes, a bizarre sight when combined with the black face of a Dark Elf.

"Ah, but I would. I've been calling your name for the last quarter-hour," he said. The bucket hadn't wavered. "Are you going to get up, or am I . . ."

Alaire thrashed around, trying to get away from the bucket but in so doing he managed to roll into Naitachal's legs. The sudden jostle dislodged Naitachal's grip. With a loud *slosh* the water and bucket landed in Alaire's lap. And yes, the water was cold. Icy, in fact.

"YYYAAaaaaaarghhh!" Alaire shrieked, throwing

the soaked bedroll off his legs and scrambling to his feet. As he made for the blazing fireplace he saw that he'd soaked Naitachal as well.

"That was not what I intended," Naitachal said. "I assure you. But it did get you on your feet. We have another long day ahead of us."

Alaire glared at him, trying to think of a clever retort. Unable to think of one, he settled for the obvious. "That water was cold!" he said indignantly.

"Then why did you knock it out of my hands?" Naitachal asked. "You needed a bath, anyway. You humans get a little *ripe* after a few days of not bathing."

"Don't remind me," Alaire said, somewhat sadly. Normally he would soak in a hot bath before bed — *without* having to haul his own firewood. Muscles he did not use in swordwork ached. At this point, Alaire had had about enough of this kind of "adventure." He could not imagine having to travel the countryside singing for his meals and bed. He no longer envied the Bards who did.

"Should we get there today?" he asked hopefully.

Naitachal glanced through the open cottage door at the sun, still low on the horizon. "If we get on the road before the sun sets, then perhaps we will. I've already cooked breakfast."

Alaire couldn't see breakfast, but he could smell it. A closer look at the fireplace showed him the delicious aroma's source, two little rabbits roasting on a spit.

His mood improved immediately, as Naitachal took both rabbits from the spit and lay one on a piece of clean bark for him. *Yum! A hot breakfast alone is worth getting drenched with ice water.*

As Alaire tore into the rabbit, he realized the water he'd awakened to was fresh, and not tainted with the leathery tang of the old bucket.

"Where did you get the water anyway?" he asked between bites.

"Ah," Naitachal said, settling down next to him and starting on his own breakfast. "There is a shallow spring down the side of this ridge. Not more than a trickle, but it was enough to water the horses and bring a bucket full up here for you. It was to be your drinking water, not your bath."

Alaire grinned, for by now the shock of the icy water had worn off. *It's hard to be mad at him for too long, especially when he lets me sleep and catches and fixes breakfast.* Then his mood brightened even more. *We could arrive in Rozinki today. There will be an inn with real baths!*

They packed and loaded the horses, but before leaving Alaire sought out the spring. It was a mere trickle, as Naitachal had said, but it was very fresh. And very cold, he rediscovered as he splashed some on his face.

When he bent to drink, he felt something distinct, and familiar. A wave of weak magic passed over him.

He froze momentarily, then resumed drinking, satiating himself while pretending to ignore the magical probe that had fixed on him. It felt warm and tingly, like a large beam of sunlight; but unlike sunlight, this had a feeling of control behind it. Who was controlling it, he couldn't guess, but he had the distinct impression it was coming from the direction they were traveling towards.

Good gods, he thought, still acting oblivious to the probe.

Who in the world could be doing that?

He returned to camp, but as he left the well behind him, the magical eye followed. *You're a mere mortal, remember? You don't know it's there. You can't know it's there. Only a Bard or a mage could feel it.*

Before he reached the horses, he felt the probe shift, weaken, then vanish. Relieved, he quickened his pace, eager to tell his Master about this unexpected intrusion.

He found Naitachal adjusting the bridle on his horse, but as soon as Alaire drew closer he felt the probe again. This time the magic only brushed past him, for it focused on the Bard instead.

The Dark Elf turned, and met Alaire's eyes with his own. Alaire nodded, ever so slightly.

"Are you ready to travel?" Naitachal asked. Tension colored his words, which seemed to say, *Ah, so you feel the probe too?* Alaire nodded again.

"Yes, I believe so," he said, trying to approximate the same tone. "I wonder if — ah — we're going to see any natives today?"

Naitachal mounted his horse, and looked down at Alaire.

"Perhaps. I suspect they'll see us first."

They rode for close to an hour, making idle conversation about the weather. That wasn't hard to manage, for it deteriorated into a cloudy, cold morning, threatening rain or, more likely, light snow. The mysterious probe followed them and Alaire tried to conceal his unease; it was as if a giant *something* was looking over their shoulder, listening to their every word.

Then, suddenly, the probe vanished.

Moments later, Naitachal chuckled. "My. That was interesting."

"It was a probe, wasn't it?" Alaire said, sensing it was safe to talk. "A Watch-Spell? Who was it? One of our mages?"

Naitachal snorted. "Hardly. It came from Suinomen. I suspect it was one of their court mages. Amateurish, if you ask me. We've been approaching their border for some time, but they're only now aware of it. And they tipped their hand."

Alaire had to agree; it was quite possible to use a Watch-Spell without alerting the subject. The wizards of Suinomen should have been more careful than that. "If we were an invading force, they'd be in real trouble by now."

"Indeed." Naitachal frowned. "It leads me to wonder if we were right, and they want our mines to the west. They certainly weren't paying any attention to *this* route, until now."

During the latter half of the afternoon, the weather continued to turn. What had been nothing more than a chill in the air became a frosty winter blast, a hard, cold wind that hit them head on, from the north.

Naitachal, as usual, seemed to be taking it all in stride. Out came the winter coats, complete with hoods that buttoned closely under the chin. Alaire's hood seemed a bit oversized and hung low over his face. This obstructed his view somewhat, but the dieren clothing kept out the cold perfectly. The outfit even included thick dieren gloves, a necessity when riding.

There was another advantage to the hoods; he saw right away that the one on the Bard's coat concealed Naitachal's ears and a good part of his face; he didn't look like an elf, unless seen from close up.

The sudden change in the weather made Alaire wonder if a mage had brought the cold down on them, to discourage further travel northwards. He said as much to his Master.

Naitachal shrugged the suggestion off. "I doubt it. This is simply what the weather is like around here. Frankly, I doubt their mages could cook something up this dramatic."

That afternoon they crossed the Suinomen border.

They found no guardhouse or barriers, just a strange stone pillar on the Althean side. Naitachal translated a series of elven runes which covered the marker. The odd message warned all elves, Dark and White, to stay away from Suinomen. It said nothing specific, according to Naitachal, just a general *stay out* to all elves who saw it. Alaire thought it might be a forgery by the Suinomen government, to persuade magic users to turn back.

The Bard shook his head. "There is a residue of elven magic on the writing," Naitachal said. "They could never have forged that."

Alaire felt strangely uneasy the moment they crossed the border into Suinomen. Not only was he leaving his home behind, he felt as if he had passed a point of no-return, and that the odds were he would never go back. . . .

Oh don't be stupid, he scolded himself. *You're seeing bogeys under the bed again. People go across borders all the time and nothing more happens to them except a pleasant or unpleasant journey. You're not a Druid or a Cleric. You can't foretell the future. You're just a bardling, and this is just a border like any other.*

The terrain leveled out as they drew closer to the sea. The fens and marshes were clearly overrunning the western side of their trail. Alaire winced as he imagined the difficulty in taking a horse through those miserable bogs, particularly in this cold. The air here was thicker and damper, and redolent with the scent of the marshlands, a mingling of sea scent and decaying vegetation.

Naitachal had trotted up ahead a few horselengths to the top of a rise, then reined his horse to stop. "Come up beside me and stop," the Bard said, before Alaire could see what had attracted his attention. "I see someone approaching."

Alaire's head came up, as if he could scent some danger in the air like a hound. Naitachal didn't seem too concerned yet. Nevertheless, his hand was on his hilt, and Alaire thought it prudent to follow his example.

Presently two riders rode over the next rise. They were several hundred paces away, and it was difficult to make out much more than that the newcomers were also muffled in heavy dieren-wool coats. The two parties regarded one another in an uneasy silence for several moments, then the others nudged their horses forward again.

"Remember who and what you are," Naitachal said. "I think they're border guards, but I don't recognize the livery, so I'm not certain. Time to assume our new roles."

Alaire said nothing as the men came closer, but was fascinated by what they were riding. The beasts certainly weren't horses. These creatures were enormous, at least four hands taller than their own high-bred geldings. Each animal had a set of enormous branching horns, like a pair of young trees growing from their heads, and larger and more dangerous-looking than any deer could ever boast of. Their hoofs were cloven, but larger than a horse's, and the length and musculature of their legs suggested great speed and agility. When he noticed the peculiar color of their coats, a rich reddish brown, and realized it exactly matched that of his coat, he realized what they were.

"*Dieren!*" he said, louder than he had intended.

Naitachal whirled around, glaring at him. "What did you think they were, rabbits? Will you please keep still while I try to establish our credentials?"

The men wore readily identifiable uniforms. Coats, trousers, boots, even saddles and saddle blankets were identical. Over the left breast of each coat was a triangular badge with the red and green colors of the Suinomen flag. One of the guards sported brass decorations; he was older than the other, and that seemed to Alaire to guarantee that he was the superior officer of the pair. They wore fur hats that looked like gray loaves of bread, and seemed more ornamental than practical.

The hats looked absolutely ridiculous at first, but as the guards drew their swords as they approached, he decided that maybe the hats didn't look quite as silly as he had thought.

He had to control the automatic reflex to pull his blade. Naitachal's sword remained in its sheath.

The Dark Elf cleared his throat, and the two men started. "King Reynard, ruler of Althea to the south, has sent us to represent him. We come in peace. We would like to speak to your ruler, King Archenomen," Naitachal announced, in his best minstrel's voice. The words carried clearly through the chill air.

The two guards exchanged muffled words before the older guard replied, "You do not look like ambassadors. Look more like bandits to me. Show us your credentials." He spoke with a thick accent, making his words difficult to understand. For one thing, the emphasis was on all the wrong parts of the words; for another, they rolled the words around in their mouths as if they were gargling. *At least,* Alaire thought, *they're using the same language. Even if it does come out a little different.*

Naitachal sighed, sounding more annoyed than anything. The younger guard, still mounted on his dieren, began to advance toward them. Predictably, both Naitachal's and Alaire's horses reared up in fright.

"Hey!" Alaire shouted, fighting to get his horse back under control. The horse half-reared again, then shied sideways, nearly unseating him. When he calmed his steed down, he looked up to see how Naitachal's beast was behaving. Judging by the froth of dark sweat on its neck, it was no happier about the dieren than Alaire's gelding.

The young man laughed nastily. Alaire decided at once that the man must be a bully by nature; he had that look of unpleasant enjoyment on his face that reminded Alaire of an oversized page who had liked to catch the younger boys alone and throw them into the horse-trough. "You must be from down south after all, to be riding such loathsome, cowardly beasts. Never seen one of our riding animals, have you? Good. That's how we like it!"

Naitachal dismounted and rummaged through his pack. Finally, after a long wait, he withdrew the envelope Alaire's father had sent, with the scroll declaring Naitachal the official envoy of Althea.

"I have a letter from my king to yours if this isn't sufficient," Naitachal said, walking towards the guard. To look up at the mounted guard he had to remove the hood; when he did so the younger guard, then the captain, froze in shock.

"Dark Elf!" the senior guard shouted. "What are you doing in our kingdom?"

Before Naitachal could respond, the younger guard pulled his beast back, away from him. They were both terrified.

Of course. These people are terrified of magic. Most Elves are active practitioners, and Dark Elves are usually Necromancers!

Naitachal simply raised a calm eyebrow, as if he found their fear as nonsensical as a child's fear of beasts in the closet.

"Nothing that would violate your honorable laws, I assure you. King Reynard chose me to be his ambassador because he trusts me. I practice no elven magics, either Dark or White. Do not fear me. I am only King Reynard's servant."

The guards regarded them suspiciously. They seemed far more concerned with Naitachal's heritage than his credentials.

The Dark Elf frowned. "Well?" He waved the packet of papers at the guard. "Are you going to look at this or not? We'd really rather not stand here in the middle of the road for much longer."

The two guards exchanged looks, then the elder said, hastily, "Please proceed to Rozinki. With our blessings. If you leave now you should reach the city before nightfall."

With that the two guards wheeled their dieren about, and rode off, back down the route they just traveled. Naitachal stood in the middle of the road, watching them ride away, and when they were a considerable distance away, he smiled wickedly.

"They rattle easily around here, don't they?" he said. Alaire sensed a chuckle under his words.

"I suppose so," Alaire said, trying to restrain his own laughter. "We should get going. Rozinki sounds pretty good right about now!"

The road they followed showed more signs of travel; the ruts made by wheeled vehicles, churned up mud and animal droppings, all dusted with the remains of a recent light snow. Naitachal strained his neck and turned his ear forward, as if he was trying to hear something ahead.

The terrain continued to be hilly, with the hills gradually rising higher and higher before them. They could see nothing from the top of one but the crest of the next and the valley between.

An icy, wintry wind blasted them at each hilltop. Alaire stopped thinking of the two guards, stopped thinking of Rozinki, stopped thinking of anything except huddling on his saddle and avoiding the wind.

When they crested the final hill, Rozinki's sudden appearance below them came as a surprise.

At first it appeared to be a city of boats, and only boats, spread beneath them on a huge bay. A complicated network of wood and stone docks surrounded it. Many of the boats looked like homes as well as a source of income, and came in many different sizes and shapes. One of these boats, a long, flat craft, docked on the shore nearest them.

"Good gods," Naitachal said. "I had no idea Rozinki was this large." He stared down at the bay in silence for a moment. "Interesting. All those ships would imply they travel, but it certainly isn't to our kingdom. So whom *are* they visiting?"

Alaire shrugged. The Bard's eyes moved upwards a bit, then stopped. "And there's the castle."

Alaire followed his gaze to what he had thought was simply a more regular outcropping of stone on the cliff above the bay. Then his first impression was that it was a military fort, not a royal palace. Then again, it was probably both, palace *and* fortification; the harsh land probably made the kind of castles Alaire knew of impossible. Squat and round, the palace perched in the cliff above the town.

"Doesn't look much like a castle," Alaire said absently, as he urged his horse to follow Naitachal down a steep section of road. "How are we supposed to get across this bay?"

The Dark Elf said nothing as they drew closer to the shore, where the road came to a complete stop. A clanking bell on the flat boat caught his attention, and as the people reacted he realized that this must be a signal the craft was about to leave. *A ferry!* Alaire thought in surprise. He had never seen a ferry large enough to take several laden carts and wagons at once. The only ferry he had ever seen could only take a single donkey and its little cart.

"They have a full load already," Naitachal observed. A man and a woman began moving about the boat, tying down wheels, herding people to benches along the sides. "Or maybe not," he added, pulling out a purse of coins.

They rode straight up to the boatmaster. He'd started to pull the ramps back onto his ship, but stopped when he saw the silver. The gray-haired boatmaster seemed as fit as a man of thirty, despite his ancient, wrinkled face. With a visible effort he turned away from the coins, shaking his head and saying wordlessly, *no, we can take no more.*

Naitachal held up a large silver coin, and the boatmaster paused, as if considering. He came over and studied the coin, and muttered something to Naitachal in a language Alaire didn't understand. After biting it, he grinned widely, and motioned for them to board the ferry, horses and all.

Alaire dismounted before they were underway and tethered his horse. With several other able-bodied passengers he helped the boatmaster pole the craft across the bay. The water never got very deep, and what had appeared to be a large bay turned out to be a marsh dotted with tiny islands, around which other boats were moored. A cold, icy wind whipped around them, and Alaire was grateful for the exercise; it helped him to limber up and keep warm.

If the boatmaster was ambivalent about them, several of the other passengers were the opposite: One man and woman, evidently farmers and wearing conservative black and white clothing, kept glaring at both Alaire and Naitachal with resentful and suspicious glances.

Must not see too many foreigners, particularly from the sunny south, he thought, remembering to smile when their eyes happened to meet.

Naitachal seemed to take this all without a single sign that he noticed or cared. Alaire thought that it might be because he got this kind of reaction from humans all the time. Perhaps he was simply playing his part, and he had no intention of showing that these folk bothered him.

Soon they arrived at the pier on the other side of the marshy bay, and as soon as they docked the Suinomen natives wasted no time in putting distance between themselves and the newcomers.

"First, a bath," Naitachal announced. "Then we change into something impressive and expensive, and go present ourselves properly. Do you see anything that looks like an inn?"

The language of Suinomen closely resembled, but was not identical to, their own. Right now the differences were enough to keep Alaire totally confused. He finally ignored the voices and concentrated on simply observing. He ought to be able to spot an inn simply by the customers going in and out!

Naitachal led the way down the pier to the main wharf. The stone dock ran along the curve of the shore, out of sight, with little activity near the ferry. People and goods appeared further on; sailors shouted and cursed in a babble of strange tongues that were more alien than the boatmaster's.

Naitachal seemed to know what he was doing; he dismounted and led his horse up a stone ramp to a higher street, and Alaire followed his example. On this upper level there were more shops, and each had a sign over the door that indicated the shop's specialty; a wooden fish for seafood, a bee for honey, wax and candles, a bigger fish with a fountain coming out of its head for oil and some kind of meat and ivory products —

That last sign puzzled Alaire. He could not imagine what a fish had to do with oil and ivory.

Finally, they came across a sign with a crude bed painted on it, and behind the inn was a small stable. Paying for the brief use of a room and bath became an exercise in pantomime, but the people here seemed to appreciate silver, no matter whose face was on the coins.

Alaire scrubbed himself pink in the communal bath while Naitachal cooked himself in the adjoining steam room. They returned to their room wrapped in woolen robes supplied by the inn. The bardling had had only the briefest glimpse of the clothing his father had supplied for them. He almost choked on laughter when he saw his Master's outfit. Now Naitachal wore a frilly, lace-dripping shirt, a scarlet, gold-trimmed coat, and scarlet satin breeches. A gold-trimmed scarlet hat with a trailing plume crowned the silver-white hair. The entire outfit was the kind of thing young and foolish nobles in Althea would wear to impress one other. The knee-high, scarlet leather boots were equally grand, and the gold heels were simply the penultimate touch of nonsense. No one would be able to fear someone who dressed like *that*.

Perhaps that was exactly what Father had in mind.

"Not bad," Alaire commented, trying on his own courtier's garb. "Even if it makes you look like a procurer."

"It does *not*," Naitachal protested, glancing at his reflection in a door-length mirror. "My father would have been proud to see me like this. Who do you suppose decided to make it some other color than black?"

"Father, of course," Alaire said, pulling on a boot. His outfit was nowhere near as grand as his Master's, but it felt good to wear fine clothes again. He had fallen out of the habit when he started training under Naitachal; after all, it hardly made sense to wear silks and satins for sword practice. "I suspect he wants to emphasize your heritage, without suggesting that you might be a *practicing* Necromancer, to gain some sort of leverage."

"Your father is canny," the Bard replied. "My race is impossible to hide, so why not announce it? As the proverb says, 'if you're going to walk on thin ice, you might as well dance.'" He strutted grandly in front of the mirror. The gesture was so, well, un*elf*like Alaire burst out laughing.

"What do you find so amusing, human?" Naitachal demanded, fiercely.

Alaire snorted to see him standing there, hands on hips. "It just looks as if . . . well . . . you're modeling a dress."

"I do *not*. I *have* not ever," Naitachal said indignantly. Then he paused, sheepishly. "Well. Truthfully, I have . . ."

He went on to tell Alaire about the time Kevin and his group dressed up as dancing girls to flee Westerin. By the time he finished, Alaire had doubled over in laughter.

Naitachal stood over him, with his arms crossed over his chest, glaring like a black-and-scarlet, pompous peacock. "Well, it *worked*," he said at last.

Alaire collected himself and straightened the fine silk shirt and suede breeches. "Think we should carry swords?"

Naitachal shrugged. "Of course. It's expected, out here."

Alaire thought he could read something else, a brief, disturbing expression in the elf's eyes.

And daggers too, he thought, buckling the jeweled

knives to his belt. Naitachal led the way out of the inn, into the streets of Rozinki.

The stable hands had done an exceptional job of grooming the horses. No doubt this and the brief rest had refreshed the beasts, which fidgeted and danced on the cobblestone streets of Rozinki. They certainly knew what cobblestones were; they came from the royal stables, and had no reason to act as if they had never felt stone under their feet before. Their antics gave Alaire something to think about besides their current situation.

"Be young and stupid," Naitachal said, as they guided their horses up the ramps and streets leading to the palace. "Everyone will be certain to ignore you, and they'll dismiss anything you might let slip. In other words, be yourself."

Alaire felt his face grow hot at the sly glance Naitachal cast him, but before he could protest, he saw for himself the wisdom of such a move. *I remember the way the elders of Fenrich always ignored the young and foolish boys of the village back home. Perhaps I should chase girls — discretely of course — I remember what that one old man used to say. About how in the springtime, when the blood runs away from the head and the mind freezes, the only difference between a young man and a goat is that you can eat the goat when you get tired of its games.*

"But don't overdo it," Naitachal hastened to add.

"Oh, certainly not," Alaire said. "I don't have a silly impulse in my body. After all, I don't go around wearing dresses, or pouring ice-cold springwater on my friends."

Even though Naitachal said nothing, Alaire saw the slightest grin of satisfaction on the dark, elven features.

They rode in silence then, to concentrate on controlling their skittish beasts. In between hauling his horse's head down and curbing his prancing, Alaire studied the city, which followed the hill's natural curves. High above, the castle presided over the town and bay like a squat, stony frog. All the city's streets led upwards to it. The cobblestone streets themselves had seen better days and there were places where the cobbles were missing altogether. Some of the less populated streets, dark in the shadows of decaying stone buildings on either side of them, stank of stale beer and urine. Though not clearly marked, these establishments were probably taverns, their doors and iron-shuttered windows open to air out the fetid interiors. The barkeepers, bleary-eyed, casually threw unconscious drunks into the limestone gutters. Alaire rode without comment. There were always cheap taverns, cheap beer, and cheap drunks to populate the first and drink the second. There probably always would be.

Then, in a more cheery section of town, the structures were all of wood, with more windows to let in light and air. Instead of thatch, lush green moss covered the roofs. This was obviously a business district, and native Suinomites swarmed markets and shops, all wearing dieren garments of one style or another. When they turned to look at the two Altheans, they stared at their horses. Everyone else rode the splay-footed dieren, if they rode anything. Not another horse was in sight.

"Do you notice anything . . . peculiar?" Naitachal asked quietly as they rode past aisles of merchants hawking fresh vegetables and live poultry.

Alaire had to admit he had, but he wasn't sure what it was. Granted, this was a foreign country. The language here seemed to be a mixture of their own and one other, a heavy, guttural tongue that was rough on the ears. The city, even back in the tavern district, was immaculately clean of trash and sewage. He could only assume Rozinki had an efficient sewer system and equally efficient rubbish-collectors. Even in Silver City one found telltale garbage, but not here. Cleanliness obsessed these humans.

Then he saw what it was that was so unusual here. *The humans. Only humans, here.*

No White or Dark Elves, no orcs, no dwarves. The signs also were in the human tongue, and there was nothing written in Elven, Dwarven or Orcish.

Alaire began to feel very uncomfortable for Naitachal. He glanced over at his Master, relieved to find his ridiculous hat completely covered the top, pointed portion of his ears. He looked human in every other way. Though he was the only *black* human among these people, he didn't seem to be attracting nearly as much attention as his gelding.

"This is a very . . . human settlement," Naitachal noted, echoing Alaire's thoughts. "Only humans."

"Yes, I see," Alaire said. "But let me point out that your absurd hat covers your ears. You look human."

Naitachal looked relieved. "Of course I do," he said, but didn't sound completely convinced. His nose wrinkled. "I must have imagined that smell just then."

"What smell was that?"

"The unmistakable odor of tar and feathers."

By the time they reached the castle, the sun prepared to set on the sea. Already the air had become considerably frostier; Alaire wished he had not packed up the dieren coat, even if it didn't go with anything he now wore.

Archenomen's palace was considerably larger than it had appeared from across the bay. A lesser wall surrounded it, perhaps for ornamentation, since it did not compare to the castle itself. Either by design or accident, it was as black as Naitachal; every stone, every metal fixture, every wooden adornment, including the twin doors of the main entrance.

Guards dressed much like the ones who had approached them earlier that day came forward with, of all the silly things, ceremonial spears. Alaire smothered a smile with faint amusement. They were thin and gaudy and would never make a suitable weapon; he would have preferred his own short dagger in a fight to one of those frail things. Alaire relaxed, knowing no fight was likely to occur, in spite of the guards and their arrogant stance.

"State your business," one of the guards said with brusque politeness.

Naitachal rode forward, and bowed over the neck of his horse. "We have come to see the king of this land, Archenomen. I am Ambassador Naitachal, representing the kingdom of Althea, appointed by King Reynard."

The two guards conferred privately, then one came forward to examine Naitachal's papers. Alaire could only suppose that he hadn't identified Naitachal as a Dark Elf, yet. His expression was bland as he took the letter and scroll back.

Nodding to the Bard, the guard said, "Go with him," indicating the other guard. "No horses," he added.

So here they dismounted, and stable hands appeared to take their horses. The doors were a good two stories high, and the knockers were so heavy the guard had trouble lifting one. One solid *boom* announced their presence.

A small window opened, through which the guard spoke to an unseen figure in the unknown tongue. He beckoned to Naitachal, who again relinquished his papers. The letter and scroll disappeared through this window, and the huge twin doors slowly opened.

The small figure who greeted them did not inspire fear or confidence. Alaire's first impression was of a man who had risen as far as he could as a servant, and still didn't like his position. He was old enough to be Alaire's father, but was thinner and more gaunt than Naitachal. The livery he wore had all the trappings of an upper servant's attire, though a little less elaborate than what Alaire saw at home. What struck Alaire as odd was the long flowing cloak that trailed behind him. The thin fabric was useless for providing warmth. The man certainly carried himself as if he thought he was serving in a place far below the rank he truly deserved. *Does he have royal blood?*

Alaire's first fear, however, was that the servant would spot him for what *he* was: royalty. Upper servants had a way of spotting these things. Alaire looked away and tried to appear submissive, bowing his head slightly, as he had seen his father's secretary act at home.

"Please, enter," the servant said nervously. "Welcome to the House of Archenomen. I am Paavo, the head of the house here. The guards inform me that you are . . . ambassadors from Althea?"

"Naitachal," said the Dark Elf. "And this is my secretary, Alaire of . . . house Turonen," he added, improvising. "I do hope we haven't come at an inopportune time. It's been a long hard ride, but if the King isn't receiving today we would be pleased to call tomorrow."

Alaire stifled a laugh. It would be rude for a king to refuse to see any ambassador with proper credentials. His Master's statement bordered on the impolite, as it suggested that Archenomen might commit a blunder by refusing to see them. *Perhaps I'm assuming too much here,* Alaire thought. *This is, after all, a foreign land, with its own rules of etiquette. For all I know we are the ones being rude, calling without prior notification.*

His first impression seemed to be correct, since Paavo quickly ushered them through a grand gallery, where three young servants were lighting hundreds of small candles on a chandelier. They stared at Naitachal as they passed, but paid no attention to Alaire.

The bardling wanted badly to gawk, and finally decided that the best way to handle this was to do just that. If he looked like a highborn idiot, the kind of young man an envoy might be saddled with, he could well be taken for harmless.

So he gawked, the young servants smirked, and Paavo looked pained. Naitachal caught the ruse and sighed audibly, and he and Paavo exchanged knowing glances.

Just as we wanted it, Alaire thought, wondering just how far to take the silly-ass routine. He decided to wait until someone took a keen interest in him before proving there was nothing interesting about him.

Paavo led them to a smaller chamber, crowded with people in gaudy, expensive-looking clothing — though nothing as gaudy as Naitachal's scarlet glory. On a dais at the end of the room, there was a gilded throne; in that throne was a man who could only be the King.

He wore a cape of purple velvet, lined with ermine, and a robe of the same material, embroidered with bits of gold and amber. A thin, delicately trimmed beard covered a thick set of jowls, and from his girth it was obvious he ate very well. His eyes peered from the white, doughy flesh like candied green cherries, regarding them with a combination of curiosity and caution. Around him lay rugs of fur, not dieren, but possibly bear.

High above the throne, set into the wall and hammered into brass or even a plate of thin gold, was a device of some kind, with the prominent letter *A* in the center.

Two young men, boys, really, stood at attention at either side of the King. Servants, Alaire supposed. They wore hose and tight, formal jerkins, with a double skirt of more purple velvet slashed into panes. The effect was striking, Alaire had to admit, and began to wonder if the King's personal servants here were relatives, or perhaps favored by-blows. He stayed several steps behind Naitachal as he approached the King, and was grateful no one paid the slightest bit of attention to him.

Everyone in the royal circle regarded Naitachal with cool detachment, though Alaire detected concealed surprise in the King. *He wasn't ready for a black ambassador,* he noted with amusement. *Wait till the King sees the rest of him!*

With an exaggerated motion, Naitachal bowed before the King as he removed his absurd feathered hat, revealing the two long, pointed elven ears.

Pandemonium erupted in the room. The King hissed as he drew back in surprise, a look of horror and dread coming over his royal features. He even held his arms up, as if protecting himself from anything originating from Naitachal's general direction. The two young servants were guards as well, and from stands behind them they drew short swords and took a position halfway between the King and Naitachal.

A moment later large double doors burst open on either side of the throne. Five soldiers, like the ones they had met on the road, charged in, but froze in their tracks when they saw Naitachal. Behind the soldiers was a tiny trio of magicians, with purple robes and ridiculous, conical hats, who immediately formed a protective circle around the King.

I think we just made a big mistake. This isn't going very well, Alaire thought as he watched their first attempts at diplomatic relations crumble to dust. Residency in the palace dungeon was beginning to look like a real possibility.

"Elf!" the King roared. "*Dark* Elf. Why have you polluted us with your presence?"

The soldiers stood their ground, shifting nervously. The young servant-guards stood defiantly, inching closer to the Dark Elf, swordtips flashing with reflected candlelight.

Naitachal yawned, discretely, and smiled.

"Your highness," Paavo interjected politely, approaching the King on his throne. Although he lowered his voice, the acoustics were such that Alaire could easily pick out what the servant was saying.

"It would seem wise," Paavo said, in hurried, hushed tones, "to remember that, despite his unfavorable heritage, this *is* the Ambassador from Althea. I doubt seriously he is here to harm you, magically or otherwise. Perhaps we should hear him out?"

Alaire cringed at the insolence. *Never would a servant presume to offer advice to the King!* he thought in indignation. Then something else occurred to him. *So. Perhaps this* is *no mere servant.*

King Archenomen seemed to consider this before snapping his fingers three times, quickly. The soldiers withdrew, slowly, uncertainly, behind the doors. The magicians, looking more like religious leaders (which perhaps they were), remained, looking down their long, pointed noses at Naitachal. The two boys returned their short swords to their stands, and took their places beside the King.

"I beg pardon, your Highness," Naitachal said grandly. "Perhaps I should have sent prior warning about my . . . family," he said, pausing at the end, as if uncertain how to phrase the statement. "But I did present my credentials and my nature to two of your guards upon the road here. Perhaps they have not yet reported this to you?"

He raised an eyebrow, and the King scowled.

Someone is going to pay for that little omission. . . .

"I bear a letter from King Reynard himself. Perhaps this will explain the situation in a little more detail." He smiled, a smile so gentle and without guile that Alaire could almost believe it himself. "I fear, your highness, that I have allowed complacency to cause an uncomfortable situation."

"Quite the contrary," King Archenomen said. His voice boomed, but the slight crack on the last syllable indicated some residual shock. "I'm afraid I've overreacted. Those of Suinomen seldom run across citizens of other countries, especially members of less — other races." He smiled broadly, and insincerely.

Lesser races, Alaire thought, completing the sentence another way, and sighed to himself. *We have our work cut out for us.*

"Please, have dinner with us tonight. You may stay in our royal visitor's suite. Will your . . . servant be staying with you, or should we put him in the servant's quarters?"

Maddeningly, Naitachal seemed to consider this. When he cast a brief glance in Alaire's direction, Alaire thought he sensed the hint of a devious smile.

You wouldn't! Alaire thought, although he knew that the Bard would, if he thought it amusing enough.

After considering this, Naitachal said, indifferently, "No, I will be requiring his presence for secretarial work. Allow me to introduce Alaire. Although he is my assistant, he is near and dear to the King's heart."

Naitachal let this last statement dangle in the air for

just the right amount of time, with just the right amount of inflection, suggesting innuendo. *Near to the King's heart? Could he be implying to His Majesty that I'm a royal bastard?* The ruse seemed to make sense. *That would explain my clothes, and why I'm with Naitachal. Otherwise, it would look odd.*

The King gazed thoughtfully at Alaire, then, with a knowing look, nodded in his direction. "I see. We will be most hospitable to you both."

Naitachal didn't seem to hear this. "If it is convenient, could we put him in an adjoining room? If not, he can sleep on the floor of my room."

What?

"Certainly, certainly," the King said. "Paavo, would you please show them their quarters?"

As they filed out of the royal chambers, Alaire thought, indignantly, hoping that Naitachal would somehow hear the thoughts — *On the floor? Really! Master, we are going to have a little talk very soon!*

Chapter IV

Alaire was glad to find a comfortable, if lumpy, goose-feather bed tucked away in a corner of his room, which turned out to be the antechamber to Naitachal's quarters. The walls were the ubiquitous stone; the floors, as they seemed to be everywhere in the palace, were reddish-gold planks of a wood he couldn't identify. This explained the pleasant, spicy aroma that permeated the rooms. Naitachal had a plush room with plastered walls and ceiling, painted with elaborate scenes of buxom wood nymphs. The room, unlike Alaire's, had its own fireplace, with a chimney of carved stone, and an ample supply of firewood. The enormous canopied bed could have accommodated a family of ten.

"I might want to sleep on the floor, anyway," Alaire said, standing in front of the fireplace. He shivered in the chill that already filled the apartment, although it was still early in the evening.

"I doubt that dragging the mattress in here would raise any eyebrows." Naitachal frowned, in a way that was particularly disturbing to Alaire. "They probably expect bizarre, eccentric behavior from both of us. I must be the first elf of any color most of these people have ever seen. I knew that intellectually, of course, but actually dealing with it is irritating."

Alaire wanted to quiz him more on his first impressions, but a knock sounded on the door. A young servant informed them dinner was ready, and that His Majesty King Archenomen requested their presence at the table.

Naitachal's look seemed to say, *We'll compare notes later*, as they walked down the torchlit halls to the dining room, where Alaire smelled the overpowering aroma of cooked meat and potatoes.

Eating with the King and his court turned out to be a complicated affair. A multi-tiered floor held several long tables, each one at a different level. It looked rather as if someone had carved narrow platforms into the side of a hill, and dropped a section of table onto each one. The lower tables were less decorated than the ones atop. The one at the apex had a huge cooked pig as its centerpiece. The King presided over the event like a judge, scrutinizing everyone who came in. No queen was in sight, and Alaire made a note to find out if there was one, or if the King had a harem of concubines, as sometimes happened in other distant lands. The servant led Naitachal to this higher tier, and automatically Alaire went after them.

"No, no, *no!*" one of the kitchen wenches admonished, waving a wooden spoon. She was hauling a kettle of gravy that probably outweighed them both. "Only the ambassador dines with the King. You sit *down there,*" she said sharply, as if he was an idiot, and went on with her task.

Alaire didn't like the sound of the phrase "down there" one bit. She led him to a section of tables almost a story and a half below the King's. Naitachal continued to the head table without him. *Oh well*, he thought. *So be it. Perhaps I can learn something useful* down there.

Those of the lowest social order ate here, he soon learned. Even Paavo sat a tier above him. The head servant sneered down at Alaire as he took his seat, a miserable little stool at a bare wooden table.

Bad manners at the dinner table are ill-advised,
Alaire seethed inwardly. *Particularly when everyone
has knives.*

Alaire found himself at a table lined with Suinomen
natives who evidently did not speak his language,
although some of the servants bringing food to the table
did. Alaire appraised their clothing with a knowing eye,
and guessed that these folk were the servants or
secretaries of those above. Except for one thing; every
one of them had a cape or cloak of fur. The dining hall
was a bit drafty, but didn't warrant the use of furs he saw
around him, and he wondered if there was something
no one had told them about. *There always is.*

He saw a flock of young girls at the tables two levels
up. None of them were particularly attractive, at least
by his standards, and some he even cringed at. They
watched his table eagerly. He glanced up, far up,
where Naitachal was sitting, and saw right away that
the Dark Elf was too far to offer advice or distraction.

Some of the young women were discreet, but others stared openly at *him.* Alaire was afraid to return
the looks, at least too directly. Even flirting could be
dangerous. *They can't know I'm a prince,* he thought
frantically. *I hope Naitachal is covering my tracks up
there. I wouldn't want to become part of a deal.* Now it
wasn't only the girls near him who watched him from
under their long, coquettish eyelashes. Some of the
girls sat at the topmost table, with his Master and the
King. *They must be his daughters. If they find out who
I really am, I could become some sort of bargaining
chip! Aaaargh!*

Halfway through the meal Alaire noticed an empty
wooden cup near his plate. Occasionally a servant
would come by and drop a single flower petal into the
vessel, and when he looked inside it was half full. The

petals had something — names? — written delicately on them in an odd script. He shuddered, considering the possible meanings and ramifications.

Could these petals be a trysting invitation? He guessed about thirty petals were in there now, and they were still coming. *Gods! There wouldn't be anything left!* he thought in horror. He took extra care not to touch the cup after that. Better to be cold and distant than get into something there would be no getting out of!

Besides the petals, the situation was hardly comfortable. Paavo had claimed they were the guests of honor, but *he* was eating with the kitchen help. The food was terrible, since the meat was unidentifiable, and nearly raw, the bread burned or still doughy, and the rest all seemed to consist of variations on dried peas and beans cooked in fish-oil.

He was here to observe, so he did his best to ignore the food and the girls and keep his eyes open. He noticed surreptitious glimpses towards Naitachal from the greater nobles, some even overtly hostile, and he wondered if this was because of his Dark Elven heritage or if it was because he represented a country Suinomen had chosen to make into an enemy.

Could be a little of both, he thought. At the first few mouthfuls of mystery-meat, his hunger had overcome his aversion. Now the edge was off his appetite, and he wished the evening could just end.

Despite Naitachal's dark presence at the board of honor, the meal became festive, with idle chatter in both languages flowing from table to table. A servant offered Alaire wine, but he politely refused, knowing that even a little bit in his exhausted state would lay him out on the floor. He seldom drank anyway.

As the meal ended, a six-piece consort struck up some dance music. Evidently there was no prohibition here against couples dancing, and a few of the more bold or boisterous joined in a lively gigue in a section of floor cleared away by the servants. Alaire took this chance to try to get back to Naitachal.

He encountered a barrier of noblemen and their assistants; apparently, during dinner, word had circulated that it might be wise to cultivate Ambassador Naitachal's acquaintance. From what little Alaire saw, the nobles showed him at least the respect his office deserved. However, they kept a certain uneasy distance from his Master, who remained a solitary black figure ringed by a moat of stark wooden floors, bridged only by the briefest bow and a few hurried words.

Later, I'll talk to him, Alaire thought. *He seems to be doing fine, given the circumstances. I would only attract attention if I made a point of joining him.*

He backed away from the impromptu receiving line, looking for something to do. He felt completely useless. But then, that was the idea.

At another table sat several apparently available young ladies (not of highborn, but of some other ranked or wealthy class). A young man, a teenager really, stood in front of the table, telling an animated tale of some sort, gesturing wildly with his arms in wide sweeping motions. The boy's striking attire impressed Alaire more than his demeanor did. His white and red cloak, embroidered with gold thread, hung to the side. He wore the most unusual gold hose the Prince had ever seen. Despite the finery, however, he looked like an unmade bed. Half his shirt hung out over his hose, and his white scarf looked ready to fall off. As he drew closer, he saw why; the boy was drunk out of his mind.

Alaire thought the boy was telling the women a humorous story in the native language. *Perhaps he's*

some kind of well-born court jester, Alaire thought.
But as he continued to watch, it became obvious that,
despite the young man's brave (and intoxicated) attempts at gallantry, the women were laughing *at* him.

He was obviously the son of one of the nobles
meeting with Naitachal, given his dress, and he'd had
far too much to drink.

Alaire's heart went out to the stranger, as he knew
too well the stresses a royal court could put on young
men and women. *He's of the age when parents start
pairing their children off, whether or not they even
know each other,* he thought, reminding himself that
his father had given him more choices than most
noble children. It could even be that the poor youngster had just been informed of his impending
nuptials . . . and that the bride made one of the dieren
look like a better mate.

*Better save this lad before he makes a complete fool
of himself,* he decided, though he knew it was probably too late. *Or at least, before he offends someone.*

Alaire wasn't even sure the young man spoke the
Althean language; he approached his target with some
trepidation, and took him by the elbow to lead him off
in what he hoped was a friendly manner. He half
expected the stranger to swing around and hit him, or
at least try to escape his "rescuer." Yet in the general
confusion, with people of all castes milling around,
and music increasing in volume, he led the young man
away from the table without arousing his suspicion, or,
apparently, his attention.

Alaire took him to a balcony that looked over the
courtyard below. No one else was out there in the
cold, and Alaire shivered in a wind which bit sharply at
his bare skin.

The young man started to shiver a little as well, as
he looked about in a kind of daze, as if he could not

imagine how the table full of young women had turned into a balcony. *Good. Maybe this will sober him up a little.* Alaire gently turned him, so lanterns burning on either side of the balcony illuminated his face.

He looked at Alaire, bewildered, as if it was the first time he had noticed him, and began babbling in his native tongue.

Alaire shook his head. "No, I'm sorry, whoever you are. I don't speak your language at all."

If I can keep him out here in this cold he might straighten up a little. Alaire had been drunk exactly twice in his life, once on his thirteenth birthday and then, more recently, at the wedding of the daughter of the Mayor of Fenrich. Both times, ice applied to the forehead seemed to take care of the more unpleasant side effects. This wind was practically the same thing.

"A southerner, then," the boy said suddenly. "Don't get many of you around here."

Though it was with a heavy accent, including a strong rolling of the r's, he spoke Alaire's language clearly, without hesitation. As the boy sobered, he examined the bardling, in a way that reminded Alaire of the King's look as they entered. The youngster even took the sleeve of his shirt and studied the fabric.

One thing was certain, this youngster was not one of the servants.

He must have said that aloud, for the young man started. "You're no peasant yourself!" the boy said loudly, but it did not sound as if he was trying to be impolite. "What brings you to Rozinki?"

"Business, of a sort," Alaire said, hesitating. "I'm . . . Alaire, an assistant to the Ambassador of Althea. The dark fellow, up there with the King."

"Ambassador from Althea? Didn't know we even had one." His face went sour, as if he'd bit into a bad apple. "Who wants to discuss kingdom business tonight, anyway? It's not even midnight yet!"

As the boy spoke, a puff of breeze blew his breath into Alaire's face, and Alaire wrinkled his nose. The boy smelled like a brewery.

How much has he had to drink anyway? Alaire wondered, since he didn't recall seeing him at the dinner earlier. There was something about the way he phrased things that made Alaire wonder: *Is he some by-blow of the royal family too?*

"Then I suppose you've already had the pleasure of meeting my *father*," the stranger continued, sardonically. The way he emphasized the word "father" suggested they didn't get along very well.

"Well," Alaire said, uncertainly. "Perhaps. I'm sorry, but which man was your father?" He knew he was probably committing a sizable blunder by admitting ignorance, but could think of no other way to find out.

A broad smile creased the stranger's boyish features, a mischievous gleam that made Alaire instantly wary.

The young man led Alaire to the balcony doors, where the supper guests were still milling about, circling around Naitachal like curious, but frightened little birds about a great black eagle.

"See the big fat man up there in the purple coat?" the boy asked ungraciously.

The only person in purple was the King. "You mean King Archenomen?" Alaire was aghast.

This is the crown prince? Drunk as a soldier on leave?

"Prince Kainemonen at your service," the boy announced, bowing an exaggerated bow, removing his hat with a sweeping gesture. "But you can call me Kai. Everyone else does. When they don't call me useless, wastrel, or ne'er-do-well." He teetered, just a little, and Alaire gently pushed him upright. "I think I was

an accident. I don't look like any of the family. Perhaps
I was . . ."

Alaire stood frozen in shock at the unasked for reve-
lations, but Kai seemed to realize that he was babbling
things he shouldn't and interrupted himself with a
shrug.

"Well, probably not. Such things would be too
much an embarrassment. I doubt they would have let
me live. But yes, gods help Suinomen, I'll be king,
whenever Father croaks."

*Holy heavens, he despises his father and himself,
and he doesn't care who knows it,* Alaire thought with
dismay. *Assuming he's telling the truth. Could be, the
ale has gone to his mind, so he thinks he's a prince. But
everything else certainly fits.* His eyebrows raised
when he noticed the boy's ring, a chunky, gold piece
that flashed when the candle-light caught it just right.
*The large letter "A." A simplified version of the Arche-
nomen Coat of Arms I saw hanging over the King's
throne. Perhaps he is the Prince after all.*

Then again, maybe he was only what Alaire was
pretending to be; a royal bastard.

*I might as well keep talking to him, whether he is or
not. Even a drunk having grand delusions can supply
a lot of interesting information.*

"The good news is," the boy continued glibly, "I
don't have to do a thing around here! Just have fun.
That's what he ordered me to do, anyway; have fun,
don't poke my nose into politics or business, and stay
out of his way."

Alaire wondered just how much to share with Kai.
At home, a prince did more than just "have fun."
Derek, the Crown Prince of Althea and the oldest of
the brothers, took a personal interest in the affairs of
the nation. After all, he would eventually be in charge
of it. What better way to learn a job than to do it?

From the age of thirteen Derek had been in on council meetings, inspected the Palace Guard regularly, and in general kept abreast of everything going on. Including, Alaire assumed, this little trip their father sent them on.

Alaire regarded the drunk lad before him, and found it difficult to imagine his caring about the affairs of Suinomen.

"Is that all you do?" Alaire asked. *He seems to be in quite a talkative mood. Why not encourage it?*

"Just about," Kai replied. Alaire eyed a marble bench nearby, considered moving closer to it, in case Kai should need to sit down. "Father told me to stay out of his business, so I do. They don't let me do anything involving the kingdom, or the Guard. And nobody in the kingdom will have anything to do with *me*, except Captain Lyam and Sir Jehan."

Remember those names. They could be important, Alaire thought. *Though it is starting to look like this Kai might be a dead end for inside information, there is a lot of general information I could get from him. Things the whole court knows, but we don't. For instance, why do they want to invade Althea?*

"Well, Alaire," Kai said, slapping his shoulder. "How would you like to flee all this pompous nonsense and go see some *real* entertainment?"

Well . . . why not?

"Sure, Kai," Alaire said, cautiously. "But I really need to inform my Master that I'll be going, first."

"Oh, you'll do nothing of the sort," Kai said, good-naturedly. "You'll get us both into trouble and someone will probably stop us. I'll have one of the servants tell him for us, after we're gone."

That didn't exactly sound like a good idea. "Well . . . I don't know about this. . . ."

But he had protested too late. "Come on," Kai said

joyfully, grabbing Alaire by the wrist. "This place is getting boring anyway."

Reluctantly, Alaire let the boy lead him away. He had both bad and good feelings about this. Good, because he knew he would learn *something* about this bizarre kingdom. Bad, because he could tell by the feral gleam in Kai's eye that they would both be rump-deep in trouble when they got back.

Assuming they didn't get rump-deep in trouble long *before* they got back.

"Got your sword with you?" Kai asked as they dashed down stone stairs at the end of the balcony, into the chill night.

Chapter V

Kai had obviously planned the deceptively hasty get-away in advance. A royal carriage, lamplit at the four corners, and gilded like a maiden's jewel-casket, was waiting for them just inside the palace walls. Harnessed to it were two large dieren, stomping and snorting, eager to get underway. But despite the finery, which left no doubt as to which family it belonged to, it was obvious as they drew nearer that the carriage had seen better days. Somewhat dented and worn, from the number of scrapes, splintered places, and missing bits of trim, it had apparently clipped many trees and lampposts. When Alaire saw the driver, a grubby sort of servant, in dark, rumpled clothes, clutching a leather wine flask, he knew why it looked that way. The driver looked to be as drunk as Kai. Maybe drunker.

"Don't worry about him," Kai said, waving casually at the driver, who ignored them both. "He can find the taverns blindfolded."

"That's a relief," Alaire replied wryly, stepping into the carriage. The carriage lurched forward, and in a few moments it was careening down the hill at full speed.

"Father always does get angry when I take off from official events like this," Kai shouted over a deafening rattle, seating himself awkwardly in the shifting, swaying vehicle. "Says it embarrasses him for me to go off like this. With any luck no one will miss me. Ah, there it is!" Kai produced a leather flask and handed it graciously to Alaire.

Glad I wore at least a thin coat to supper, Alaire thought, watching his frozen breath, visible even inside the carriage. *Gods, Kai probably doesn't even feel the cold, in his condition.* He braced himself in the frigid, plush seat, stained with wine and beer and who knew what else.

He took only a small sip and returned it. *Not too bad. A red, fruity party wine. Just the thing for young, inexperienced tastes.* Nothing like the wine he would have had at home, for supper. He respected good wine — Naitachal would have killed him if he had simply gulped the stuff with no care for anything but alcohol content. And after that bout of sickness and hangover at thirteen, he had learned to respect what *bad* wine could do. Kai, naturally, took a long swallow of the decadent stuff. *Probably strong, too. A quick, cheap drunk.*

It was difficult to talk or drink, in the swaying vehicle. They rode for some time, while Kai did most of the babbling, sometimes shifting into his native language. Mostly useless blather, Alaire realized after a moment. Although it was hard to hear over the loud clatter. The wooden cage Kai had imprisoned him in was going full tilt, as fast as the dieren could go, Alaire guessed. Twice, huge potholes violently jostled the carriage contents, landing Alaire in the floor, and then Kai on Alaire's lap, laughing hysterically. The rear axle made a strange grinding noise, which got louder as their journey progressed. What lethargy Alaire felt earlier had evaporated. Now his blood roared in his ears; he clutched the sides of the carriage and feared for his life.

"Whoooooeeee!" Kai said as the vehicle slowed to a

halt, then gracelessly stopped. He tumbled onto the floor as the carriage lurched once more. "Wanta go back and do that again?"

Alaire, politely, but vehemently, refused. *"No. Where are we?"*

"Where do you *think*?" Kai said, getting off the carriage floor, where he had landed. "Where the real fun is. In the happy part of town!" He tumbled out the door, leaving Alaire to follow.

Alaire emerged from the carriage, knees shaking, and stepped down onto cobblestone. Without comment, he noticed one of the carriage lamps had shaken free and fallen to the street, somewhere behind them. Also, a spoke in one of the wheels was missing.

Grateful to be on solid ground again, Alaire looked quickly around the street where they had stopped. It was a narrow, cobblestone avenue in an old part of town, lined on either side by many cheap, ill-kept taverns. A few torches lit the streets, with too many shadows for Alaire's comfort.

A small group of men staggered out the door of the tavern nearest them, singing and leaning on each others' shoulders. Alaire had hoped to be able to let his guard down, but when he saw the great contrast between their clothing and everyone else's, he shuddered. *Might as well paint a target on our backs. Attack us, we're rich,* he thought. *Good thing Naitachal's got most of the money.*

But strangely, no one seemed to pay them any particular attention. The street crowd, rough workers, ne'er-do-wells, loafers, probable thieves, who knew what else, all seemed hell-bent on getting drunk that night. As did Kai.

The Crown Prince led him down the long, four-story canyon of bars, brothels and places that offered "entertainment." Alaire's eyes nearly fell out of his head when he saw an advertisement for a show. *Something for everyone*, he thought. *That is, everyone except non-humans. Not a sign of elves, orcs, or dwarves anywhere.*

Kai led him directly to the first tavern on the right. Carved on the wooden sign hanging over the door, dulled with age, was the image of a large dragon on its back, its legs sticking straight up. The tongue lolled lifelessly to one side. THE DEAD DRAGON INN, Alaire read, deciphering the strange but legible Suinomen script. *Charming.*

"Here we go," Kai said cheerfully, stepping over an unconscious man blocking the doorway. "First stop."

"Of how many?" Alaire asked, not expecting an answer.

The tavern was small, cramped and smoke-filled. Through the haze Alaire made out about a dozen tables, lined up on either side of a long, narrow room. Barmaids scurried from table to table, balancing wooden steins on teetering trays, serving rowdy customers, fending passes, keeping up with the orders. In one corner, a musician played a harp, singing some ballad in the Suinomen tongue. His presence surprised and cheered Alaire, who had resigned himself to enduring the bellows and howls of drunks. *Beautiful. Maybe this will be fun after all.*

Kai stood glaring at everyone in the tavern. When Alaire finally noticed this, he thought the boy was looking for a place to sit. Then he saw he was looking for something else entirely.

"You, there, in the pansy outfit!" a large, drunk man roared, from the nearest table. "This here be the adult's bar! The nursery, it be down the street. Now git!"

An odd silence fell over the tavern, with the exception of the harpist, who continued playing —

Though Alaire clearly saw the harpist's muscles tense, and his legs brace for a quick escape.

Alaire's hand crept close to the hilt of his blade. Fully half the tavern turned to look at them, as a few got up and made a hasty exit.

The table in question glistened with spilled ale. Five men, sailors perhaps, had claimed it as their own. The candle burning in the center was cheap, fat and guttering, illuminating their bearded faces in brief, unpleasant flashes. These were not pretty men; nor, from the number of broken noses and scars, were they strangers to a fight. A fight that would probably not stay or even start fair. Alaire saw far too many scars on hands and arms, marks which could only have come from sharpened steel. And given their present mood, a joyless, surly one that could quickly turn to violence, they seemed ready, *eager*, to add a few more scars to their collection.

Kai seemed to revel in the attention. He gazed at them belligerently. Five sets of bleary, ale-shot eyes glared back.

Actually, four and a half. One of them has an eye patch.

Kai grinned nastily. "Looks to me like you boys need a mother to clean up after you. *Look* at that table!" Turning to Alaire, he added, "I think we've already walked into the nursery. Orphanage, more like. Orphans so ugly no one wants to take them in."

Kai! Shut up! Alaire wanted to scream. *I'm good with the sword, but not that bloody good!* He briefly considered pulling the boy out of there before a fight started. By the hair, if necessary.

Except that he didn't think he'd be able to get them out of there intact. Kai would certainly fight him, probably yell further insults at the sailors and without a doubt would precipitate the fight the Prince seemed to want.

Instead, Alaire did the only thing he could do; he watched the table, waiting for the tensing of muscles that would signal an attack.

"What about your friend there?" one of the toughs asked. "Pretty boy as he is. Makes me wonder, is he your wife, or do you two like to dress up like girls to make people *think* you're highborn?"

"Don't bother to guess," Kai snorted. "Don't bother to think, you're not equipped for it. Where'd your mothers find you five, anyway? Under a rock somewhere? No wonder they didn't want to keep you." He grinned slyly. "Not a chance they could ever find five men, or even one, ugly enough to claim paternity."

The five were slow to react, but they reacted. Probably the bit about paternity, Alaire suspected. That last jibe triggered the expected muscle-tensing. They might have been dense, but they weren't *that* stupid, and Kai had just called them all bastards.

"Now come on boys, we don't want no trouble at The Dead Dragon Inn," one of the barkeeps said in a wheedling voice. But it was too late. The men ignored him as if he was a fly, annoying, but powerless. They rose as one, with fire in their eyes and snarls on their faces.

"I was beginning to wonder if you boys were too drunk to stand up," Kai said laughingly, and pulled his sword.

As Alaire pulled his. The two nearest them came after Kai, armed with short curved swords of a kind he'd never seen before. *How the devil do you counter those?* he thought in confusion. *And are they going for blood or . . .*

They were.

The tall, uglier one, with a full face of hair that looked like a bird's nest, smelling of ale and sweat and salt water, charged him with a blood-curdling scream, swinging his short blade in a way that left no doubts in Alaire's mind. Kai had managed to work this one, at least, into a killing rage.

Wonderful. Just wonderful . . .

Alaire engaged; the short sword clashed with his longer blade, and Alaire suddenly discovered why the blade was curved. The sailor bound his longer blade before he had a chance to think, and nearly pulled it out of his hand. He disengaged, only to find his blade bound again. This time he backpedaled a few steps and freed his sword again; the tough came after him, still full of fighting fury.

Can't let him take my sword . . . He still had his jeweled dagger, tucked away under his shirt, but that would never do against their weapons. The sailor bobbed and wove like a snake, forcing Alaire to make desperate deflections that were nothing like any of the fighting styles Naitachal had taught him. If only Naitachal was here!

But knowing the Dark Elf, he would probably sit back and watch Alaire get out of this one himself. He walked into it without Naitachal's help, after all.

I was only after information. . . .

Kai moved into the periphery of his vision, a blur of flashing metal and fine, white fabric, fighting two of the uglies by himself.

He might be drunk but he sure fights well.

In fact, he was keeping up amazingly well with his two opponents, each by himself twice Kai's size. One of them had a gashed and bleeding wrist; Kai was still untouched.

In fact, Kai was having the time of his life.

He wanted this to happen. Just like I thought. Alaire flushed with sudden anger. When he got hold of Kai, he'd beat the living daylights out of him!

But first he had to survive this brawl. . . .

To do that, he had to stay calm and think his way out. *Easy, now. Anger and fear are the mind clouders.* He calmed, as Naitachal had taught him; concentrated everything on the moment of *now*. His opponent seemed to slow — and Alaire saw the disadvantages of that odd little sword.

The moment of opportunity opened, and Alaire struck for it.

This time Alaire bound the tough's blade, and pulled it away; it dropped to the floor between them. Before the sailor could reach for it, Alaire kicked it into hidden shadows under the tables. Weaponless, the man lost all the courage that ale had given him. He turned and fled, leaving Alaire to find another opponent.

Get these two off Kai, he thought. *But there were five. Where'd the other —*

A sword flashed at the edge of his vision, and he ducked out of the way just in time, the *shwwooooosh* of the blade loud in his ears.

In the corner, the harpist was manfully trying to play on, singing "I'll Go No More Roving" as a strange counterpoint to the dance of death in the front of the tavern.

Alaire did not even bother to reflect on how close that last strike had come, for this new opponent had committed a little too much to the stroke and was off-balance. Before he could recover, Alaire slapped his blade aside, and thrust. It was not even a serious attack, but it caused the other to stagger hastily backwards, tripping and falling backwards over one of the frail little stools. In an effort to save himself, arms flailing wildly, the man fell into three tables, knocking their contents, wooden steins, mostly, clanking and splashing in all directions. With a roar of anger, one of the customers grabbed his emptied stein and broke it over the tough's head, taking him out of the fight completely.

Kai! Where —

He glanced frantically around, at first unable to see his companion. Then, the white blur reappeared from the shadows, an angry little whirlwind that showed no sign of exhaustion.

By now half the bar's customers had cleared out, prudently, but a fair number remained, some waging bets that Kai would come out unscratched. Amazingly, this lot acted as if the fight was some kind of entertainment staged for their benefit. Almost as if they had expected it.

That little maniac, Alaire seethed. He wasn't fighting two anymore, but *three.* And they were huge — but their size was a handicap in the bar's compact interior. Kai was still wearing that grin of sardonic enjoyment, and he had already given them a few bloody nicks.

Alaire paused at that, before throwing himself to Kai's rescue. *Is he* playing *with them?* he wondered. Kai had a wild, feral look on his face, no sign of fear, only pleasure of the most animal sort.

Instead of flinging himself into the fight, Alaire joined the spectators for a moment. Given the skill Alaire had seen him display so far, he came to the conclusion the Crown Prince could have killed all of the toughs by now, if he had truly wanted to. He was in no danger; he never *had* been in any danger, not from the very first! He *was* enjoying this!

And that explained the relaxed attitude of the onlookers. Probably regulars, and familiar with the Prince, they had *known* this was going to happen the moment Kai walked into the bar!

Alaire was angry all over again. *His attitude really stinks. Reckless, foolish, starting fights when he has no*

*business doing so, and pulling me right along with
him! He didn't know I could fight! He could have gotten me killed!*

"All right! Break it up!" a loud, authoritative voice
boomed behind him.

Alaire turned to see three uniformed men, guards
of some kind, standing in the doorway. They wore gray
cloaks with gold braid, shiny, black boots and a single,
silver star badge over the breast. And disapproving
looks.

The Watch, Alaire thought. *Constables. Wonderful.
Now he's going to get us thrown into the local gaol!*
Alaire tried to sheathe his sword before one of the
constables could catch him with it in his hand, but it
was too late; the one nearest him caught him in the
act. *Oh, Gods, now what?* he thought, dismayed.
What have I got into?

The entire population of the tavern froze. Kai
glanced over, his sword raised in mid-slash, looking
disappointed. His opponents backed away, slithering
towards the rear exit, where more of the official-looking
men appeared, blocking their way.

"You, and you," the first man said, pointing at Kai
and Alaire. "Come with me. *Now.*"

Alaire briefly toyed with the notion of running like a
scared rabbit once they got outside. Heaven only knew
what penalties were waiting for them. He didn't think
diplomatic immunity extended to tavern-brawling.

He looked to Kai for cues. But the boy seemed
defeated, sullen, as if cheated of some bizarre pleasure. He sheathed his sword with an air of disgust.
Alaire did the same, and followed the uniformed men
into a store room stacked high with ale kegs. No
chance to run here. . . .

He noted however, with interest and hope, that the
constables didn't ask for their blades.

Diplomatic immunity, after all? Do they know me already? I must have some kind of diplomatic immunity in this situation. . . .

Alaire thought frantically. No, they couldn't possibly know who and what he was yet, not down here in the city. *But Kai, he has something better. He's the Crown Prince! Does he do this often enough for the constables to recognize him? Would his rank cover me as well? Could I try a little Bardic persuasion — no, better not!* He paled, remembering there were severe penalties for using magic. *Better not even think too directly about that.*

The uniformed men instructed them to sit, and Kai sat on the top of an upturned keg, carefully dusting it off first, so as not to soil his clothing. His long legs dangled awkwardly over the edge. He didn't seem too concerned about the situation.

But then, he hadn't been concerned about picking a fight with five men who were all much bigger than either himself or his companion.

"What's going on?" Alaire said to Kai, finally, unwilling to play the guessing game any longer. "Are we going to gaol, or do we need to bribe someone?"

Kai waved the question away, as if it didn't matter. "Don't be silly. Neither. I just need to see —" he started, then another man entered the door to the storeroom, and his face lit up. A broad, slightly ridiculous grin spread across his boyish features.

The uniformed man, this one in solid black, with a larger, golden star on his lapel, perhaps indicating higher rank, strode in, sweeping them all with a single glance. From the way the others deferred to him, he was obviously their superior.

"Ah, what do we have here at The Dead Dragon Inn this time?" he began, then stopped when he saw Kai.

"Well hello there, Mac," Kai said, legs dangling against the keg. "What brings you to this infamous part of town?"

"Oh gods," Mac, said, his face falling. "Is this what I get for being a Watch Commander *and* your father's friend from University? Putting up with your antics whenever you get a wild idea and a little too much wine in your belly?"

He walked over to Kai, shaking his head. "And this time," he continued, glancing over at Alaire, "you brought an accomplice. Just what I need. I suppose it's the same old story —"

"I didn't start it," Kai and Mac said in unison. One of the Mac's men laughed discreetly behind his back.

Mac sighed. "Of course, of course. But why can't you 'not start it' in your own playground, hmm? Don't you have enough young swordsmen in that court of yours to keep you busy?"

"We've been through this before," Kai admonished, shaking a finger reprovingly at the Watch Commander. "They would never kill me, or even dare to spill a single drop of my royal blood. That takes all the fun out of it. Here, on the other hand, at places of such high repute as this inn and others in the neighborhood, I have a more sporting chance of fighting someone *not* afraid to kill me. Therefore, the challenge. Therefore, the fun."

"Therefore, my headache," Mac retorted. "At least you can take care of yourself. You seem to be unhurt. And, strangely, not dead drunk. *Yet.* You drink more than all of my men! *Combined.*"

Kai laughed, as if he found that terribly funny. "Ha! But the evening is still *so* young!"

Mac grimaced. "It's an hour past midnight!"

Kai waggled his head from side to side, mockingly. "My day is just beginning."

Mac seemed about to reply, but instead he just gave

up, abruptly. "So be it," he said, after a long pause. "Just do me one small favor?"

"Yes?" Kai said sweetly.

"Don't kill anyone tonight, hmm? There's no more room in the morgue. All the slabs are full." And with this parting sally, the Watch Commander turned and left, the black cloak swirling behind him. His minions followed him out the door.

Kai jumped down to his feet, his enthusiasm apparently renewed.

"Come on! What are you waiting for? Let's go!" His infectious grin was back. "There's *hours* left till dawn!"

"Where?" Alaire wanted to know, though he had a sinking feeling he already knew the answer.

"The next tavern. *Of course!*"

Alaire sighed.

The street's population had doubled in the brief time they were in The Dead Dragon Inn.

Party time in Suinomen, Alaire thought sourly.

The crowds parted for them, most apparently recognizing the Crown Prince. *It isn't just the clothes,* Alaire thought. There was something else about the way he carried himself, despite his relative small size, that commanded the attention of everyone around him. He acted like he owned the street, the buildings, the town. And, being the Crown Prince, this was probably not too far from the truth.

But without a doubt, given the way the Watch Commander had reacted when he had seen Kai, the Prince was no stranger to this part of town. Those who made this place their regular haunt probably *did* know him. And given his propensity for picking fights, by now it was very likely that there wasn't a local who would rise to his challenge, though they also wouldn't bother to warn a stranger.

Probably he provides a lot of entertainment for them, given the way the people in The Dead Dragon were acting. Lovely. The clown *Prince.* Though right now he was walking and strutting like a bantam rooster, eager for another fight, swaggering about with an air of importance that Alaire found distasteful.

This air seemed to coincide with Kai's increased consumption of alcohol, he also observed, but he didn't know what to do about it. Or even if he *could* do anything about it.

The next bar, called, ominously, The Hair of the Dog, turned out to be a discreet drinking establishment for noblemen looking for cheap thrills, but still wanting some of the trappings of home to make them feel comfortable. A man dressed suspiciously like the palace guards carefully checked their "credentials." After Kai vouched for his companion, they entered an establishment which bordered on the luxurious. Discrete amenities, like well-cushioned chairs, elegant crystal glasses instead of the awkward wooden tankards of the previous inn, and a guard or two, placed inconspicuously in the shadows, lent it enough of an air of wealth to satisfy most highborn. Alaire liked the place, at first.

"Sir Jehan!" Kai shouted, almost as soon as they were in the door, waving to someone. He grabbed Alaire's elbow. "Come over here, Alaire, I want you to meet someone."

He headed straight for a small gathering around one of the wooden tables. No doubt, the center of attention was Sir Jehan, but this worthy was not the young nobleman Alaire had thought Kai would introduce him to. Jehan was closer to the King's age, in fact. And that made him oddly suspicious, for Kai had no reason to greet someone like this as a cup-companion. *Why would he befriend the Prince when nobody else would?*

Sir Jehan was a dark, handsome fellow with graying beard and hair, sitting in a thronelike chair, surrounded by rough-looking men (bodyguards?) and tavern wenches. Without a doubt, he was holding court.

"Ah, Kai, my dear boy," Sir Jehan said condescendingly. "I wondered when you would be out and about tonight." Three or four of the entourage greeted their entrance, but for the most part the attention remained affixed to the nobleman.

Without waiting for an invitation, Kai pulled up a bench and sat at their huge table, motioning for Alaire to do the same. Immediately, two barmaids appeared, eager to take his order and his money. Kai ordered two carafes of vintage red wine and two glasses, one for himself and one for Alaire.

Wine on ale? Ye gods, what a fool! Alaire thought. The last time he had gotten drunk — and ill — was with this same combination. But he'd barely had any of the ale at supper, and he was too busy dealing with the fight Kai created at the last stop to have any more. *It will probably be all right — if I'm careful.* After sitting down with this group, he had pretty much resigned himself to drinking a little, for appearances. *At least here I can have the good stuff. Hangovers from cheap wine are horrible!*

Sir Jehan stared at Alaire for a long moment before returning his own attentions to the bevy of blowsy beauties he had gathered about him, like ants swarming a drop of honey. *Please don't ask about me,* Alaire prayed, not knowing what he would say if the nobleman did inquire about him. *I'm just a nobody, a nonentity. Remember that, everybody.*

But does the Prince usually keep company with nobodies? With anybody? Time to play the fool again.

The wine arrived, and before the barmaid had set

the tray down, Alaire managed to jostle her clumsily, just a little, in an awkward and inexpert attempt to steal a kiss. It was enough to topple one of the glasses, and invoke laughter from the table.

Alaire grinned his most stupid grin, and tried to look as silly as possible. Sir Jehan no longer paid attention to him, apparently having decided he was no longer worth paying attention to.

"Oh, don't worry about *that*," Kai said, righting the glass. "See? You didn't even break it."

"You aren't going to drink from the carafe again, are you, my dear child?" Sir Jehan said, over the breast of a young woman who had managed to drape herself across his lap. "You looked like someone had run you through, with all that red wine covering you."

A titter of laughter rippled among those assembled, but Kai didn't seem to mind. "Of course not. I'm not a total barbarian, after all." He poured two glasses expertly, and gave one to Alaire. "Drink up. The evening's still young."

"Was that a rumor I heard about you picking a fight over at The Dead Dragon?" Jehan said, obviously baiting him. He held a large wineglass in one hand, and helped his lap decoration drink hers. "Or did you really get into trouble so soon?"

A wicked grin passed across Kai's face, before an audible gulp from the glass smothered it. "Would *I* do such a thing?"

"Yes," Jehan replied.

"Well, then. There's your answer."

While Alaire sipped his wine, and Kai guzzled his, he observed Sir Jehan discreetly. The litter of empty wineglasses and carafes suggested some heavy imbibing, but he soon realized that they were not all Sir Jehan's. Those around him were in various stages of drunkenness, and indeed, Jehan was encouraging this,

pouring wine the moment someone's glass was empty
or only half empty, toasting, laughing, ordering more.
But Jehan wasn't really drinking — perhaps as much
as Alaire was, a sip occasionally. While the others were
going through entire carafes, Sir Jehan nursed a single
glass.

Odd, Alaire thought. *He's not really as drunk as the
others. But he's sure acting like he is. Why? What is
Jehan doing here? Spying on Kai, perhaps?*

That could be it, but he doubted the man's efficiency, given the circumstances. Jehan seemed more
interested in the dubious charms of the women
around him, and at any rate, he could only spy on Kai
when Kai was with him.

But he already knew about the disturbance at The
Dead Dragon. Were other spies watching them? Did
Jehan have a network of watchers, who brought him
word while he sat at his ease here, like a spider in the
center of a web?

That was an unpleasant, perhaps unjustified, anal-
ogy. Sir Jehan could be keeping an eye on Kai for his
own good.

That had to be it. *He's watching the Prince to see
that nothing happens to him while he's out carousing.
Since I doubt anyone could stop him, at least this
keeps him from getting himself into real danger.* Kai
definitely needed someone to watch over him, keep
him out of trouble and bail him out if he found it.

Alaire felt a great deal of relief at that. So Jehan was
not someone he needed to be terribly concerned
about, he decided, since he wasn't betraying his mission to Kai or anyone else. He only hoped his
performance thus far into the evening was convincing.

Absentmindedly, without meaning to, Alaire finished his glass, and Kai refilled it instantly. *Can't
afford to get drunk tonight.* He touched his lips to the

rim and since no one was looking, lowered it without sipping.

"I bid you all good evening," Sir Jehan said grandly, rising to his feet. "My little flock and I have other plans, don't we, pretty ones?" Amid a chorus of giggles, all of the females seated also stood, and for a moment Alaire thought he was going to invite the Prince to share his companions.

The other men left the table wordlessly, seeking the exit, some visibly disappointed at Sir Jehan's highhanded appropriation of every woman at the table. Sir Jehan and his "flock" vanished up a flight of stairs, saying no more.

If the Crown Prince felt left out, he didn't show it. Alaire's opinion of him raised considerably. While not a prude, Alaire had been more than a little uncomfortable with Jehan's blatant pawing of the tavern girls. *He might be a drunkard, but Kai would seem to set higher standards on women than on wine.* A small miracle, given his youth and his lust for adventure. *No, not adventure,* Alaire corrected himself. *Misadventure.*

Together they sat, alone at the big table, while barmaids scurried to refill the carafes, and Kai proceeded to tell him his life's story. It would have been easier to understand him if he hadn't lapsed into his native tongue a time or two, but Alaire caught the gist of what he was trying to say, anyway.

"You know, Sir Jehan is one of the best men in the whole country of Suinomen," Kai slurred. "He's been my friend since I was thirteen, and was the only one who showed any interest in my future. Why, Sir Jehan, he gave me my first drink! In this very bar. Four, five years ago."

And you've been drinking ever since. You really are a decent person, I'll bet, when you're sober. Did Sir

Jehan turn you into a drunk, or did you do that all by yourself?

Alaire, trying his best to play his role though he was, found himself becoming quite annoyed with his princely friend. That Kai could get them both killed, particularly if he picked another fight in his worsened condition, didn't bother him nearly as much as Kai's deteriorated personality. He had been drunk at the start of this carouse, true, but now he was becoming disgusting.

But Kai was rambling on, in that disjointed fashion of drunks everywhere. "And you, my friend, you must have been here before. I know you from somewhere, and we used to be best friends, are best friends. You saved my life back there, with those sailors, did you know that. . . ."

Alaire finished off his glass of wine, and Kai, of course, refilled it. As he sipped this one, he recalled what Kai just said about Sir Jehan, and this bar. *Jehan got him started drinking. And he encouraged Kai to drink himself drunk, just now. And the man wasn't a drunk himself. Very odd, that.* Back in Fenrich, he remembered the drunks were usually the ones who encouraged heavy drinking, particularly in those who drank little.

Now Sir Jehan seemed sinister again. For Jehan didn't fit that pattern; he had hardly drunk enough for the wine to affect him, but acted as if he was as inebriated as Kai. He might have another motive for helping Kai become, and remain, a drunk.

There was more to the picture that he wasn't seeing. Whatever Jehan's motive's were, they couldn't be good. *What is it about that man that rubs me the wrong way?* Meeting him had shed some light, however dim, on Kai's relationships within Suinomen. *Meanwhile, let's encourage this notion that I'm an old friend. Likely as not, he won't remember a thing tomorrow, if he's like the other drunks I knew back at the village.*

"I might have been here, some time back," Alaire began. "My parents, they liked to travel. In fact, I met someone who looked an awful lot like you."

"You *did*? How long ago was this?"

"Oh, I must have been about fifteen. Four years ago? Anyway, we stayed at this wooden lodge, on a large lake." Although he was making a wild guess, he knew there had to be a large lake somewhere, based on the amount of water he'd seen in the land so far. And since most buildings consisted of wood, he figured a "wooden lodge" was a pretty good bet as well.

Kai's eyes widened. "Was that *you*?"

Alaire shrugged. "Might have been," he replied, distantly.

Kai gestured excitedly in his chair. "Oh, it was! It must have been! It was you, Alaire, I remember now, I remember it all, that summer the royal family decided to have a 'peasant's holiday'! And *you* were there. My best friend! We swore that oath of eternal friendship, but my father didn't approve — I thought he'd forced your parents to take away to some awful place like Althea and I'd never see you again!"

Kai leaned over and hugged Alaire for what seemed an eternity. The barmaid gave them an odd look. Alaire rolled his eyes.

Not the impression I meant to convey, Alaire thought, although this new level of trust promised to be very useful.

At the next tavern, Kai got down to some serious drinking.

This place had no sign, no real front door. To find the tavern, they had left the main street, to a darker, more shadowy alley, through which Alaire walked clutching the hilt of his sword.

"Is this really a place we need to go?" Alaire had whispered, as Kai led him into the darkness. He found it difficult to envision the tavern that would be in this end of the district. Twice they stepped over motionless forms lying across their path, one of whom had lost his belt and whatever had hung on it, his cloak, and anything that had been in his pockets, which hung inside out. The other was probably passed out drunk.

Kai seemed more in his element here than at the previous two places. They entered the establishment through an entrance practically invisible from the alley, which was just as well. If you didn't know where the place was, you probably didn't belong there. The tavern keeper knew him by name, greeting him simply as Kai, not "sir," or "your highness." *Do they even know he's a prince?* Alaire wondered. But then, they didn't use titles at the other taverns. And Sir Jehan certainly knew Kai was the Crown Prince.

It's almost as if he is ashamed of the title, Alaire considered, as they settled down into a semi-private booth, this one with blood stains on the wall. Kai didn't appear to notice. *He might have been responsible for them being there in the first place.*

"So, what'll it be this time?" Kai asked enthusiastically.

Alaire had managed to drink only four glasses of wine or ale that evening, in spite of the pressure to drink much, much more. He even managed to act a little drunk, to blend in with the masses. But his stomach, and his head, were both sending warning signals to him. If he drank much more, he would get drunk, or worse, and be completely useless in a fight. Which, in this area of town, seemed highly likely.

"Oh, whatever you're drinking," Alaire said, and Kai

ordered up three large steins of some foul looking brew called "dogbolter." Two were for Kai. One was Alaire's. When he looked down, he saw that twigs were floating around in it. Heaven only knew what else was in it.

"Tasty," Alaire said, without trying it. *If I dump this on the floor, he won't even notice. The floor is already so sticky anyway that another quart of muck won't matter.*

Alaire made ready to anoint the floor with his gift from Kai when a disturbance at the door distracted him.

The Watch. Again. Alaire saw the four uniformed men before Kai did; the boy's powers of observation had dwindled to next to nothing. They were halfway across the bar before the Prince noticed them, turned pale, and ducked behind both of his steins, peering furtively between them.

"They're not after us," Alaire whispered, not sure if this was even true.

The four uniformed men turned towards the rear of the tavern. In the shadows Alaire could make out a terrified middle-aged man and an equally terrified older one, sitting at a small table at the very back.

Kai exhaled loudly. "Glad it wasn't us," he said. "Thought for sure they'd changed their minds and decided to take me in. Show me a 'lesson.'"

"Different group," Alaire observed. "Different uniforms, too. They're all black, like the Watch Commander's, instead of gray."

"*Black* uniforms?" Kai asked, and peered around the booth at the unpleasant scene developing behind him, apparently seeing the men clearly for the first time. "No. Not here."

"What?"

The barkeep went over, rattling something in their

native tongue. It looked like he was trying to vouch for the two sitting at the table, but was having no luck. Finally, the barkeep handed over several gold coins.

"They were going to take him in along with those two, for serving them," Kai informed him. "Gold is the best bribe of all, here."

"Why are they taking those people in?" Alaire asked, but Kai stared without answering. The uniformed men took the two away, roughly shoving them towards the door. The moment they were gone, Kai returned his attention to the table, and his brew.

"Magicians," Kai snorted in contempt. "Unlicensed magicians. Damn fools don't ever learn!"

This is what Naitachal was talking about, Alaire thought, in sudden fear. *Careful, now, don't want to pry too blatantly here.* He noticed Kai fishing one of the twigs out of his brew. With a silly grin, he used it to stir his drink. *But then again, as drunk as he is right now, is it going to matter? I'm his long-lost best friend, after all.*

"Those guys weren't the regular Watch, were they?" he asked.

"Oh, no. They were Swords of the Magicians' Association. Special law-enforcement troops, there." He took another long swallow from the stein; Alaire blanched. "Then they ba — brr — ah . . ."

Kai's eyes rolled up in his head momentarily, as his head tilted forward. Alaire thought he was going to bang his head on the table, but he recovered just in time.

"Ah? What was I saying? Is it dawn yet?"

Alaire had no clue what time it was, though it couldn't be too far from daybreak. "The Association. You were telling me all about them."

"Oh, right. The troops. The elite of the enforcement arm of the Magicians' Association."

Alaire strove to look innocent and interested. "Are they the ones who enforce the laws regarding magic?"

Kai stared at him for a long moment, his head wobbling slightly. *Should I continue this discussion tomorrow?* Alaire wondered. *He looks like he's ready to pass out. After all he's had to drink, he should have passed out hours ago.*

"Not them. The Association. That's all they do, look for unlicensed magic going on." Kai blinked owlishly. "Then the Association sends out the Swords to bring the poor fools in for punishment. That's what that was probably all about, there at the table."

Alaire tilted his head to one side, and looked puzzled. "*Unlicensed* magic? How does one go about getting a license?"

Kai wrinkled his nose. "You don't *know*?"

Alaire shrugged. "I haven't been here very long."

"Takes a lot of gold. More than that barkeep had." Kai shrugged. "But without one — too bad."

"Licenses which, I'm assuming, most of your citizens don't have." Alaire continued probing, thinking that it was a miracle Kai was so coherent.

Kai nodded, and took another pull of his mug. "That's right. The nobles think they should be the only ones to have magicians. You can only perform magic in the Association Hall, with very rare exceptions, arranged well in advance. And paid for in advance."

Sure — but what about people like the two in here? "And those who don't want to bother with that?" he continued delicately.

Kai laughed nervously. "The Association sends out their troops to catch the perpetrators, then fines the one who paid for the unlicensed magic double what the licensed version would have cost."

A good incentive to pay for the license. "And

what . . . what about the magician? The one who actually did the magic?"

Kai's face lost all expression, and he leaned forward to whisper, "*He* goes to the Prison of Souls."

Alaire shivered at the name. "Gods, that sounds awful."

"Well," said Kai, showing some real, if ghoulish, interest. "It is. Let me tell you about it."

He did. Alaire wished he hadn't.

"They put their bodies in casketlike boxes for a minimum of one year, and use crystals to capture their souls. They do everything in a room deep under the Hall."

Alaire shook his head; this was magic unlike anything he had ever heard of. "I can see the point of imprisoning them but — crystals? With souls in them? Why?"

Kai lowered his voice still more. "They use the souls to help fuel the *licensed* magic so that *they* don't have to expend personal energy for spell-casting. That's the real punishment, you see."

Alaire fought to maintain a neutral face, but inside, he was frantic. *This is Necromancy!*

"Tell me more, Kai."

"It gets worse," he said, with a kind of ghoulish excitement, like a child telling a ghost story. "For every year a magician spends in the Prison, his body ages twenty. So a young man of twenty will come out a year later as a man of forty — if he is stupid enough to get caught for a major crime-of-magic or to get caught a second time, sixty or eighty! I even hear of a mage who got sentenced to a term of five years. When they let him out, he staggered into the light. Hardly more'n a skeleton. Fell dead on the spot in the Association Hall."

The story horrified Alaire. *A completely non-violent*

way to mete out the most cruel punishment. That must be why the people, the King's people, put up with it. It works no violence on the mage directly, so it must be perfectly just and equitable.

No, I'm not likely to be working any Bardic Magic in Suinomen!

"But don't worry. There aren't any magicians around *here*." The Prince glanced back at the empty table. "At least, not anymore."

Kai polished off the two steins and ordered another. Alaire wondered if he should say something about Kai's consumption.

No. I doubt that would be useful. He's going to drink whether or not I try to stop him.

So it proved. After a while, Kai slipped into his own tongue, and Alaire simply nodded and grunted at appropriate intervals. Some time later, after Kai had been babbling on in his own language for a good long while, Alaire did manage to get him to his feet and pointed towards the door. When they got outside, it was already daybreak.

Kai groaned when the early morning sun hit his face.

Alaire felt a certain amount of pleasure at that. "You weren't expecting that, were you?" he asked, but got no reply.

He escorted Kai back to the main street, a curiously silent place now that the sun was out, save for one loud drunk singing in the gutter. Soon he found the carriage, with the driver passed out inside. Dumping Kai on the seat, he roused the driver and, with gestures, managed to convey the need to return to the palace.

Slowly, and with considerably less enthusiasm than when they arrived, the carriage moved forward. Though not hung over, Alaire felt tired. Kai's little rampage had taken quite a bit out of him.

Maybe, if I could just sleep a little on the way back . . .

But he couldn't. Tired as he was, sleep wouldn't come. He couldn't get the awful image of caskets and crystals out of his mind.

"The Prison of Souls," Alaire murmured to Kai's sleeping form. "Gods, Naitachal, what are we about to get into here?"

Chapter VI

As Naitachal had expected, the dinner "in their honor" was a grand affair, with all the correct seating strategies to turn it into a political event as well. The Dark Elf sat with the King and other nobles at a high table, giving him a bird's-eye view of the dining hall. The King, however, seemed more intent on making a favorable impression on his subjects than discussing politics with Naitachal. They exchanged perhaps a half-dozen words during the entire dinner, after which King Archenomen excused himself — though not before promising Naitachal a formal meeting the next day in his chambers to discuss matters of state.

Which was just fine with Naitachal, given his exhaustion. Wine poured freely, but he only pretended to indulge, knowing that if he did in his present state he would likely make a fool of himself and, in turn, of Althea. *No, that would not do. At all.*

He was a little put out that they did not seat Alaire next to him, but to maintain Alaire's false identity, he said nothing. After all, Alaire was a servant. *It won't kill him. And he might even learn something.*

After supper, Naitachal spent what seemed like hours getting acquainted with the highborn of Suinomen. But as he became accustomed to some of their nuances of speech, he realized he was little more than an oddity, and they were more interested in his race — an elf, and a Dark Elf at that — than his appointment as

Ambassador of Althea. From what he gathered from their fragments of conversation, no one really seemed to want a war, or even know that the King had made threats.

That the King allowed him to mingle so freely seemed odd. If these folk intended a fight with Althea shouldn't they spirit its ambassador off to his private quarters after supper to better control what he saw and heard? Instead, they left him to his own devices. The worst was the surreptitious glances as he walked past their huddled groups. He soon grew tired of their impolite stares. Until these people grew used to him and treated him as something other than a freak, he preferred the company of Alaire, the King, or no one at all.

One particular nobleman, a count, or the closest equivalent to that title, showed a little more respect than the others. He was a middle-aged man, wearing a fine fur jacket, trimmed with silver, which matched his thick head of gray-white hair. He had also been indulging generously in the wine at dinner and was eager to talk. In short, an excellent source of dropped information.

In spite of his desire to find his bed and sleep for a day, he entertained this Count Takalo, slyly turning the conversation around to international relations between Althea and Suinomen.

"Couldn't be better," the Count brayed, in a fine baritone voice that rattled all the crystal goblets within reach. "In fact, I'm hoping to establish free trade soon."

Naitachal nodded wisely. "I'm sure Althea would reciprocate. Particularly if the trade involved dieren. That is, if you were willing to part with some of your herds."

The Count's expression turned crafty. "I wouldn't

know about that. The plan I like best involves selling *dieren* of only one sex. Is that why you're here? To talk trade?"

Naitachal smiled smoothly. "King Reynard sent me to discuss several things."

During this conversation, he noticed Alaire talking to someone who appeared to be of noble birth, given his elaborate dress. At first this alarmed him, since Alaire's role put him lower on the social ladder than this other highborn lad. Then he relaxed, realizing that if the stranger chose to speak to Alaire, they might learn something useful. And if Alaire *did* commit a social blunder, it shouldn't really matter much; they were, after all, silly foreigners.

Emphasis on silly *for Alaire. Hope he doesn't overdo the stupid, naive, country-lad pose. If he gets into any trouble, he's likely to be on his own.* But Naitachal noted, with satisfaction, that the bardling was still wearing his blade.

Count Takalo apparently noticed the direction Naitachal was looking, and nodded at Alaire and the other young man. "Would that be your assistant I saw you with earlier?"

"Yes it would," Naitachal replied. He raised an eyebrow at the younger man's antics; the boy was obviously drunk. Very drunk. "Who's that with him?"

The Count shrugged, as if the boy's behavior was of little importance. "Oh, that's the Crown Prince, Kainemonen."

The elf raised both his eyebrows at this. "The Prince?" *But he's making a complete fool of himself in public. Doesn't his father care?*

"Ach," the Count said, in obvious embarrassment. "I'm afraid he drinks a little more than he should. He's young. But I hear the King was the same way." When the Count spoke of the royal family, his voice lowered.

"The King, he's afraid the Prince might want the throne a little early, if you know what I mean."

Naitachal decided to feign naivete. "Well, no, I don't. Do you mean a revolt?"

"Perhaps." The Count shook his head. "I'm not so certain of this, but the King seems rather fearful of the prospect. I can't imagine anyone taking Kai seriously, but there is always the possibility of someone using him as a puppet, I suppose."

No doubt. "Is the Prince always, well, intoxicated?" Naitachal asked delicately.

The Count considered this a moment. "Not always. There are some lucid moments, when the sun's up."

Naitachal sighed, as if contemplating the sins of youth. "This younger generation. I just don't know. I wonder how such a lad could inspire enough trust for a revolution. It doesn't seem likely."

"I must agree," the Count replied. "Yet, the fear still exists." He seemed uncomfortable, discussing such delicate matters, and promptly changed the subject. "How long will you be staying here?"

"That much I'm not certain," Naitachal said. "But perhaps you can recommend some sights while we are here?"

The conversation continued in a less dangerous vein, and soon a large, bosomy woman, apparently the Count's wife, snatched him up. The Count bid him good night.

Weariness settled over the Dark Elf like a heavy cloak. He knew he should stay and fish for more information here among these men, but he was just too tired from the journey to make the effort. Also, the remaining noblemen had begun talking among themselves, and didn't seem to be receptive to admitting any stranger into their pockets of conversation. The evening had suddenly become *boring*.

Now I remember why I can't stand Court functions. Thinking of soft beds and warm fireplaces and a much-needed rest, Naitachal extracted himself from the gathering and strode out of the great hall, seeking his quarters.

But the information he had gathered left him with plenty of food for ponderings. *The Crown Prince. Strange,* Naitachal thought. *Very, very strange.* As he puzzled over the exchange with Count Takalo, he wished Alaire's mother, Queen Grania, were here. *She would have dissected and devoured that group back there with ease, and they would have divulged far more than they intended before they knew what was going on.* Very wise, very crafty, famous for being able to charm information right out of people, Grania would have been of far more use here than Naitachal was.

Being a male and a Dark Elf, I'm at a disadvantage.

Not all of Grania's power was due to charm, though. Some of it — as Alaire's Bardic ability proved — came from another source entirely. Did Alaire know his mother was a powerful mage in her own right before she married his father? Surprisingly, Naitachal didn't know the answer to this. She knew whenever her offspring were in trouble without casting a single spell, though she no longer used formal magic. *Oh I think that's where Alaire got his gift, all right,* Naitachal decided.

She often said that the court mages were enough to take care of any problems magic could cure. Queen Grania preferred being Reynard's right hand "man" to any kind of magery. Naitachal wished again that he had her with him.

She could get to the bottom of this mystery in no time on pure personality alone. Looks like we're both going to have to do it on intelligence and stealth.

Naitachal returned to their room from memory, through ornate halls, steep, rock staircases and then smaller, damper halls, all lit with torches or candles. The closer he got to his room, the more spread out were the sources of illumination. Large swaths of darkness separated the tiny islands of light. Few people, evidently, were staying in this part of the palace this evening.

When he arrived at his room, he found the door slightly ajar. His first thought was that Alaire had arrived before he had, but Alaire would never have left the door open, particularly in unfamiliar and potentially hostile territory. Then, while he puzzled over this, the Dark Elf sensed a sudden movement of air behind him as someone moved closer.

He started to turn — but too late. The garrote slipped expertly over the Dark Elf's neck, then tightened over his windpipe.

Naitachal reached for the rope and stepped backwards, gasping for the breath that had so quickly been shut off; he could not see the attacker, but judged him to be bigger and stronger than himself. He pushed harder, trying to force the man against the wall. The attacker held on, unyielding. His lungs screamed for air.

He reached up, clawing at the attacker's wrists. The thought formed unbidden in his mind.

Archahai Necrazach. Sceptre Touch. Touch of . . . Death . . .

As he readied himself to reach for the powers he would need for the death spell, his first, instinctive defense, he caught himself. Just in time.

I can't use magic in this land! Much less that magic!

Quickly, he groped for a knife he had hidden in an arm sheathe, partway up his forearm. With one frantic move he slashed at the hands controlling the garrote.

The pressure on his neck fell away, as Naitachal whirled, and confronted his attacker, face to face.

The man didn't seem particularly alarmed that Naitachal had freed himself. Through his blurred vision, which cleared quickly now that he could breathe, the Dark Elf stared at his attacker, who stood in the shadows, poised for another assault.

Why isn't he running?

Because he thinks he can still kill me. And he's probably right. . . .

They squared off, weapons raised, circling each other like cats about to fight. Naitachal realized with sickening clarity how much he relied on magic in battles like this, the ones that really mattered, when his life or that of someone close to him was at stake. Even Bardic Magic was a combative weapon —

The human, garbed completely in black, wore a gauzelike wrapping wound tightly around him, giving him free movement. The Elf saw nothing in his eyes but cool calculation, no fear or panic, as if he wasn't worried that the garrote had not worked on his quarry. And there was something about his stance, a professional air Naitachal had come to associate with a certain class of hirelings. An air that said, without a word being spoken, that murder was not new to this man.

The man's a professional assassin, Naitachal thought, with a sinking feeling. *Which means he probably can kill me.*

Reflexively, the Dark Elf briefly thought of all the spells he might be able to use on those eyes, but couldn't, given the restrictions of Suinomen.

But then, now that the garrote was gone, he was unarmed, giving the elf a definite advantage.

"Who are you?"

No response. *Well, it was worth a try.*

The assassin snatched up the elaborate brass candlestick from a marble shelf set into the wall, extinguishing the candle.

"You don't really think that's going to bother *me*, do you?" Naitachal said, as darkness fell.

His eyes adjusted quickly, just in time to dodge as the assassin struck out with the heavy brass candlestick.

Clumsy, Naitachal thought, countering the strike with one of his own. His knife drew blood as it sliced into the assassin's hand, severing tendons.

He heard no yelp or exclamation of pain at the strike. Again, evidence of intensive training. Instead, the assassin dropped the candlestick and ran.

Naitachal ran after him. The chase took him to the end of the hallway, which branched into more halls. After only a few turns the elf lost him, and gave up the chase.

Must have disappeared down a secret passage, Naitachal thought glumly as he returned to his room, wary of anything that might be lurking in the shadows. *There's no way to know. If he vanished through a hidden door he must be familiar with the palace layout. Which could, in turn, implicate the royal family, or possibly someone loyal to the King.*

He didn't like this one bit, and was uncertain what to do next. If he alerted the palace guards to the attack, they might be able to find the intruder. However, there was another option, and that was to do nothing. What the palace staff did in the next few hours could be very revealing to their true intentions, particularly if he pretended this never happened.

Before sheathing the knife he noticed a glint of blood on its blade. *The assassin's.*

He regarded this tantalizing bit of evidence like a starving man would a steak. *What a remarkable relic to leave behind. What a shame I can't take advantage of it.* There was more than enough blood left on the blade to call the man back or track him down with magic. They may have calculated this into the plan, to lure him into the practice of magic, so as to discredit himself, his King, and his mission. This may, in fact, be an *excuse* to launch an attack on Althea!

If I could only . . .

Naitachal was suddenly sympathetic to the magicians in Suinomen; he knew there were a few, at the very least. *What they must endure in order to practice their craft!* Another alarming possibility came to him. *What about Alaire? If they're going to attack me, wouldn't that make Alaire a prime target?* As he made his way back to his room, he shook the thought out of his head. *Of course not. He's just a silly servant, not worthy of a moment's attention. Unless the fool of a child has somehow revealed himself!*

The Dark Elf didn't think that Alaire would let his identity slip, but he worried anyway. Naitachal had no idea where Alaire and Prince Kainemonen had gone, or what this city was like at night. If it was anything like the coastal cities in Althea, he could have found some pretty rough trade lurking in the taverns. Company that Alaire, though he was far from sheltered, might not know how to handle.

Once in the room, the Bard stoked the smoldering fire to get some heat going. Instead of lying down on the huge canopy bed, Naitachal decided to sit up and wait up for Alaire. Despite his efforts to stay awake, he fell asleep sitting in one of the chairs.

Several hours later, he woke to find Alaire entering the room. Sunlight poured in through the partially drawn shades. Though he would have rather slept horizontally on the bed, the brief nap in the chair had restored a good deal of his strength.

Alaire tiptoed carefully into the room, his eyes fixed on the shadow-shrouded bed, holding his boots in one hand. Naitachal saw his breath fogging in the room, reminding him that the fire had gone out. He evidently thought Naitachal was in the bed, and hadn't seen him yet.

"Good gods, look what decided to drag its weary tail in from the night," Naitachal said softly, but the quiet words made Alaire jump. Startling the bardling granted some satisfaction. That his apprentice had been out all night still perturbed him.

"Naitachal," Alaire said, clearly flustered. "I didn't see you sitting there."

"Obviously. Care to tell me where you've been?"

It was at times like these that he felt most like a parent, even though the boy was a very mature nineteen, and quite capable of taking care of himself. *But Gods, it's dawn! Where in the seven hells could he have been all this time?*

Alaire had been in at least one fight. Ale and wine streaked his rumpled clothing, and dirt smeared his face. His excited, feral look didn't fit his otherwise disheveled appearance.

Ah, Naitachal thought, understanding. *He's had what the humans call a "Good Time."*

"Are you *drunk*?" Naitachal asked.

"Oh, no," Alaire said, sitting down on the edge of the bed. "Though I've been hanging out with a lot of people who were *roaring* drunk."

Naitachal raised his eyebrows. "Including the Crown Prince of this kingdom. Kainemonen, was it?"

"The very same," Alaire said. "So. What have *you* found out so far?"

The Bard shrugged. "Very little. The perception of some of the nobles is that young Kainemonen is after the Crown." He wanted to save the best for last, so as not to taint Alaire's memory of his own evening. *If I told him what happened to me, he might remember all sorts of people following him that weren't there.*

Alaire proceeded to describe Kainemonen in the most lurid detail. Appalled, Naitachal could not imagine what the King thought he was doing, letting the boy run riot like that. Fighting, drinking — though Kai was young and bright, Alaire observed sadly that Kai had the most unsatiable thirst for ale he had ever seen in a person. "He drank enough to put you, me, and my entire family under the table."

"Even your brother Craig?" Naitachal asked, fascinated in spite of himself

Alaire sighed. "He makes Craig look sober. I drank a little, but did my best to stay unintoxicated. It was a lot more difficult than I thought, but before the evening was over he believed me to be a long-lost friend from some time ago. Could this help us?"

Well, that was a promising development. "*If* he remembers tomorrow. At this point, he may not even remember meeting you last night."

Alaire shook his head sadly. "This is true. But there is something else. Something far more . . . threatening."

Naitachal didn't like the tone Alaire had suddenly taken. Threatening? Could assassins have come after Alaire as well?

He nodded, as the bardling paused. "Yes, Alaire. Please continue."

Alaire stared at the wall for a moment, as if he was thinking of something too horrible to describe, or even react to. Rubbing his temples, looking like he was summoning the nerve to discuss what he'd learned, Alaire finally continued.

"Kai and I were in a tavern. The local constables came in and arrested two men. Kai told me right away they were unlicensed magicians, and that the Swords of the Magicians' Association had caught up with them."

Naitachal calmly held up a hand. "The Swords of the *what*?"

"The organization responsible for enforcing the magic laws. They wear black and operate in groups of about six, with a leader, and seem to presume anyone they're arresting is guilty without trial. But that's not what's so scary about this place. When I asked Kai to elaborate on what was going to happen to those men, he told me about the Prison of Souls."

At once, Naitachal felt a darkening of his spirit, as if someone had drawn the curtains, snuffing out the sun, and a chill crept over him that made him shiver in a way that had little to do with the cold air of the bedroom. But the sun continued to shine, warming his feet on the carpeted floor. There was more to the name than the suggestive language. He imagined the darkness this prison contained and saw the tortured souls stored there. *Yes, stored. Was this what Father encountered, that time he traveled afar? Had he traveled to Rozinki?*

The cold chill Naitachal felt seemed to have touched Alaire with its spectral fingers, for the bardling shivered as well. "It's not like any normal prison, like we have at home. Its more like a, well, mausoleum. They store the bodies in caskets, but somehow they extract the souls and keep them separate, storing them in crystals somewhere deep beneath the Association Hall."

"*Aie*," Naitachal said in dismay, shaking his head. "Even my people have yet to come up with something so . . . malevolent. Or cruel!"

"Oh, but that's not the half of it." Alaire was on his feet now, making broad, animated gestures in the air, as if by movement he could drive away the chill of fear. "Not nearly. For every year they imprison someone, his body, stored away elsewhere, ages twenty!"

"Which means — let me see if I have this right —"

"Which means," Alaire interrupted, "If they imprisoned me in this *thing* for two years, I would be sixty years old when they released me. Think of it! And if one was stupid enough —"

"Or desperate enough," Naitachal interrupted back. *Good Gods, what an evil device! But consider the source.*

"This came from the mouth of a young drunk, who was, by your accounts, intoxicated. Are you certain he wasn't exaggerating? This is almost too horrible to believe."

Alaire paused, considering. "I don't think so. At least not this. The arrest there at that tavern seemed to sober him instantly. For a moment or two he was lucid enough to convince most people he hadn't been drinking. This place *scared* him as he described it. I could see it clearly in his face. And it scared me."

Though not completely convinced, Naitachal was almost ready to accept the story at face value. *I must confirm this with someone else. But for the time being, I'll assume this to be true. Alaire is shaking, talking about it.*

"I think someone wanted me to use magic tonight," Naitachal said, and told Alaire about the assassin. "I came within a breath of summoning a rather nasty dose of Sceptre Touch to do away with him."

"Did you stop yourself in time?" Alaire asked, visibly shaken.

"Just barely. As tired as I was, I was operating on reflexes only. I wonder if this assassin realized how close to dying he really was. He wasn't trying to kill me, I don't think. Just trying to get me desperate enough to fling a spell at him."

Naitachal decided to try and make light of the situation. There was no point in frightening the youngster any further. "And, if I had used magic, it would not have been the end of the world. I am, after all, a Dark Elf. Who knows, I might be able to make friends in a place like that. They might have decided I made a better teacher than a body in their prison."

Alaire made a sour face.

Naitachal forced a laugh. "And with my elven constitution, a year or more wouldn't make much difference, nor would the aging effect."

Alaire frowned, and pointed out the obvious. "But in that year, the war between our two kingdoms might come to pass, with you out of the way."

Naitachal waved the comment away. "Never mind that. We both managed to get through this night without mishap, and now we know the dangers. You must promise me that you will not use magic of any kind while you are here, unless it is to save your life, or someone else's."

"You don't need a promise from me. I'm not about to use the Gift in this place!"

Naitachal nodded, satisfied. "Is there anything else I should know?"

Alaire's expression turned puzzled. "Well, this Sir Jehan. I met him in one of the taverns. Strange sort of fellow. He's an older man, middle aged, one of the nobles, and he *seems* to be the kind of profligate someone like Kai would turn into after a few years. Not sure what his rank is. Kai is very fond of him, and I'm not sure why. It might be because he is the only noble from the court who will have anything to do with him. But there's something suspicious about him; I got the feeling that everything he does is a calculated pose."

Interesting. "You couldn't be a little more specific?"

Alaire shook his head. "Not right now, no. Just a feeling, a hunch. He's manipulating Kai somehow. And also there's this Captain of the Guard, another friend. I didn't see him out there last night, but from the way Kai spoke of him, he's another 'friend' in the Suinomen Court."

Very interesting. "We must look into this. It could be important, or it could be nothing. Meanwhile, it looks like Kai is likely to be our best source of information."

"I have to agree," Alaire replied. "What I need to find out is how I stand with him when he's not drinking. Could be a world of difference there."

Naitachal regarded the sun, peeking obtrusively through the window, like an unwanted guest. "Looks like my day is beginning. You, my young friend, had better get some sleep. Which, I presume, is what Kai is doing now."

Alaire looked pained — or perhaps, merely embarrassed. "Oh, yes. Passed out in the carriage on the way over here. I delivered him to the servants, who seemed to be expecting him to be in that condition, and knew exactly what to do with him."

Naitachal motioned Alaire into his bed, and the young man barely took the time to strip off his boots and outer garments before tumbling in. On the whole, the Bard was proud of his apprentice. He was making wise judgments, thinking on his feet, and had a good grasp of the dangers of the situation. Now Naitachal's only concern was that he embroil himself *too* deeply, take *too* many risks. He was a clever young man — but those who opposed them were likely to be just as clever.

Naitachal summoned the energy to rise to his feet, and started toward a washbasin filled with water. As he splashed water on his face, Alaire's muffled snores came out of the heap of bed coverings behind him.

Chapter VII

As Naitachal emerged from his bed chamber, he sensed the castle awakening around him. Even though he had slept very little he didn't feel as tired as a human would have under the same circumstances. In fact, he had only begun sleeping vaguely human hours in the last half century of his life, a sure sign of elven middle age. These humans rose slowly in comparison with elvenkind; he heard them, making muffled noises from the rooms and down the hallways, grumbling like bears waking from a winter-long hibernation. Given how much sleep they needed, and how short their lives were, he wondered how they were ever able to build a civilization.

In the dimmed hallway he stopped a young servant girl to ask where he could find the head servant, Paavo, who apparently had been the only representative Archenomen assigned to them. She muttered something back in the native language and held her hands up in the universal gesture of *I don't understand you* and continued extinguishing the candles in the hallway. Interestingly, she did not seem to notice the missing candlestick that had stood beside Naitachal's door.

The Dark Elf regarded the stony halls with equal parts of distaste and frustration. *Not even a civilian guard to watch these halls*, he thought, mildly annoyed. Althea afforded the highest degree of protection to diplomatic guests.

This could be carelessness, or it could be something else altogether. I was, after all, attacked in this very hall last night. Time to see the King, he thought, and tried to remember if King Archenomen had left directions for their meeting. At dinner the King had seemed determined to watch the behavior of his subjects, rather than engage in any kind of conversation with a visiting diplomat.

It would be easy right now to dip into deep pools of paranoia and find a knife-wielding assassin, specially groomed by the Royal Archenomen family, in every shadow he passed. But a small part of him told him this would be assuming way too much. *Easy, now. It's still too early to say who's responsible. There could be a valid reason why I have no guards — perhaps they honestly feel I'm in no danger.* There did seem to be a lack of concern, one way or the other, this serene morning.

Time for answers. The longer they lived in the shadows, the greater chance the forces of darkness had of gaining some advantage against them. And without the advantage of his magical tools, the sooner he and his apprentice learned the truth, the better. At the moment, knowledge, his diplomatic skill and his sword were the only weapons available to him.

Naitachal made his way to the main hallway, keeping in mind the route back to his room should he suddenly need refuge. Here servants were more numerous, and a group of them were picking up after what looked like a late night party. Paavo was among them, issuing orders, supervising the cleanup, but doing very little himself.

From across the hall, Naitachal tried to get the servant's attention, but Paavo appeared to be ignoring him. In fact, the man quickly turned his back on the Bard. *He's pretending he doesn't see me,* the Dark Elf realized, and this small insight angered him far more than it should have.

He decided to press the issue, and walked to within a foot of the servant. Standing behind Paavo, Naitachal spoke again. "Perhaps you can help me," he said, loud enough for another servant, further away, to hear. Two other servants turned and gawked at Naitachal's black countenance. Paavo did nothing.

No you don't my friend. "Excuse me," Naitachal said, stepping around the man, and standing right beside him. *Patience now. Perhaps the man is hard of hearing,* he reasoned, though the servant had shown no sign of deafness the day before.

Paavo, slowly, reluctantly, turned and faced Naitachal. "Oh, Ambassador. Forgive me, I didn't see you enter the hall."

Naitachal gave him a sharp look, and Paavo winced. "I seek an audience with the King. To whom may I speak to arrange this?"

"I am only a servant," Paavo said, apologetically. "I doubt that I would be very effective in arranging this."

You didn't have these problems yesterday, when you took us directly to the King. The second letter, the one from King Reynard to Archenomen, remained in his breast pocket. It would be more than enough of a reason to justify an audience-on-demand, but he had already decided to hand deliver the letter to the King, per instructions. *It may . . . disappear, otherwise,* he mused.

The elf waited a moment, giving Paavo a chance to continue, to answer the second half of his question. Paavo offered a blank but polite smile, lacking in comprehension, as if Naitachal had addressed him in a language he didn't understand.

Naitachal tried again. "Well then. Could you direct me to someone, perhaps on the King's staff, who could arrange what you cannot?"

Paavo seemed distressed, as he struggled to answer the question. Or — *not* answer the question. "That is a good question, Ambassador. Let's see, who is not on vacation this month. . . ." The servant scratched his chin and looked thoughtful.

"Perhaps it would save you the trouble by taking me directly to the King? *Yesterday,* this didn't seem to be a problem," Naitachal replied pointedly.

At this suggestion, Paavo adamantly shook his head. "I am simply not of a high enough rank, you see. If I could . . ."

Indeed. Well, there is no point in forcing the issue. Or reminding him that yesterday *his rank was high enough for him to advise the King. He'll only make some other excuse — or tell me that the person I saw was his twin brother. . . .* "Then please tell me, who *is* of a high enough rank," Naitachal said, his patience slipping.

"This may take some time," Paavo replied. "Have you broken your fast yet this morning?"

Naitachal stared at him, strongly tempted to strangle the man. *What in the seven hells is going on here? What has changed between last night and tonight? And why is this fool blocking my access to the King?*

"No. I. Have. Not. Eaten," Naitachal said, slowly and deliberately pronouncing each word. "I spoke with the King last night, and although dinner was not the appropriate time or place to discuss matters of our two kingdoms, he did indicate that he wanted to meet with me today. Could we please arrange this? Today, please."

"Did you make an appointment?" Paavo asked meekly.

Naitachal paused, wondering if he should lie. "No. None seemed necessary."

Paavo frowned. "Perhaps if you could go to the great hall, we can arrange a meal for you, and I will do what I can to arrange your meeting. I recall that the King designated a member of his staff as your liaison."

Then why didn't you tell me that in the first place? he seethed, but kept the biting words to himself. And kept from biting Paavo.

"Very well," Naitachal said, and before turning towards the dining hall, added, with heavy irony, "Thank you, kind sir, for all your — help."

As he walked away, he cursed himself for forgetting to ask him who exactly this someone was, and what his position was on the staff. But on the other hand, was he really in a mood to deal with whatever sidestepping dialog Paavo would use to avoid answering him directly? *With time, and with a great deal of luck, I might even meet this person before spring.*

He found the great hall empty, but a young maidservant appeared immediately, showed him to a table, and vanished. Between the long rows of tables he noted her passage through two huge swinging doors leading to the kitchen. Two other servants, cooks by the look of their aprons, stared over the top of the doors and conferred heatedly among themselves.

I sense a conspiracy, Naitachal thought. A maidservant appeared with a plate of food, a pitcher of ale, and a basket of bread, all of which she balanced precariously on a wicker tray that had seen better days. *There is absolutely nobody else here, or signs that anyone else has eaten here this morning, and they had food prepared in advance. They could not have conjured a more effective stalling tactic.* The maidservant deposited the food before him and vanished into the kitchen. He wondered when the rest of the castle had breakfast, then realized that very few of the evening's guests had stayed overnight, or if they had they had been absolutely quiet and invisible during his trek down from his room. Most likely, meals went directly to the rooms of the palaces' permanent occupants. That, or the others had known he would be here and had chosen to avoid him.

Naitachal regarded the food with annoyance. The bread was cold and hard, and the wooden implements would not penetrate the dense crust, so he resorted to gripping the loaf and slamming it impolitely against the edge of the wobbly table. This action, which he had to repeat, nearly tipped the table and its contents over, which would have been no great loss. The pheasant, or small chicken, or game bird, he couldn't tell which, was cold, its juices congealed in a greasy puddle on the wooden trough. Fearing intentional, or even accidental, food poisoning, he declared the bird-thing uneatable, and filled his copious time gnawing on the bread, bread which more closely resembled a brick than a loaf.

When he looked up, he saw that he had quite an audience himself. The cooks, the maidservants and a half dozen others, peered over the door, exchanging amused looks, with even a giggle or two for guaranteed embarrassment.

This could take forever, he thought, ignoring the onlookers as he chewed on the barely digestible bread, and ventured to conclude that this might have been the intention, since every exchange so far had delayed his meeting with King Archenomen. He imagined the King, this very moment hurriedly boarding the royal carriage for an impromptu picnic in the forest, arranged for the sole purpose of avoiding him. *They've had more than enough time to plan this,* he thought darkly. *Gaining an audience might be more difficult than I first thought.*

He glanced back towards the entrance to the hallway and saw Paavo conversing with a short, squat fellow partially hidden from view. They seemed to be arguing about something, casting distressed looks in his direction. Apparently the topic of heated discussion was Naitachal.

Naitachal was about to leave the sumptuous feast to go meet the new fellow himself, when Paavo's companion began walking, without much apparent enthusiasm, towards his table. *Finally, someone to take me to the King. I hope.*

He came directly to Naitachal's table, his posture becoming more self-important as he neared. And to Naitachal's eyes, his costume hardly warranted such puffed-up pride, for he looked as if he wore the spare clothing of six or seven different folk. He wore a broad, black hat with a silver satin scarf draped over it, and a baldric of blue velvet, which was tucked into a belt of gold braid. The tunic was a dull orange, with large, billowing sleeves, and had a skirt that terminated at his knees, over hose of green. Black boots thumped against the bare wooden floor of the hall, the noise ceasing suddenly as he stopped to stand regarding the Ambassador as if he found himself confronted by a freak of nature.

"Please, don't stand," the man said, although Naitachal had no intentions of getting to his feet. "I am Johan Pikhalas, assigned to you by the King to deal with your needs." He smiled greasily, reminding the elf of the uneaten bird in front of him. He was younger than the elf had expected, perhaps in his forties. Even wearing the broad hat, it was very clear that Johan was losing his hair. He had the appearance and attitude of someone assigned an important, but unwanted and unpleasant task.

"Please, sit," Naitachal said, gesturing at an empty chair opposite him. *And have some dead bird with me.*

But Pikhalas seemed to prefer the psychological advantage of standing. He shook his head politely. "I understand you seek an audience with the King."

"I do," Naitachal said. "I spoke with him last night at supper, and he indicated he would be happy to speak with me today."

Pikhalas seemed to be choosing his words carefully. "I see. Paavo told me that you had arrived only today. What subject, may I inquire, did you wish to discuss with King Archenomen?"

"I am the Envoy from Althea," Naitachal said, slowly, and keeping a rein on his temper, "and this is concerning a rather delicate matter, which I am under orders to discuss with him directly. Forgive me if this intrudes on some custom of your land that I am unfamiliar with. I understand the need to protect your ruler, but your court accepted my credentials last night, and an envoy and ambassador has certain privileges as well as duties."

Naitachal reached for the letter, but Pikhalas raised a hand in protest.

"That will not be necessary. Your credentials are not in question. But the King is a very busy man, and you have arrived at a rather awkward time. You see, it is late harvest, and the King has been receiving counts from all over the kingdom for the past week. Internal matters. Taxation. We keep a rather tight rein on our various Houses. The accounting of their properties requires his undivided attention."

The Dark Elf was not going to buy into this. *Harvest? Even a late one, in the winter? Agriculture may be more critical, this far north, but why should the King play a personal role in inventorying crops?*

Pikhalas might know of the attack on him last night, or might have even arranged it. *Or might not. Don't jump to conclusions.*

Still, it was time to take off the gloves. "Let me cut straight to the matter, here. Are you telling me in a roundabout way that the King is refusing to receive an Ambassador of Althea?"

Pikhalas flinched at the accusation, but Naitachal let the question stand without apology. "Certainly not, Ambassador. The King will be willing to speak with you, but not today. And since you seem unwilling to discuss your business with me, it would seem we are at an impasse."

"Perhaps," Naitachal said evenly. "What I came to discuss is rather important, and involves the future relations of our two kingdoms. I am a patient being, willing to adapt to whatever schedule the King requires of me. But I have traveled quite a distance to be here. In Althea, King Reynard would have wasted no time to accommodate a representative of your land. While I do see the importance of keeping accurate books, we usually assign such a task to servants and underlings."

He paused, waiting to see Pikhalas' reaction. His expression was as blank and unreadable as a death mask. Naitachal continued. "May I respectfully ask when the King's schedule might allow my vital meeting with him?"

Pikhalas was quiet for a long time, and finally his expression changed as the mask dropped. Now he glared at Naitachal with unconcealed contempt. When he spoke, his voice held a world of disdain. "We have an expression in Suinomen, which would seem appropriate now. Loosely translated to your barbaric tongue, it says, 'Guests should remember that they are guests.' If you are a patient man, Ambassador, show us by your actions, and not your empty words. I will discuss this with the King. Tomorrow I might be able to arrange something, but I promise nothing. If this is insufficient to your rather trying demands, I suggest that you take to the road, and return to that home from which you came."

Pikhalas turned brusquely, and tossed a final salutation over his shoulder, as Naitachal stared at him. "Good day, Ambassador."

He stamped off to whatever "important business" Paavo had interrupted, his stiff gait and posture telling the world how annoyed he was at having to deal with the Dark Elf.

Naitachal gazed after him, suppressing the urge to work the tiny magic needed to make him trip and fall on his nose.

When he had left, the boot thumping fading into the distance, Naitachal stood. Summoning as much serenity as he could, which wasn't much but enough to mask his own hot feelings, he left the dining hall with a little more composure and a lot less noise than Pikhalas.

If I'm cautious, perhaps I can do a bit of investigative work in places they would rather not see me, before they declare such sites off limits. It seems to be all I can do.

Demon-dogs! Even Alaire is accomplishing more than I!

Chapter VIII

Alaire set out to find Prince Kainemonen, pausing to change into something simple but clean. *Something black, that wouldn't blind him or give him a headache. I doubt he'll be feeling his very best today.* The clothes he chose were more appropriate for night-crawling, and he could only pray they wouldn't be giving Kai any ideas about another round of tavern-hopping. An upper servant or lesser noble *might* wear the black hose, tunic and small cape, in another land.

His alertness had slipped once or twice the previous evening, when he was out with Kai, but after hearing about Naitachal's visitor his senses were keyed to a high pitch. And although it might seem logical to suspect the Crown Prince — who, after all, had dragged Naitachal's companion off, leaving him alone — in his gut he knew that Kai wasn't responsible for the attack, or even knew anything about it.

There simply wasn't a devious bone in Kai's body. Foolish, perhaps, but not devious.

He puzzled over how much to tell Kai about his own life. Most of his background was secret in Suinomen *and* Althea, for benefit of his disguise. *If I'm going to get through to him I've probably got to level with him completely — well, almost. I'll have to do it without mentioning my Bardic Gift. To let him know I'm as well-born as he is as well may open some doors.*

Or alienate him completely.

It was a chance he had to take. Satisfied he had struck the proper balance in his attire, so he wouldn't look like a degraded peon or a well-appointed noble, the kind Kai appeared to dislike the most, he began looking randomly through the halls for a servant to take him to Kai.

In retrospect, he decided it was a good idea after all not to mention the tavern fight to Naitachal, although the elf must certainly have seen the signs all over him. *And that's all it was, at The Dead Dragon Inn. A simple fight, in a rough part of town. It had nothing to do with the attempt on Naitachal's life. So, no need to tell him anything about it. If he thought I was going to be walking into trouble, he wouldn't be suggesting an alliance with Kai.*

While Naitachal saw that ingratiating himself with the lad would provide practical information for their mission, Alaire wanted it to be more than that. *Kai needs a real friend here. One day the Watch might not come in time to break up whatever fight he's in. If nothing else, he needs people along to save whoever he's fighting! One day he may kill someone, quite by accident —*

Alaire frowned as something else occurred to him. *What if that's what someone wants?*

It was easy to see a conspiracy behind every one of the closed doors he passed, in this early stage of the game. The reality of it was he was no closer to the real conspiracy than he was last night — unless Sir Jehan was at the middle of it.

He found Paavo dusting shelves in one of the grand hallways. When he turned and saw Alaire, his distaste was evident.

"*You,*" he said softly. "Is there somewhere else you could be right now?"

Alaire bristled at the attitude, but restrained

himself. *They should treat me like this. I am a foolish assistant, nothing more. A hanger-on.* "Why, yes, as a matter of fact. Could you show me Prince Kainemonen's chambers?"

The elder servant's eyebrows lifted ever so subtly. "Why would anyone want to see him? Particularly at this hour. It's daylight, after all."

Alaire thought he did a credible job of looking stupid. "Why? I wanted to thank him, in person, for showing me such an entertaining evening. Is he not receiving today?"

"That is not the point," Paavo sniffed. "He's always receiving, but nobody wants to see *him.*" He sighed, apparently resigned to the task. "Come this way. If you want to waste your time with that drunken child, you are more than welcome. At least you'll be out of my way."

An odd way to talk about his Crown Prince. As if he didn't matter. As if — he never will take the throne. . . .

While Paavo led him down another hallway, this one painted on both sides with primitive woodland scenes, Alaire wondered why even a mere servant in this castle would treat the Prince with such contempt — even if he was a drunk. Alaire had known a few servants back at home who had such familiarity with the royal family, but they were never as presumptuous as this man.

Take notes. File away for later. We can figure Paavo out some other time.

He'd expected a more regal setting for the Prince, but the door they stopped at was no more suggestive of royalty than his own front door in Fenrich.

Paavo waved at the door with an air of one who has done more than his duty. "You may let yourself in. I have other, more important things to do today."

With that Paavo turned and walked swiftly away,

leaving behind a palpable cloud of petulance.

Shrugging, Alaire opened the door, and strode into a darkened room unannounced. The room had no windows, or wind hole, and reeked of (what else) stale wine and ale. It was now high noon, and Kai had evidently decided to sleep in, under cover of artificial darkness.

"Kai?" Alaire ventured, as his eyes adjusted to the dimness. "It's Alaire. Are you awake?"

Silly question, he thought, closing the door behind him. He did this reluctantly, because there was no other source of light. But he needed privacy to discuss the things he wanted to, and an open door would only attract idle ears, possibly Paavo's. The room, he discovered, had windows after all, but something solid and black was covering them. Thin lines of light made an outline, giving him enough light to avoid bumping into the larger pieces of furniture.

He became aware of a large canopied bed shoved into a corner of the room at an odd angle. Heavy velvet curtains cut off his view. Presumably, it was even darker in the bed than in the rest of the room.

From the bed he heard a muffled grunt, then a more articulated "unngh" as somebody stirred inside.

Alaire stood uncertainly in the middle of the room, wondering if he would even be visible, wearing his black outfit. Then it occurred to him that Kai might not be alone. After a moment, though, he dismissed the idea, remembering the unconscious condition he'd left Kai in.

There was a table against the wall, with something on it that might be a lantern. When Alaire felt his way over there, he discovered that it *was* a lantern, with the shutters pulled; one that was still burning dimly. He turned it up. It didn't help much, but now he could see something more than mere outlines.

The bed-curtains quivered slightly as someone pushed them aside a crack, revealing half a face and a bleary, bloodshot eye.

"Unnnngh. Alaire. What are you doing here at this ungodly hour?"

Alaire turned with the lantern in his hand. Kai winced away from the light. "This ungodly hour happens to be noon," he pointed out. "Do you plan on sleeping the day away?"

The curtains shut, but Kai kept moving around, from the sounds within. "That's precisely what I had in mind."

Alaire ignored him, and began searching the area around the windows for a means to open them.

The curtains opened again. Kai had thrown on a pair of breeches, from a pile of clothing strewn over the bed. No one else seemed to be with him. Barefoot, shirtless, Kai dangled his legs over the side of the high bed. He muttered something inarticulate, rubbing his forehead.

"Might I suggest having breakfast with me today?" Alaire offered. His own stomach was rolling over with hunger. He guessed, from the boy's wan appearance, that Kai's stomach was rolling over for completely different reasons.

"Oh, gods, no," Kai replied fervently, sticking his tongue out. "What's breakfast anyway? I don't eat breakfast."

"Then maybe I could light another lantern, or a candle. Or open a window."

"Leave the windows shut please," Kai said firmly. "If you must have light, you could blow some life into that stove and light a candle. A *single* candle."

The tiled stove was much like the one in Alaire's room, except it had a bellows built into one side. It was a little chilly here, but not as much as his own room had been when he awakened. He suspected servants came into Kai's rooms periodically to keep the fire going. Certainly Kai would never have noticed.

Soon Alaire had a roaring fire going again, and stoked it with wood from a log-holder tiled to match the stove.

By the time he had carefully lit a candle, Kai was up, rummaging through the room. The place was a shambles. Discarded clothing covered the floor, except for a pie-shaped area where the door opened. Kai was poking through the debris as if salvaging usable items from a burned house.

"What are you looking for?" Alaire asked.

"What do you *think*?" Kai said irritably. "Got to get the day going somehow."

The reply left Alaire completely baffled until Kai extracted a wine flask from a heap of clothing.

Oh no, not again, Alaire thought. *That's the last thing he needs.*

But fortunately, the flask was the one Kai had carried with him the night before, and was quite empty. Embarrassed, Alaire watched as the boy shook the flask out, as if he were perishing of thirst. Despite his best efforts, not so much as a drop trickled out.

Despondent, Kai dropped the flask to the floor and stood there, staring at nothing. He looked ready to cry.

Alaire tried to rally him. "Looks like it's empty," he said cheerfully. "Come on, Kai, do you really need a drink this early?"

Kai ignored him, and began to search frantically through the mess. "Damned servants. Paavo tells them to take my private stock whenever I come in late." His face lit up. "But I have a contingency supply! That is, unless those twice-damned servants found it!"

He opened a wardrobe next to the bed, and ran his hand up and over, along the inside. "Ah! There it is!"

Kai turned around, holding a wineskin larger than the flask he had carried the previous night. The leather pouch quivered with fullness. Alaire looked away.

"You don't approve, do you?" Kai said. Alaire thought he heard genuine concern in the boy's voice, but when he turned back, Kai was drinking deeply from the skin.

Well, why not? Maybe it'll have an effect. "In a way, yes. Do you *ever* stop drinking?"

"Only when I run out," Kai said, a note of defiance in his voice. "Why shouldn't I?"

Alaire considered this. *How to reason with a drunk?* He'd never done so successfully. *If I don't try . . .*

He remembered Kai mentioning that Sir Jehan gave him his first drink, and that the man had encouraged his consumption the evening before. But Sir Jehan was in no way responsible for Kai's overall condition; that was Kai's doing, and no one else's.

Why do some people drink more than others? How can one person have one drink and put it down, while the man next to him orders another, and again another? He never had really thought about it.

Try the obvious. "Well, for one thing, it will destroy your body, and your mind. Not necessarily in that order."

Kai offered a feeble shrug. "Does that really matter? I'm a *drunk*. Everybody says so. Nothing I can do about that." He glared at Alaire, again with that hint of defiance. "I could stop whenever I wanted to. But I just don't *want* to, is all!" He paused to take another swig. "And it doesn't matter if I'm a falling down drunk. My father hates me and would rather see me dead than on the throne!"

Ah. Here we go. The opening I was looking for.

He cleared his throat delicately. "Have you ever really wondered why I'm here, and how I was able to meet you, the Crown Prince, so many years ago? Granted, it was a 'peasant's holiday,' but you know, not just anyone could get close to the King's son."

Kai was looking at him strangely, and sat down cross-legged, in a sort of nest of clothing on the floor. "You know, you're right. You couldn't have got that close to us, unless there was another reason behind that so-called 'holiday.' Huh. You're here now on some sort of diplomatic mission from Althea, right?"

Alaire nodded. "Exactly. The Dark Elf is the Ambassador sent by King Reynard."

Kai seemed to find this amusing. "Right, the elf. Caused quite a stir, in our little court. Heard a little bit about it before supper began last night. Is your father a diplomat, perhaps?"

Alaire took a deep breath, and told the truth. "I am the son of King Reynard, ruler of Althea."

Prince Kainemonen sucked in his breath suddenly, a short exclamation that conveyed the proper surprise. "Good gods, are you the *Prince*?"

That *got his attention. But now that I have his ear . . .*

He grinned, shyly. "A prince, actually. One of a horde. Father sent me here to have a look at diplomacy firsthand. How do you really know what your father is thinking? I doubt he really hates you at all. I used to think the same thing about my father. I was so far down the line of succession, I didn't think I was really worth much to him. But I found out differently, a while back."

Kai stared. "Down the line? You aren't the Crown Prince of Althea?"

Alaire laughed. "Oh, no. That would be Derek, my oldest brother, the firstborn. I get to choose what I'm going to do with the rest of my life!"

"I see," Kai nodded. "In a way, I'm glad. You certainly didn't act like a prince."

Alaire opened his mouth to comment, something like, *and you do?* but thought better of it. Instead, he continued with the family tree.

"I'll take that as a compliment. My identity is a secret, so I guess my acting must be pretty good!" He grinned, and Kai managed a feeble smile in return. "I'm the youngest of eight brothers. The others had their destinies planned *for* them. Grant, the next born, is a natural fighter and is in training to become a War Lord. Trevor, number three, will become Kingdom Seneschal, given his high intelligence and wit. Contemplative Phyllip was our family's 'gift' to the priesthood and Church. When Father suggested Roland start studying to become the Court Researcher and Librarian he nearly had a fit, he was so pleased —"

Kai stared at him, apparently fascinated that King Reynard had taken such pains to suit his sons' destinies to their talents.

Alaire restrained a smile. "As the more obvious positions became filled, as it were, it became a little less obvious what to do with my brothers. I remember Father once asking Mother why she couldn't have had some *girls* for a change! But we coped, you know; and when Drake, who's number six, turned out to have a temper as fiery as his name, Father decided that he'd better serve under Grant and have that temper tamed with military discipline. The seventh, Craig, still doesn't know what he wants to do. Last I heard, Father was just going to leave it up to him." He left out the fact that Craig was proving something of a black sheep, idling his way among the ladies of the court, and thinking of little besides clothing, wine and women. *Best not give him any ideas.*

"And you're number eight —" Kai left the sentence unfinished.

Alaire nodded. "Even as a child I felt like an embarrassment, with nowhere to go. The 'extra extra prince.' I thought Father hated me after I heard him tell Mother that bit about daughters."

Kai's expression was sour. "I think my father would prefer a daughter."

But Alaire shook his head. "Don't be so certain. When I thought Father had given up on *me*, he surprised me. I remember the day clearly. I was only six, but I remember when he came into the palace nursery and shooed all the nurses away so we could talk, just the two of us, 'man to man,' he said. He asked me what I wanted to do, that I could be anything I wanted to be. At first I didn't know what to say."

"And then?" Kai said. He was hanging on every word, fascinated by Alaire's story.

"I told him I wanted to be a B-Minstrel." Alaire stuttered. *Sure hope he didn't pick up on that near slip!*

Kai laughed. "A B-Minstrel? Is that like a bar minstrel, paid less, seen and heard only in bars?"

Alaire chuckled nervously. "Ah, no, just a garden variety minstrel. He asked why, and I told him that —" *Think quickly, Alaire!* "— that minstrels go everywhere and see everything and no one notices them. They become part of the furnishings, and they learn a lot. I wanted to do that, you see, to become Derek's eyes and ears, and learn the things no one would tell him to his face. And I had already chosen an instrument. A harp."

He realized that he had wasted his frantic thought when Kai ignored the long speech and focused on the last words. "A harp! Did you bring it with you?"

He shrugged. "Well, it's back in my room."

"Please, you must play for me!" Kai urged, as excited as a child with a promised treat.

Alaire assented, glad to be able to play at long last. *It's been a long few days since I've played anything, with Bardic Magic or not. I have to admit it would be a pleasure, and if anything it would give me a chance to practice.*

"Later," he promised. "After we've eaten. I'd be happy to."

Kai seemed pleased all out of proportion to the promise. "I didn't know you could play an instrument. I tried to learn the lute, but I just didn't have what it took, I guess." Then his expression fell. "Like everything else in my life."

"That isn't true," Alaire responded automatically, but couldn't think of any reason why this was so. *I wish I knew him better. I might be able to get a handle on this, know which words to use to lift his spirits. But here he is, getting all maudlin again.*

"Father never talked to me that way," Kai continued, miserably. "I've never been more than a nuisance to him. At least since I was ten. Before then we got along just fine, but after that, well, something happened."

"It's not unusual for fathers and sons to have problems. Though they usually get worked out," Alaire soothed, trying to guess what could have happened when Kai was ten. *A peculiar age for problems like that to start. Early puberty, perhaps?*

"But not *our* problems. He'd rather see me dead." Kai took a long drink from the skin, licked his lips loudly and burped defiantly. "It doesn't matter. What's the point, after all? I can't please him, so I might as well enjoy myself!"

Alaire shrugged. *I chipped away some of the ice, at least. For a little while, anyway. All this I'm seeing*

*now, this drunken fool of child, is his only defense
against himself and whatever or whoever he views as
his enemy.*

"Well?" Kai asked. "You game?"

Alaire shrugged. "For what?"

"Another round of enjoyment, what else. After all,
you're useless too!"

He didn't really want to give in, and go through
another drunken evening, this one beginning much
earlier, at noon. But he remembered his promise to
Naitachal. *Be a friend to Kai, and find out as much as
he can.*

Well, Kai certainly needed a friend. And this was
something he felt he could become, given time. But
Alaire did not think he would see much useful information out of Kai.

Alaire half expected to find Kai leading them back
to the tavern district; much to his surprise, however,
Kai took him out for a short walk on the palace
grounds. The day was unseasonably warm, so they
needed no coats. Alaire had no idea of their destination, however, until they reached the vineyards. These
grapes were, he soon learned, Kai's pride and joy.

"I had this strain planted myself," Kai said proudly,
before the rows of brown, dormant vines. Even without the spring foliage, it was obvious that these were
particularly robust and healthy vines. "Over there is
the winery," Kai said, pointing to a rough rock building
up against the palace wall. Alaire sighed. It made perfect sense that the Prince had his own private
wine-making operation, given the amount the lad con-
sumed.

"Are we going there today?" Alaire asked. He'd
wanted to grab a bite to eat, but Kai didn't seem to
care about food. The hunger pains had subsided

somewhat on their own, but Alaire knew that wouldn't last.

"Not the winery. I have something else planned for us."

Kai led him through an overgrown garden, brown with winter. Alaire appreciated how these people relied on natural growth to give form to their gardens. In Althea the gardeners planted and pruned and trimmed the palace garden into a sterile facsimile of neatness, which required constant upkeep, even in the winter. He hoped to see this place in the spring, and perhaps bring some of these ideas back home.

They came upon a large wooden building that gave Alaire no clues to what it contained — until they entered it.

Good heavens! he thought, gazing about at the racks of weapons, the open floor. *This is a fighting-practice arena!*

It made sense to have sword practice indoors this far north; what he found inside was clearly a training area with a dirt floor. On the wall hung several weapons, both of the wooden practice variety and the real, lethal thing. He recognized fifteen distinct species of sword, several spears, a cabinet of different knives. The place smelled of leather, sawdust and sweat. And someone was waiting for them.

"Young Kainemonen," a big, burly man growled. "You're late."

"I apologize, Captain Lyam," Kai said solemnly. "I've brought a friend. A . . . diplomat from Althea."

Captain Lyam ignored the introduction. The man was huge, easily as tall as Alaire's father, and it was obvious that all his immense weight was muscle and sinew. His huge boots looked like something Alaire could row across a lake, with room for fishing gear. His scarred face looked like someone had ripped it apart and clumsily reassembled it. One eye was slightly higher than the other. He wore no insignia on the loose shirt or the dark breeches, but his stance, solid as a boulder and unmoving, commanded all the authority that seemed needed. Kai withered, and looked away.

The Captain sniffed the air. "As I thought. Drinking already, are we?"

Kai looked to deny this, but instead nodded meekly. "Yes, sir," he squeaked. "I'm sorry."

"Oh, that you will be," Lyam assured him, in an ominous tone that made the hair on the back of Alaire's neck stand up. "That you *will* be!"

The scene was making Alaire uncomfortable. And nervous; Lyam was easily five times the size and weight of Kai, with longer arms and legs, both definite advantages in sword fighting. Plus, Kai was hungover, horribly hungover, a fact which Lyam appeared to take great displeasure from.

Kai seemed resigned to his fate as he went over and selected a sword from the wall, as Lyam did the same. By the time they had taken positions in the center of the practice ring, that same feral look he'd seen the night before returned to Kai, as if touching the blade had restored the madness that got them into that fight with the sailors.

They wasted no time. They saluted with their blades and immediately plowed into each other, a blur of flashing steel that Alaire had trouble keeping up with. Lyam advanced, pushing Kai backwards, yet the boy was holding his own, deflecting every one of Lyam's thrusts. But he wasn't making any headway with the big man. Purely defense, this time; he just didn't seem to have any energy today.

But Lyam did not look like he was making things easy on purpose. The Captain gave all appearances of delivering everything he had, a frightening prospect no matter what Kai's condition was. The swords continued to clash, but despite Lyam's best efforts to corner the boy, Kai expertly sidestepped, proceeding to circle backwards, leaving his path clear. Alaire saw that Kai had an advantage, after all. Though he was much smaller than Lyam, this allowed him mobility. He could move faster than the hulk he was up against, and Kai took advantage of this.

Two other men appeared in the ring, dressed much like Lyam, but neither had about him the same air of authority. The bearded one had a skin tone that suggested long years at sea. The other was a bit stockier, but built like Lyam.

"You, take over," Lyam said to the shorter of the men, who stepped in and began sparring with Kai. The boy was sweating profusely now, but launched into aggressive swordplay with the other, chasing him around the ring the way Lyam had been chasing *him* moments before.

Alaire relaxed, once Lyam paired Kai with a more even opponent. The man was only a little taller then the boy, and didn't seem to be too enthusiastic about the practice. But he was fresh, and not suffering from a night of drinking. Despite the lackluster challenge, he was still a viable opponent. And the swords they were using were real, lethal tools even a novice could kill with.

As the new man warmed up to his work, he began to display a certain sadistic enthusiasm. The new man got a few good strikes in, slapping Kai's backside hard with the flat of the blade to get his attention as Kai grew wearier. He was also using street fencing and underhanded tricks — exactly the kind of thing that Kai could run across in the tavern district.

His relief on Kai's behalf was short-lived, however. He felt a strange uneasiness, as if someone was staring at him, and turned to see that Lyam was regarding him with a hard, cold gaze.

"So, young Kai, how good do you think your friend is here?" Lyam said after sizing Alaire up, gesturing with his swordtip in Alaire's direction.

"He's passable," Kai shouted over the clashing swords. The brief shrug didn't interfere with his thrusts. "Give him a go if you want."

Me?

"Arm yourself, young man," Lyam said, grinning. "Alvar, see what he's made of!"

The other man took a position in the ring, as Kai and his opponent continued fighting. Alaire wasted no time in arming himself, selecting a simple wooden practice blade about the size and weight of the one he used at home. He saluted Alvar, and immediately regretted his choice. Alvar's blade was a good two hands longer, and the man's reach was longer as well.

But Alvar was not very quick; the longer blade made for less mobility all around, and Alaire quickly touched him in several vulnerable places, once cracking the blade hard against the man's arm, delivering a bruise he hadn't intended. Alvar didn't seem to notice, and continued sparring like the trained practice-dummy he probably was, keeping Alaire alert, but not inflicting any real damage.

Lyam, now rested, took over for Kai's partner, who Alaire noticed was beginning to waver. He couldn't figure out where Kai's energy was coming from; he parried and thrust with the same skill Alaire had seen the night before — but oddly, with none of the pleasure. This was simple mechanics, the skill of the sword, but this time Lyam seemed determined to make headway.

Lyam drove Kai out of the ring and into the wall, hard. Kai ducked under the huge man, somersaulted, and landed on his feet, sword ready.

Alvar took advantage of Alaire's distraction, thrusting all too close to his torso, a controlled lunge that could just as easily gone through his heart if they had been using steel, like Lyam and Kai, instead of the blunted wooden blades.

Lyam took over Alaire's practice, setting the other stocky man on Kai again. He loomed over Alaire like a giant, but Alaire saw that the man was getting tired. Nevertheless, he was a consummate professional, and he didn't make mistakes, even when weary. It took everything Alaire had to keep up with the Captain, even to the point of using some of Kai's evasive tactics, but he didn't make the same mistake he had made with his first opponent. His concentration didn't waver. Lyam looked for an opening, but couldn't find one.

"*Hold!*" Lyam boomed, and at once all swordplay ceased. Alaire didn't catch on right away that this meant practice was over, and made ready to thrust again. A warning look from Lyam froze him in mid-attack. His sword dropped.

The entire exercise couldn't have taken a quarter of an hour, but Alaire found himself quite exhausted. His practices with the Dark Elf were nothing like this. It was as if they were training for a battle the next day in which only one side would walk away.

In an odd way, Alaire felt terribly pleased with himself. He hadn't let Lyam score on him. He'd even managed to pick up some new tricks from the Captain, and looked forward to using them with Naitachal the next time they sparred.

Kai was breathing heavily, his hair and clothes soaked with sweat. The boy's exhaustion was no real wonder, given Lyam's special attentions and the rotation of partners. He had no doubt sweated out every drop of alcohol he'd ingested since the day before.

"Well done," Lyam said, and Alaire grinned shyly, uncertain which of them he meant. Some unspoken cue had dismissed the two assistants, who had disappeared to parts unknown without a comment.

Lyam turned to scowl at Kai. "If you come into practice drunk tomorrow, I'm going to *really* wear the drink out of you!"

Kai bowed slightly, but as Lyam turned and left the ring, Kai made an absurdly comical face at his retreating back, mouthing some mute retort Alaire could only guess the content of. The ridiculous expression caught Alaire at an unguarded moment, and he almost laughed out loud. He stifled his outburst with a great effort, saving it for when Lyam was far, far away.

Moving a little slower now, Kai took his blade to another rack. Althea had a similar arrangement at the palace guardhouse, although it was more ornate, and the minions were always present to take them personally for sharpening. Metal though they were, these *were* practice blades, and a lot sharper than Alaire felt comfortable with. Alaire racked his weapon as well, suddenly aware of muscles he didn't think he had.

"Gods, Kai," Alaire said as he lay the sword beside his friend's. "Is that typical for a workout?"

The familiar, arrogant look returned. "You didn't think that was *hard*, did you?"

"Well . . ." Alaire began, unwilling to admit just how soft his own training with Naitachal had been, in comparison. "Does he usually trade off partners like that?"

Kai grinned, like a fox. "All the time. It's why I can kick the behind of anyone I want, whenever I want."

Alaire allowed that this made sense, but he didn't like what it implied about Kai. He hadn't thought the lad was a bully. . . .

"Now it's time to get cleaned up in the *sowna*," Kai said, shaking some of the sweat out of his hair.

"The what?"

"Come on. I'll show you."

Alaire didn't know what to expect, but this wasn't anything he could have imagined for himself. Kai led him to a part of the palace grounds somewhat concealed by trees, where he found a crystal clear pond fed by a generous freshwater spring. Near the shore was a short, squat building made of timbers, built into the side of a small, and clearly artificial hill. Smoke poured out of a chimney, its fires apparently stoked by servants prior to their arrival. The sweat was chilling on his back, and he was looking forward to getting out of the stiff breeze that had suddenly arisen.

"This is the *sowna*," Kai explained as they entered the small structure through a narrow door. "I heard you didn't have these down south. Shame, really. They're really good for getting rid of muscle aches."

Within the *sowna* were two smaller rooms, the first furnished with towels, bottled perfume and soaps, a large wooden bucket of water, and a shelf where someone's clothes were drying. A strong, acrid smell of pine and cedar made him briefly dizzy, and cleared his head in the process. Kai immediately began shedding clothing.

Alaire hesitated, but began doing the same, wondering if the ritual included females. Kai sported a lean, wiry frame, well developed for a seventeen-year-old. Though Alaire was two years older, he found himself comparing his own larger but less muscular body with Kai's, sucking in a bit of baby fat that had taken residence around his middle. He envied Kai's build; but then, Kai had a torturer for a trainer.

When Kai opened the door to the second room, a wave of heat and steam nearly knocked Alaire over, and he recoiled reflexively.

"You get used to it," Kai assured him, but Alaire bent lower, where the air wasn't as hot. Inside were a few wooden stools, and mixed with the steam was a strong scent of smoke. In one corner a hot bed of coals heated a cluster of pitted, round rocks.

"What is this, an oven?" Alaire asked, sitting on one of the stools. He yelped as his backside touched the hot wood; he leapt up again, and did a little dance around the stools.

" 'S not funny!" Alaire wailed. Kai chuckled. "You could have at least warned me!"

"You are new to this, aren't you?" Kai said. He'd brought the bucket of water in with them, first pouring some on Alaire's stool, then sprinkling some on the hot rocks. The temperature rose sharply.

"It's good for you," Kai said firmly. "Do you hurt anywhere, after that match?"

"A few places," Alaire said. In truth he had strained several muscles. Before practice he would normally do several stretching exercises, but today he hadn't enjoyed that little luxury. Also, he had unconsciously tensed when he had realized Lyam was going to run him through the same meat grinder he had Kai, and that had added to his injuries.

"This will take care of that. Sit down. *Relax.*"

He did, finally, breathing the steam in through his nose and exhaling through his mouth, as Kai demonstrated. More water went on the coals, hissing an angry protest. Little droplets of sweat ran down his back and face. The heat relaxed him, and the steam cleared his head.

"See what I mean?" Kai said, stretching his arms. "You should take this idea back with you when you return to Althea."

"I just may do that," Alaire said, feeling a little light-headed.

"I didn't realize how good you really were," Kai said off-handedly. "Lyam wasn't holding back when he had at you. And those two he had sparring with us, those are a couple of his best men. Who trains you, back home?"

"The Ambassador," Alaire replied without thinking. "The Dark Elf."

Kai offered a low whistle of surprise. "Remind me not to try taking *him* on! He's a good trainer. Must really know the sword."

Alaire was about to boast about some of Naitachal's previous conquests with the blade, but thought better of it. *It would be too easy to mention the magic. I really have to watch how much I tell.* He eyed the boy slyly, but Kai was only working a strain out of shoulder muscle. *Is he fishing for information? Better be on guard.*

"Where I come from, everybody trains for the sword," Alaire said casually. "Even farmers. You never know when someone might declare war on us."

If the last remark made any impact on Kai, the boy didn't show it. "But you must admit that being a prince does grant you certain privileges. Best trainers, best equipment. What you did back there really impressed me. And what's one better, it impressed Lyam. He doesn't impress easily."

Alaire didn't know what else to say. His pride fully swollen, he could easily forget the heat; the muscle strains were melting away in it like butter on a skillet.

"What did you want to do this evening?" Kai asked at last.

"First I'd like to get something to eat," he said. The hunger had returned after that vicious practice session with a vengeance. *He can't be suggesting another night on the town, could he? Not again!*

"Then after that, what about going out to the tavern

district again?" Kai suggested hopefully. "You're good company!"

Alaire hid his dismay. "Well, I don't know. I'd really rather not, if you want to know the truth. And Naitachal might need me. I *am* his assistant." *Does he do this every night?*

Kai made a face, but relented. "The day is yours, my friend. Whatever you like."

It sounded as if Kai might be willing to do without his wine for once —

But Alaire was already suspecting that Kai was going to come up with a way to get drunk anyway, no matter what Alaire said or did.

Chapter IX

Naitachal returned to their room to see if Alaire was up yet, but arrived to find him gone. The Bard found this surprising, since he'd had little sleep, and often slept past noon at home. *He must be chumming around with the Prince. Good. Maybe he can find the answers that I, so far, have failed to obtain.*

Paavo's and Pikhalas' behavior confirmed, for the Dark Elf, that a dark, sinister conspiracy reached to the highest levels of Suinomen royalty. But this conspiracy did not seem to include the Crown Prince —

Odd, that. They still knew little about Kai, but what Alaire had managed to observe pointed to a lack of complicity on the child's behalf. If anything, the conspiracy targeted the Crown Prince as well as himself and Alaire.

Kai is a black sheep, an outcast within the kingdom that by rights he should one day inherit. This would make him both an easy and desirable target for anyone seeking to gain power, or even to seize the Crown altogether.

The whole thing was troubling. *Have we stumbled into a coup in progress? Or are they — whoever "they" may be — simply laying the groundwork for one, and we happened to come along at a most inopportune time?*

He had the feeling that men close to the King were intentionally trying to shield him from foreign visitors, while the King himself had no idea that anything of the sort was going on. Naitachal certainly had the impression at supper that the King intended to receive him.

All right; let's assume that he wanted to talk to me, but his minions are keeping me from seeing him. If that is true, then enemies surround the King, and so far that list includes Paavo, Johan Pikhalas, and perhaps this Sir Jehan that Alaire mentioned last night.

Naitachal became suddenly worried for Alaire as well as himself and Kai. *We are the first and most likely targets. If there is a coup, we'd be the first to die.*

As the Dark Elf pondered these ominous thoughts, he heard a soft knock on the door. Though the knock was quiet, he started, reaching for his blade. The knock sounded again, and Naitachal approached the door, sword drawn.

"Yes? Who is it?" he said, ready for a garrison of soldiers to come storming through the door. "What do you want?"

"Came to clean your room, sir," a young male voice replied timidly.

Naitachal relaxed, but not completely. *Could still be a trap.*

"Come in then," he said. *Remember, no magic, just good swordsmanship, if this is another assassin.*

The door opened slowly, and a young boy, of perhaps thirteen years, came in carrying a feather-duster and a rag. He wore the simple clothing that the rest of the servants wore, a tunic of soft suede, and short boots that were little more than slippers. His long brown hair fell over his face, but his eyes peered through it, as he used it as a veil to hide his features. When the boy saw the blade in Naitachal's hand, he stopped dead in his tracks.

No threat here, Naitachal thought, and put the

blade away. "Never mind that," he said, gesturing for the servant to come in. "Just practicing."

The boy smiled, apparently relieved, and stepped closer to Naitachal. He looked up at the Dark Elf, and his hair fell away from his face, which was full of wonder. He stared for several moments, speechless, almost to the point of being annoying.

I'm the first elf this boy's ever seen, Naitachal realized, and softened even more. In most circumstances he would not have appreciated this awkward attention, but because of the treatment so far from the adults of this land, a smile, even a curious one, was a welcomed sight.

"You speak Althean," the elf observed.

"Yes. A little," the child said shyly. "They teach it in school. I'm a little keen on it. The teachers say it's important to speak the southerner's tongue, since we're going to be trading with you more soon."

"Do they really," Naitachal replied, a little more dryly than he had intended. He had wondered why so many of the natives spoke fluent Althean. *But are they teaching their youth our language to trade with us, or to conquer us? In either case, a grasp of our language would be useful.*

The boy giggled, hiding his mouth with a grimy hand.

Naitachal raised an eyebrow at him. "Did I say something amusing?"

"Your *ears*. They pricked up, just then."

Naitachal felt blood rushing to his face, a mild but uncontrollable response to an old, familiar embarrassment. Whenever a human noticed his ears, his reaction was always the same; perhaps it had something to do with growing up in a relatively closed elven culture? This time, though, he was more amused than anything.

"They did that because you said something interesting to me," he told the boy, with a conspiratorial grin. "Tell me, what do the grownups say about Althea?"

Naitachal made his ears wiggle; the boy giggled again.

"Well, that it's warm, and beautiful, and seldom snows." The child sighed as if that in itself was a wonder. "And we can make lots of gold selling male dieren down there."

"But no female dieren?"

"Oh, *no*," the boy said, as if he'd uttered something incredibly stupid. "Then you could breed your own."

Naitachal burst into laughter. The boy was charming the shoes off him. The child's eyes widened, but in delight, not fear.

This boy can be helpful, in many ways, he thought, his mind turning to the practical side of their mission. *Ironic how the only information we've been able to obtain on this country has been from their youths.*

He grinned, and the boy grinned back, now sure of Naitachal's harmlessness. "Tell me your name, lad."

"Erik," the boy replied, proudly. "Son of Eliel, House of Lieslund."

"And I am Naitachal," the Bard replied, with a courtly bow. "Now what does your father do?"

Erik hesitated for a moment, then replied. "He's a teacher at the school. I wanted to be a teacher too, but my father says it's a great honor to serve the King, even if it's only cleaning the rooms for his guests." Erik looked around the room, and shrugged. "Doesn't look like there's much to do here. Nothing like the other rooms I've seen."

"I recall a late party," Naitachal replied, absently. "Perhaps you can help me. The King's liaison has asked me to appear at the Swords of the Magicians' Association Hall. I need to be there in an hour, and

I haven't the faintest notion where it might be."

The boy's fresh innocence became a mask of horror. "Oh, you *don't* want to go there! Are they going to punish you for something?" He started walking backwards towards the door, as if proximity to Naitachal would somehow taint him.

"It's quite all right," Naitachal said, somewhat puzzled by his reaction. "We have a similar institution in Althea. They just wanted to show me how their system works."

"You didn't work magic without paying the gold?"

"Of course not," Naitachal said, crossing his arms and looking away stubbornly. "I don't *look* that stupid, do I? They wanted to explain exactly how the Association enforces the laws. In my own land, I am a kind of law-maker myself."

This seemed to make only a slight difference; Erik's gaze fell to the floor. "Then I guess I can tell you." He walked over to the window. "Over here. You can see it from here, outside the palace walls."

Erik pointed to a short, squat building, surrounded by barren trees, but plainly visible in the winter sun, just beyond the palace grounds. "Over there, near the south wall. Don't look like much. But it's where they keep —" He was about to say something else, but evidently thought better of it.

"Where they keep what?" Naitachal asked casually. "The Prison of Souls, perhaps?"

"I can't say. I mean, I'm not supposed to say. Think I've already said too much." Erik turned, and made ready to leave. "Is there anything I can fetch for you? Clean sheets? A blanket?"

"Well," Naitachal said, wondering if he'd finally run out of useful information. *For the time being. This boy is receptive and curious. At another time, I think he could tell me many things about this palace the adults never would.* "We seem to be a little short on wood. But before you leave, I just wanted you to know. I won't be telling on you. What we talked about is a secret. If you shouldn't talk about something, then *I* never heard it." He gave the boy a wink that he hoped was reassuring.

"Oh please don't say anything to Paavo," the boy pleaded. "He'd have my hide for sure."

"That fool?" Naitachal laughed at the name, for good measure. "I say as little as I can to that —" he was about to say *that human,* and stopped himself. "Well, that *fool.* That's the only word I can think of to describe him."

Erik giggled again, reassured. He bowed, and said, "Thank you, sir. I'll be back with your wood soon."

The boy vanished, his light, quick footsteps padding down the hall.

Naitachal listened to him leave, then closed the door firmly behind him.

Well, it looks like I've at least one *ally in this godsforsaken place!*

No one challenged Naitachal as he passed through the corridors of the main palace, though he felt someone was watching him, noting his movements. He said nothing to Paavo as he let himself out through the front doors, but he was aware of the man's beady eyes, tracking him as he left. *So be it,* he thought. *Let them know where I'm going. Perhaps they'll arrange my meeting with the King when they realize their childish tactics are not going to douse my curiosity.*

The day was unseasonably warm for what he had come to expect from this land. Though the trees were barren of leaves, the grass brown, the vines in dormancy, it felt almost like a spring day. For some reason this reminded him of his harp, and in particular, how little he'd practiced it lately. The beauty of nature reminded him of music. He'd had no music at all in his earlier years —

Well, he'd had little pleasure at all, devoting his life to Necromancy; the only beauty socially allowable was that found in the woodlands. Until he'd met Kevin in the days of the famous Carlotta conquest, he had never realized what a talent he'd had for music. Now his true nature was tugging at him, and he resolved to practice later that day.

Without Bardic Magic, of course.

And he would have to nudge Alaire about his own practicing; in spite of the court intrigue they'd found themselves involved in, the boy couldn't afford to get rusty. Bardic Magic was a weapon of defense, but music was an art.

Gods help us if either one of us are ever in a bind serious enough to break these thrice damned laws of Suinomen. Given the severity of the laws, and the enthusiasm this kingdom appeared to have for enforcing them, he doubted even the gods would be able to do much on their behalf.

All he knew of this so far had come at secondhand from Alaire; while he didn't doubt what the boy had said, he needed to verify some of the things the bardling had told. *This whole mystery could hinge on what I find in this Association Hall.*

The uncertainty of how they would receive him put a spring in his step, and heightened his awareness. In no time at all he found the building Erik had pointed out, somewhat reluctantly, from his bedroom window. Everywhere but *here* the buildings stood so close together that there wasn't a hand's-breadth of space between them.

Except here.

There were no other buildings *here,* only a sad

tangle of trees and bushes, setting it apart from the rest. Behind it, the hill rose steeply; too steeply to build upon, perhaps. To the right was the wall of the palace gardens. To the fore, the street. And to the left —

To the left, a wide distance, full of tangled vegetation, separated the building from its neighbors, as if *no one* wanted to build too near it.

There was a thin trail leading to it, blown over with leaves, that indicated very little foot traffic. But there was an odd feeling to the place itself, as if something hidden deep below the ground was — wrong. Very wrong. Twisted.

To investigate further, however, he would have to use magic to probe, and he had no desire to spend any time in prison. This close to the Association Hall, he expected that he would have very little time before the wizards and magic-makers came storming out of the squat building, looking for whoever was stupid enough to cast a spell so near.

The Hall had no obvious guards, though he suspected there were probably alarm-spells to notify those within that a stranger was approaching. But as he came to the entrance, its front door badly in need of repair, he sensed nothing. Either they had used no spell at all, or they were better at this than he suspected.

He came to believe in the former, having seen nothing so far during his visit to suggest any exceptional skill in the magical arts. *They would have had to be quite impressive to surprise me*, Naitachal thought. At times he found it easy, living with the humans, to forget his Necromancer's past, his teachers and his clan of Dark Elves. The elves' grasp of magic went back many thousands of years, whereas the humans had only recently mastered some of the rudiments.

Yet, that was often enough. In the hands of novices, magic can be quite dangerous.

He knocked once on the large plank doors, noting the worn paint, the bare places where the weathered wood showed through. A few moments passed before he considered letting himself in.

Presently, he heard footsteps advancing towards the door, followed by a loud creaking as it opened. A small, nervous man looked around the door, peered at Naitachal, and made ready to shut the door in his face.

"Don't be so hasty," Naitachal said sternly, not using a magical, controlling Voice, but with a normal, mundane voice delivered in an authoritative tone. "I've only come to see what this place is all about." The Dark Elf advanced a step. "What wondrous magic you must work in this place. You don't even need light to work by."

"Oh, but we do not permit elves here," the man said timidly.

But Naitachal ignored him. "Don't be silly. I am a visiting diplomat. If this place is off limits, then no one has bothered to tell me." He entered a darkness punctuated with dim, flickering candles, some no more than stubs. No windows in this place; one or two would make all the difference. "Who's in charge here?"

"I am," a loud, booming voice announced. "Why has an elf dared to darken the doorstep of the Association Hall?"

"Soren!" the man who opened the door exclaimed. "He forced his way in here. It wasn't my fault!" He ran off into the shadows, and stopped there, gesturing with agitation.

The second speaker answered him in an impatient voice; the little man whined his reply. Naitachal stood in the darkness, listening to them argue. As with any elf, his eyes adjusted to the gloom quickly. An over-weight wizard wearing a gaudy, tawdry robe glared at him from a spiraling staircase. Naitachal wondered how the flimsy staircase could hold the man's weight, but evidently the wizard had no worries about it.

At the top of the stairs, Naitachal saw an opened door. Naitachal only caught a glimpse of the room beyond, but from where *he* stood, it looked like an — establishment of dubious repute.

Scantily clad females appeared in the doorway and peered down, confirming his suspicions, before retreating nervously and closing the door behind them.

"Please forgive my intrusion," he began evenly. "I am Ambassador Naitachal from the kingdom of Althea. While I respect your laws and do not wish to violate them, I would like to see how precisely," he paused, glancing up at the now-closed door, "the practice of magic is sanctioned and administered in your fine land."

The wizard flushed, then blustered forward. "We do not allow beings such as yourself in the Association Hall."

Naitachal raised an eyebrow. "And why not?"

"It is — ah — forbidden."

Naitachal considered his situation. *I can either leave, or I can turn this into an international incident, and then leave. But something tells me this is important, that I need to see the inner workings of this place, or at least as much as I can persuade them to show me.*

"Perhaps I should leave then," Naitachal began. "Soren, is it?" He coughed, politely. "I have to admit, I am a bit disappointed at what I've seen already. In Althea, we have granted our mages homes to equal those of the wealthiest nobles, and they engage in the councils of the King as equal to any there. I was under the impression that *your* mages enjoyed equal power and prestige, but it appears that I was mistaken. Perhaps there isn't much for me to see here after all."

The elf turned to leave, arranging his face in a mask of disappointment.

"Now wait just a minute," Soren began. "It's not entirely fair to judge our Association by just what you've seen here. *We* have power and honor!"

Naitachal paused, then said casually over his shoulder, "Frankly, I have not seen anything yet that would lead me to agree with that statement. Unless you would like to show me the inner halls of this place."

The wizard hesitated, as if he was tempted to prove to the Bard that his words were no boast.

"What could it hurt?" Naitachal added. "My liaison has never said this was forbidden to me. Go ahead. Impress me. If you can."

The wizard stammered unintelligibly; Naitachal shrugged and started for the door.

"If you would follow me," Soren sputtered. "I will escort you to the heart of the Association Hall, the place of our deepest and most powerful magics. Only if you promise not to wander off by yourself."

"Very well," Naitachal agreed, and turned back. Soren descended the rest of the stair and motioned to him to follow.

The wizard led him through a short passageway, opened a door with a flourish, and gestured grandly. "Behold!" he said, proudly. "The heart of the Association!"

"This is *it*?" Naitachal almost said. He couldn't believe it. *All the kingdom's magic is performed in this little place?*

Though considerably larger than the great hall of the palace, this place left much to be desired. At least here some sunlight came in through two narrow windows, high at the top of the rafters. It was enough light, though, to show the sheer barrenness of the room, the pale wood planks that served as wall and floor, the brazier that hung above them, the unpainted walls. Hanging in the air was a nasty aroma reminding him of burning tar.

"So, as I understand it — all magic must be cast here, and only by license." He raised an eyebrow. "To someone from my land this seems somewhat — restrictive."

"The King is very generous when he grants licenses to practitioners," Soren replied defensively. "He almost never turns anyone down."

"Interesting." Naitachal tried to look as if it *was* interesting. "How much does a license cost? For say, a simple spell of good luck?"

Soren beamed. "Oh, that would be three thousand crowns. More, depending on the duration of the spell."

Naitachal wasn't sure what that translated into Althean currency, but it sounded high. Nothing he saw explained why such things were regulated; and nowhere did he see a sign of all the *official* mages that were supposed to be here. All those wizards that had burst into the Audience Chamber the day they arrived were nowhere in sight. Perhaps they resided in the palace on a more or less permanent basis.

Perhaps not. Perhaps, despite the robes and silly hats, they hadn't been wizards at all. Perhaps this whole thing was a facade.

But if that were the case, who was finding the "unlicensed" mages last night? And who had cast that spell of magic-detection that had come sweeping over himself and the boy before they ever arrived here?

The hall wasn't empty. At one end, sitting outside a circle of what was probably salt, crudely drawn inside a pentagram, a "wizard" sat staring at the contents of a jar which was set at the middle of the pentagram. He sat cross-legged, looking utterly bored. As Naitachal watched, he yawned.

"He's been there all day. I'm not sure what he's up to," Soren said. "I hope *you* didn't have something in mind. He's booked the Hall for the rest of the day."

"And if I did?" Naitachal asked, shrewdly. "And I had the coin?"

Soren shook his head nervously. "I'm afraid that simply wouldn't be allowed. First of all, you're not a citizen."

The Dark Elf suspected this was the least of the reasons.

"And —" the wizard continued. "You're an — elf."

Naitachal chuckled, surprising the wizard. "I know that. My parents told me, long ago; my mirror repeats that information every day. What special significance does that have?"

Soren frowned, looking down at the wood floor. "I think perhaps it is time for you to leave." He started towards the door. "This way, sir."

Naitachal shrugged. Nothing he had seen here shed any light on his problems. And he wasn't happy that not one of his main questions had been answered.

This is not where they practice the real magic. Instead, this is just the place where they let the amateurs sit and stare at pentagrams and crystals. The answer must be somewhere in the palace, in a place I haven't seen yet.

As Soren led him to the front door, Naitachal sensed something beneath the hall, deep underground. It was the same ominous darkness he'd felt earlier, but stronger now, and obviously coming from directly beneath him. Soren seemed oblivious to it, which only made sense; the Dark Elf had already decided he was far from being a "real" magician. *His magical abilities are probably only a notch or two above those of the poor chap back there staring at the jar.*

But there was an — entity — down there, beneath the Hall. Alive, malicious, and very, very much aware of his presence. *Something is down there, something not of Earth, and it's watching me.*

He wanted to probe, to see what this thing was, but that would mean using magic. *So tempting . . .*

Perhaps this is exactly what someone has in mind.

Chapter X

After sitting in steam for as long as they could stand it, Kai led Alaire out of the *sowna* and immediately went charging into the small lake just outside. He instructed Alaire to follow.

"Trust me!" Kai shouted.

Alaire shook his head, and regarded the lake dubiously. Under pretense of making certain of their privacy, which was in doubt given the leafless state of the trees separating them from the rest of the palace grounds, he hesitated for several long minutes before immersing his bare body in what had to be ice-cold water. Then finally, after increasingly scathing comments from Kai regarding his masculinity, he tested the water by dipping a single toe in the frigid lake.

"Aaaarrrrgh!!" Alaire shouted, leaping back from the water's edge. A thin skin of ice was forming around the shore. *"You've got to be kidding!"*

Kai stood waist-deep in the lake, and his expression said clearly the Prince considered Alaire's manhood to be in question after all.

A gust of chill breeze reminded him that it was winter above the water as well as below. Gritting his teeth, he forced himself to plunge into the lake. *If it will impress Kai . . .*

The icy water instantly numbed his body. He immediately turned around, intending to get out as quickly as he had got in, and stepped into a deep depression. Cold water closed over his head. He flailed his arms in panic until his feet gained purchase on higher ground. When he lurched up to the surface, clutching his sides, he tried to scream. But his voice wouldn't work.

"That's more like it," Kai said. He was getting out of the water, heading back to the *sowna*, where their clothes were.

"Where are you going?" Alaire managed to gasp.

Kai grinned. "Back where it's warm. It's *cold* in there!"

Alaire could have strangled him. But he figured this would not bode well for any future diplomatic relations with Suinomen. He followed Kai out of the lake, hip-hopping to the shore, hoping to speed up his circulation. Chagrined, he noticed that certain important portions of himself had retreated in terror into his body.

The sacrifices I make for Althea, he thought, shivering his way back to the *sowna*.

He had no idea where Kai was taking him. They'd donned their simple clothes and headed back to the palace, without a word said about their destination.

"Where are we going?" Alaire asked casually as they entered the warmth of the palace. "We're not going out *again* are we?"

Kai smirked, giving his companion the impression he was keeping an amusing secret to himself. "I've already said we weren't. Besides, do you think I'd be caught dead in public in *these* clothes?"

Alaire shrugged, resigned to the fact he would find out where they were going when they got there. He had to admit, after the steam in the *sowna*, followed by the brisk dip in the icy lake, he was very much awake now. His strained muscles now felt better.

Alaire mentioned this to Kai, who replied, "The

heat in the *sowna*, followed by the cold water, helps that. I'll bet you feel it tomorrow, though. But it won't be nearly as bad. I told you there was a good reason for everything!"

Alaire grumbled under his breath about barbarians and torture, but the boy pointedly ignored him.

They strolled through some of the more highly decorated portions of the palace, halls covered with murals of rustic revelry. Intricate scroll work decorated the trim and moldings — or rather, appeared to. On further examination, he saw that this was an illusion; a skilled artist had painted the flat wood surfaces, giving the impression of sculpted plaster with cleverly depicted shadows. He wondered if this was some obscure comment on Suinomen society.

Servants stopped what they were doing and bowed deeply as they passed, but Kai didn't bask in the attention as much as Alaire thought he might. *He doesn't feel like a prince,* Alaire said to himself. *Perhaps he does feel as worthless as he says he is.*

The end of the hallway opened onto a grand, completely enclosed, glassed-in balcony, which overlooked the bay. This portion of the palace perched vertically upon the cliff face, as much, he reasoned, for security as for the sheer beauty of the view. Boats wallowed at their anchorages in the shallow waves of the harbor below. The sight, combined with the abundance of sun warming the balcony, made him feel slightly drowsy.

"Ah, Helena, my sweet," Kai cooed as a well-endowed maiden came flouncing over from a window seat and pecked him on the cheek. "You ready to marry me yet?"

Helena giggled, as did three other young women sprawled about on the cushioned benches set below the windows. Two of them could have been twin sisters; when Alaire appraised them from a discreet distance, he realized they probably were. Long, silky curtains hung on the walls, giving the balcony a very feminine atmosphere.

He started to feel uncomfortable as he tried to assess the kind of situation Kai had introduced him to. This did not look like his mother's solar — but it also did not look like anything else he recognized.

He was afraid that the young women here might be something other than the kinds of young women he should be associating with.

The prospect made his stomach quiver.

Alaire was, even at the not-so-tender age of nineteen, still a virgin, and though naturally desirous of rectifying the situation, he knew it would be madness to even dream of doing so *here* and *now*. "Assume every friendly female you meet is in the employ of our enemies," Naitachal had said. Wise advice, Alaire reluctantly knew. Naitachal had often commented that his upbringing had an odd mixture of naivete and street smarts.

Don't get ahead of yourself, he thought. *You don't know what's going on here yet. There could be an innocent explanation for all this!*

Right. These are Kai's schoolmates. And those boats down there are going to take to the air and fly away like a flock of gulls.

"And who's *this*?" Helena said, moving closer to Alaire. He unconsciously took a step backwards. "A new *friend*?"

"Allow me to introduce . . ." Kai began, pausing at Alaire's warning look. "One of the ambassadors from Althea. Meet his Lordship, Alaire Re-Risto. Alaire, meet Helena."

Helena bowed slightly, offered her hand. Alaire took it and kissed it gallantly.

The twins giggled hysterically. Alaire's face burned. Kai proceeded with the introductions.

"And over there," Kai gestured grandly towards the twins, "are, in order of appearance, Heikki and Aini." He leaned closer to Alaire, whispered, "And I think they like you. They like to share, if you know what I mean!"

Alaire fought back a wave of dizziness. "Pleased to meet you!" he said, to no one of them in particular. His words came out a full octave higher than usual.

He leaned over to Kai, whispered back, *"No! I don't know what you mean!"*

"And the fourth lady," Kai continued, indicating a more modestly dressed lady a bit older than the others, "is Rajanen. She will be entertaining us today on the harp."

"On the . . ." Alaire started, glancing around the room. What he had first thought was an oddly shaped piece of sculpture was a harp indeed, the large, non-portable kind that remained in music rooms and moved only rarely.

Rajanen smiled politely and stood up. Gracefully, she made her way over to the instrument, seated herself on a small stool, leaned the huge instrument against her shoulder, and began playing. It was a soft, lilting tune, evidently selected to tranquilize. Or, as in Alaire's frame of mind, calm the jitters. Perhaps she observed this; the prospect made his face burn even more.

"Come. Let's sit." Kai led them over to the flat couches, and clapped his hands three times. "Now we will have that meal you've been begging for since this morning."

At first he thought Kai was referring to something besides food. *Out here? In the open? Better come up with some kind of story, something conventional, something believable, and something that would make me* . . . He thought about it a moment. *Got it!*

"I'm engaged back home," he blurted out. His announcement passed without comment. As they sat on the cushioned benches, now out in the full sun, two servants appeared with trays of food. *Oh.* The two young men didn't seem to notice the women as they entered. They stared straight ahead, unblinking. They opened small folding tables and set the trays down, taking the silvered covers with them. Kai hardly acknowledged them as they marched back into the palace.

Alaire regarded the food in a mixed mood. He was hungry, yet his stomach was in knots. Still, the sword "practice" had taken a lot out of him, and the romp in the royal ice water had put an edge on his hunger.

"Pheasant!" he exclaimed, in approval. "And — what's that?"

"That's dieren ribs, of course! You do eat meat in Althea, do you not?"

"Of course we do," Alaire said, picking up one of the ribs. He saw no silverware, so he assumed this to be proper etiquette. "But remember, we don't have dieren. I'd never even *seen* a dieren until I got here."

"You hadn't?" Kai asked, momentarily perplexed until his attention suddenly shifted back to the fair ones who had joined them and were hanging on his every word. Intoxicated by rank.

Helena had firmly planted herself next to Alaire, and proceeded to lightly run her fingers across his thigh. He found himself sweating profusely.

Rajanen continued to play her harp, oblivious to everything but her music.

After lunch the servants came in and took the trays and tables away, replacing them with an iced-down bucket of bottled ale.

"Ah, that's more like it," Kai said, reaching for one of the bottles.

"Oh, don't be such a barbarian!" Helena said playfully. "You're shoving the cork *into* the bottle!"

"Ah, but I am a vulgar barbarian," Kai replied. "I always shove the cork in the bottle. When you tip it over, it doesn't drain away as fast!"

Unamused, Alaire pretended to laugh along with the rest. *It's starting all over. Another day, another drunk for Prince Kainemonen. At least this time we're safe inside the palace instead of out tavern-hopping with the ugly crowd.* He reconsidered this, remembering Naitachal's clash with the assassin, and all the unanswered questions about the political climate of Suinomen, and frowned. *Perhaps we would be safer in The Dead Dragon Inn!*

Kai handed him an ale, and opened more for the ladies, then, finally, one for himself.

The Prince began a long, exaggerated account of their adventures the night before, throwing in hordes of drunken sailors, mobs of villainous ruffians, an elaborate chase through the city streets with the constables hot on their heels, and an encounter with an illegal magician who supposedly performed a spell that set the tavern they were drinking in afire. The ladies listened avidly, evidently believing every word he said. For good measure, he threw in a few heroic words for Alaire, explaining how Alaire had — with Kai's help, of course — beheaded four of the sailors with a single sword blow. Kai drank and fibbed, emptying one bottle of ale after another. Soon a noticeable flush came over the boy; he was almost as drunk as the night before.

"Well," Kai said, wrapping his arms around the two sisters. "Please excuse me for a moment. I'll be right back."

Alarmed, Alaire watched as Kai, Heikki and Aini rose, Kai winking at him for effect. They disappeared down a hallway, which led presumably to a bed somewhere.

Now what? Alaire thought, looking around nervously, but pointedly not looking at Helena. Helena leaned closer. He looked for the harpist to request a tune to break the ominous silence, noticing the music had stopped sometime during Kai's long tale, and saw that Rajanen had vanished too. *Discreetly*, he thought. *She knew what was about to happen.* He glanced over at Helena, who somehow moved closer still, almost purring. Her hand, stilled during Kai's story, recommenced its work.

In panic, Alaire leaped to his feet, intending to pace the balcony. It was a moment before he realized what his sudden move had done; Helena sat sprawled on the floor.

Oh gods! he thought, rushing over to her. "I'm so sorry!" When he helped her up, he saw, thankfully, that she didn't seem angered. "I don't know what came over me."

As he offered his hand, Helena took it, running a long fingernail seductively across his palm.

At the sudden, unexpected sensation, his hand spasmed; Helena went sprawling a second time.

"Oh no! Helena, I . . ."

When he saw her face, words failed him. This time, he thought she was going to slap him. He wanted to slap himself. He offered his hand again, but this time she refused his help. *Wisely*, he thought.

"I think I can manage," she said softly, but the slight edge to her voice was unmistakable. "Is something wrong?"

Alaire sat beside her on the bench, his face in his hands. He hoped this posture would elicit the right amount of sympathy for him, but he doubted it.

"I'm sorry," he said. "It's just that, I'm engaged to be married."

"I didn't see an engagement ring," she sniffed. "But I suppose I shouldn't have assumed."

"It's a long story," he said, hoping she wouldn't probe his weak lie any further. "You are very beautiful, Helena. Prince Kainemonen has . . ." *Good taste? Attractive friends? Pleasant company?* "Misjudged the circumstance. I wasn't expecting —" *A harem?* "This balcony. Please accept my apologies. I meant no insult."

She smiled, this time with visible regret. "Shame," she said whimsically, getting to her feet. She regarded him with a gamin pout. Alaire's stomach quivered. Again.

"Your lady is a fortunate soul," she said simply, and left the balcony by way of the same exit Kai and the twins had taken.

Alaire stared after her for several long moments, wishing the whole thing had never happened, or at least gone . . . well, differently. Suddenly he was filled with vain regrets and longings. Lucky she had left when she did!

Now what is Kai going to think of me? Will he believe my story about the fictitious fiance? Probably, though he may wonder why I didn't mention her before.

Then it hit him. *She's gone to join them! Three? In one afternoon? No wonder he wasn't looking for women when we were out last night.*

The whole incident left Alaire feeling both embarrassed and depressed, a very unpleasant mix of emotions. *I'm not a prude. Am I?* The tavern wenches of the night before behaved better than these ladies. *Courtiers should act better than this.* Then again, perhaps he was assuming too much. *This isn't Althea, after all. I shouldn't expect their people to have the same social rules we do. But they were in the company of the Prince. And evidently good friends.*

"You don't approve, do you, young ambassador?"

Alaire turned violently at the sudden spoken words. Captain Lyam stood in the doorway, his arms folded, with a wry grin of amusement on his rough face. The young man got to his feet, feeling and acting like a schoolboy caught at something naughty.

The Captain entered the room casually, as if he owned it. It might not have been obvious to anyone else, but Alaire has seen that kind of careful, too-casual looking around before. *He's making sure we're alone,* he thought, and relaxed. It didn't feel like an intrusion. It felt, instead, like a rescue.

"I didn't mean to eavesdrop," Lyam began. "Sound carries quite well from this particular room, and Kai made no secret of who was in here. And *why.*"

Alaire felt his ears burning again, wondering what exactly the Captain had heard, particularly of the exchange between himself and Helena. *Oh gods,* he bemoaned. *Did this man hear me turn down the direct proposition of a beautiful lady?* This was no longer a question of his behavior as a visiting ambassador of another nation; this was a question of his own masculinity. *This is getting personal.*

"Helena seemed intent on entertaining you, young man," Lyam said, strolling over to one of the benches, and sitting down as he if owned the place. "What was the *real* reason you turned her down?"

Alaire successfully stifled a gurgle. "I —" he began, and stammered. *He must have seen through the fiance story.* "She was, how shall I say it, too, too —"

"Brash?"

Alaire shrugged.

"Forward? Brazen?"

Alaire nodded mutely. *Close enough.*

"I agree," Lyam said. "She's a little — well, light-minded would be the *polite* term."

Alaire looked up, somewhat dazed. *He was going to call her something else, and I bet I know what that something else was!*

"Some women are worth courting," Lyam continued, scratching his bearded chin thoughtfully. "For a long time. Months. Years, sometimes. And then, when the moment is right, and you love the woman and she returns it, the results that come with that love are appropriate."

Alaire started to relax with this man; this was not the same person he had been sparring with earlier that day. Lyam was more like a concerned father now; not a vicious opponent. His bump of caution told him he should be a little more wary around this man, but his heart was telling him it wouldn't be necessary.

"Where did the Prince go?" Lyam asked suddenly.

He must know the answer, Alaire knew, but he humored him anyway. He nodded towards the door.

Lyam's eyes rolled, and he slowly shook his head.

"And you don't approve," Alaire said.

The man grimaced. "I gather you do not, either."

Since it was clear to him his masculinity was no longer in doubt, he felt free to speak. "No, sir, I don't. In our kingdom, ladies do not behave that way. Or if they do — well, they are not ladies, and their conduct is not appropriate. And — sir, no prince should have friends of that sort."

"Those women are no friends of his," Lyam spat.

"Nor is Sir Jehan," Alaire blurted.

Lyam regarded him with a hard stare. Alaire instantly regretted the slip. *What are you saying, you fool!* he screamed at himself. *You don't know what side he's on!* The stare softened, and Lyam nodded, in agreement.

"Indeed he isn't." Lyam replied, regarding him further, with an expression that made Alaire think of hidden blades, and ambushes in dark places. "I just don't know what to think of you, young bardling. You are — a careful observer."

But his eyes told Alaire that he had made up his mind already —

Wait a minute! Young bardling? How does he know that?

Yes. How *could* he know that? Alaire wondered about his safety then. *Lyam. I'm sitting in the same room, unarmed, with a master swordsman who could only know I was studying to be a Bard if he were the King's Spymaster as well as the Captain of the Guard —*

Alaire tensed suddenly, looking for an escape.

Lyam sat without motion, his gaze unwavering.

"I would not speak, or move very quickly, if I were you," came the deep, reassuring voice of Alaire's Master, from somewhere behind the length of curtains. The curtains fluttered, and Naitachal stepped out from behind them, as casually as if he'd entered the room under common circumstances.

Lyam did not react, nor did he seem surprised. His expression remained bland.

Naitachal offered no explanation of his presence, and Lyam didn't ask for one. The Dark Elf's black cloak fluttered in the breath of air that came in from the hall; he paced forward with his flowing, graceful walk, as smoothly as a cat. He stood a few feet away, looking as serene as he'd ever been.

How in the world did he get back there? Alaire wondered. He had no idea how his Master done so without using magic, but still Alaire was very grateful to see him there. *I might live now.* He could only guess that Naitachal knew, somehow, that he and Kai would come to this balcony, and had crept behind the curtains unnoticed before they arrived.

Lyam continued to sit very calmly, showing no sign of alarm. "Believe me, Ambassador, if I had wanted your protégé dead, he would be so now."

"Using the same tactics your underling employed against me last night?" Naitachal asked smoothly.

For the first time during the encounter, Lyam was visibly rattled. "Last *night*?"

Naitachal studied him further, saying nothing. Alaire knew his Master's expression well; it boded soft speech and clever verbal maneuvering that could pull the words right out of one's mouth, and get one to confess to almost anything. *I sure hope he's not using magic to help him right now. . . .*

"Ambassador, are you claiming you were attacked?" Lyam stared at the Dark Elf with narrowed eyes. "Why didn't you summon help?"

Naitachal shrugged. "None seemed available at the time, and afterwards, I doubted it would make any difference. So. You *didn't* send an assassin to kill me?"

Lyam seemed flustered. "What possible reason would anyone have to do *that*?"

Naitachal frowned. "I did not think you to be so obtuse, Captain. To trigger a war, of course. But if you did not —"

"I most certainly did not!" Lyam exclaimed. "I was looking for an ally in your company, not a target for assassination!"

Silence, for a long moment. "Then who could have?" Naitachal asked, grimly.

Alaire caught a key word in Lyam's last statement. *Ally. That would imply an inner political struggle of some sort, one that this man would want us to take sides on. Perhaps our guesses weren't so far off after all.*

Naitachal seated himself on one of the benches, folding his hands comfortably, and unaggressively, on his lap. The posture had the desired effect; Lyam relaxed slightly, emphasizing how little he'd tensed up.

Naitachal began. "My researches lead me to trust you, sir. In fact, I came looking for *you*, Captain Lyam. I wish to lay my cards on the table, so to speak."

Lyam nodded cautiously.

"I have . . . questions. The first, and most obvious to me, is why are there so few non-humans in this land? This was not the case several years ago. Though other non-humans were not plentiful, the dwarves, who are excellent artificers and makers of weapons — and never had much love for magic either — were present in great numbers."

Lyam nodded in agreement, opened his mouth to say something, then apparently thought better of it. He let Naitachal continue uninterrupted.

"My own people, as well as the White Elves, visited Suinomen often enough that most folk knew, at least, what an elf looked like. Your own Guard employed many orcs upon the northern border. But all of this has changed." Naitachal raised a single eyebrow, inquisitively. *"Why?"*

Lyam cleared his throat, but Alaire could see it was only a stalling tactic, designed to give him time to formulate an answer. *Yes, Captain of the Guard. Why is that? If anyone would know, you would.*

"Well," Lyam said. "The non-humans were at one time more numerous, I must admit. But about twenty-five or thirty years ago, the government encouraged them to leave. Something happened back then — what, I do not know, but it was decisive, and sudden. I was a child herding dieren in the hills then; I remember nothing except that suddenly the non-humans were gone. And this didn't happen over several years. It happened almost overnight. And now, the government advises those who cross our borders to cross back as soon as their business is complete. Once they hear about the Prison of Souls, they usually find urgent business elsewhere."

Naitachal nodded sagely. "Was this about the time magic became illegal?"

Lyam frowned. "Suinomen has always regulated magic," he corrected carefully. "At that time, however, it became more difficult to practice. That's when the Association came into existence. And, of course, the Prison of Souls."

"And the Swords of the Magicians?" Naitachal persisted.

"The same. They are the enforcement arm of the Association. Actually, magic isn't illegal, it simply requires a permit."

Naitachal snorted. "Let us not spar with words, my dear Captain. Semantics is my specialty. Magic is, for all intents, illegal in Suinomen. I've seen the Hall, and the farce it really is. No magicians of any reputation would bother with it. And how much is the price of a 'license'? More than most can afford. It is a common tactic, my friend — if you wish to make something difficult to obtain without actually making it illegal, you put a high price upon it. And I am sure, if someone like myself actually had the gold to pay for such a license, there would be other obstacles to obtaining it than mere money."

Lyam seemed chastened, but didn't seem eager to leap to the defense of Suinomen's magical policy. "Of course, the magician in question would have to pass certain criteria. He couldn't have a history of non-compliance with Suinomen law."

"He couldn't have a criminal record," Naitachal translated. "I'll agree with that. What else?"

"His political view would have to align with the King's."

Naitachal shrugged. "And?"

"It would be helpful, but technically necessary, to have a friend within the Association."

"That goes without saying," Naitachal said dryly. "Now, assuming one had all those things, what would be the price of an unlimited license — the kind the mages of the Association have?"

Lyam sucked in his breath, shook his head. "Ten thousand crowns."

"That's outrageous," Naitachal said, echoing Alaire's thoughts. "How can anyone, much less professional magicians, afford such a fee?"

Lyam raised his upturned palms in helplessness, a strange gesture from a man as strong, physically and psychologically, as he. "I don't make the rules, Ambassador. The answer is, they don't, because there are no professional magicians in Suinomen, save for the ones in the King's employ. The Association, in other words."

Naitachal nodded. "And it goes full circle. Magic is legal, but it isn't, and the only magicians who can practice their trade are for all intents and purposes dancing to the tune called by the King. Am I leaving anything out?"

Alaire cringed at the last statement his Master made. *If he doesn't watch out, he's going to alienate Captain Lyam, and we need this man.*

But Lyam did not take exception to Naitachal's evaluation of Suinomen; if anything, he appeared to be in full agreement.

"No, I don't believe so," he said simply. "As I said, I don't make the policy."

"Yes, I know. Another thing," Naitachal said, leading

the conversation. "What gave the King the notion that his son is conspiring against him?"

That Lyam didn't seem surprised indicated this was probably a common rumor. "I'm not in His Majesty's confidence. However, I am the Prince's friend as well as his swordsmanship tutor, and I do not think there is any truth in the idea."

Naitachal cast a questioning glance towards Alaire, as if to confirm this. Alaire picked his words carefully. "Captain Lyam here is an excellent swordsman, and from all I could see, he and the Prince have a unique friendship. I think that the Prince needs friends. He is nowhere near as — ah — mature as he would like to appear."

Lyam nodded. "The boy is raw, that is for certain; he's like a cornered wildcat if the wrong blades come after him, and he won't hesitate to defend himself in a fight, but I know for a fact that he has no designs on the throne. In fact, I think he would rather *not* have the throne. He dreads the day he will have to sit in it, because he knows it will be the end of his freedom when he does. And — I think he fears that day as well, because he knows how ill-prepared he is to rule."

"I suspect this might be the reason for his hedonistic lifestyle, then," Naitachal said. "Which, because of his extreme youth, has yet to affect his health."

"The Captain keeps him in shape," Alaire offered.

"If it's not the other way around," Lyam said. "He'll never believe I said this, so I feel confident telling you. That young hothead gives me a greater run than he thinks when we spar."

Alaire disagreed. What he had seen earlier that day did little to convince him this was true. *He's belittling his own skill, perhaps so we will underestimate him. Shrewd, but not necessarily suspicious. This doesn't mean he's an enemy; it means only he is not willing to divulge everything yet.*

Naitachal gazed off into the distance, over Lyam's shoulder. "If Kai isn't after the throne, then who is?"

Lyam frowned. "I'm not certain that's what's afoot. I am not privy to all the information this palace contains."

Naitachal's tone was heavy with irony. "But surely, being the Captain of the Guard . . ."

. . . and Spymaster . . . Alaire added to himself.

"That does not guarantee my complete knowledge of royal affairs," Lyam replied firmly. "This may have been true at one time, but I suspect that I got this position because I was an outsider. That may sound odd to a foreigner, but the true power doesn't lie with anyone in a martial appointment."

Naitachal looked faintly surprised. "Where then, does it lie?"

It was Lyam's turn to snort. "With the *magicians*, of course. The palace has a monopoly on the powers of the mages, you see. Powerful wizards, who can level the walls of this palace in mere moments with their raised energies."

Naitachal chuckled. "Please. What I saw in the Hall didn't impress *me*."

Lyam simply smiled. "Who said they were in the Hall? Only the amateurs operate there. When you first met the King, and his bodyguards — and wizards — came charging out to defend him against an unexpected elf, where did they come from?"

Naitachal considered this. "Of *course*. From behind the King's throne. They reside in the palace."

Lyam got to his feet, calling a halt to the discussion. "We've spoken long enough here." He turned to Alaire. "I would be grateful if your pupil would continue to keep company with the young Prince. If I cannot keep him from folly, I would like to know there was someone at his back that I can trust."

He started toward the entrance, then paused and turned back for a moment. "Oh, and another thing. Avoid magic. I'm not certain diplomatic immunity would protect you. And also, if you wish to confer later tonight, my room is one floor above yours, and I think two doors to the north. It's the corner suite, which the King has been gracious enough to provide for me. But be discreet. It would start tongues wagging if anyone saw you paying me a visit. Good day, Master Bard."

Master Bard? Alaire thought, stunned. *Is there anything Lyam doesn't know about us?*

He and his Master watched the large man leave; he noticed this time that the Captain's head barely cleared the doorway as he passed beneath it. Naitachal stared after him thoughtfully.

"He is, or was, the King's Spymaster," Naitachal said, after a long moment. "Was, I think. He keeps his network of spies still, but it is a small one now and he is no longer in the King's confidence."

Alaire wanted to ask how precisely he knew this, but experience had shown the Dark Elf would not waste his breath, and precious time, explaining. If anything, Naitachal would berate him for not figuring it out for himself.

And in a moment, he *had* figured it out. "He's friends with the Prince, but he doesn't know why the King mistrusts his own son, and he hasn't been able to do anything about that mistrust. That means he isn't close to the King anymore."

Naitachal nodded. "Exactly. In fact, supporting the Prince may have been the reason he fell from grace. But he doesn't know who's behind the troubles between the Prince and his father, or his land and ours. I'm certain of it."

Alaire sighed, and stood up. "What do we do now?"

"You, my young friend, must stay with Kai." Nai-tachal considered something else, then added, "And I believe *I* shall seek this Sir Jehan and pick his brains myself."

Chapter XI

Naitachal left Alaire on the balcony. The first thing he did after leaving the room was to see if anyone was in the hallway who could have overheard them. He found no one, not even a servant, and trusted his conversation with Captain Lyam had been a private one. The talk with the burly swordsman had convinced him that they were both in danger here, and he contemplated returning to Althea for Alaire's protection. *They should have sent another ambassador. Someone who's had experience with this kind of political mess,* he thought, stopping short of using the term "expendable." *This situation is more dangerous than I had ever suspected.*

But to leave now would only humiliate Alaire without accomplishing anything for Althea, and they would be vulnerable on the road out of here. He could imagine the ease with which the opposing faction could have them both eliminated, without witnesses, and then be able to blame their demise on hazards of travel: natural predators, bandits or just simple bad luck. In many ways they were safer here, in this pit of wolves, because any harm that came to them would be most difficult to explain to an enraged King Reynard.

While this didn't grant them any immunity from hazards *within* the palace, it did give them some leverage. Provided of course Suinomen didn't declare an all-out war against Althea. In which case, questions of their fate would become moot.

Better to deal with it now, he thought, resigned to the task ahead of him.

He found the huge antechamber to the King's suite, a grand room nearly the size of the great hall, tastefully decorated with ornate, upholstered furniture and several heads of dieren and other creatures of the forest mounted on plaques, hanging on the pale, plastered walls. The floor, as it was in just about every corner in the palace, was light, unfinished pine. Thirty or so individuals of obviously high rank lounged or talked fervently in groups, in their native language. A raging fire burned in a large fireplace, around which most of the courtiers gathered. Somewhere beyond the double doors at the end of the room was the King's reception hall, and the chamber for his private audiences. It was maddening to be so close and yet be unable to pass those doors. If he could only have used magic, to make himself invisible. . . .

Well, he couldn't, and that was that.

No one seemed to pay any real attention to him as he entered. *Perhaps these people are too polite to stare.* He could only hope.

From the doors at the other end of the room, Johan Pikhalas emerged. There was a graying noble with him, and at that moment, one of the group by the fire called something out to both of them. And Naitachal recognized at least one thing in that hail. The name of Sir Jehan — who was, obviously, the man Pikhalas had just taken to speak with Archenomen.

Hmmmm. A confidant of the King. Interesting, Naitachal thought. *Very, very interesting.*

Pikhalas spotted the Dark Elf immediately. While Naitachal feared he would take Sir Jehan and flee through the nearest exit, the King's aide did the opposite. He whispered something to his companion, who nodded and regarded Naitachal evenly. They both came over to him without hesitation.

What remarkable luck, Naitachal thought. *Or is it?*

"Ah, my dear Ambassador," Pikhalas offered. "How fortunate we both are." He extended his hand and shook Naitachal's black one warmly. "Allow me to introduce Sir Jehan. He would like to speak to you."

Pikhalas quickly excused himself, leaving the elf and human to fend for themselves. "I think we should go somewhere private," Sir Jehan said, glancing furtively around him. "This room is full of folk with acute hearing and loose tongues."

Naitachal nodded solemnly, following the noble to a smaller, adjoining library, leading off the antechamber. It had a single window, also looking over the bay, but this side of the palace was colder than the sunny warmth of the balcony. On the opposite side, next to the window, was a large set of wooden doors, with golden handles. A dying fire threatened to sputter out in a stove, and as Sir Jehan stoked it, heat flooded the library.

Naitachal took this opportunity to study the man. He was certainly no commoner, not if the ermine that trimmed his heavy winter cloak was real and not rabbit made up to resemble that royal fur. He dressed in shades of gray and black silk, with tall, soft, black leather boots, the toes tipped with silver. Though Alaire had described a rascally sort of man, this Sir Jehan seemed the very opposite. The gray in his hair and beard gave him a distinguished air, which was entirely at odds with the description Alaire had given.

"There is a new chill in the air," Sir Jehan said amiably, turning to the elf. "I'm afraid the pleasant weather we've had during your stay is about to come to an abrupt halt."

"I was wondering if this was typical weather," Naitachal said cautiously. "It has been rather enjoyable."

Sir Jehan waved at one of two leather chairs. "Please, have a seat. We have much to discuss."

Naitachal did so, finding the padded leather chair unexpectedly comfortable. Sir Jehan took a similar seat, leaned forward and studied his hands. In spite of his fashionable dress, his dignified manner, there was something about him that put the Dark Elf on guard.

Whatever he's hiding, he's not going to share it with me, Naitachal thought. *At least, not now.*

"I'm not certain how to phrase this precisely," Sir Jehan began slowly, "so as not to offend you, sir."

"I believe we can resolve whatever differences exist between our two kingdoms," Naitachal readily supplied. "That is, of course, my mission."

A puzzled look passed briefly over Sir Jehan's face. "No, you misunderstand. While I am happy to hear that, that's not the situation I'm referring to."

"I see," Naitachal replied, carefully. "Then what situation *are* you referring to?"

Jehan coughed. "Your assistant. Alaire, I believe his name is."

Oh gods, Naitachal thought, keeping his expression neutral. *Do they know he's the son of the King? Perhaps I should have spirited him away when I had the chance.*

Jehan's smooth expression gave nothing away. "It is no secret that, since last night, when you two arrived, Alaire has become a companion of our dear Prince."

Does he suspect something shady about this? "Yes, I believe they met shortly after dinner last night. Prince Kainemonen invited my secretary out for a night of . . . light entertainment." *As if you didn't know that first-hand! Or did you think Alaire hadn't told me?*

"Hmmm, I think I see what you're getting at. Such an

acquaintance, between prince and a visiting diplomat, even the diplomat's secretary, would not seem terribly out of place in Althea. Have we perhaps violated some rule of social order in your fine land?"

"Oh, no," Sir Jehan said blandly. "On the contrary. I'm grateful to see such informal mingling between people of our two lands. Your assistant has done no wrong by befriending the Prince, although I do understand they ran into a bit of trouble in town. I heard through the network of contacts in the tavern district that the Prince picked a sword fight with some unruly sailors. Regrettably, the brawl drew your assistant into it. I'm afraid such behavior is quite common with our young ruler-to-be, and I have to admit to some embarrassment over the incident."

Naitachal nodded, still wondering what the man's point was. "Alaire may not seem to be very old, but he is capable of handling himself. Suinomen has nothing to apologize for, however. He went with the Prince willingly, without my knowledge or consent. Not that he *needed* permission from me, you understand. . . . He is not the envoy. I am. And as you know, young men *will* have their little excitements."

"I became aware of this last night." Now Sir Jehan produced a cool smile, and one that did not reach his eyes. "From what I've heard, your secretary is a rather remarkable swordsman." Sir Jehan's right eyebrow raised at this, but he made no further comment about Alaire's training. He continued, in a lowered voice, "If I may, I would like to speak freely, but in confidence. Just between the two of us, and with no diplomatic matters involved. My concern is for your secretary, Ambassador. Our young Prince is a bad influence. Even though your secretary is an adult and can take care of himself, this doesn't make him immune to certain unsavory influences in our land."

"I was under the impression that they were only out drinking," Naitachal said in defense of both young men. *What influences?*

"There may be more to it than that," Sir Jehan said, and there was a certain sly shading to his words. "Though I cannot be more precise. There could be more to Kainemonen's nightly jaunts than we know. He does this drunken tavern-hopping regularly, in the very worst parts of town. No lady of good blood will associate with him, even incognito."

This answered a question that had been gnawing at the Dark Elf since he spied on Kai, Alaire and their cluster of "maidens." *Those women were of a much lower class — no higher than servants, I should think. I should have guessed as much.*

"I still think Alaire is safe," Naitachal said. "He has enough good sense not to become involved with women who may ultimately seek to cause him trouble. Unless there are other factors you haven't mentioned yet."

If Sir Jehan took offense at this, he didn't show it. "I do hope that having a friend his own age will settle Kai down a bit, but I'm afraid that Alaire does not have a strong enough personality to resist Kai's depravity. If I may speak frankly, Alaire seems to be rather young for a diplomatic mission — even as a mere assistant."

"He is here to polish his skills under my tutelage," Naitachal informed him simply. "But he is very close, *very* close, to the King's heart."

Sir Jehan gave him a knowing look, as if he understood all too well that yes, Alaire was indeed a favorite bastard. *Good. His disguise seems to be holding.*

Naitachal smiled faintly. "I agreed to take him as my assistant largely to please King Reynard. I admit he is a little raw, and I had hoped that some of your fine culture would rub off on him during this visit. He's never been outside of Althea. Please forgive any uncouth behavior you may observe in him. But I do assure you, his personality is strong and fundamentally good, his morals secure."

Sir Jehan sighed, and shook his head woefully. "Kai's debauchery is the root of the troubles between him and his father. The boy simply refuses to behave like a civilized adult, or even a civilized child; and he certainly refuses to behave like a prince."

Naitachal shrugged. "Then why is it critical that Kai be the Crown Prince? Certainly, if he had a younger brother . . ." He raised an eyebrow. "The solution seems a simple one to me."

Sir Jehan shook his head sadly. "Kainemonen's birth was a most difficult one. The Queen is unable to be a mother again. Disgraced, she seldom appears in public. Unlike other kingdoms, it is not acceptable for the King to rid himself of her, or select a — favored by-blow. It is the way of our land."

"So, it is Kai who will inherit the throne, or nobody." Naitachal pursed his lips in an imitation of thoughtfulness. "I think I'm beginning to see the problem."

Jehan waved that off as not important. "All that is immaterial to this discussion, however. My concern is with your assistant. His close association with Kai could very well discredit your mission here."

This took Naitachal by surprise. Still, there was no hint they knew Alaire's true identity.

"And why is that?" he asked, making no secret of his surprise.

"The motives of someone who befriends a potential problem in our kingdom are somewhat in question," Sir Jehan replied. "And he *is* your assistant. What he does will by necessity reflect on you. I expect no trouble, either for you or for your young man. But it looks . . . suspicious, for you, for your assistant, and for your kingdom in general."

This, too, Naitachal was beginning to get the gist of. *Is this Sir Jehan a part of the opposing force in Suinomen politics that Captain Lyam warned us both about?* He was not going to let this man intimidate him. The direction their discussion was taking was starting to sound like an attempt to threaten the mission, despite the gentle tone Sir Jehan was using.

An old family proverb came to the Dark Elf's mind. *Never try to frighten a Necromancer.* Granted, he wasn't a Necromancer any more, but still . . .

"Am I to understand," Naitachal returned, in an irritated tone, "that a friend of the *Prince* is not an ally of the *King?*"

Sir Jehan shrugged, palms upturned, a gesture which conveyed very little to Naitachal.

Time to show some of my cards. And to prove that Alaire confides more in me than this Sir Jehan thinks. "I was under the impression, sir, that the Prince considered *you* one of his friends."

"Well," Sir Jehan began, sounding like the elf had caught him in a subtle deception. "I do my best to heal the rift between father and son, but there is very little I can do when the boy refuses to reform. There's still hope; he's still quite young. Perhaps when Kai comes to his senses, if ever, I can do something about the problem."

Which neither confirmed nor denied Sir Jehan's double role in all this. Naitachal decided not to pursue that particular question. Instead, he formulated an appropriate cover story that would both protect Alaire's identity *and* flush out some bits of information Sir Jehan might not otherwise volunteer.

"What can one do?" Naitachal said, sadly shaking his head. "This was not the sort of problem I had planned to deal with on this mission. *If* there is any trouble — and I trust Alaire enough to doubt that he will become involved in anything he perceives as counter to the interest of either our kingdom or yours — any trouble Alaire happens to get into is his own problem. He knows this. I rely on his good sense; it may even be that he can exert the steadying influence that you feel your Prince requires." Naitachal leaned forward, as if about to impart a confidence, and continued. "My family has a long tradition of magic use. Are you familiar with the term *Necromancer?*"

A flicker of recognition passed over the neutral mask Sir Jehan was trying to maintain. *Yes, he knows exactly what I am. But will he admit it?*

"I'm not familiar with the term," Sir Jehan said, his eyes shifting to the side, indicating a lie. "I know that it describes some sort of magician."

Naitachal smiled thinly. "Yes, a magician. A *very powerful* magician. Using magic is as natural to me as breathing air is to you. Though I would not dare to demonstrate these abilities to you now, in this land where it is illegal. I could raise a corpse from the dead, or force a soul to answer my questions. And — there are more ways available to me to destroy an adversary than I have time to tell you, all of them painful. This training began many, many centuries ago."

Sir Jehan gazed at him thoughtfully, without comment.

Naitachal continued to smile. "There are certain ways in which I could use these powers to defend myself. Ways which, given the laws of your kingdom, I could easily guarantee a long residence in your Prison of Souls."

Naitachal watched his eyebrows raise appreciably. "So you know of this."

Naitachal gave him a look which said plainly, *What, did you think I was deaf, blind and a fool as well?* "Yes, I do. And I would never want to find myself imprisoned in such a place."

"You needn't worry," Sir Jehan assured him. "Our laws apply in fact to the peasants, the lower classes, not to those like you or me. We created the Association to police potentially dangerous magic among the peasants, so that they couldn't use arcane powers to oppress each other, or as tools in a revolt." He steepled his hands together, and put on a thoughtful expression. "And that, I fear, again puts you and your assistant into jeopardy. Though I cannot verify this either way, rumor has it that Kai has been actively recruiting mages in order to overthrow his father, and take the Crown now. This would be a tragedy of the highest magnitude. We must prevent this at any cost. You may find our laws regarding magic confining, even unfair, but I assure you that there are good reasons for regulating it. Surely you can see the wisdom in these precautions."

"Of course," Naitachal said evenly. "I didn't mean to suggest that these precautions were unnecessary. And I surely would never do anything that would make someone think I was willing to use my powers against your King. That would be more than foolishness!"

"Actually, I'm glad you brought it up," Sir Jehan said, standing. His smile was crooked, as if he could not bring himself to produce a real smile. "This is one of the things the King wishes to speak to you about." He gestured grandly towards the set of double doors. "This way, please."

When they entered the chamber beyond the double doors, Naitachal saw King Archenomen gazing at the barren winter countryside through a tall bay window. Framed in the pale afternoon sun, he seemed extremely worried about something.

Sir Jehan cleared his throat. "Sire," he announced. "May I present Ambassador Naitachal from Althea, Envoy of King Reynard."

Eyes still fixed on the landscape beyond, he said, "Thank you, Jehan."

Sir Jehan bowed slightly, and quietly left the chambers.

Naitachal stood boldly in the center of the floor, wondering what could be so fascinating outside that it would hold the King's attention. He didn't know if he should take offense or feel complimented by the complete lack of attention the King was giving him.

"Please, make yourself comfortable," the King said, turning. "Would you care for some ale, Ambassador?"

Refusing would be impolite, so he nodded and said, "It would please me, indeed, Your Majesty." Warily, he took one of three heavy wood chairs, set about in a semi-circle. The throne faced him squarely, a tall, velvet-upholstered artifact raised on a platform that would put the King's toes about eye level when sitting.

The King turned and regarded Naitachal with some visible apprehension, then forced a smile. A servant appeared with two large steins of ale, offered one to the Dark Elf, than served the other to the King. As Naitachal took his, he suppressed a grimace. He did not care for ale, and this was a heavy, bitter brew.

Still, the King's wish was an order. Naitachal relaxed and tried the ale, wondering briefly if it had been poisoned. Since he had a choice of either of the steins, he decided this was unlikely.

The King drank from his stein and seated himself in one of the other smaller chairs next to Naitachal, forgoing the use of the ostentatious throne. Though he wore yesterday's purple robe, his clothing seemed rumpled; shadows lurked under his eyes and stubble stood out on his tired face. Stress lines showed on his forehead. *Either the King is ill, or he is worried sick over something.* Naitachal drank his warm ale and tried to look composed.

"I come directly to the point," the King said. "It has come to my attention lately that there is considerable renegade magic going on among the peasants. There are suggestions that some of these magicians are connected somehow with your land."

Oh? This was a new accusation, and it baffled Naitachal. *Now what?* he wondered, thinking this might be smoke, sent out to conceal the real issue, whatever it might be.

"If there are magicians practicing magic covertly in Suinomen," Naitachal began with an even voice, "I am hardly in a position to know of it. Though my kind does have a long history of the practice of mage-craft, I have carefully avoided this practice since arriving here. And you, sir, have never sent any communication to my King making any suggestion that such renegades are troubling your land. What, exactly, is the link to Althea you speak of?"

"Nothing . . . specific," the King admitted. "And I am not accusing you of anything. It does raise some issues, which I would like to discuss with the understanding that we intend no offense. It is most opportune that you are here to negotiate. It saves us the trouble, and time, of sending an ambassador to *your* land."

At the mention of the word *negotiate*, Naitachal's ears stood straight up. *Are we finally going to discuss these "war threats"?*

The King stirred restlessly. "This mage-craft was once a threat to our kingdom, many years ago. That is when we created the Swords of the Magicians, and began policing the land of unauthorized magic. Since then, things have been quiet here. Until lately. There hasn't been much in the way of travel between our two kingdoms, but in the last half year

what little there has been has increased twofold.
Perhaps it is no coincidence that the unauthorized
magic using has increased as well."

Naitachal saw the King's point, and he didn't like it
at all. *He's trying to blame Althea for the failure of his
policies, for his inability to stifle magic in what is obviously a land rich with those who have the abilities, if
not the training, to practice the art.*

But the King's next words took him entirely by surprise. "I think it would be a great benefit to both our
lands if you recognized the superior policing ability of
the Association and permit them into your kingdom. It
is clear to me that your land is the source of this
scourge, and if you let our Association in, for the
express purpose of dealing with mages, we can solve
this problem once and for all."

The King gazed at him hopefully, obviously finding
nothing wrong with the request.

Naitachal stared at him for a long, long time. The
request appalled him so much that he had to reassess
everything he'd learned about Suinomen and its king.
*Did I hear that correctly? Fearful of magic. Suspicious
of his son. Influenced by unknown political forces. Perhaps completely misled about Althea. He thinks we
want to clean up magic in our own kingdom? Badly
enough to let a foreign force in, from a country whose
intentions are in serious question? He really believes
this is a reasonable request!*

"I see," Naitachal said, forcing a most urbane manner in spite of his desire to demonstrate a little high
level Bardic Magic and wipe the King's mind clean of
even the shadow of such an idea. "Of course, I am in
no position to grant such a request. It might be a very
good idea, after all, and I will *certainly* inform the
King of your request."

King Archenomen's brow furrowed, as if he had

expected immediate agreement. "But surely, you can understand the need . . ."

Naitachal made a conciliatory gesture. "Of course I see how important this is to you. But you must understand, this would mean ridding Althea of most non-humans, elves, fairies, Arachnia as well as the human mages. I'm not even certain this is possible; the non-humans occupy much territory within our borders, and have established themselves as indispensable to the commerce and prosperity of our land. You see, non-humans simply will not allow humans to regulate magic. Magic is the core of their existence. To take it away would cause serious political problems for our King."

"I would have expected the King of Althea to send a stronger soul to discuss matters of state," Archenomen said, looking disappointed.

"It is not a matter of strength," Naitachal said. "Only of prudence. Within our government we have many non-humans, in positions of power. Non-humans such as myself."

"Oh, yes, that's right," the King replied, clearly annoyed, and shaking his head as if he simply had not seen the sable skin and pointed ears of the being right in front of him. "You are a Dark Elf, aren't you?"

Is he a half-wit? Or is his mind going? This is incredible! Naitachal schooled his expression to give no hint of his thoughts. "To impose such rules would be, at the very least, an insult to many powerful beings. But the matter isn't up to me."

Archenomen's face brightened. "That's right, it's not. Relay the message to the King, if you would, please. I think we will be sending our own ambassadors along soon anyway, to make certain he gets it." The King stood, clearly ending the audience. "You may leave."

Naitachal immediately rose to his feet, bowed and backed himself out; grateful the discussion was over, and proud of himself for not converting the King to a pile of ash.

Naitachal returned to their room hoping to find Alaire, so he could discuss this new — and highly disturbing — information with his protégé. *The boy is in more danger than I suspected*, he admitted to himself, guiltily. *Sending him home now would be even more dangerous.*

The Dark Elf realized as he entered the room that he had got about as far as he was going to get with the King. *Reynard should have sent a human*, he admitted glumly. *Only a human can make any progress now.* The monarch of Suinomen was far more phobic about magic than he'd ever imagined, and if Archenomen ever learned that he and Alaire were Bards, it could be a catalyst for war. It seemed almost certain now that they were looking for an excuse for one anyway; that was the only *rational* explanation for such an outrageous request. Surely that act the King had put on was only that — an act. Surely he could not be so stupid, senile or mad enough to believe King Reynard would spend a single second considering such an outrageous idea!

Sending the Swords of the Magicians into Althea — no, surely no one could be that mad. I do believe it is time for us both to find a way to leave this dreadful place, Naitachal decided. *If we left now, we might take them by surprise. Yes. We will be on the road, headed back towards Althea, tonight.*

"Alaire?" Naitachal called softly, as he closed the door behind him. He found only an empty room.

"Good gods," he muttered, picking up a note on the bed.

Your Darkness,
I have gone out again with you-know-who. I
promise to be careful. Don't worry about me. And
don't stay up; it may be late.

Alaire.

Gazing at the note, Naitachal began making soft, strangling noises.

Chapter XII

While Naitachal went off on his diplomatic search for Sir Jehan, Alaire returned to their room to catch a few hours of his lost sleep. The drink with the Prince's bevy of beauties had made him sleepy, and this seemed as good a time as any to catch up on some rest. Just before he fell into deep slumber, he wondered belatedly if he had remembered to lock the door or not. . . .

Alaire woke to someone shaking him by the shoulders. "Wake up, sluggard!" Kai shouted in his ear. "We've got to go out! Hurry! We're losing time!"

The boy roused him with such intensity in his voice that he struggled out of the tentacles of sleep in a panic, wondering what emergency was upon them.

"Wha—" Alaire managed, feeling about for a weapon.

Kai let go of his shoulders, and laughed sardonically at the expression on his face. "Oh, relax," Kai told him. "If I had known it was so hard to wake you up I would have been in earlier."

Alaire finally focused on Kai, who sat on the edge of the huge bed. He wore a new outfit of court clothing, topped with the embroidered red cloak, but he still looked like he'd thrown his clothes on in a hurry. "We're going into town tonight."

"Oh, not again," Alaire started to say, but as he sat up, he realized that Kai was not in a good mood.

Sullen, stormy, perhaps even angry; there was nothing teasing or playful about Kai at the moment. "What's wrong, Kai?" he asked, completely awake now.

"Sir Jehan told me I should —" Kai hesitated, then shook his head, his jaw tensing. "Nothing," he finally appended. "Nothing at all. I'm going to go get drunk. You can come if you want to."

He flung himself off the bed and started out the door.

"Wait a minute," Alaire said, getting up.

Kai paused, and looked back over his shoulder. "You coming?" he asked hopefully.

"Well, I —" Alaire shrugged.

"Good," Kai interrupted. "Bring your harp. You can cheer me up with it."

"— guess I am," Alaire finished.

They took the carriage to the edge of the tavern district, under cloudy skies that grew darker by the moment. Tonight's driver seemed sober, so the ride into the heart of town wasn't as exciting as the previous evening's. The tavern they ended up in was a notch or two below the other places they'd gone to; it took them a moment to find chairs and a table that hadn't been damaged in a brawl. Even so, the night was still young, and according to Kai the very best of the establishment's stock hadn't run dry yet. It appeared that this was the only thing that cheered Kai up — a steady supply of liquor, the prospect of total oblivion.

All he wants out of life is out, Alaire thought. He wondered if going with Kai had been a good idea. Now he felt as if he were inadvertently aiding the Prince in his quest for that oblivion.

This evening's poison was not ale or wine, as had been the choice the night before. This place, The Deadman's Drunk, its name burned into a tombstone-shaped wooden sign above the door, served only the hardest of liquors.

"They distill *aakaviit* from a tuber that grows wild in the hills," Kai explained easily as he downed small glasses of the stuff. He drank it like water. Alaire couldn't understand it. He stared at his own small glass. A single sip had set his mouth and throat on fire. He eyed the burning candle between them nervously.

This is almost pure alcohol! he thought.

Now he wished he hadn't brought his harp. There had been some heated discussion over taking it along, but Alaire had finally relented, thinking that perhaps Kai wouldn't drink as much if he did. The harp was the most important possession he owned, and here it was, exposed to danger in this wretched place. Though wrapped in a thick canvas bag, and looking like a random sack of possessions, it would not fare well in a fight. He placed it so a bottle of *aakaviit*, if spilled, wouldn't drench it. The potent fluid would probably eat right through the finish.

He had hoped the liquor would loosen Kai's tongue a bit. That cryptic sentence about Sir Jehan had him wondering just *what* the man had said to Kai, and if they would see him out again tonight. For additional clues Alaire had suggested they go to the tavern where Sir Jehan had been last night. Seeing them together might yield useful information. But Kai had insisted that place would be closed so early in the afternoon; The Deadman's Drunk was going to be their destination for now, and when Kai started to get a little testy about it, Alaire shut up and sat back in the coach.

Kai had confined his discussion to trivial matters; the good time he had with the twins, this year's grape crop, which had been poor, and the turning weather. When they had left the carriage and started walking, Alaire noticed the air had become considerably colder than he remembered it being last night. A biting cold singed his nostrils. Breath clouded visibly before them. Snow fell lightly as they reached this place; Kai predicted it would get worse.

"I love getting drunk when it snows!" he said. "Any bad weather. Thunderstorms, floods, as long as I'm not in it, and snowstorms. Don't ask me why. Maybe it's the hint of anxiety in the air that makes it exciting!"

Snow was not unusual back at Fenrich, but it rarely fell early. It snowed enough to accumulate about a month before midwinter, and usually melted off by spring equinox. But Suinomen was further north, and the shift in temperature had been rather drastic this evening.

"How much does it snow up here?" Alaire asked.

"Oh, I guess it will probably be waist-high by morning," Kai said casually. "Why?"

"*What?*"

Kai laughed, finished his glass of *aakaviit*. "You act like you've never seen snow before."

"Well, I have," Alaire said, proudly. "But not waist-high!" He tried to imagine what it would look like. "How do the roofs stay up? Don't they collapse under the weight of the snow?"

Which sent Kai into another round of laughter. "Whatever gave you *that* idea? What are your roofs made of down there, thatch?"

Alaire frowned. "Some of them are."

"Of course," Kai said, as suddenly subdued as he had been roused to laughter.

Alaire was more concerned with the effect the snow was going to have on the state of the streets. "Well anyway, if it's really going to snow that deep tonight, perhaps we should make it an early evening?"

"Not a bad idea," Kai said, but his mischievous smirk indicated he didn't take the idea very seriously.

"But if it gets too bad we can always stay at an inn. 'Not exactly fit for royalty,' as his highness Sir Jehan would say, but do I look like I care? Gods no! I've passed out many a night in places far worse than that!"

Alaire's ears pricked at the mention of the nobleman's name. *Yes? And?* He waited for the boy to go on.

A fight broke out behind them, but Kai remained oblivious to it. Alaire watched the two combatants who, from the little he understood of the screaming imprecations, fought over a bottle of *aakaviit.*

Kai had ordered another, and at that moment the barkeep scurried over, and most apologetically explained that the gentlemen behind them were fighting over the last bottle of *aakaviit.*

Kai turned to regard the fight, now interested in the outcome. As the two men struggled with the bottle, Kai reached for the hilt of his sword, but didn't draw it. The barkeep paled when he noticed the weapon, and promptly vanished.

Alaire thought he was going to get sick. The sight of the men fighting over the bottle, and Kai apparently willing to kill for it, was a little too much.

"Here," Alaire said. "Have the rest of my glass."

There was still a half glass left; the little Alaire drank went right to his head, so he had stopped drinking. Though mildly intoxicated, he hoped he still had possession of his fighting skills. *One of us needs to stay at least partially sober,* he worried. *Kai's not going to be worth much, if he keeps this up. He's probably not worth much right now. I've never seen anyone drink as much as he can and still walk.*

The fight continued; Kai watching the two men avidly, his tongue licking his lips as if he were hungry. Suddenly there was a *crash,* signaling the demise of the bottle of *aakaviit* as it fell to the floor. But the fight continued; the two men, now driven to a rage by the loss of the bottle, went directly for each others' throats. A third man had crawled into the area of the affray and was trying to drink the spilled stuff from the floor.

Alaire wanted out of there, badly — but how to persuade Kai? The Prince seemed fascinated by the fight, by the drunk lapping up liquor from the floor —

Then, the fighters knocked over a candle, which fell to the floor, igniting the *aakaviit* with an audible *woooooopf*.

The stuff was as flammable as Alaire had suspected. A roaring fire spread across the floor, away from them, licking the cheap, wooden furniture with fiery blue tongues.

People panicked and ran out of front and rear exits. Somewhere, amid the flames, a man screamed. The bartender beat at the flames with a rag; he only made them spread faster.

The fire was spreading, quickly; *too* quickly. Soon the flames would block the exits!

"Come on, Kai! Let's get out of here!" Alaire shouted, grabbing Kai's arm and tugging him upright.

"Oh, awright," Kai said, sullenly, as if Alaire was trying to get him to leave a bit of high entertainment before it was over.

Alaire grabbed the harp's canvas bag with one hand and Kai's arm with the other and led him through the press of bodies to the front exit. As they reached the door, he glanced behind him to see if anyone else was trapped in there. The place was empty, except for the two original combatants, still locked in struggle, silhouetted by the rising flames.

Forget them, he thought. *Let's get back to the palace before we're snowed in down here.*

He turned — and blinked in surprise. *Snow.*

Gods — Kai wasn't joking about the snow! A thick, white blanket had wrapped itself over the tavern district, and huge, coin sized flakes dropped in sheets. He looked down, and saw he was standing ankle-deep in the stuff. He stumbled out of the doorway, still towing Kai, and took shelter in another doorway across the street from the bar.

People in the street began to shout now, as it became apparent to the passersby that one of the buildings was on fire. Smoke poured out of the front door. The barkeep ran about helplessly, slipping in the snow; no one seemed to be doing anything about the fire except watching.

Suddenly Kai seemed to notice the snow. "All right!" the boy whooped, running into the thick whiteness. He promptly made a ball out of the mush and threw it at Alaire, ignoring the fire licking out of the doorway behind him.

At that moment a number of men appeared, with a purposeful air to them. They formed a human chain and began passing buckets of water to throw on the fire. It occurred to Alaire that maybe they should help —

Then again, maybe that wouldn't be a good idea. Kai was still whooping and playing in the snow, and Alaire didn't think there was any likelihood of getting him to do something as *responsible* as putting out a fire. *No. Let's get out of here, while we have a chance. The snow still looks shallow enough for the carriage to make it back to the palace.*

He followed Kai, who slipped and slid down the street, laughing like a fool. "Kai, you know, maybe we should go back to the palace?"

"Naw," he said over his shoulder, and hiccuped. "Still early."

Alaire persisted. "But getting back while we can . . . don't you think . . ."

Kai muttered something about the next place, and started off down the narrow street without him. Though he walked fairly well, it was clear to Alaire he was very drunk. He started rambling on to himself, as if Alaire was standing next to him.

The situation was starting to anger him. *Why should I care if he cares for no one but himself? Do I really need to go along with him?* He resisted an urge to start walking back to the palace by himself, after taking a few steps in that direction. *I don't know the way that well, and in this snow, everything looks different. And, it's cold! Maybe I'd be better off in a tavern somewhere. Bound to be a fire burning. That way I can keep warm. And keep an eye on Kai.*

He groaned, knowing he had talked himself into being Kai's keeper once again.

Alaire scrambled after the Prince, cursing his footing, and taking excruciating care not to slip and fall on his harp. The sun had set by now, and torchlights and lanterns again provided the only illumination. Foottraffic had diminished, and now only a few people braved the snow.

"So where are we going now?" Alaire said irritably. He clutched the harp tightly, as if holding it closer would shut out some of the cold. Kai's coat was wide open, and he wore no warm hat, as Alaire did; evidently, as drunk as he was, he didn't feel the cold.

"Oh, let's try The Dead Dragon Inn again," he said, matter-of-factly. "They probably won't throw us out."

The clamor surrounding the fire faded, and a new, muffled silence fell about them. In spite of his annoyance with Kai and with himself, and his discomfort, the snow fascinated Alaire; he'd never seen this much falling at one time, so suddenly, and with flakes this large. They fell about the two of them in swirls, landing on his face, his clothes. He stuck his tongue out and caught one. The large flake melted instantly in the warmth of his mouth, reminding him how thirsty he was for simple, plain water. *Maybe at The Dead Dragon Inn, I can get some*, he thought. *After all, Kai drinks enough for both of us.*

He hoped they would reach the place soon. The cold was beginning to eat through his clothing.

He heard something behind them, and turned just in time to see a dark figure vanish into a shadow.

A chill that had nothing to do with the weather ran up his spine, and he felt for the hilt of his sword, slinging his harp over his back. Saying nothing to Kai, who babbled something to himself in his native language, he continued the slow trudge through the snow, keeping his ears open for another telltale noise. When it came, he knew for certain they were being followed. He didn't turn to look this time, but as he listened, he heard the same footsteps trying to match theirs, using the noise they were making as cover.

Maybe it's one of Sir Jehan's men, keeping tabs on the Prince, he thought hopefully, but the prospect didn't comfort him as much as he thought it would.

I'd better say something. He's still a good fighter, even if he's drunk.

He whispered to Kai, "I think we're being followed."

Kai glanced up, and shrugged. But in spite of the bravado, Kai acted a little more wary. Then, finally, he whispered back, "How many?"

"One, at least. Maybe more." *Was that a second set of footsteps, or echoes of our own?* The effect of snow on sound was maddening.

Two figures jumped out in front of them, swords drawn. Kai hissed as he drew his weapon, clumsily, and staggered backwards.

Alaire's nerves were already keyed up, and he was

ready. His sword out, he went after the closest of the two and closed for the attack. His opponent seemed surprised at the aggressive tactics. *Figured I'd be drunk, too?* Alaire thought briefly as their swords engaged.

Within moments he knew that these were no average cutpurses. *These are professional killers!* Alaire thought in dismay, taking in their black clothing, the scarves wrapped about their faces to hide their identities. Why they would be wearing black escaped him; they stood out against the snow. *Unless the snow caught them by surprise too.*

Swords flashed through the falling snow, and soon Alaire was separated from Kai and the other assassin. Alaire heard them, somewhere behind them, clashing away, and didn't like the idea of not being able to see anything but his current opponent. And what of the men who had been behind them? Where were they?

Street-fighting meant street-tactics. He managed to distract the fighter for a moment; his blade lashed out, nicking the man's wrist. Bright ruby-red spots appeared on the snow beneath him. First blood.

The assassin snarled an evident curse in a language he'd never heard before. Alaire feinted, and parried twice, pushing the killer near a torch on a rock wall. In the flickering light he saw the man's eyes, and the dark, olive skin around them. His wrist bled brightly into the falling snow, and Alaire knew his wound must be a great liability to him; he didn't change hands, as Alaire would have done in the same situation. Evidently his teacher had not been as good as Naitachal.

Alaire stepped back, saw an opening, and lunged.

Metal pierced flesh with more difficulty than expected, reminding Alaire he hadn't sharpened his blade since the fight in The Dead Dragon. Even so, his sword found a rich target, and as he withdrew his steel, blood followed it.

The assassin groaned, dropped his blade, and pressed a hand over the wound. The stain spread beneath him as the snow captured the fresh blood. The man stared at him, his eyes hollow in the torchlight, then staggered off into the dark and snow. In a moment, he was lost to sight.

Alaire turned and looked for Kai; there was nothing to see but snow. Then, around a corner, he heard blades clashing. He ran to the sound, staggered as his foot slipped on the fresh snow, and found the two next to another building, their arena brightly lit by street torch. The tip of Kai's blade was broken, giving the assassin the advantage. The boy's face was a mask of pure terror; he knew he was in serious trouble.

And Alaire was a good twenty feet away.

He shouted, hoping to distract the killer, but the man ignored him.

As Alaire rushed at the assassin, the man lunged, piercing Kai in the abdomen. The boy screamed in pain and fell back into the snow.

The killer looked up, apparently satisfied with his work, then ran off.

Alaire scrambled to Kai's side; he was lying face up in the snow, still waving his sword and moaning.

Alaire gently deflected the weapon with his own and took it from his hand.

He knelt over Kai, calling his name.

But the boy just stared blankly, his skin now the color of the snow around him. A red stain spread over his tunic and shirt, but Alaire saw no wound. He pulled the slick fabric of his shirt up, revealing a neat puncture next to Kai's navel. The wound bled a thin, pulsing river. A gut wound. The worst.

He's going to die.

Kai opened his mouth to speak, but he was already too weak to say anything. He was going to die.

Unless —

No! his mind screamed. Without really thinking, he began looking for his harp. He ran, staggering, back to where he thought it would be. *Where is it? Did someone take it?* he thought, just as his eyes fell on the instrument. He grabbed the canvas bag and rushed back to Kai.

Alaire ripped the bag open, with stiff fingers; his heart pounding frantically. Kai's eyes glazed; the thin plume of breath over his nostrils lessening with every moment. Hot tears coursed down Alaire's cheeks. He fought the urge to scream, curse, moan in helplessness —

Don't think of that. Don't think of anything. Just the magic . . . just the power . . .

He took a deep breath, steadied himself, and started to play.

The strings were out of tune, the music sour, his fingers cold and numb. But he played anyway, ignoring the one broken string. He reached for the only song he knew that might work, a short tune Naitachal had composed when one of their favorite horses had suffered an attack from a pack of wolves. The horse had been near death —

Like Kai —

Bardic Magic had healed it, had saved its life.

As Alaire played the tune from memory, his fingers loosened up, and the notes came easier. He ran through the song once, looked down at Kai. He remained still, even peaceful, in the snow. Then, with one spastic motion, the boy exhaled a single breath. Then nothing.

The Magic had failed.

"*No!*" Alaire screamed. Tears streamed down his

face, blurring his vision. He felt an empty space form in the center of his chest, and as he stared at Kai's lifeless face, the space grew larger. He choked back a sob.

Snow began to collect on Kai's face, instead of melting, as it had only moments before.

Alaire wept, unable to help himself, unable to stop. He held the harp loosely, until it was ready to slip out of his hands. Then, suddenly, his Master's words echoed in his head:

The essence of Bardic Magic is the ability to make, and unmake.

To unmake Death — and make Life?

He reached deeper, into his soul, for the power. Willing his arms and hands to move, he began to play the song over a fourth time, automatically, but this time his mind and heart focused on something else altogether.

His mind's eye followed tendrils of life-source downwards, to the ground. Here he found vast pools of untapped power, seldom used in this land, just beneath the surface. Yearning to be released. He imagined Kai's wound, closing itself, healing the injury the assassin's blade had rendered; the tiny folds of tissue, reassembling, knitting, binding, sealing the blood vessels, cauterizing them with light. Then the new blood, slowly filling his veins, restoring what had been lost. At some point, he stopped playing Naitachal's tune and began a new one of his own, one that seemed to fit the magic he was weaving, that complimented the interplay of power and Power. . . .

When Alaire opened his eyes, he found himself and Kai enveloped in a cloud of bright stars, points of light that were pulsating with the harp's music. The untuned strings played a haunting melody that echoed in the drifts of light, of green, blue, red, weaving a spell of life.

The music stopped, interrupted by a shrill, rasping cough.

Kai!

Kai inhaled sharply as his eyes widened with fear, and his lungs struggled for air. He gasped again, clawing at the stained snow with one bloodied hand as the other reached for a sword that wasn't there.

Alaire had a moment to exalt — a single moment of joy at his accomplishment.

Then the harp fell from Alaire's hands as a wave of exhaustion seized him and dragged him down into darkness, while stars of a totally different kind clouded his fading vision. Vaguely aware of someone calling his name, he fell into nothingness.

Chapter XIII

Naitachal flung the note back on the bed. *Why did he have to leave now, of all times?* In the moment it took for the note to sink in, his annoyance darkened to fear. Something was wrong, something very wrong . . .

He cursed Alaire, cursed himself, cursed their luck — and most of all, cursed the Prince.

Soon, it would be time for supper, but if he attended, the rituals of dinner would trap him for gods knew how long. He had little time to waste now.

Wearied by the situation, the Dark Elf sat down heavily on a chair, rubbing his face. As he sat, pondering the circumstances, he had a terrible premonition about Kai and this latest venture into the tavern district —

And not about Kai alone; he sensed that Alaire was in danger too. To probe this further he would have to invoke powers that were illegal here, and he wasn't willing to jeopardize the diplomatic mission or his freedom by bringing the Swords of the Magicians down on them.

I must see Captain Lyam immediately. If anyone can help me in this mess, he can. He might even know where they went.

Poking his head out the door, he glanced down the hallway. Palace guests and noblemen filed toward the great dining hall. If he left now to look for Lyam he might be dragged into a nonsensical conversation before he even got to the stairs. *No, oh no. And going somewhere besides the hall, in view of everyone, would attract unwanted attention.*

Then he sighed. *There is, of course, another way out of the room besides the door.*

When he opened the window, a biting wind ripped into the room, reminding him to don something a little warmer than his usual black cloak. He put on a thick dieren coat and a pair of flexible leather gloves, and climbed over the sill to a narrow ledge along the castle wall, and closed the window behind him.

Their room was only three floors up, but ice had formed on the ledge, and the wind was particularly stiff out here. He had second thoughts about this rather foolhardy venture, but decided to continue. Wasn't he an elf? Didn't he have twice the agility and strength of any human born?

Wasn't he a complete idiot?

Two doors north, one floor up . . . a corner suite. He peered up through the gathering darkness. *That must be it up there. The only room with a light. Gods, I hope he's there.*

He found a section of the ledge above him that had no ice, and pulled himself up, a move which would be difficult for most humans.

His muscles complained bitterly at him; elven he might well be, but he was *not* accustomed to gallivanting about on ledges in the middle of snowstorms. He swore, gritted his teeth, and forced himself up and onto the ledge —

He lay there for a moment, panting with effort.

But that was the worst part; in moments he was looking in the window of Captain Lyam's room. A warm room, with a fire raging in the stove. The Captain was sitting at a desk, with his back to the window.

Good thing I'm not an assassin, Naitachal thought as he let himself in through the window.

"Please close the window behind you, Ambassador," Lyam said politely. He hadn't bothered to turn around. "There is a rather stiff chill in the air tonight."

The Dark Elf stepped down to the pine floor and closed the windows behind him. "I hope this is a discreet enough entrance, Captain," Naitachal said, lazily, impressed despite himself with the Captain's composure and keen senses.

Lyam rose as soon as he stepped into the room, and offered him a cup of heated, spiced cider. Naitachal accepted it with a sigh of gratitude and went to stand beside the stove for a moment.

Elven or not, it had been cold enough out there to freeze the ears off a marble horse.

But as he took his place beside the fire, he saw that what he had thought was Lyam's calm nonchalance was something of a mask. The Captain was obviously concerned about something. Naitachal had a shrewd notion he knew what it was, too.

"Kai has vanished again," the Captain said, abruptly. "Jehan informed me — *after* Kai ran off — that he had set a servant to watch him. I sent a watcher after the watcher. My own man just sent me back word that he found Jehan's 'keeper' dead, with blood spilled in such a pattern as suggests an attack. Because of the amount of blood, we suspect a second person died."

"The Prince?" Naitachal asked, his mouth going dry with fear. He remembered his earlier premonition —

Lyam shrugged. "We don't know. The Swords of the Association are searching the tavern district now."

What? Naitachal stared at the Captain. "Why the Swords?"

The Captain returned the stare, and the Dark Elf had the impression he was looking for signs of deception. "Someone, probably an unlicensed mage, worked some powerful magic in that area. Sir Jehan dispatched the Swords to track the perpetrator down. Then they discovered traces of that same magic at the scene of the killing." The Captain shook his head sadly. "As we speak, the entire force is searching for the mage responsible."

Naitachal's gaze didn't waver. "And if they find the source, what then?"

"They will arrest him. Or both of them." Lyam stared at the Dark Elf broodingly. "Mark you, they do not *know* who the mage is at the moment, but if it was your apprentice, the traces will still be upon him. They will charge Kai with treason."

Naitachal's knees felt a little weak. The Dark Elf seated himself in a chair, opposite Lyam.

Captain Lyam continued. "Is there anything you would like to share with me?"

Naitachal maintained his mask of calm. "I know nothing of the incident. However, I returned to our room to find a note, left by my secretary. Apparently Alaire went with the Prince for another night on the town. To the tavern district, I believe he said."

Lyam nodded. "This we already know. Paavo, the Seneschal, saw them both getting into a carriage a few hours ago. The driver let them off near the district." Lyam leaned forward, his voice lowered. "This discussion is in complete confidence."

Naitachal nodded warily. "I appreciate that. But if you suspect that Alaire used magic to kill, I really must object. That is not the sort of training I have given him, nor is it something he's sought on his own. He's quite capable of defending himself with the sword."

Lyam's mouth tensed. "As I am well aware. No, I don't think he used magic to kill. But *someone* used a powerful spell, after the killing, or killings. They found only one body."

Naitachal frowned, shook his head. "Is there anything to connect either young man with the killing or the magic use? Could they be somewhere in a tavern, idling time away?"

Lyam said warningly, "The Association knows that Kai and Alaire were in the vicinity. An agent saw them at the site of a tavern fire tonight. The Association thinks the Prince and his companion were involved."

Naitachal grimaced. "This is — not good."

"Perhaps it's not as bad as you think," Lyam replied. "I'm the only one who knows you're a Bard, since I haven't shared this information with anyone. Your secret is safe with me. My main concern is how this incident will discredit the Prince. The King believes Kainemonen is raising a secret cadre of mages to take the throne. Though these are only rumors, men close to him are making sure the King believes them."

Naitachal stared off for a moment, his eyes fixed on the blazing fire. *Could Alaire have performed powerful Bardic Magic? I wouldn't have thought that possible at this stage of his training. Why would he, unless there were no other choice?*

"Yes?" Lyam said cautiously, apparently reading his expression. "You had a thought?"

"I had a talk with Sir Jehan this afternoon," Naitachal replied. "He seemed convinced Kai had designs on the throne, using the same means you just described. He was very eager for me to believe that anyone who befriended the Prince would not be considered a friend of the throne. I had the feeling that he would have done anything to persuade me to order Alaire to stay away from the Prince."

"Of course," Lyam said dismissively. "They weren't expecting you two to come along, and they certainly were not expecting an outsider to befriend Kai. If Sir Jehan is behind this, he would use whatever powers of persuasion he had to divert your attention from Kai."

Something else was nagging Naitachal. "What about these so-called 'keepers'? Is this usual? Alaire never mentioned bodyguards when they went out last night."

Lyam shook his head. "When I say 'keeper' I'm only quoting Sir Jehan. More likely they were spies, looking for more stories to bring back to the King about Kai. They probably stayed well out of sight, hoping to observe without being observed."

"And if Kai discovered their presence, would this prompt Kai to eliminate them?" It was a valid question, or so Naitachal thought. "Could this be why they found only one dead man? Could Kai have wounded one and killed the other?" That would be better news for Alaire — and it would point to someone other than Alaire as the unlicensed mage.

Captain Lyam stood, towering above Naitachal, and began pacing back and forth, past the window. For such a large man, he made very little noise. In his uniform, he was an even more imposing figure than he had been at their first meeting, though Naitachal felt more protected than threatened. "He would do no such thing," the Captain said, after apparently giving it some thought first.

"I meant no insult."

Lyam waved the half-apology aside. "None was taken. I appreciate your candor. You have been straightforward with me from the beginning, and I thank you for that. And I admit, on the surface, and especially to someone whose opinion has been colored by minions like Sir Jehan, that is precisely what it *does* look like. The King is convinced a revolt is at the gates."

Naitachal remembered that supper was being served, and stood. "In view of these new circumstances, I think it would be wise of me to attend supper. My absence would be missed, may even be seen as suspicious."

Though how I'm to even pretend to eat, with my stomach in anxious knots —

He started for the door.

"Before you leave, I would like to mention one thing," Lyam said. "I believe that this was a trap, perhaps a trap gone wrong, and I think you will eventually be implicated in this mess, if you aren't already. Please be careful. And remember: you were never here."

Naitachal bowed, and left the Captain to his own anxieties.

The Dark Elf arrived at the dining hall in time for supper, amid a sea of curious stares, some openly hostile. *So. My reputation precedes me. At least, the reputation someone wants me to have.* Pikhalas saw him from across the room and scurried over to intercept him.

"*There* you are," the timid, frail man said, clutching a small felt hat in both hands, nervously twisting it into an unrecognizable lump of fabric. "We've been looking all over for you. You weren't in your room, and we were beginning to wonder."

"Oh, about what? Is something wrong?" Naitachal inquired innocently.

"A situation has developed," Pikhalas said, reluctantly. "The King is having a private supper tonight, and he extends his warmest invitation to join him."

"By all means," Naitachal said cheerfully, stretching his mouth in a smile. "Lead the way."

Adjoining the great dining hall was a smaller, intimate dining room with a long marble table in the center. King Archenomen sat at the head, with Sir Jehan sitting on his right. A score of others sat to either side, with one empty place still at the King's left. Pikhalas showed Naitachal to this seat. Posted at either end of the room was a burly guard.

As Naitachal approached the table, a hush fell over the gathering of nobles, and all eyes fixed on him as he bowed deeply to the King, nodded politely to the rest, then seated himself at the table.

"Good evening, Your Majesty," he said, as urbanely as possible. *Was I supposed to bow when I entered as well as just before I sat? Oh well, too late now.* "I understand there is a problem of some kind tonight. I trust this will not interfere with the enjoyment of the meal and the conversation." *What am I supposed to know? Nothing. Nothing at all.*

The meal had already begun, and once Naitachal seated himself, everyone resumed eating. Sir Jehan cast surreptitious looks in his direction as he gnawed on a piece of cooked bird. Its huge skeletal carcass made a grim centerpiece, which fit Naitachal's mood, though not the mood of cheer he was attempting to project.

As a servant poured him wine, the King said, after a long pause, "Where is your secretary tonight?"

Naitachal didn't even blink. "I understand he is out with the Prince again," he said. "He left me a note to that effect — and truly, I did not expect to see him here, the snow is falling so thickly. I fully expected him to urge the Prince to take some private rooms in a good inn until the weather clears —"

He blinked, as if suddenly realizing that the King and Sir Jehan were gazing at him as if his words held important secrets. "Good heavens — your most efficient liaison informed me something has come up. This 'situation' wouldn't involve the Prince and my secretary, would it?"

"It would," Sir Jehan said suddenly. His look was venomous. "Our agents found the Prince's bodyguard, dead, this evening. The Prince is missing. And so, presumably, is Alaire."

Naitachal froze, allowing the appropriate shock and surprise to surface on his dark face. He turned to the King. "Why, Your Majesty, what has happened? Have you sent the guards to look for them? Is there any hint of foul play?"

"You see!" the King exclaimed. "He doesn't know a thing! And you were wanting to risk a war —"

He broke off abruptly, and returned his attention to single-mindedly devouring his meal. *Good gods,* Naitachal thought, gazing at Sir Jehan blankly. *What have I walked into here?*

All assembled looked appropriately embarrassed. Naitachal cleared his throat, and their eyes went to him again. "Your Majesty, if harm has come to the Prince, then what of my secretary? He *would* defend young Kai, and I confess that now I am growing very anxious. And as I gather from Alaire, Kainemonen is a skilled swordsman himself. What happened to them?"

"We know very little, as yet," the King said, slurping loudly from a goblet, showing no concern whatsoever for his son. "The Swords of the Association are looking for a mage. You see, magic is involved. Signs of it were found with the body. I pray that both boys are safe, but you see, they are in a very disreputable part of town." He turned to Naitachal again, with his face set in an inexpert mask of care. "It is a testament to my failings as a father that he would choose to seek entertainment in such a place. I know that your servant only meant well, but this has become a rather difficult situation."

"How may I help?" Naitachal offered, now free to display all of his considerable anxiety. "I am as interested as you are in securing their safety. If there was —"

"It would be best," Sir Jehan interrupted stiffly, "under the circumstances, that you remain distant from —"

"Let the man finish!" the King shouted. "I'm still not convinced that Althea is behind this!"

Naitachal glanced up at Sir Jehan, who looked away nervously. "Althea?" the elf said softly. "That would be — an unwise assumption."

"Of course, *I* don't think Althea is to blame," the King blustered. The wine sloshed over the rim of his goblet. "And neither does anyone else at this table. There are forces behind this, this, this *conspiracy* that are still a mystery. I'm afraid you've become involved in a rather nasty civil dispute."

Naitachal spread his hands, helplessly. "I don't mean to pry, Your Majesty, but what is the nature of this dispute? I know nothing of it, and King Reynard knows even less. We seem to have become implicated only because we are foreigners in your land. My main concern is for the safety of the two young men. If I may help in some way —"

Sir Jehan stood suddenly, glared at Naitachal, and stormed out of the dining room. The Dark Elf tried not to stare, with little success.

"Ignore him," the King said. Sir Jehan's footsteps thumped loudly down the corridor, audible for a surprising distance. "We are not blaming you. He sees a traitor behind every closed door."

As perhaps you should, Naitachal thought privately.

"I didn't warn you when you first arrived," the King began. "The Prince is an immature youth, filled with ambition. I believe his ambition grows too great, and he has begun to cast envious eyes on the powers and positions he cannot have. But he fails to understand just how powerful our mages are. I am in no danger."

But what Naitachal saw in his tone and mannerisms told a completely different story. King Archenomen's eyes shifted from side to side, his voice quavered, his drinking hand shook ever so slightly. He seldom met Naitachal's eyes. *Is he afraid of me?*

Regarding the other dinner guests with cool detachment, he took in their faces, and social rank as indicated by their clothing. Of those assembled, he recognized one as the Count he met the first night. Others had been present in the waiting room when he met Sir Jehan.

One was without a doubt a mage, masquerading unsuccessfully as a noble.

All seemed to ignore the interplay between the King and the Dark Elf. In fact, they were listening, very carefully, while at the same time trying to be as invisible as possible.

The King shook his head. "If there is a danger to me, which I doubt, it would be in the form of going too far to defend against hazards which do not exist. Sir Jehan will calm down. When he does, then we can settle down to business."

The dinner proceeded in silence, and slowly the other guests excused themselves. It seemed all very strange to the Dark Elf, who would have expected at least *some* show of concern for Alaire and the Prince. Naitachal permitted himself to display his worry about Alaire, as he wondered what had *really* happened in the tavern district.

After supper adjourned, the King took Naitachal aside. "We will keep you informed, Ambassador," the King said, evidently thinking he had to smooth ruffled feathers. "I'm sure there's nothing to worry about. By dawn they'll both come staggering home, with youthful tales of wine and women. Oh, and before you leave," he added. "It would probably be best if you remain in your quarters."

To Naitachal's accusing look, he quickly amended, "So that we can find you on short notice, of course. And for your safety."

Naitachal raised an eyebrow. "I didn't know my safety was in question."

The King waved the comment away. "Just a precaution. Good evening, Ambassador."

"Thank you, Your Majesty," Naitachal said, bowing deeply. "And good evening."

As he ascended the stairs to his room, he saw Sir Jehan standing in the shadows, talking with a handful of noblemen. He stopped as soon as Naitachal came into view, and sent the others about their business before turning pointedly to go himself. But he managed to cast a cold, calculating look towards the elf, complete with nauseating smile, before he was out of sight.

Chapter XIV

Alaire awakened, confused and rather groggy, buried to the chin in a pile of hay in a loft above a stable. Below him, he heard horses blowing and stamping. Dim gray light filtered in through closed shutters at one end of the loft. Kai was nowhere in sight. Weakly, he struggled to sit up.

It was very cold, and the hay was all that had been keeping him warm. He took in his surroundings, wondering why he was there, and how. A single ladder lay against the loft edge within arm's reach, and it looked like the only way up. In his mouth lingered the unpleasant aftertaste of liquor. *Did I get drunk and forget what happened?* He'd heard about blackouts from his brother Craig, who on numerous occasions had been unable to recall an entire evening of drinking. More than once Alaire had helped put him to bed after too much ale, after one of his Required Familial Visits to the palace in Silver City. But this had never happened to him.

Yet.

Then again, he'd never tried to keep up with a sot quite like Kai before.

There's a first time for everything. Did someone carry me up to this loft because I passed out? Gods, what happened to me?

A single round ventilation grille above him allowed some light in. Beyond the piles of hay he made out the wood-slat floor, which creaked as he stirred, and the vague outline of his harp in its canvas bag, leaning against the wall. Beside it was his bloodied sword, glinting in the weak light.

Blood? What in —

The blood was dull and brown on the blade. Suddenly he remembered everything.

"Oh. *No*," he whispered to the chill air. The words froze like little clouds before his nose. Another sort of chill settled into his spine, and he suppressed a violent shudder. *Gods. I used* magic.

Total wakefulness came with the realization. Though still drained from the ordeal, he struggled to his feet, a little unsteady, but more or less alert to every sound in the stable. Within moments he was numb with cold. From below him came the odor of horse, or possibly dieren. The beasts made little noise in the stable, and Alaire guessed it was fairly late now, and they were asleep. *Best to let it stay that way.*

He considered the likely prospect that Kai had left him here, to fend for himself, and had returned to the castle alone. *Staying with me would serve no purpose,* he admitted. *Better that he's gone when the Swords of the Association come take me away.*

Climbing to the top of a mound of hay, he peered out between the slats of the small, round window and studied the snow-covered street below. A thick layer of white covered the entire landscape, and dotting the streets of what had to be the edge of the tavern district were the staggering remnants of the evening's revelers. He thought he saw the two men who'd fought over the bottle of *aakaviit,* but that did not concern him. What *did* matter was that he didn't think he was far from the scene of his "crime"; he puzzled over why the Swords hadn't picked them up already.

Isn't arrest for Magic simultaneous with the spell-casting? Maybe not. Maybe the mages here weren't good enough to catch the perpetrator in time.

Before the arrest of the two magicians the previous night, the officers had talked with the barkeep first. *Could this man have been an informant, telling them who to arrest? Maybe,* he thought with a thin ray of hope, *the Swords rely on snitches to make their arrests, giving the impression of "omniscience" to enhance their authority.*

The man who ran Kai through fled when he saw me. He was long gone by the time I found the harp. If there were no witnesses to the Bardic Spell, then just maybe —

If he stayed in the stable much longer he'd freeze to death. Any warmth to be had in the place was down there, with the beasts. And their owner would likely appear at dawn to tend to them, if not sooner.

A door creaked open at the other end of the stable, and Alaire held his breath. His heart was beating so fast he was afraid it would give him away.

He saw nothing of the level below him, but whoever came in didn't stop at the animals. The ladder began to rattle as someone climbed it. Alaire reached for his sword and stood ready with it.

Kai's head popped up over the edge, and he froze, with the tip of Alaire's sword at his throat.

The boy stared at him, then the blade, then back to Alaire before saying, softly, "I see you're up. How do you feel?"

Alaire let his breath out, and withdrew the blade. "Better. Come on up here."

Kai did so, with two canvas sacks slung over his shoulder. "I brought breakfast. And clothes. We can't go around looking like we're highborn anymore."

Kai seemed grim, but alert and sober. "So," Alaire

said, dropping his voice in response to the obvious need for quiet. "The Swords are looking for us?"

"Everybody's looking for us," the Prince whispered urgently, dropping one of the sacks between them. Although dried blood covered his clothes, his recovery seemed to be total. If he had any pain from the wound, he didn't show it. "The Swords of the Association, the Constables, the Royal Guard. You should be asking, who *isn't* looking for us!" He fixed Alaire with an angry look. "You have a lot to answer for!"

"Huh?" Alaire replied, completely confused. "I only —"

"Why didn't you tell me you were a Bard?" Kai demanded. He opened one canvas bag, presenting a banquet of food. Sausages, cheeses, bread. Even a flask of wine. The sight of it all made Alaire's stomach clench with hunger. *Gods, I'm starving!* he thought, forgetting Kai's wrath.

They started eating, using Alaire's knife to carve up the food. Once Alaire got some of the food in him, his stomach quieted, and he felt much better prepared to face whatever came.

"As I was saying," Kai said sternly, gesturing with a sausage. "Why did you have to use magic, of all things? We had those toughs beaten! Now we've got everyone in the kingdom looking for us. There's a reward for us, too. Ten thousand crowns!"

"Dead, or alive?" Alaire asked, carving another hunk of sharp cheese off the enormous round.

"I'm not joking," Kai protested, filling his mouth with bread and sausage.

Alaire regarded him askance. Then, it fell into place. *He doesn't remember anything from the time the assassins attacked us to when the spell healed him. Either from drinking, or from the magic. I still can't believe I pulled that off.* He looked at the harp, sitting behind Kai, and wondered with awe, *am I a Bard now?*

Kai continued to seethe at him, plainly thinking that Alaire had taken a stupid and cowardly way out of the fight.

"For one thing," Alaire said, patiently, "I'm not a Bard. I am only studying to be one, and I've not achieved that status yet. We didn't mention that before, because we were under instructions from our King, my *father*, remember, to keep that to ourselves. Would you have allowed us into your kingdom had you known? No," he said, answering for Kai. "Anyway, the question is moot. I tried the spell that I thought would work, because if I hadn't you wouldn't be talking to me right now. You'd be dead. You suffered a fatal wound. Remember?"

Kai's look made it clear the Prince didn't believe him. "What are you talking about?" he asked irritably.

Alaire sighed. "What *do* you remember, Kai?"

He thought this over briefly. "We left the tavern, two robbers jumped us, you took one and . . . and . . ."

"And what?" Alaire persisted

Kai's gaze grew very distant, and a strange, bleak, frightened expression crept over his face. "I don't remember. At least, I don't think I remember. Something happened back there, something that . . . it must have been the magic."

Alaire looked at him narrowly. "Is that all?"

Kai looked ready to fling the cheese round at him. "What else is there?"

His anger concealed what had to be fear. *He does know,* Alaire realized. *He knows what happened, and he doesn't want to admit it. Who can blame him? Would I want to relive that?*

He decided to take control of the discussion. "The robbers, as you called them, were no such thing. They were assassins. And they were there to kill us, not take our purses. I know, because the same ones or some-one just like them tried to kill Naitachal, my Master, within the very walls of your palace. I got lucky with one; I killed him without so much as a scratch to myself. That round with Captain Lyam probably saved my life. I learned some things from your teacher that put me at an advantage. Remind me to thank him."

"He's the best," Kai said proudly. Then he frowned in accusation. "If you got so good at this, then why did you have to invoke magic?"

Alaire sighed. "Because the assassin you were fight-ing killed you. Or at least, he wounded you badly enough that you almost died."

Kai smirked. "Sure he did."

"You don't remember?" Alaire asked, annoyed. "You don't remember when the assassin ran you through? Or falling? You don't remember bleeding all over the snow, or me singing over you?"

"Well — I —" For a moment, the arrogance was gone. Then it returned. "Prove it to me!" he demanded belligerently.

Humph. "All right," Alaire said immediately. "I will. Lift your shirt up."

Boldly, the Prince did, without hesitating, revealing a flat, white belly. "What are you looking at?" Kai asked with a smirk, then looked down.

When he saw the fresh scar, still red and a little puckered, he sucked his breath in. "Gods," he whis-pered. "How did that happen? That wasn't there yesterday."

"That was where the assassin ran you through," Alaire informed him grimly. "I came just in time to see him do it, too. He saw me and, I guess he assumed his job was done. He turned and fled. You were lying in the snow, with a gut wound, and bleeding enough to fill a lake."

The revelation, and the proof, clearly disturbed Kai. "All that blood," he said, weakly. "I thought it was the robber's."

Alaire snorted. "No. It was yours. I knew you would die if I didn't do something about it, so I took my harp and wove a spell I saw my Master perform once. It brought you back." He spread his hands wide. "I had to," he said simply. "You're my friend, Kai."

Kai stared at him in disbelief. "You risked everything so I would live," he said slowly. "Nobody's ever done that before. I can't think of anyone who would, except maybe Captain Lyam." He looked away, wiping his face with a sleeve. When he looked back, a tear rolled down a cheek.

"I was *dead*?"

Alaire hesitated before nodding. "Something in my magic, something I don't understand yet, brought you back." He didn't know what else to say. "I guess that was why I passed out," he finished.

At first Kai simply sat and stared at him. His face grew pale, then he began to tremble; his stony facade melted, and tears began to trickle slowly down his cheeks.

At first Alaire thought he might still be drunk; he certainly still reeked of *aakaviit*. He'd seen many drunks get weepy this way.

But then Kai collapsed into a ball, leaning towards Alaire, sobbing. *This is different*, the bardling thought then. *He's not just drunk.*

Hesitantly, he patted Kai's back, and offered his shoulder for support. Kai took it without pride. As Alaire held him closer he broke down completely, burying his face in Alaire's shoulder, stifling the sobs in the fabric of his coat.

They held each other for a long time in the cold loft, Alaire listening to Kai's incoherent grief and the sounds of sleeping livestock. He kept silent, knowing the value of it, as any Bard would. Finally the last of Kai's grief drained from him, and Kai pulled away.

He peered at Alaire through swollen eyes. "If I hadn't been drunk you might not have had to do that. If I had been sober that assassin wouldn't have stood a chance. And you wouldn't be in trouble for saving my life."

"I don't know that," Alaire lied. "Those two were experts."

"Horseturds," Kai said. "It finally got the better of me. I never thought it would."

"The sword?"

He shook his head. "No. The *bottle*." Kai frowned, and looked down at the gore stiffening his clothes, with growing horror. "Demondogs! This is *my* blood!"

He started shedding the clothes, as Alaire watched in amusement. *Now he believes me. He's willing to freeze his behind to get those bloody clothes off his skin!*

Pale, skinny and naked, Kai hopped over to the second bag he'd brought with him and pulled out a pair of leather trousers, boots, a flannel shirt, a leather tunic. In his already disheveled state, and with these new garments, he looked like an ordinary peasant boy.

"Now tell me," Alaire said. "How did you get *me* up here?"

Kai shrugged. "After that — spell, I guess it was, you got all wonky. Like you were walking in your sleep. I got you as far as this stable, and you sort of helped yourself up the ladder, flopped over on the hay, and passed out. I thought you were going to get cold, so I covered you with hay."

Alaire managed a smile. "The spell took a lot out of me, I guess. I'm better now, and the food helped. Thanks."

Kai flung clothing at him from the canvas bag. "You'd better change. If we don't look like peasants, we'll stand out like peacocks on a chicken farm."

Alaire hesitated before exposing himself to the frigid air, then started dressing quickly. *Kai's a native here. He knows more about this place than I do.* "Where are we, and where did you get the food?"

"The stable is in the care of Gallen, the owner of The Dead Dragon Inn, and belongs to a Count on the eastern border. He comes into Rozinki twice a year, and he's not due back for months. The dieren down there belong to traders who come into town for supplies. I chose this place for two reasons, one being if any of those traders saw us, they would look the other way. They'll want nothing to do with the Association, or the reward. I know too many things about them, things that they do that aren't exactly legal, like using unlicensed mages when they're on the edge of the kingdom. They know I know, and they know I wouldn't hesitate to turn them in if they turned *me* in, so we're pretty safe. But not for too long. By daybreak, this street will be crawling with Swords."

"Then where will we go?" *And what will you do?*

Kai looked thoughtful. "Well, Gallen is on our side. For months I've been bribing him with promises of protection and favors once I'm King. My father taxes these places heavily, and I've promised to cut their taxes down to almost nothing. And besides, I know that half of the liquor he serves there hasn't got a tax stamp. I know who smuggles it to him, and how."

Which explains why most of these places let him in the door.

Kai looked a little more confident now. "He has a warm basement where we can hide for days, if need be. The Swords and the Constables have already searched there. They might go back, but I don't think so. They believe Gallen is loyal to the Crown. It's the best place I can think of."

Alaire considered his options, saw that he had very few of them. *Do as the natives do.* He pulled the last of the clothes on, a tunic that was a little too big. The boots were better than the ones he'd had before, since they were fur lined, and designed for the cold. Long, threadbare woolen scarfs were wrapped around their heads and necks, giving them an undeniable poverty-stricken look.

But Kai still hadn't really answered his question. "Kai, what's going to happen? What are we going to do?"

Kai finished tucking the scarf into his tunic, then said slowly, "We're both wanted for 'questioning,' but that really means they've already convicted us." His brow creased with thought. "I *might* be able to explain what happened. I can say a mage came along, that it wasn't you. Or something. As soon as I convince Father someone tried to assassinate me, it might make a difference. Father has the power to pardon us both."

Kai said nothing about the Prison of Souls, but the omission emphasized it, highlighted it, drew circles and arrows around it. *Prison of Souls.* He desperately wanted to ask Kai more about it, but was more afraid of what the answer might be.

Not might, would. Minimum sentence, one year. They put the bodies in caskets, their souls in crystals. Fuel for magic. Limbo. Nothingness? Or is there pain, a slow burning, or is it like roasting on a spit? Aging twenty years for every one. No, I can't let that happen.

A lump of fear settled coldly in his stomach, which threatened to expel his breakfast. But Alaire forced his gut to settle, and turned his thoughts to other concerns. A lesser, but nonetheless important concern, was Kai's going back to the palace. This seemed, at the best, foolhardy. *Would they believe him?* he wondered. *Could he really convince the King to overlook this little incident?*

Is he my only chance?

Kai seemed now to be blithely certain of success. "As soon as you're secure in the basement, I'm going back to the palace to talk to Father. Gallen will take care of you. Just cooperate, do as he says, and everything should be fine."

"I doubt that," Alaire said sadly. "Our so-called diplomatic mission is now a disastrous ruin." He looked up, suddenly concerned for his Master. "Any word on how they're treating Naitachal? Is he under arrest?" Alaire guessed that his Master and friend would not fare well in a Suinomen gaol. Althea would view this as an act of war.

They stared at each other, apparently having the same thought.

"How *stupid* of me!" Kai said, slapping his forehead. "That was the whole reason for the attack! Your Master is an elf, and I'll bet they figured you had to be some kind of mage too! If they didn't kill you, they would force you to use magic. These enemies, whoever they are in the palace, thought this through completely. Yes, Naitachal will probably be arrested. Would Althea go to war over *that*?"

Alaire's stomach lurched again. "Maybe, but if they imprison one of the King's sons, even unwittingly —" He seized his head in both hands, as it threatened to explode from the pain of headache and heartache. "Oh gods — I don't know what to do! Unless I escape Suinomen and explain what's going on to my father, we have no chance of preventing war."

How had all this turned into such a horrid mess, so quickly?

Kai looked grim. "There are probably watchers and

checkpoints at the port and the roads. Still, there are ways. If worse comes to worse, I can put you on a boat for Althea."

"If it comes to that. I hope it doesn't." He shook his head unhappily, some of the exhaustion coming back. "Gods, what a mess this is! Does someone in the palace want a war with us that badly to go to so much trouble?"

Now Kai looked completely baffled. "I see no possible benefit from it, for anybody. But it sure looks that way. I have to convince Father of what's going on. It's the only chance we both have."

They made ready to leave for Gallen's. Kai eyed the harp suspiciously, then suggested he keep it with him, in case he needed to protect himself. Alaire slung it over his back, on its wide leather carrying-strap, to give his arm free movement if he had to use his sword.

He overestimates my Bardic ability, Alaire thought wryly, though it was flattering that the Prince would do so. But then Alaire remembered last night. . . .

Who knows, maybe I can raise the power to defend myself against an army. Yes, and pigs will turn to swans when I do so!

They gathered up all the old clothes and stashed them in one of the bags. Kai gave instructions to Alaire to burn them as soon as possible.

In the dark of the early morning, the two peasant boys crept out of the stable. The snow had diminished to a mere dusting, though Alaire had trouble negotiating what had already accumulated.

"You can do better than that. Someone will notice you," Kai admonished. Alaire didn't know what he was talking about. "If we look like we're drunk, maybe it won't be so noticeable if you slip and slide a little."

Alaire took the flask of wine out of the bag, took a drink, and, hesitating, handed it to Kai. The boy stared at it for a long moment, then wrinkled his nose, and refused.

"No. Thanks. I'm not really . . . in the mood for it right now."

Alaire gawked at him. *Never thought I'd hear that.*

To give the impression he'd been drinking all night, he dribbled a little on his tunic, then splashed some on Kai as well. Now they both smelled like a winery. A *cheap* winery. He capped the flask and held it in plain sight.

Alaire guessed by the hint of daylight on the horizon that dawn would arrive soon on the deserted streets. *I hope I'll be safe enough to be able to sleep in this place,* he thought, stifling a yawn. *I'm ready to fall over right now.*

He recognized some of the taverns, most of them closed, as ones they'd been to on Kai's last carouse. A few were still open to greet the dawn, now an undeniable brightness on the eastern horizon. The burned-out tavern where their misadventure had begun earlier that night was a charred husk, still smelling strongly of smoke. As they passed it, there was a bit of warmth coming from it still; it felt good, but they had no time to stop. At the end of the street a mounted figure in a uniform appeared, and Kai stiffened.

"Do what I do," Kai said quickly. The uniformed man saw them and directed his dieren towards them. It was quite appallingly surefooted in the snow, and Alaire realized that it would have no trouble overtaking them and running them down if they tried to flee.

Alaire thought he was going to lose his breakfast again, this time from the other end of his body. As the man approached, he saw that it was a lone member of the Swords of the Association. His throat became dry, his knees turned to mush. Their swords, though concealed beneath their thick fur coats, were well within reach. *Am I going to kill twice in one day?* At this point he would do anything, short of sacrificing Kai, to avoid the Prison of Souls.

"Don't even think it," Kai whispered. "There would be fifty of them on top of us in moments. Follow me. Say nothing."

Horrified, Alaire watched Kai run to the soldier. *Kai, what are you* doing!?

"Alms!" Kai cried, jumping up and down like a little kid, holding his hands up to the soldier. "Alms for a poor beggar child who hasn't eaten in three days!" He held his hand higher, and the soldier stopped, momentarily confused. Alaire ran over and held an open palm up, looking hungry and desperate, the latter not requiring much acting.

"Oh, please, kind sir!" Kai wailed pathetically. "Can you spare us a little coin? A copper? Please, sir, we're starving!"

"Ho! Get away, you little beggars!" the solder cried. The dieren came to a complete stop, the beast itself disinterested in the two peasants. The soldier sniffed the air. "You're hungry because you've been too busy drinking wine to spend money on food!" The soldier shouted. "Look! It's a wonder you're hungry now!"

The soldier was pointing at Alaire's wine flask, which he still had in his other hand. He grinned sheepishly, opened it and offered it to the soldier.

"Go home and to bed, peasants! I have criminals to look for!" He kicked his beast and the dieren trotted off down the street, in search of the Prince of Suinomen and a renegade Bard.

"Tightwad," Kai spat, watching the retreating soldier. "They get paid six hundred crowns a month, and yesterday was payday!"

✻   ✻   ✻

Alaire remembered Gallen from the night they first went to The Dead Dragon Inn. He was one of the barkeeps who tried, in vain, to prevent Kai from taking on the five sailors. He seemed too young to be bald, and Alaire guessed him to be around thirty, with a large, knobby nose and beet-red complexion, as if perpetually embarrassed about something. His expression was not exactly welcoming when they reached the rear door of the inn; he glanced up and down the alley nervously, then hurried them inside.

"So this is your friend, who caused all the trouble," he said gruffly. "Well, can't be helped. In for a lamb, in for a sheep. Follow me."

He took them down steep, narrow stairs into a maw of darkness. Rich odors of wet earth, and stale beer, and fermenting yeast wafted past them. There were no handrails, and Alaire tiptoed nervously on the uncertain steps. Once down, light bloomed when Gallen struck a match, and lit a single candle.

"This is where we keep some of the premium ale, and it's also where we brew the cheap stuff. Do not disturb any of it, or you'll interrupt the fermentation. Come on, the place I have for you is back here."

Past the kegs was another, even smaller passageway, lined with planks. It looked like an old mine. When Alaire asked about it, Gallen confirmed it.

"Used to mine crystals down here, centuries ago, before the Crown made magic illegal. It doesn't go back very far, but I've got a place set up that's not very easy to find. There is a single flue connecting with the main chimney above, and it will only handle small fires. Got one going now."

They entered a hollowed-out section that looked as if it might once have been part of a cave, with a curved, rock wall. A stove glowed warmly in the corner. A row of bunk beds with hay mattresses lined one wall.

"Mac was here after you left," Gallen informed them. "Your friend the constable. Thought you might be back here. I tell you, I don't like it, Kainemonen. This is not a safe place."

"It's the only place we have," Kai admitted sadly. "I won't be here long anyway. I'm going back to the palace tonight. Last night was an attempted assassination, not a robbery. My father must know about it."

Gallen seemed resigned. "If you must. Whatever you do, please don't say anything about this! They'll execute me for treason!"

Kai nodded, an oddly adult expression on his face. "Don't I know it," he said. "Alaire will think of something for you to tell them. Something that will get you off the hook."

Thanks, Kai! But better that they got their stories straight now, he supposed.

Alaire stowed his harp under the bottom bed, then sat on the edge. The warmth of the room acted like a weight on his eyelids.

"Kai, I need to know something," he said suddenly, forcing himself awake. "How good are the Swords in tracking magic users? When they captured those two the other night, were they led there by a snitch, or did they have some way of 'seeing' them, and where they were."

"They're not as good at that as they say," Gallen said. "Usually, someone turns the magic users in. If no one saw you, then they would have no way of knowing *who* was responsible. They can 'feel' magic being performed, but can only narrow the search down to a particular portion of town. If we can keep you under cover long enough, the traces of magic still on you from what you did will wear off, and they'll never be able to prove you did anything."

But he turned back to Kai and his face showed pure

desperation. "If you would reconsider. Another part of town, on the north side, perhaps, would be much safer."

Kai set his jaw stubbornly. "I don't know anybody up there."

Gallen looked just about ready to cry. "But you're a Prince!"

Kai glared at him. "But all my friends are here, in the tavern district. I don't *know* anyone up there. And remember the things I know, Gallen."

The man's red face paled.

"If you are my friend," Kai continued, "then you will help me. Please take care of Alaire, protect him, feed him, conceal him. I will be back as soon as I can."

These last words faded quickly as exhaustion overwhelmed him. *Whether or not I'm in a safe place now, I can't — hold — out,* he thought as he collapsed back on the bed, and his eyelids dropped closed.

Chapter XV

In their room, Naitachal prepared for breakfast in the great hall. A knock sounded at the door; he reached for his sword, but didn't draw it. He recalled that the last time someone knocked on his door it had been little Erik, come to clean the room. He relaxed a little. It wouldn't do at all for the boy to walk in a second time with a sword pointed towards him, and he didn't think the poor child would believe the "practice" story again.

"Come in," Naitachal said, carefully.

The door opened, and a cart pushed by Erik came rolling in. "Your breakfast," the boy said happily. "Paavo sent me in with it, sir."

The Dark Elf raised his eyebrows when he saw what they'd sent. Dieren steak, fried eggs, a fresh loaf of bread, a round of cheese, a pot of jam. Compared to the "repast" of yesterday, this was a veritable feast.

Hmm, he thought, trying to unweave the tangled web they were spinning before him. *They're serving me in my room, on the third day of the visit. They must want me out of the way, so as not to mingle with anyone who might ask me questions about the whereabouts of Kai and Alaire.*

"Where would you like it?" the boy asked, eager to please. At least they had not managed to contaminate Erik's mind.

"Anywhere," he said. The cart became a clever

table, and he pulled up a chair to make the best of the meal. *Something tells me this is going to be a trying day. I'll need my energy.*

Erik made ready to leave. Naitachal spoke up. "You don't have to leave, just yet. Come sit. I'll be happy to talk with you, if you like. You had a lot of questions yesterday."

Shyly, the boy complied, but his hesitancy indicated he either had something else he had to do, or Paavo had instructed him not to talk to the Dark Elf.

Naitachal cut a careful piece from the dieren steak, and ate it as casually as if he had not a care in the world. Young as this child was, and guileless, he could still be used as a source of information. "So. Have the Prince and my secretary returned to the palace yet?"

"That's your secretary they're looking for, too?" the boy replied, clearly shocked.

Naitachal ate a piece of bread. "Evidently," he said with careful casualness. "What's the news?"

"Well," Erik began, eying the door. "I — uh —"

Is someone watching him, making sure he returns promptly?

"Yes?" the elf asked.

"They're both still missing," Erik said, quickly, "and Sir Jehan threw a flying fit when the Swords failed to find them last night. He sealed the port, permitting no ships to leave or enter without a search."

I never considered escape by sea, Naitachal mused. *Gods forbid that ever becomes necessary. It may be the only route out of this land.* He tried some of the cheese. It was excellent.

"Interesting," he said. "I can't imagine why they think Alaire would want to escape. His place is with me, after all. I should think they ought to be looking for whoever has kidnapped him and is trying to create an incident."

There. Plant a rumor of my own.

The boy stared at him. "Why are they keeping you here?" Erik blurted. "All the servants are talking about it."

Well, that didn't make much sense. "Keeping? You mean, 'boarding,' don't you?" Naitachal asked.

Erik made a face. "I mean, why aren't they letting you leave the Palace? Why don't you go look for your secretary yourself?"

Now it was Naitachal's turn to look surprised. "I wasn't aware this was the case. They must really think I'm important. Or perhaps they *do* think someone has kidnapped Alaire, and they fear for my safety if I venture into town."

Erik glanced at the door again, then stood, and said, "I'll be by later to clean the room. Are those Alaire's things over there, in the corner?"

Alaire was a tidy traveler, and was careful to keep his clothing and assorted belongings in one place, so as not to get mixed up or get in the way of his Master's possessions. "Indeed. Why do you ask?"

Erik was visibly nervous. "I wanted to make sure, so I wouldn't disturb them."

And he was gone.

Puzzling, the Dark Elf thought. *He is a rich source of information. Erik would make an excellent spy, if he isn't one already. After all, who would suspect a child? Except an evil Dark Elf, who would suspect his own mother in this place. . . .*

Still, the boy seemed innocent enough. *But his tongue certainly does wag a lot if he's working for the King in that capacity. And if I'm a captive in this place, I must be the last one to know.*

He finished breakfast, and was about to ignore the King's request that he stay in his room when someone knocked on the door again.

He had his sword out this time; the knock was harder, and was higher on the door. An adult.

Captain Lyam let himself in without invitation. He glanced at the sword indifferently, not particularly surprised or offended. Naitachal returned it to its sheath.

"We have news about the Prince," Lyam said soberly. "This morning he returned. He's in the King's chambers right now."

Naitachal did not bother to hide his elation. At least he knew that the boys were still among the living! "And Alaire?"

Lyam's face was grim. "He, unfortunately, has *not* returned. Went off on his own in the tavern district, according to Kai. The Prince is probably protecting him, but so far the story holds water. King Archenomen urgently requests your presence, at once."

"So how *else* was I supposed to get onto the palace grounds unrecognized?" Kai was shouting shrilly when Naitachal entered the King's chambers, with Captain Lyam at his side. "You have half the kingdom out looking for me. You've accused me of a crime I didn't commit, you've offered a reward for my *head*, and you ask me why I look like a pauper? Of course I'm dressed like a peasant. Maybe you should be asking that stupid guard why it was so easy for me to get in, Father!"

The King looked as if he had a splitting headache, one which was getting worse with each passing second. Captain Lyam looked away, visibly trying *not* to look embarrassed. He was, after all, in charge of the guard in question. Sir Jehan was standing to the King's right, evidently enjoying the show while attempting to look concerned. Beside him stood Soren, the rotund wizard, dressed in an even more gaudy robe of burgundy silk, decorated with silver moons, stars and symbols of unknown meaning. The wizard seemed intimidated by Kai's brazen insolence, while trying, without success, to exude authority as the King's head magician. Behind these men, against the rear wall of the King's chambers, stood ten heavily armed guards, some holding shackles and chains at their sides, open and ready to use.

Prince Kai sat in a heavy wooden chair in the center of the room, his feet dangling above the floor, glaring at everybody present.

"Ah. You must be the Ambassador of Althea," Kai said as his eyes settled on Naitachal. "Alaire has told me much about you. I'm glad you're here. I was saving the best for when you arrived."

Naitachal bowed graciously. "Pleased to make your acquaintance."

Kai continued, with a certain amount of glee in his voice. "Last night someone sent two assassins to kill me and Alaire. And they almost succeeded."

"Assassins?" Lyam spoke up. "Are you sure?" Despite the surprise the large man was feigning, Naitachal knew the man had expected this. *Why else would he be training the boy so hard with the sword? Captain Lyam has anticipated this for months.*

"Oh, don't be silly," the King said, petulantly. "You probably got attacked by a couple of pickpockets. What did you expect, carousing in such a place?"

"Were they by chance dressed in black, with black wrappings concealing their faces?" Naitachal said, loud enough for everyone in the room to hear.

"What are you talking about?" the King demanded, distracted by Naitachal's question and the sudden odd turn the interrogation had taken.

"Yes, they were," Kai said. "They were professionals, wearing black costumes and black scarves about their faces. So Alaire was right. They were like the ones who came after you."

"Only one, my lord," the Dark Elf corrected. "But otherwise the same."

"Ambassador, were you attacked? Why didn't you say anything about it?" the King said in a softer, dangerous tone. "When did this happen?"

"The first night we were here," Naitachal said, stepping closer. "I didn't report it because — there were things about your land I did not understand. I wanted to find out more first. The incident, however, left me with the feeling this assassin was not trying to kill me, but to goad me into using magic against him. While this was tempting, I remembered in time where I was, and refrained. The attacker fled, and if he were really trying to kill me he would not have abandoned the job."

"Now why would someone want to force you to use *magic*?" Sir Jehan said, in a oily voice. He was stroking his beard casually, pretending he was relaxed during these proceedings, but a nervous tic at the side of his face gave him away. "Certainly you're not suggesting the King had anything to do with it?"

Naitachal made no secret of his contempt for such a suggestion. "No, I am not. But whoever it was knew the castle, and apparently knew of secret passages. The man who attacked me vanished, and he went down one of these, I suspect."

The King's eyes narrowed with suspicion. "I find it very disturbing, Ambassador, that you have chosen to keep this to yourself," King Archenomen said. "This raises questions. Can you prove this? Did anyone see this?"

"There were no witnesses," Naitachal said, "save myself. And that was precisely why I said nothing, for with no way to prove what happened, who would ever have believed me?" He faced the King squarely, meeting him eye to eye. "I, on the other hand, find it even *more* disturbing that someone attacked me, a guest of this palace. From our conversations I have gathered that you feel there is a conspiracy afoot. Perhaps elements of this conspiracy are responsible for these two attempts at murder — one upon me, and the other upon my secretary and your Prince."

"We are not doubting your word," Sir Jehan said evenly. "If you had reported the attack when it happened, we might have been in a position to do something about it, but I fear the evidence, if there were any, would be a little stale by now, don't you think?" His face hardened. The time had come for him to make his move. "No, the situation, I fear, is something other than the Prince claims. It appears your secretary has broken one of our laws, and is hiding from our justice."

"Alaire did no such thing!" Kai shouted at his erstwhile friend.

"Silence!" the King roared. "You've had your say."

Naitachal regarded Sir Jehan with a cold, unwavering stare. "Those are strong accusations to be making against Althea. What evidence have you? And what law did Alaire allegedly break?"

Sir Jehan met his stare and promptly blinked, then looked away. "When the boys went out last night, I had two of our men follow. This was only a precaution, you see, and something I do from time to time anyway. Our men caught Kai trying to recruit magicians in the tavern district, and when he saw our men he went after them, killing one. The other lived to tell about it."

"Interesting," Naitachal replied. "If true. Why wasn't this information available last night? Certainly you must have known at dinner that this alleged incident had taken place. Why did you say nothing?"

King Archenomen cleared his throat. "It would be wise of you, my dear Ambassador, to remember that you are a guest of the palace, and not a member of my staff," he said sternly. "There are things to which you are not privy. Sir Jehan, please continue."

"Our man saw Alaire cast the spell," Sir Jehan said smugly. "And a rather potent one, at that. It was for show only, to impress the Prince. It would also seem that the Ambassador's secretary has been in the process of allying himself with the young, traitorous Prince, while his Master is presenting the illusion of Althean decency here in the palace."

He turned to the King, his tone silky, but full of menace. "Your Majesty, there can be no mistaking the factions that threaten your land. We have seen a clear pattern of deception, cloaked with diplomatic propriety. Althea has been infiltrating mages into your land to aid the Prince in disposing of you, and last night my men caught the Prince and an Althean mage red-handed carrying out plans to overthrow you. I see no reason for further debate."

"Well, I do," Prince Kainemonen interjected. "Sir Jehan is a *lying traitor.* There were no keepers as he describes, only two ruffians who tried to kill us both, without provocation. Sir Jehan sent assassins, not guardians. Please, Father, you must believe me! I am your son! I am telling you the *truth!*"

King Archenomen gazed at his son thoughtfully, rubbing his temples as if this would make it all go away. Then he shook his head.

His voice was sad and heavy, but determined. "Son, in the past year I have seen you go through some disagreeable changes. You have completely ignored your responsibilities here at the palace in favor of carousing with the scum of our society. You have consistently shamed Suinomen before visiting dignitaries, important men of the trades, and our own nobles; you have shamed the throne, and worst of all you have shamed me personally.

"Do you have any idea how bad you make me look when you show up too drunk to stand at official gatherings? Do you know how humiliated I am whenever you arrive at the palace at daybreak, reeking of ale, with women in tow, singing at the top of your lungs? Your mother won't *speak* to me, she won't even show her face in public, because of the monster you've become.

"You've shown no interest in the well-being of this Kingdom, unless it happens to coincide with your own selfish needs. You're more interested in your grape crop than you are in the farmers' wheat! Sir Jehan, on the other hand, has been a trustworthy confidant of mine since before you were born, has consistently performed his duties with no regard for his own welfare, and up until now he's put out every one of the little political fires you've started, protected the throne, put the kingdom's needs before his every waking moment of his life, *and you want me to take your word over his? How dare you insult my intelligence that way!*"

The silence in the room was thick enough to cut. Nobody moved, or breathed. The King was on his feet, his face a hand's width away from his son's, and purple with rage.

"Why should I believe you?" the King said, his voice dripping with contempt, and he turned on his heel and returned to his throne.

Kai didn't answer right away. His attitude during his father's tirade had gone from cocky to neutral to submissive.

He spoke softly, into that horrible silence that had filled the room.

"Because I am telling the truth, Father."

"Nonsense!" the King spat. "You've been conspiring against me for a long time now. Admit it! And you thought you had an ally in Althea. Didn't you?"

"I thought no such thing, Father."

"Where is this secretary?" Sir Jehan demanded. "If you're not a traitor, then why are you protecting him?"

Kai shrugged. "I told you, we parted, last night. Check the brothels."

"If I may interject something," Naitachal said cautiously. "If Alaire is allegedly guilty of performing magic without a license, then why haven't the Swords of the Association picked him up already? They're magicians, *with* a license. Surely this shouldn't be a problem. Any Althean hedge-wizard can track the scent of magic to whoever has performed it. One of your Association mages should have found Alaire long ago, *if* he is guilty."

All eyes turned to Soren, who had all but vanished during the exchange. It looked to Naitachal rather as if he had attempted to slip out the door.

"Your Majesty," he said, sweating profusely, "this is a very powerful mage we're talking about here. He must have — must have cast some sort of concealing spell, so that we can't find him. The moment he cast the magic, the entire Association Hall trembled with the power, and we knew immediately where it came from. The tavern district. As soon as our staff of magicians began tracing this power source back to the culprit, the trail mysteriously vanished."

Naitachal rolled his eyes. *What a charlatan.* "Are we speaking of the same young man?" he asked mildly. "A *powerful mage*? At *nineteen*?"

"You've never had this problem before," the King said suspiciously. "Why the problem now?"

Sweat was pouring down Soren's face. "If we had some personal possession of his, it would make it much easier."

"Such as?" Naitachal asked politely. *First Alaire is a conspirator, now a mage. Not even a hint that he's a Bard. Good. Up to a point.*

"An article of clothing, jewelry. Anything will do."

"Then perhaps we should escort Naitachal back to his room," Captain Lyam suggested. "Where Alaire's possessions are." The Dark Elf's heart sank; he had hoped Lyam would be an ally, but it looked otherwise. *Perhaps he still is. There's enough smoke in this room to smother a horse.*

"Before you go anywhere," the King said, yawning. "Arrest Kai. Throw him in the dungeon, until further notice."

"No!" Kai shrieked, leaping to his feet. "You can't do that! I'm your son!"

"You *were* my son. No longer. Take him away."

Two of the guards came forward with shackles. The boy looked ready to fight, but all his energy drained out of him before Naitachal's eyes. Once shackled, feet and hands, he walked out of the King's chamber with a loud rattle, his head down. Sir Jehan looked positively gleeful.

"Oh, and one more thing," the King said, addressing Naitachal. "Any idea why Althea would be massing troops near our southern border?"

"Your Majesty? Are you sure about that?" *Certainly there must be a mistake!*

"Quite. I await your response."

"I know nothing of this, either," Naitachal said. *Someone must have lied to him.*

The King smiled. "That is an unacceptable answer, Ambassador. Now, you were saying, Soren?"

The wizard trembled. "I need a relic. A possession of the secretary's, if I may."

The King waved at him. "Take what you need. Sir Jehan, you go with them. Ambassador, until we resolve this matter, I ask you to place yourself voluntarily under guard of Captain Lyam. If you resist, or try to return to Althea, you will share the dungeon with the former Prince Kainemonen, and a state of war will exist between our two kingdoms. It would seem by the actions of your own army that such a state may already exist. Do you understand the severity of this situation, Ambassador?"

"Indeed I do," Naitachal replied. "I will assist you any way I can. I cannot explain why our forces are gathering on your borders, but I doubt they are considering an invasion."

The King only smiled a little more, as if he had expected this answer; it pleased him. "Your lack of *total* conviction is disturbing, Ambassador. The only thing we would like you to do now is provide a possession of the young man's to Soren, then confine yourself to your room. Captain Lyam will be personally responsible for your continued residency here."

"Then by all means," Naitachal said, "let's go and get what you need."

The grim procession of four to Naitachal's room attracted a great deal of unwanted attention. It looked for all the world like the group was on its way to an execution, and Naitachal was the guest of honor. Several of the palace guests stood and stared at the group, the news of the situation and the return of the Prince having spread quickly through the halls. This treatment was nothing new to Naitachal; the natives of this wretched, backwards kingdom gawked at him anyway.

The Dark Elf knew it wasn't time to direct blame. He must remain calm and professional, and play along with whatever they wanted. They hadn't thrown him in prison yet —

Sir Jehan stayed behind them several paces, keeping

a distance from Naitachal. The nobleman had made a habit of avoiding his eyes, perhaps because he knew what a Necromancer was.

In the old days we killed with a look, made all the easier if we made eye contact, Naitachal thought stormily as they approached the room. *And I have a very good reason to kill you; you are the one behind all of this.*

He berated himself for being so stupid. He knew he should have concluded this long ago, but had not — because it was too obvious? Naitachal hoped that was not the case . . . but feared it was. Oversubtlety was a character flaw of his, no doubt about it.

Naitachal noted with a kind of reluctant admiration — in the way that one admires the efficiency of a poison, or the potency of a snake's venom — that Jehan had conveniently and convincingly accomplished both these deeds over a single evening. It would seem that *somebody* in the King's circle of confidants would take notice, but evidently nobody did. Or else — they were all in Jehan's pocket as well.

Do they know Sir Jehan patronizes the tavern district too? Perhaps not. The man is shrewd, to bring this off as far as he has. He planned all this from the beginning; my arrival was never more than a slight inconvenience. He's planning on my use of magic to save myself and Alaire. The question is, does he think his magicians are better than I am? Not only has he declared war on Althea, he's declared war on me.

He doubted Suinomen magicians were much of a challenge, at least the ones he'd seen already. Lyam said they dwelled in the Palace, but only Soren had appeared at this little meeting. Though Soren did seem like an incompetent, giving him a relic of Alaire's made Naitachal a little uneasy. *Even amateur magicians can go far with relics. . . .*

When Captain Lyam opened the door for them, he winked at Naitachal, ever so subtly.

Erik cleaned the room, as promised. However, one thing was *not* as Erik had promised. Alaire's things were gone. Not a single stitch of fabric remained which belonged to the lad. Naitachal tried not to look surprised.

Instead, he pretended as if nothing was missing.

"It doesn't seem to be much," Sir Jehan noted. "Which are his things, Ambassador?"

"This must be it," Captain Lyam said helpfully, picking up a saddlebag the elf didn't recognize. Inside were garments about Alaire's size, resembling what he had worn before. But they were not his; Naitachal was as sure of that as he was certain of his own name.

"A favorite piece of jewelry would be most beneficial," Soren said, his chest puffing out importantly. "Does he have any such thing?"

"But of course," Naitachal said. He reached for a smaller bag belonging to himself, made a pretense of searching, and pulled out a shiny silver ring with a human skull, a death's head with tiny rubies for eyes. "This was one of his most prized possessions."

"Charming, isn't it?" Soren said sarcastically to Sir Jehan, holding it up to the light. "But if it belonged to him, it will be most helpful."

Without so much as a thank you, Sir Jehan and Soren left. Captain Lyam stood with him for several moments, listening to their retreating footsteps. A moment or two later, when it was safe to talk, Lyam inspected the hallway briefly then closed the door.

"So when did you have time to replace Alaire's possessions with someone else's?" Naitachal asked, folding his arms over his chest. "I wish I'd known; I might have been able to do something useful."

"I didn't. Little Erik did. We can trust him, he's

working for me. If I had more time to warn you, it wouldn't have been necessary to give him that ring," Lyam said, his face grim. "As for your predicament, I can arrange safe passage on a ship for you and Alaire. It will have to be tonight, because tomorrow will be too late. They will have found the justification by then to put you in the dungeon with Kai."

The Dark Elf frowned. "I am more concerned with the state of affairs between Althea and Suinomen. If I leave, there will be war. My mission here was to prevent it."

Captain Lyam shook his head, and his expression grew even darker. "Your mission was doomed from the beginning. War with Althea is inevitable at this point, I'm afraid. Getting you two home is the only way King Reynard will know that Sir Jehan is behind this sad folly."

Naitachal let out his breath in a sigh. At least there was *one* person still in a position of power that was not Jehan's man. "Do you know where Alaire is?"

"No, but Kai does," Lyam replied confidently. "He'll tell me. And if you would like, I can recover that ring for you."

"Oh, don't bother. It wasn't Alaire's," Naitachal said, with a sly grin. "It belonged to my father. I do think the relic of a long-dead master Necromancer will muck up Soren's search spell in very interesting and entertaining ways. It will eventually find its way back to me, all by itself."

He leaned back, studying Captain Lyam closely without appearing to. *Can I trust this man?* he wondered. *Is there something peculiar about his total commitment to returning us to Althea, when he has everything to lose?*

"Why are you doing this, Captain?" the elf asked at last.

"You're wondering why I'm sacrificing everything." Lyam dropped his masks for the first time since Naitachal met him. He looked old; old, tired and defeated. "Well actually, I'm sacrificing very little. One of Sir Jehan's nephews is about to replace me as Captain. My next post is to be a remote wasteland in the north. It stays dark for months at a time, and it's not a place where anyone would ever go willingly. I'm ready for a career change and a change of climate. I would rather return to Althea with you, on the whole. If necessary, I could find work as a mercenary." He sighed. "I cannot save my King or my country. I might as well save myself."

"That I can accept," the elf said. "What about this blockade I've heard about from Erik? Will that be a problem?"

The Captain shook his head. "You forget who I am — however temporary my power may be. In the late hours, when they have the green recruits watching the port, I will have no trouble impressing them with my rank. We can get through with no trouble."

"And the ship," Naitachal persisted. "Is one ready to sail?"

"There is an Arachnean-owned ship, crewed by humans, that is due to leave in the morning. A trader, loaded with dieren goods." Lyam seemed to have thought of everything — there were few even in this kingdom who would care to interfere with the trade of Arachneans. "If you explained who you were, perhaps they would leave a little early."

Naitachal smiled grimly. "That shouldn't be difficult, given my heritage." Most traders would probably be ambivalent about the troubles of an Ambassador and a Prince, since most had more loyalty to their trade than to the Crown of Althea. But no one would risk the anger of a Dark Elf, since so many of them were Necromancers, and those that were not, were formidable warriors.

If they refuse to take us, I will be very, very angry. "If you can find out where Alaire is and get us as far as the port, you have a deal. I will get us the rest of the way."

"Deal," Lyam said. They shook on it.

The skies remained overcast, but didn't shed anymore snow on the already blanketed ground. At noon, and again at suppertime, Erik brought meals on the cart, bearing no new information to Naitachal. After dinner Lyam put a young recruit, a lad of about seventeen, on guard duty. The Captain said that he had been pulling double guard duty, and was likely to fall asleep around midnight. The Captain disappeared around dusk, to gain access to the dungeon and have a little talk with Kai.

Shortly after midnight, Erik appeared for the last time to take the food cart away.

"This time, you get to ride out inside it," he whispered. "You're leaving now. We know where Alaire is. Guard's asleep, but Cap'n Lyam said to take no chances. Put a bundle in the bed to look like you. I'm taking you down to the kitchen. This way no one sees you."

"Inside *this*?" Naitachal asked, regarding the cart doubtfully. He sighed and, taking only his sword and harp, squeezed into the cramped space of the cart. A tight fit, but manageable; Erik draped the cloth on either side, opened the door, and rolled him out.

The trek was uneventful until just before Erik pushed him onto the dumbwaiter; Naitachal recognized Paavo's voice, and they chattered in their native language, for some time. Then Paavo walked off, and Erik rolled the cart into the tiny elevator, and moments later he had descended to the brightness of the kitchen. Oil lamps illuminated the now cleaned and polished palace kitchen, empty of staff at this hour save for Erik and Captain Lyam.

"Hurry. This way," Lyam said, ushering the Dark Elf out the back door to a waiting carriage. Erik bundled up in a heavy dieren coat and a fur hat and jumped into the driver's seat, while Lyam tucked Naitachal's weapons under the seat, and threw a black cloth over him.

"With any luck, they won't see you. Duck down to the floor when I say," Lyam said urgently. "Not much going on this time of night. The most difficult part was getting to the kitchen. Did you have any trouble?"

How would I know what was trouble, unless it arrested me? "Paavo stopped Erik to talk about something. I don't think he knew what was going on."

"Dammit all," Lyam muttered. "That might have blown the whole thing." He leaned out the window. "Erik, let's go *now.*"

The carriage lurched forward, and Lyam told the elf to get down. "Best not to take any chances."

They traveled for a short distance before they stopped, presumably at the outer wall. Naitachal stayed close to the floor, flattening himself against it like a cat. Outside, he heard several voices, speaking the strange Suinomen dialect, to which Lyam responded. Then they were moving again.

"That was too easy," Captain Lyam said, his tone very uncomfortable. "I'm not sure if we should go on."

"What choice do we have?" Naitachal asked, from beneath his drapery. "I'm already gone. We're free of the palace. Is anyone pursuing us?"

He heard Lyam shift in his seat. "It may be difficult to tell. A professional is always hard to spot. But I suppose you are right, we are past the point of no return."

Naitachal squirmed uncomfortably. "Is it safe to sit up?"

"For now," Lyam said, and Naitachal got up off the floor and seated himself across from the Captain, rearranging his black drapery. "Perhaps their guard *was* down; after all, the Prince is back in the dungeon, and the real search is taking place in town. We will have to be careful once we get closer to the tavern district."

Trees quickly gave way to brick buildings, tile roofs, the rock walls of the larger estates, all towering over the carriage.

"So where is Alaire hiding?" Naitachal asked, curiously, wishing there were some way to ease the knot of tension in his back and neck.

Lyam rubbed an old scar nervously. "A place called The Dead Dragon Inn. The owner is hiding him in the basement. Kai did well, putting him there. The owner is a good friend and dislikes the Crown for the taxes they weigh against the taverns. With the Swords of the Association wandering about down there, that would be the safest place to hide."

Provided that the reward does not tempt him to regain some of the money gone in taxes, Naitachal added, but only to himself. *And provided that the owner is not aware that his "protector and friend" is currently languishing in the King's dungeon.*

Chapter XVI

Alaire emerged slowly from a deep, but restless, sleep. A confused and disturbing dream melted away as he became aware of his surroundings. First, the lumpy hay mattress, then the dank, musty odor of the room and finally the warmth and the humidity, and the sweat that had beaded on his forehead. He opened his eyes and tried to focus. The room was dark except for the orange glow of the stove.

He sat suddenly upright, banging his head on the bunk bed above him; the sudden pain forced more wakefulness into his stiff body, his slow, numb mind. *Where am I?* was his only thought.

Loud tavern sounds filtering down through the ceiling answered his question. *I'm under The Dead Dragon Inn. Kai brought me here.*

The room had no windows, which added to his confusion. Uncertain how long he'd slept, he didn't know if it was day or night.

What about Kai? he thought, with a sick suspicion that something terrible had happened to him. *And my Master. Naitachal, what are you up to right now?*

He felt exhausted despite the long, deep sleep. *The spell. Right. I've never reached that far, that deep for the energies before. Naitachal told me of mages who reached too far, even after years of experience, and scorched their own minds with energies too powerful for even them to handle.*

His raging headache was a good indication he'd done the same thing, on a smaller scale. *What should I expect? The spell turned back death. It reassembled flesh, it restored blood. Looks like my head is going to pay dearly for it now.*

He must have slept all day, and he was tempted to go ahead and sleep another day, but something told him it was time to get up, that something was afoot. *The Swords of the Association are all over the place by now,* he thought. *Would they ever think to look down here?*

Evidently, they hadn't yet. The sounds overhead, the singing, the stamping of feet, indicated the tavern was open and doing business, meaning it had to be night. He reached under the bed to make certain his harp was still there; it was, along with his other possessions. *Kai must have left as soon as I was asleep,* he thought. *Gallen must be upstairs working.* So that left him with one question. *What am I to do now?*

He remembered that Kai had warned him they had to destroy the old clothes as soon as possible, and groped under his bed for the bag that held them, finding it by touch alone. He tossed the canvas sack with the bloodied garments into the stove, then added more wood to it. In moments a raging fire burned, destroying the evidence. The wool clothing stank as it burned, but it was something he was going to have to put up with.

As the stove crackled and popped and the light increased, his eyes fell on a crude oak table, and the food left for him.

Well, they aren't taking too bad care of me, I guess. Though his head hurt, his stomach was in good shape, and complaining bitterly about how little he had been putting into it lately. The food they'd left him wasn't bad; a plate of meats, cheeses and a warm stein of ale.

There was also a kettle, a mug with dried herbs, and a rough note scribbled on a piece of parchment. He had to hold it up to the light of the now-blazing stove to make it out:

> *Alar,*
> *Ki sed you wood haf a baad hed wen you wok up,*
> *so i lef a mug o willow*
>
> > *Gallen*

Alaire read the note twice before he understood what the barkeep was trying to tell him. "A remedy, for exactly what I have now," he thought with gratitude, although the remedy sounded a little dubious. He set the kettle on the stove to heat up. "Willow bark," he said to the mug, without much conviction. "Right now I'd try anything."

Waiting for the water to boil, Alaire stretched and scratched. He felt grungy, particularly after sleeping in his clothes; a hot bath would be really nice right now. But the only hot bath he knew of was at the palace; it might as well have been in Althea.

Not bloody likely they'd let me get a bath if I went back to the palace now, he thought dismally. *Gods, a good long soak would be heavenly. Or maybe an hour in that sowna. Now that was a great bathing invention!*

A loud clatter came from up the staircase, followed by voices and footsteps. His heart leapt into his throat, and every nerve felt afire.

Oh gods — they've found me!

Alaire jumped to his feet and reached for his blade, and stood beside the entrance to the small chamber, in the shadows. A desperate measure; but that was all he had left, were desperation measures.

The group of three, he guessed by the footsteps, approached the chamber without talking. His heart was beating so hard he might just as well have been running.

Closer. Closer.

He now wished he hadn't thrown more wood on the fire, since the flames were climbing within the little stove, casting bright light, making it impossible to hide. He took cover in the little pool of shadow next to the bunk. The intruders drew nearer.

A shadow entered the room. No, not a shadow — the Dark Elf.

"Naitachal?" Alaire said incredulously, sword still raised and ready. His Master had been the last person he'd expected to see!

He relaxed until Lyam walked into the room, gripping the hilt of his sword tighter as the huge man's eyes met his.

"Lyam is on our side," the elf said simply. "However, there is a complication."

"Oh gods, what now?" Alaire asked although he didn't want to hear it.

"I'll be goin' back up, now," Gallen, the third person to come in, said. "You mind that tea, it will take care of that headache real quick. And I'll let you know when those chaps are through snooping around. The sooner you're out of here the better for all of us!" The barkeep trotted back up the stairs and shut the door.

"We won't be leaving right away," Lyam said, taking a seat on the edge of the bunk, looking as exhausted as Alaire felt. "There are a couple of Swords nosing around upstairs. More likely they're looking to cadge a few free drinks, but we can't take the chance that they might spot us."

"Swords?" Alaire said, alarmed. "Here?" He looked around frantically, half expecting the Swords to appear at any moment.

Naitachal laughed softly as he motioned to Alaire to

take a seat, and began an examination, first checking his eyes, and then feeling over his forehead and scalp. "Nasty bump there. Recent." He glanced over at the bunkbed Lyam was sitting on. "Didn't know where you were when you woke up? You sat up too fast?"

"You can tell all that by a bump?" Alaire replied, a little sullenly. "They should have you tell fortunes by bumps at court, I'm sure it would be very amusing."

Naitachal didn't seem annoyed by his attitude. "Nasty mood, too. You must have a headache, given the sort of spell-casting you've been up to."

It almost sounded like an accusation. Well, if he hadn't done what he'd done — they wouldn't be in this predicament. "I don't want to talk about it," Alaire said. "Kai would have died had I done nothing."

Naitachal shrugged. "I don't doubt that at all. I'd like you to tell me about it, if you would. It has a bearing on your ability, after all."

Slowly, Alaire told him the whole story of the assassins, Kai's fatal wound, and the Bardic Magic he raised to save his life. Naitachal listened quietly, nodding occasionally as he poured the hot water over the willow bark.

"Well. You certainly are a credit to my training," Naitachal said, handing him the steaming mug. "I would have shown you ways to protect yourself a little better, had I known you were that far along. As it was, you fully exposed your mind to everything you were pulling in, and that's the reason for your headache. I know exactly what it feels like. My head isn't that different from a human's. What you did was right, Alaire, even if it did create problems for the rest of us."

In a way, Naitachal's reaction made it all worse. "But I messed things up so badly!" Alaire wailed. "We were here to try to prevent a war. Now I've probably started one."

"Don't blame yourself, Alaire," Lyam said, trying to soothe him. "Sir Jehan had already made certain there would be a war before you ever arrived. You are not to blame. You simply became a convenient excuse for what he wanted to do anyway." Then he explained Sir Jehan's machinations.

But that left Alaire with a number of unanswered questions — one of which was very important.

"What about Kai?" Alaire asked, hesitantly. "They've got him now, don't they? What happened when he got to his father?"

Captain Lyam answered, not Naitachal; his face and voice completely expressionless. "He tried to explain what happened. Kai's word was against Jehan's; he had little credibility and his father, of course, didn't believe him. They put him in shackles and sent him to the dungeon. They charged him with treason, with conspiracy involving mages sent by Althea to overthrow his father."

"The *dungeon*?" Alaire said, his eyes darting back and forth between his Master's and the Captain's. "Now they're looking for me. It's me they want! We can't go off and leave Kai in prison!"

"And what do you propose we do?" Naitachal said softly. "We barely got out of there ourselves, and that was only because Captain Lyam was my jailer."

Alaire shook his head vehemently. "I don't care. We have to go back. Kai saved my life when he brought me down here."

"Which would make you about even, hmm?" Naitachal said shrewdly. "You saved his life, and put your own in jeopardy by performing magic; he saved yours by hiding you. The scales balance, in my opinion."

"There's nothing we can do, Alaire," Lyam said sadly. "Sir Jehan is just too powerful right now. He had the King eating out of his hands, and it would take a miracle to change that. If you go back to try to save Kai, and fail, do you know what will be waiting for you then?"

"Yes, I know," Alaire said sadly. "Prison of Souls."

"You do not want to go there," Lyam replied, emphatically. "Kai's fate won't be nearly as terrible. Trust me, his father will not deliver him to the usual fate of traitors. He'll probably be disowned and made into a slave, under Paavo. Slavery is the usual fate of those traitors who are not considered clever enough to be dangerous." He coughed, embarrassed. "Jehan will probably urge this very move on the King. He would obtain far more enjoyment out of seeing Kai shining his boots than swinging at the end of a rope."

Alaire could not imagine this.

"Kai will never serve anyone but himself," Naitachal said. "I've seen enough of the boy to make that prediction."

"But you're wrong," Alaire protested. "He's changed. No, really! He's not the same. When I brought him back, he saw how close he was to dying. Something happened to him, I'm not sure what." He groped after the words he needed to describe Kai's transformation, but failed to find them.

"Which is all moot, at this point," Naitachal said. "We can't go back. It would be the three of us against the entire Royal Guard and King's mages, and the Swords. We don't have a chance against them.

Alaire slumped, and put his head in his hands. "I guess you're right. But how do you plan on getting us out of *here*?" Alaire downed more of the tea, which helped his headache tremendously. "What's going to happen to you, Captain?"

"I am going with you, young man," Lyam said, wearily. "I've burned my bridges to get Naitachal here. They'll be offering a price for my head as soon as they realize I'm gone, and who I took with me." He scratched his chin, reflecting. "I hope they don't go too hard on that boy I put in charge of guarding you."

"I'm more concerned about Erik," Naitachal said. "They knew he was driving the carriage when we left."

"That's something I haven't told you yet," Lyam said reluctantly. "He's going with us too. You see, Erik's my son, in spite of the tale he spun for you about a teacher and the House of Lieslund. More like House of *Lyam*." He beamed proudly, despite his obvious worry. "Right now, he's leaving the carriage somewhere on the other side of the tavern district, to throw the Swords off, and will meet us at the dock."

Alaire looked up, surprised. "We're going by ship?"

"No other way," Naitachal said. "An Arachnean trader, by the looks of it. The problem will be getting to it. Sir Jehan sealed the docks."

"Speaking of which, shouldn't we be getting out of here?" Lyam said, standing, with a visible effort. "If we wait too long, my rank isn't going to carry much weight with anyone. I won't *have* a rank. Or a life."

Gallen came puffing back down the stairs, wiping sweat off his forehead. "Looks like the Swords are gone," Gallen said. "But I'd be careful. They went north, towards the palace."

"Good," Lyam said, loosening his sword in its sheathe. "We're going —"

"Don't tell me!" Gallen said, holding fingers in both ears. "I don't want to know. Now you three, you'd better get on before someone else comes looking for you."

"My thoughts exactly," Naitachal said, helping Alaire to his feet. "Are you ready?"

The movement renewed his headache, which pounded in both temples and put a tight band of pain across his brow. "As I'm going to be," he groaned in reply.

❀   ❀   ❀

They took the dark and half-hidden secondary alleys instead of the highly visible, lamplit streets. Lyam remained wary, leading the way with a drawn dagger, checking each shadow for a potential attacker. The snow had turned to a thick gray mush in the alleys. Alaire had gotten a little more accustomed to the slippery stuff in the short time he had been in Suinomen, and Naitachal, graceful as a cat, predictably had no problems with it at all.

Alaire couldn't stop thinking about Kai, and what was going to happen to him. He didn't believe Lyam's story about slavery; despite the elaborate explanation, he knew it was nothing more than a story to make him — and possibly even Lyam himself — feel better. Most likely the King would sentence him to die, given the circumstances. He doubted Lyam's motives in helping them. *There's something in this for him, and we don't know what it is yet.*

Still, Naitachal had always been a good judge of character. Granted that he probably had little choice in the people willing to help him escape from the palace, Alaire didn't think the Dark Elf would permit Lyam to join them if he had any doubts about the Captain's trustworthiness and veracity.

Kai was going back to try to clear me. Instead, they arrested him, and will probably execute him. And there isn't a thing I can do about it.

Logic told him there was no going back, that the only thing left for them to do was to return to Althea with what they'd learned. But Alaire found himself walking a little slower when he thought about the Prince and his fate, as if the palace was a magnet, drawing him back. *If I explained to Naitachal how I felt about this — Surely I can do something to help him! After all, I'm not what they think I am, my father is the King of Althea. Now that I think about it, Nai-tachal is technically my underling, not the other way around. If it actually came to that, if I put my foot down, pointed out that I was, after all, Althean roy-alty, would he back down and agree to rescue Kai?*

This was not something he really wanted to do, and not a course of action he took lightly. He watched Nai-tachal furtively as they passed through the alleys, and everything he saw in the elf's face told him he wanted to get home.

Not likely to work, Alaire thought. *I've never thrown my weight around like that before, and if I did now, it would create a rift between us that might never mend. If we return to Althea, I will still have to live with him. Or else find another Bardic Master. Right. Bardic Masters don't exactly grow on trees — and who would take me if I pulled rank on Naitachal? No one, that's who.*

The network of alleys took them out of the tavern district to a small residential district of peasant's homes. The place was definitely the poor side of town, complete with raw sewage in the gutters, piles of refuse beside the street, and large, hungry-looking rats; the likes of them strolling through this cesspool raised no eyebrows. A young gang of adolescents pre-tending to be rough threw some insults in their direction, but made no serious attack. Lyam ignored them, then laughed shortly as soon as they were out of earshot. "That might have been me, thirty years ago," he said, shaking his head reminiscently.

The smell of the sea became stronger, and Alaire knew they were closer to the bay. Lyam held a hand up, signaling danger. Without a word, the three of them took cover in the remains of a burned-out house. As they crouched behind the remains of a wall, ice-covered and ready to fall at a breath, two mounted dieren trotted down the main street, several paces away.

Swords. There was no mistaking those uniforms.

The two Swords, a larger, older one and a younger man, perhaps a student, pulled their dieren to a halt and looked around. Naitachal, Alaire and Lyam crouched even lower, keeping as still as possible. Their hiding place was not a good one. If the Swords looked closely they would probably see someone skulking there.

Lyam's left foot began slipping; to avoid falling, he shifted his weight to the other foot. In so doing, he inadvertently pulled it free of the mud and slush. The sucking sound was terribly loud in the still night air. Alaire cringed. He clutched the warming hilt of his sword so hard it hurt.

But the Swords just looked around, without paying any attention to the sound. Evidently they expected to hear things like that. After several long moments, the riders resumed their journey.

As soon as they were gone, Lyam motioned Alaire and Naitachal to come closer. They put their heads so closely together the steam of their breath mingled into a single plume. "We're not far from the dock. My men are closer to the piers. They're not likely to recognize you, but the Swords, if they happen by again, will. Be ready to hide." He checked the street, and declared the way clear.

Along the pier were a few noisy taverns, catering mainly to sailors. Not people who would know of the crisis in the palace, or care even if they heard. Until, of course, whatever the King did up the hill affected them, personally. *Perhaps the Arachnean sailors are here,* he thought. *If I listen, maybe I'll hear the right accent.*

But this was not the Captain's destination. Lyam led

them past these taverns to the edge of the pier, a long shelf of stone constructed along a rocky shore, with tongues of wood sticking out into the bay. Alaire stiffened when he saw the three Royal Guardsmen, standing casually at the end of the pier.

But then he realized that three men were not enough to patrol the area effectively — not if they were expected to look for fugitives. *Is this what they call sealing the port?* Alaire wondered. He had imagined legions of Royal Guardsmen on the alert, watching the pier, patrolling the side streets in numbers. But no, there were only the three, one of whom seemed to be half-asleep. *All the better for us,* Alaire thought. And for the first time, he began to have some confidence in the Captain's plan of escape.

Lyam led them to the pier boldly, as if he was escorting a couple of sightseers on an evening expedition. When the three guards saw Captain Lyam approaching, all three leaped to attention, the drowsy one visibly trying to feign alertness.

"At ease," Lyam said. The three young soldiers were clearly nervous. Apparently Lyam caught them doing something they shouldn't while on duty: relaxing. "Any sign of trouble tonight?"

"None, sir," the largest, and apparently eldest, reported. "The night has been quiet."

"Indeed," Lyam said thoughtfully. "Chances are, it will stay that way. The search for the renegade magician has concentrated in the tavern district. Reports of sightings have all come from there. Nevertheless, stay at your post until further notice. We are going to inspect the docks."

"Yes, sir," the soldiers said, in unison. Lyam and his party of two proceeded unhindered. It was that easy.

Under the full moon Alaire saw a long row of dark, lifeless ships moored to the wooden piers. Apparently their crews were down below, or in the taverns. *Must be later than I thought.*

"Erik should already be here," Lyam said, but worry was evident in his voice. Then, from a shadow beside them, sprung a small shape.

Erik grinned up at them, spirits undampened. "Here I am, Father," he said with his high-pitched voice. "The Arachnean ship is at the very end. It's a schooner, with a wooden lady up front."

His father smiled. "Very well, then," Lyam said. "Shall we proceed, gentlemen?"

Alaire should have felt exhilarated at this point, but something was keeping him from any such emotion. Partly, he thought, this was because Kai was doomed —

But partly he had a horrible feeling that something was wrong with this escape, that Lyam had overlooked something. The dock seemed impossibly long in the moonlight, but the sea was calm, with only a mild breeze in the air. Water lapped lightly against the dock.

In the bright moonlight he caught a glimpse of Naitachal, clutching his harp, his expression grim. Their eyes met briefly, and Alaire knew that he, too, felt impending doom. Alaire reached under his cloak and clutched the hilt of his blade again. It was still warm.

Then Naitachal stopped walking. Lyam looked back, with a questioning look. Alaire paused also, turning to see what, if anything, was following them.

"What's wrong?" Captain Lyam asked. "Did you hear something?"

"This isn't right," Naitachal replied in a whisper.

"*What* isn't right?" Lyam responded, impatiently.

Naitachal shook his head. "I don't know. A missing piece of this picture. Just a . . . strong sense that something's not quite right."

Lyam frowned, glanced down the dock, towards the ship, then back to Naitachal. "Would you like me to go on and hail the ship?"

Again, the Dark Elf shook his head. "No. Just stand here. Make no noise."

The four of them stood on the dock in perfect silence; Alaire studied the ships, all seemingly empty, abandoned.

Captain Lyam was impatient. "I don't hear anything," he said, clearly anxious to get going. "Our ship is near. I think we should go to it at once."

There is no sound. That's the problem, Alaire suddenly realized. There should be card playing, there should be drinking, there should be at least a watch. But all the decks were empty. There was not a sailor in sight. Even the lamps for the nightwatch were dark. *No one. Nothing.*

From one of the ships came a low, ominous laugh. All three drew their swords, on an enemy who hadn't made himself visible yet.

"Did you really think you were going to just sail out of here, without a problem?" came the unmistakable voice of Sir Jehan.

A moment later, Jehan stepped out of the shadows, onto the deck of the nearest ship, alone. "Ah. I see you've done me the favor of finding our young magician, Captain Lyam. Decided to turn traitor, did you?"

Lyam stood firm, his face set in a cold mask of anger. "Did you think you were going to maneuver the King into a war with Althea, with no one noticing?"

Sir Jehan didn't answer right away. For a moment he looked doubtful, unsure. The reply must have surprised him, because it was some time before he regained his composure.

"Why, war is the last thing I want with Althea," he replied, bowing sardonically to Naitachal. "However, we made it clear to the Ambassador that we would consider any attempt to leave the kingdom an act of war. I suspect this is exactly what the Ambassador has in mind right now."

"You do not consider keeping an Ambassador prisoner an act of war here?" Naitachal said evenly.

Jehan shrugged. "That was only a formality, until we clarified the situation. You made a big mistake by leaving the palace, Ambassador. By doing so you have implicated yourself in this sad state of affairs."

"It's not his fault," Lyam said. "I convinced him that he was in danger. For my own purposes, I assure you." Alaire blinked, surprised at that answer. The Captain was actually trying to protect them!

Jehan shook his head with mock-sadness. "I wish I believed that. I really do. Clearly, you have betrayed the King. But the Ambassador is responsible for his own actions. And as for *you*, Lyam, you have neither rank nor friends to protect you. You will hang for this."

Alaire scanned the dock for Sir Jehan's men. *No one. If we made a run for it now . . .*

Sir Jehan continued, his tone and posture completely casual, as if they were discussing some trivial matter over tea. "I must admit, Captain, that you have done the kingdom a service by rounding up both the Ambassador *and* his criminal servant. This will save us a great deal of time. Now, if you would be so kind as to drop your weapons, my men will escort you back to the castle."

"I don't think so," Lyam said, whispering something to his son. The boy took off running, and vanished over the edge of the dock without a sound.

"*Where* are *his men?*" Lyam whispered. Alaire was looking too — Sir Jehan wasn't planning to take them alone, was he?

Behind them, two Royal Guardsmen surfaced from

the ship's hold. Then two more, from the ship Sir Jehan stood upon.

"You make it difficult for yourselves," Sir Jehan said indifferently. Addressing his men, he waved in their general direction. "Take them," he said indifferently. "But don't kill them."

The two on Lyam's end charged, and the big Captain engaged them both, handily; Alaire charged the one that came for him, surprising him with his quick defense. Swords clashed in the moonlight; Alaire knew he had nothing to lose, and took chances he normally wouldn't have. The man he fought still valued his life, and was clearly under orders not to take one; Alaire took full advantage of this situation. A strange sort of excitement came over him, and he laughed recklessly, startling his opponent considerably.

He thrust once, twice, leaving himself vulnerable both times. In so doing, Alaire managed to slice the leather armor on his opponent's right arm. The pieces fell, and Alaire struck without thinking.

Blood spurted, forcing the wounded man to drop his sword. His first instinct was to kill the man —

No. Not another death! Instead, he rushed at the wounded Guard, and pushed him over the dock's edge. The Guard hit the water, with a scream and gratifying splash.

Alaire turned, only to find that already there were others to replace him, dozens more, pouring off the ships like hungry ants. The narrow dock limited how many came at him at once, and he fought each one as they came within reach.

It was a downhill battle, there was no mistaking it, and he began to loose some of his energy and reckless abandon. *Should I die now, or go to this thrice-damned Prison of Souls?*

The impulse was to die now; a clean death, and not

a slow wasting away, trapped by magic. He swung wildly with the sword, leaving his midsection open, then he swung again against three guardsmen, who all stepped backwards.

They collided with each other, suddenly leaving a space between two of them.

He seized the moment by shoving through them, screaming a hideous battle cry.

Before he reached the end of the dock, four more guardsmen stepped in front of him, bearing shields. The wild sword swing wouldn't work here. Behind them were three more, aiming at his chest with crossbows.

In his head a voice spoke, urging him, *wait until the odds are in your favor, then try for escape. Nobody ever won by dying.* He glanced wildly about, looking for an escape. There wasn't one.

Abruptly, his energy ran out, and he gave up, deflated. He threw his sword down on the dock, where it landed with a dull *thud.*

From behind him came two sets of arms, one wielding a dagger, placed near his throat. The metal bit into his windpipe. A sudden move, and it would cut into a major artery. For the moment, the desire to live overcame his fear of the Prison.

He dropped his arms to his sides and stopped moving.

Thick arms grabbed his wrists, pulling them behind his back. Shackles closed around them, and the cluster of guardsmen pushed him back up the dock, towards Naitachal. Lyam was nowhere in sight. Four Royal Guardsmen had surrounded Naitachal. With blinding speed the Dark Elf deflected the blades, giving no hint of backing down.

"It's useless to continue," Sir Jehan said lazily from his safe haven on the ship. "Look, we've captured your secretary. Give up, while he still lives."

At the far end of the dock, a score or more of Royal Guardsmen lined up, wielding a mixture of swords and crossbows. They charged Naitachal.

When the elf saw what was coming for him, he raised his hands, and closed his eyes.

The guardsmen saw this and froze, confused and afraid; they must have known what a Dark Elf was. Alaire struggled against the cold metal against his throat. A hand closed over his mouth.

He's going to raise Bardic Magic, Alaire thought, knowing that Naitachal was good enough to do so without needing an instrument. It hadn't occurred to him to do the same, before they shackled his hands; for him it took time and undisturbed concentration to raise any useful power, neither of which he had as the guardsmen attacked him. The instrument still hung at his back, but he had no way of using it.

The three holding Alaire pushed him closer to the elf, the knife biting into his neck, a sudden sting of pain, followed by the warm trickle of blood down his throat.

These idiots are going to kill me by accident if they don't watch out! he wanted to scream. *What is Naitachal trying to do? What sort of spell would get us out of this?*

But he hadn't begun the spell yet; hadn't even begun to sing a single note.

Sir Jehan seemed to recognize what the elf was about to do, however. "Stop what you're doing! Put your hands on your head! Or your servant will die right here on this dock!"

Eyes closed, lost in concentration, Naitachal stood motionless. The air about him began to hum.

"*Stop it, Necromancer!*"

His eyes fluttered open just long enough to see Alaire, with the knife at his throat. The elf paused, his black hand barely beginning to glow.

"On *second* thought," Sir Jehan said, smugly. "Go ahead and cast a spell. Raise the magic. Break our laws! It would give me a reason to throw you in the Prison of Souls along with Alaire!"

Alaire bit into his captor's hand, and in the moment it pulled away he screamed, *"No! Don't do it, Master!"* The knife cut deeper into his throat. More blood trickled down his neck. The hand closed over his mouth again.

The guards surrounded the Dark Elf with crossbows carefully aimed in his direction. He heard a scuffle, then rattling shackles. They hurried Alaire off the dock to a crude wagon. Bolted to the floor of this was a series of iron rings. They made him lie down, belly first, and his chains rattled as his captors locked his shackles into place. He looked up at the sound of a footstep, and saw Soren, the fat wizard, holding a little wooden club.

Powerless oaf can't even use a spell to immobilize me, he has to use fetters!

A brief discussion in the Suinomen tongue followed. Soren climbed onto the wagon and stood directly above him. Then, light and agonizing pain exploded at the base of Alaire's skull, and he knew no more.

Chapter XVII

"Stop it, Necromancer!" Sir Jehan screamed at the Dark Elf.

Naitachal's instinct was to ignore a command, any command, especially when trying to concentrate on raising magic. *Why should I?* he thought, torn between complying with the demand, and blasting Sir Jehan and his men into the sea with Bardic energy.

But this was Suinomen, and they were renegades, and now both he and Alaire were in serious danger. He opened his eyes and saw the Royal Guardsmen holding Alaire, with a dagger at his throat.

They had the boy. The game was over.

Defeat and despair settled over him as he accepted whatever fate Sir Jehan had for both of them. There was no way to raise enough power, even Bardic power, in time to do any of them any good. It looked like they'd even nicked the boy a bit already.

But he didn't drop the harp; he set it down, carefully, so as not to scratch it, and stood solemnly.

The guardsmen swarmed around him. Those who did not bring crossbows to bear on him shackled his hands and feet, and pushed him towards Sir Jehan. One of them picked up the harp, holding it gingerly, as if he thought it might come to life in his hands.

Naitachal stood calmly before Sir Jehan, who remained on the ship. He avoided meeting the elf's eyes. He threw his men a black cloth. "Blindfold him," he said simply.

He said nothing as they put the cloth over his face. *It's the King who I must speak with again. I have not used magic, though it is obvious Alaire has. If there's any chance I am immune diplomatically, somehow —*

The guardsmen shoved him forward. The rattle of a wagon or carriage pulled up in front of him, followed by the creaking of a steel door. They threw him into the back of whatever had arrived, and he landed in a heap on a cold, iron floor. *There's someone in here with me,* he sensed. Behind him, the door slammed shut, followed by the sound of a key turning a lock.

They started off immediately as the Dark Elf struggled to sit up in the lurching wagon. Strong hands assisted him, and when he was sitting against the wall, someone pulled the blindfold off his face.

"Lyam," Naitachal whispered. Even in the darkness of their moving prison, he saw the Captain's outline. There were windows on three sides of the iron box, which allowed moonlight, and cold, in.

"They took Alaire in another wagon," Lyam said dismally. "The Swords have him now. I think my son got away before the troops moved in. I can only hope." Lyam looked directly at the Dark Elf, his face full of apology. "I'm sorry I got you into this. I had no idea Sir Jehan was this clever."

"Nor I," Naitachal said. "I admit, we are running out of options. But as long as I still breathe, all is not lost."

Lyam's look was of disbelief. "No?" he said wearily, running a hand through grimy, tousled hair. His own shackles clanked loudly against his chest. "What options have we left?"

Naitachal glanced out the back of the wagon. A hundred or so Royal Guardsmen were following closely behind on dieren, a shifting, moving thundering shadow blanketing the road. "I don't suppose picking that lock would be very productive," he said.

"No," Lyam admitted. "I think someone might notice."

This would be amusing, if our deaths weren't imminent. "It seems odd they would shackle us, and then not chain us to something else."

"They know we can't go far with these," Lyam said. "Had no idea how heavy these were," he added, lifting the chains with some difficulty. "You were saying? Options?"

"I'm still the Ambassador of Althea," Naitachal said stubbornly. "That must count for something."

Lyam stared at him. His expression was for a moment unreadable. Then his face broke into a smile, followed by loud, bellowing laughter. "Oh *are* you now?" Lyam said, when he paused long enough to speak. "You've just been taken prisoner. You're wearing chains. Do you think it matters what your official office is in Althea? In Suinomen, you're a prisoner. And a non-human one, at that."

"And what bearing does being non-human have on this?"

Lyam grew serious. "These days, it means instant death, usually. Elves, fairies, dwarves, Arachnids, anyone who isn't human, simply are not taken prisoner. They are conveniently killed 'trying to escape.' That they haven't bothered to eliminate you already is a good sign, I suppose."

Naitachal leaned back against the side of the wagon and tried to think. "So what do you think is going to happen now? Any ideas?"

"Well, for starters," Lyam said, scratching his chin thoughtfully, "Alaire's on his way to the Prison of Souls. No doubt about that. He's been tried, convicted, and sentenced already, in his absence. And, let's see, I'll probably be executed. Hanging is the preferred method, although given the circumstances, Sir Jehan might arrange something a little more private in the dungeon. It will depend on the King's mood. As for Kai, I doubt he's still alive. He's probably already been executed."

Naitachal was amazed at the offhanded way the Captain discussed his impending demise. Then again, this man was no stranger to death.

"And your son?" the elf asked.

"No one in the palace knows he's my son. To them, he's just another servant child." He turned and gave Naitachal a threatening look. "And if you tell them he is, or it accidentally slips out of those black lips of yours, I'll personally kill you myself."

Naitachal shrugged, deciding not to take offense at the remark. "What I meant is, how can he help us?"

"Help? Against the Royal Guard or the Swords?" Lyam uttered a short, humorless laugh. "Not much, I'm afraid. He's only thirteen. The place we're going to is quite secure. But the boy has surprised me before. He might again."

They rode in silence for some time, the cold creeping into the wagon, chilling the elf to the bone. "This Prison of Souls. Has anyone ever broken the spell before?"

"The incarceration spell?" Lyam asked, and considered it. "There's no breaking it. Not before it wears off. It's been tried, believe me."

"By *Bardic* Magic?" Naitachal countered.

Lyam considered this carefully before answering. "To my knowledge, that has never been attempted. But then, Bards have never been allowed in Suinomen. They've always been turned back at the border."

Not this time. Perhaps we will have that chance to

try Bardic Magic, Naitachal thought, seeing a slight glimmer of hope in the situation. *No one knows that we are Bards; they think that I am a Necromancer and the boy is my apprentice. Their spells may not be ready for our power. Alaire has invoked the magic once already, when he brought Kai back. Can he do it again, to save his own hide?*

Can I?

Under armed escort, Naitachal and Lyam were introduced to their new quarters in the palace dungeon. The elf had expected dirt floors, but these were lined with stone and mortar, and had no furniture. In the center of their cell was a large iron loop, to which their shackles were padlocked. One of the guards adjusted his shackles so that he didn't have free movement of his hands. This was unfortunate, since the padlocks were simple, and easily picked if his arms hadn't been pulled so tightly behind him. *I still might be able to do something, though.*

The dungeon cells were built in a semi-circle, facing a group of guards stationed at a table. Naitachal counted four guards, with a fifth who went on a walking watch shortly after they arrived. They put Lyam in a cell opposite his, chaining him to the floor in the same fashion. The elf had hoped they would be close enough to assist each other out of the shackles, but this was not to be.

In the cell directly between the two Naitachal saw another prisoner.

"Prince!" Lyam exclaimed. "You're still here."

Kai was crestfallen when he saw who his two prisonmates were. "Aye, I'm here all right," he said, his words empty, without hope. "Since you're here that must mean Alaire's captured."

"I'm afraid so," Lyam said. "Sir Jehan had us

followed, I suspect. Something gave us away. At any rate, he was waiting for us at the docks. We didn't have a chance."

Kai turned his gaze on Naitachal, obviously dreading the next question. "Is Alaire in the Prison of Souls?"

Naitachal didn't know how to answer; Kai clearly cared far more for the bardling than the elf had expected. In fact, he was surprised. The Prince's own situation was grim, yet he was worried about Alaire. Kai moved closer, glancing at the table of guards, who had brought out flagons of wine and were playing cards. They were paying no attention to their prisoners.

Naitachal chose his words carefully. "I was blindfolded, so I didn't see what became of him. According to Lyam, the Swords took him. That's all we really know."

"You don't have to sweeten the answer for me. I know what's happened to him. And it's all my fault!" Tears welled in Kai's eyes, and a drop splashed on the rock floor. "He did it to save my life."

"Yes, he told me," Naitachal said simply. "But you mustn't blame yourself. Something like this was likely to happen to us, given the situation we walked into. If I'd known a fraction of what I have learned about Sir Jehan and his machinations, I would have asked my King to send someone a little more skilled in difficult diplomatic situations than I." *Or I would have asked him to send a practicing Necromancer; someone who would not have hesitated for a moment to strike these people dead with a single spell!*

"I wish I had acted sooner," Lyam said. "Sir Jehan had this entire plot in motion by the time I decided to do something."

"You *knew* this was about to happen?" Kai said,

incredulously. "Then why didn't you tell me?"

"I tried, a couple of times," Lyam said softly. "But you had other things to do. You didn't seem too concerned with the affairs of the kingdom at the time."

Crestfallen, Kai looked down, studying the floor. "I suppose you're right. I had no idea how selfish I was. Too busy getting drunk and fooling around with women. I should have seen it myself! How that man played me like a fine instrument, the same way he's playing my father. If only Father would come down. If he would listen to me! But it's too late for all of that."

Lyam looked like he was about to disagree, then apparently thought twice about it. "Perhaps it is," he conceded, his shoulders sagging with defeat.

A guard entered the dungeon, whispered something urgently to the four others. At once, they gathered up the cards and wine and stashed it all away in a hurry.

"What's going on over there?" Naitachal asked. *Maybe it's Sir Jehan coming down here to gloat. Or perhaps he wants one last wheedle for information on Althea before he executes us all.*

Two more guards, each wearing an elaborate uniform more suitable for the King's chambers, looked around the dungeon carefully before whispering to someone unseen in the outer corridor. Kai looked up from his sitting position, in time to see his father, King Archenomen, cautiously enter the dungeon.

Kai leaped to his feet, the chains rattling loudly around him. The boy opened his mouth to speak, but nothing came out.

Naitachal also got to his feet, as did Lyam.

No one spoke as the King approached the cells, his footsteps echoing loudly in the dungeon.

There was something peculiar about this visit. The guards who were "watching" them seemed rather disturbed that the King was present, while the King's personal guards glanced at them suspiciously.

Did they listen to us? Are the King's personal guards beginning to notice something wrong? Are they starting to see what Jehan is doing? Naitachal thought hopefully.

The King first went to Lyam's cell. "Sir Jehan claimed that you were trying to overthrow me by taking control of the guard," the King said, sounding a little surprised. "He also *denied* that he had taken you and the Ambassador prisoner. He said you were still at large. Yet, here you both are."

King Archenomen turned to look at the Ambassador. Naitachal bowed respectfully, but said nothing.

He turned back to Lyam. "What exactly is going on here, Captain?"

Lyam cleared his throat. "If I may speak freely, Your Majesty. Sir Jehan is conspiring to start a war with Althea. I suspect he may be plotting to overthrow you, in the confusion that such a war would engender."

The King shook his head, bewildered. Naitachal was beginning to feel confused, himself. There seemed to be two Archenomens, or possibly more! One was a simple-minded man who believed everything Jehan told him. One was a frightened child, cringing at every hint of magic. One was a shrewd ruler, and one a senile old man who could not remember what was happening from day to day. Which Archenomen was real? All of them? Or none?

Right now it seemed to be a combination of the simpleton and the child. "But that makes no sense, Lyam. He has everything he could want."

Lyam replied carefully. "No, Your Majesty, he does not. He doesn't have the throne. Kai was quite correct in saying that assassins were sent to kill him and Alaire; one struck a fatal blow to your son. Alaire raised magic in order to save his life. Kai was not trying to raise an army of wizards to defeat you. These were all clever stories by Sir Jehan to appeal to your fears, and to turn you against your son. I admit Kai has been less than responsible in the last several months, but he is far from being the traitor Sir Jehan would have you believe."

The King went to his son's cell, looked through the bars at him. Naitachal began to hope. There was more intelligence in the King's eyes than he had seen in a long time.

And he began to remember certain drugs that could befuddle even the wisest man. Had Jehan been drugging the King?

"Is this true, son?" the King said, softly.

Kai swallowed, but looked his father in the eye. "Yes, Father. Sir Jehan is the traitor. Look at what he's done so far. In a single evening he's assured a war with Althea, and discredited me in the process. I'm out of the way now." His voice dropped to a whisper, and he walked as far to his father as the chains would allow. "Who do you think is *next*?"

The King looked away, visibly disturbed by his son's words.

Kai continued. "I know that I haven't been much of a son. I am very sorry that I've humiliated you — this is unforgivable, I know. But please, give me another chance. I can make you proud of me. I *know* I can!"

The King gazed at his son fondly. Then, gradually, his face broke into a broad, toothy smile. "I know you can, too. This time, I think I believe you. For one thing, you don't reek of ale. That's a start."

The King stepped back from his son's cell, and addressed all three captives. "I don't know that Sir Jehan is a traitor. But it seems that you are in prison under less than legitimate pretenses. Until we resolve this matter, I think you should all be set free."

At last, he went to Naitachal. "Ambassador, I am embarrassed beyond measure by all of this! I had no idea you were to be imprisoned here. It was Sir Jehan's idea to confine you to the palace — not mine. I allowed him to persuade me you were plotting a war against us. I have just learned that the information regarding the Althean forces massing on our border is false, and it is beginning to look as if Sir Jehan fabricated the whole story. As long as I am King, there will be no war with your fine kingdom. You are free to leave and do as you wish. And I will see to it that your secretary is pardoned immediately."

Naitachal bowed graciously, watching the King's face. Yes, there definitely was more sense in the man's eyes. "I believe Alaire, my secretary, has been taken to the Prison of Souls. I suspect they may be in the process of incarcerating him as we speak."

The King's face flushed crimson with anger. "And I wasn't notified!" He turned to the guards, milling about by the corridor. "Why wasn't I notified? It is Sui-nomen Law!"

No answer came from the guards, who stared stupidly at the King, apparently at a complete loss of words.

"Release these three *immediately*!" The King roared. "Have them escorted to my chambers. We have a *very great deal* to talk about!"

At this fine example of royal rage, Naitachal expected the guards to leap into action. But the guards did nothing, averting their eyes; one began slithering towards the corridor.

The King marched over to the largest guard, his face directly in front of his. The guard looked terrified.

"Release these men immediately or I will personally skin you alive with a butter knife!"

The man gulped, looked down at his boots. "I would be most happy to, Your Majesty. But you see, we don't have the key. Sir Jehan does."

"He's lying!" Kai shrieked. "Sir Jehan was never down here. One of them has the key."

"Is this true?" the King said. "Do you have the key? I believe the rules require the attending jailer to have the key to all the cells. Which one of you has it?"

Naitachal had a sinking feeling that they wouldn't be leaving the cells for a while after all. *What kind of game are they playing with the King now? Are they that certain Sir Jehan has complete control of Suinomen, or are they under a spell, cast by Soren and his incompetents?* Naitachal studied the guards, now for the first time. Indeed they had a glassy, sort of dazed look, but then so did most of the natives here. He couldn't know for certain without closer observation — which didn't seem to be forthcoming, since the key was still "missing."

"I'll return with the keys to this horrid place," the King said. "I think I know where there are some spares kept."

He glared at the guards before leaving, and said, "You may even live to regret this." His two personal guards followed him out of the dungeon, into the corridor. Naitachal wondered if they would ever again see the King alive; now that he knew what Sir Jehan's intentions probably were, he would soon learn who was still loyal, and who wasn't. Whoever had the most men would win.

Shortly after the King left there was a brief, hushed conference among the remaining guards. Afterwards they all left except one, a small, frail man, who stayed at the table, eying Naitachal and Lyam nervously.

"This doesn't look good," Lyam said from his cell. "Those men have already turned against the King; one of them I'm sure had the keys. You know, Ambassador, if you wanted to work some magic to make that pitiful little guard over there come up with a way to let us out, I doubt very seriously the King would have you prosecuted."

"Good idea," Naitachal said, turning his eye on the remaining guard. "Come over here, little man. I would like to talk to you."

The guard yelled, "You'll be working no hellish magic on me!" and fled the dungeon. Naitachal heard his running steps fading down the corridor.

"Well, so much for that," Lyam said. "I guess we'll wait until the King returns."

"Or somebody else. I don't particularly like the idea of waiting. It might not be the King who returns first." Naitachal thought for a long moment. "Captain, are you certain there's no other way out of these cells? Some kingdoms have secret means of escape, should the rulers be imprisoned in their own dungeon by enemies."

Lyam exhaled his breath in a long, deep sigh. "That is a brilliant idea, but no, I'm afraid we never developed such exits in this dungeon. This palace is, however, over a thousand years old. There just might be —"

Before Captain Lyam finished the sentence, Naitachal became aware of a new presence in the dungeon. Lyam stopped speaking, evidently noticing the newcomer at the same time.

"You won't be going anywhere, traitor," Sir Jehan said as he came closer to their cells, Soren was close behind him, holding a wooden reed of some kind.

Does he know the King was here? Naitachal thought, as Kai looked in his direction. The Dark Elf gave him a warning look. *Don't say anything,* he mouthed, hoping the boy understood.

Jehan smiled. "With one exception, that is. You, Kai. You'll be joining your friend in the Association Hall now."

Soren stepped forward, went over to Naitachal's cell, and as if he was about to play the reed instrument, held it up to his lips. The sudden expulsion of breath launched something that pricked Naitachal in the leg; he looked down, and plucked the little dart from his flesh.

"What have you —" Naitachal began to say, but the paralysis of the drug the dart delivered was already having an effect. He crumpled like a wad of silk, his body folding over as if he had no bones left. He lay on the dungeon floor, spread uncomfortably across a length of chain, unable to move.

I suppose the drug will kill me next, he thought, with an amazing lack of emotion. But in a few moments it became evident that, at least for now, it would leave him very much alive. Whatever it was, its effect was new to him.

It seems that Jehan and Soren are quite the experimenters with drugs. This one — and one they use on the King? If it works the same on humans as it does on me, it must wear off periodically, as it did just now.

He tried, but found raising magic impossible; the drug had paralyzed his ability with complete effectiveness. Even the power of Necromancy was lost to him. He reached for the energy, the dark energies of death that once came so naturally to him, but found only a thick wall, blocking him. In the few moments before Soren hit him with the dart, he might have been capable of shielding himself. But a poisoned dart was the last thing he'd expected.

Bravo, Soren, he thought in frustration. *What do you do for an encore?*

Naitachal observed the goings-on in the dungeon

passively, completely helpless to intervene. Captain Lyam watched in equal frustration as the four guards entered after Sir Jehan, unlocked and entered Kai's cell, and seized the boy. The Prince flailed with the chains helplessly as the much larger men pulled him towards the corridor.

"As I expected. He's not going to cooperate," Sir Jehan said. "Soren, would you please do the honors?"

Without objection, Soren aimed, and fired a dart at Kai, which hit him in his right buttock. The boy yelped, spat back at Soren, and then collapsed in a fleshy puddle much as Naitachal had. The drug's effect was total. Kai lay there, eyes open, panting like a frightened puppy, but clearly unable to move.

The largest of the guards picked the boy up, flung him over a shoulder, shackles and all, and followed Soren and Sir Jehan out of the dungeon.

Chapter XVIII

When Alaire came to, wizards of the Association were lifting him out of the wagon and laying him on a small, flat cart. His first urge was to struggle, to try to get away, but his arms and legs wouldn't respond; in fact, he couldn't *feel* his arms and legs. All he could feel was his head, pounding. He could see and hear just fine, but saw only what was in front of his eyes, for he could not even move his head. As they wheeled him towards the Association Hall, he developed a sinking feeling why he was paralyzed, and how it had happened.

They've immobilized me with magic, Alaire thought, in panic. *Or with a drug. First they rapped me on the head so I would stay still long enough for them to perform the spell, or whatever they did.* The ball of fear in his stomach was cold and hard, like a ball of ice. *What are they going to do with me?*

They wheeled him into a great hall, brilliantly lit although he couldn't see the light source. Wizards leaned over him, their faces concealed by hoods. A half dozen of them picked him up, like a sack of roots. His head lolled backward, and from the skewed and upside-down perspective, he saw what surrounded him.

The entire hall was filled with wizards, each holding a red, lit candle. Another wizard was pouring a circle with white powder, perhaps salt, around Alaire and the group holding him. A strange monotonous chant began among the wizards, and grew in pitch and volume until the entire hall was chanting the strange Suinomen verse.

The box they laid him into was of oak, shallow and tapered, lined and padded with black silk. Altogether too much like a coffin for his sanity. He watched helplessly as they picked up what had to be the lid to the thing, unable to scream.

They dropped the lid over him, leaving him in total darkness. He couldn't feel anything, and the lid cut off sound as well as light. He was lost in a formless, shapeless darkness.

He couldn't even cry out in terror.

His fear was beyond anything he'd ever felt before; there was nothing left to him *but* fear.

They were going to rob him of his soul and store his body somewhere. They might already have done so! He had no way of telling. How long would he be in here? A year? Two? Forever? They had no reason to let him go; he was not a Suinomen citizen. Only Naitachal knew where he was, and they might kill the Dark Elf before he could get word home. He could be condemned to an eternity of this darkness —

Blackness became light. His body melted away completely, as if he were made of wax, and held over a flame. He had thought he could not feel anything — but now he realized there had been a feeling of weight, of solidity, and of connection. Now that was *gone*! There was no "Alaire" anymore, only a spark floating in the light.

And light became cold, deep, chilling cold. It was the cold of a thousand winters, of being frozen in ice, of freezing blood, of skin turning blue. It was a cold beyond numbness, but he could not shiver, for his body was elsewhere.

Now he was the ice itself, his new body an ice crystal, among several other ice crystals. He could see, after a fashion; a revelation that gave him no relief. Instead, to his horror, he realized that he was one of a row of crystals, lining a shelf, with other shelves before him and to either side. His "vision" through the crystal was fogged, unclear, blurred with tiny cracks and fissures. On his surface these were minute imperfections, and he was aware of every little flaw and blemish.

The terror ebbed, and as it faded, he tried to recall why he had been frightened. There was no reason to be frightened, was there? Not in Suinomen . . .

Why am I in Suinomen? he wondered, then. *I'm from . . . the south. Al . . . Althe . . . somewhere south. Somewhere else.* It didn't matter. Here mattered, and now. Right?

Distant recollections of a Dark Elf, a Bard, were somehow important to him in ways he could no longer remember.

If he could not remember them, then they weren't important. The elf faded in his memory to a dark blur, and vanished.

Father . . .

But the thoughts slipped away, like swiftly swimming fish, leaving behind only the biting cold and the vague awareness of being in a prison.

Prison of . . . what? Of where?

His identity continued to slip away in pieces, like falling shards of glass, until he could no longer recall his name.

Who am I? How did I come to be here?

What is here?

What is . . .

It was a moment later, and an eternity; it was both, and neither.

Fog shifting within ice, freezing over his soul. Drifting amid vague fears, vaguer longings, he no longer knew who he was, or what he was; captured in crystal, the soul sought memories, found nothing but ice and fog. Ice and fog, and a fear that hounded him and kept him restlessly searching for someone, something, while the ice urged him to sleep, to let it numb him to everything, to make him forget completely.

He needed help. For what, he did not know, only that he needed it. He tried to call for that help —

Then, piercing the stillness, a sound. A sound so sweet that it cut through the ice surrounding him, so pure it could only have come from the mouth of a goddess. The goddess called to him from across the ice, sounding in his mind from all directions.

She's singing to me, he thought with wonder, suddenly recognizing the *sound* as *song.* Thoughts became a little clearer. *Who is she?*

He turned his attention inward, away from the room of crystals and into the light. The light surrounded him, then broke into a delicate snowfall, falling around him with muffled softness.

The snow cleared, parted, like the parting of a thin white curtain. The goddess stood at the edge of a large lake, beside a tree that, despite the season, bloomed with tiny, white flowers. She wore a gown of white that flowed over her body in gentle folds, like a frozen fountain, and she sang a song of sweetness and power, calling to the birds and animals, gentle commands to do her bidding. As she raised her hands, the beasts surrounded her, ready to obey. The birds opened their beaks and joined her song with a hundred songs of their own.

A shaft of light suddenly illuminated him from above. She turned to him, smiled, and began singing directly to *him* again, this time calling a name.

"Alaire, my son," she sang, and he became confused, disoriented.

Son?

Alaire?

The light spread from him to her; it illuminated her clearly, and he saw that this was no goddess, but a mortal woman, older than he —

Mother?

She smiled. With that identification came other memories. And recognition; she was performing some kind of magic. Anxiety for her overcame him. She should not do this, magic was dangerous!

Is this why I'm here?

"You see who I am. Remember who you are," she sang. "Remember what you are, and sing yourself into being!"

What I am? he thought. He had a name, Alaire —

He had a mother. He must have had friends, companions. *The Dark Elf . . . he was a teacher, he helped me become what I am. What am I?*

"I will help you," she continued. "With music. With what brought you here. You will use your music to break free of this spell imprisoning you."

Imprisoning me? How was he imprisoned? He seemed free enough at the moment.

And yet, the dim memories that flitted just out of reach seemed to argue against that.

"*I will help you,*" she repeated. "I will help you remember. When you were an infant, there was a creek that flowed near our summer cottage in the mountains. You used to sing with it, gurgling like any baby, except that your baby-sounds were music —"

He saw the cottage, a rustic chalet on a ridge of hills, surrounded by fields of daisies and lavender. He wondered how the woman — *no, my mother* — was putting these things in his mind, and then saw these were *memories*, of things he actually experienced before, in another form. *I wasn't like this, then,* he thought. *I was a human, a baby barely able to walk.*

"Then when you were six, we brought you a lute, and then a harp, and you began to play in the palace nursery —"

He remembered more as the woman spoke. And as she talked to him, her story became a song, and then she was singing to him, about his past, his hopes, his aspirations.

"And then you met Gawaine, who told you about the magic that went with the music. And you began to learn what that magic could do."

He held tightly to the memories, the clear and perfect slices of his life that now sprang free of the light and cold that had stolen them. With every memory came the hints of more, and he used those hints to retrieve others, and his life began to take shape —

His mother's voice faltered, and she herself faded, until she was gone and her voice was a barely audible murmur, echoing in the distance.

Mother, no! Come back!

"Remember," she sang, a mere whisper of sound. *"Remember and sing. . . ."*

He struggled to retrieve the words and the music, and suddenly, he *did* remember singing. The song came from within him, vibrating against the prison of the crystal, surrounding him with light and warmth, and millions of memories. He sang as loud as he could, until the song roared against the walls that held him here. Cracks appeared, and then fissures; lancing through the cold light.

Pain lanced through him as well, pain such as he had never felt before. He knew he was destroying the crystal that held him — but he also knew that *this* was not his body, his real body was elsewhere, and he sang a song that would make soul and body whole again, ignoring the pain, singing through it.

Light and lightning vibrated around him, vibrated until he was all pain and sound, vibrating until his song reached a crescendo that was unbearable —

And he shattered.

In that moment, he was aware of each of the millions of shards of crystal that scattered through the room, their size, their shape, their velocity. It was as if his very *soul* had fragmented into all those pieces, each with a distinct set of eyes, and tiny chunks of himself were skittering hither and yon against rock, rafters and shelves containing other crystals.

Then, darkness.

Darkness, and a sense of weight, of *being*. Of arms and legs, of head and torso. The scent of wood and musty satin; the feeling of cloth beneath his fingertips.

He opened his eyes on darkness, and he knew he was back in the coffin again. But now he was no longer paralyzed, and he reached up with his hands and pushed the lid of the coffin up. The panel slid easily off, and clattered on the floor somewhere far beneath him.

Every muscle was stiff and sore, but he was perfectly able to sit up. He looked around the darkened room, seeing the vague outline of what appeared to be other coffins lined up on shelves.

Suddenly the enormity of what he had just done flooded over him. *He had broken the spell!* He was free!

Filled with elation, he felt all over his body, making sure it was real and not some kind of illusion.

It was real, solid, and indisputably *his*. He was even wearing the same clothes he'd been captured in.

Now what? he thought, half-drunk on his joy, and half still in terror that he might be cast back into the crystal at any moment. *Now — I get out of here!*

He crawled over the edge of the coffin and slowly let himself down to a cold, stone floor.

"Naitachal!" Lyam called over from his cell. "Can you move yet?"

It had seemed like several candlemarks since Soren's dart struck his leg, paralyzing him. The Dark Elf had succumbed to sleep for part of that time on the cold dungeon floor, a shifting, semi-wakefulness that came and went. But now the drug seemed to be fading; after a bit of experimentation, as his legs and arms flopped in crude approximations of what he wanted them to do, he gained control over himself again.

Slowly, he moved from his sprawled position on the floor, and just as slowly got to his feet.

Lyam had been spared the dart. Naitachal supposed that the purpose of the drug was to prevent him from using magic, and not to physically incapacitate him. He reached deep for the energies of his magic, to create the most rudimentary shields —

But there was still a strange, black wall preventing him from doing anything magical. Whatever was preventing him from using his power was not the drug.

"I can move," Naitachal said. "But I can't work any magic. What *was* that Soren used on me?"

"I don't know, but I think it's the same thing they used on Alaire before they hauled him away." Lyam clutched the bars desperately, his knuckles white. "You can't do *anything* magically?"

Naitachal shook his head. "Not yet. But the drug's wearing off. If I pretend I'm still incapacitated by it, they may forget to dose me again. As long as I'm able to move, I still might be able to do something. Any idea where they took Kai?"

"The Prison of Souls," Lyam said dismally. "It seems Sir Jehan is incarcerating anyone there who might be a threat to him, whether or not they've used magic."

No guards stood watch over them now; but down the long hallway, from somewhere within the palace, he could hear the distinct sounds of fighting. Shouting, screaming, the clash of metal and leather. The sounds were distant, mere echoes down the hallway. But unmistakable. The coup was in progress, and Jehan could spare no man to watch over them.

"There may be another way. Something I was going to look into, before we were interrupted," Naitachal said absently, trying to get to the cell door. But the chain pulled taut, stopping him before he could get within arm's length of it.

Fine, then, I'll look to that first!

He examined the padlock that fastened the chain to the floor. It seemed deceptively simple, but the key hole was curved, and narrow, nothing like he'd seen before. Though large and bulky, the mechanism inside didn't rattle around like the Althean locks Tich'ki had taught him to pick.

Fairies. You can't rely on them for anything.

He looked around for something that would work as a pick, and realized how much he relied on magic to get himself out of fixes like these.

But before the search for a pick got too far underway, a ruckus at the end of the hallway interrupted him. King Archenomen's voice bellowed out of the darkness at the end of the hall, followed by the clank and rattle of chains and shackles.

"How *dare* you imprison your King!" roared the King. "I'll have you all boiled in oil! Every last traitorous one of you! I'll have you skinned alive! I'll bury you in wasp nests! I'll see you wrapped in hot wires until you scream in agony and you're dead, dead, *DEAD!*"

Guards shoved King Archenomen into the dungeon. Shackled around the neck and wrists, the King struggled as three large guards pulled him along, like masters leading a reluctant dog at the end of a leash. His face was the color of overripe tomatoes. Stripped of his royal finery, he was now shivering half-naked in nothing more than a pair of breeches.

"Into the cell," one of the guards said indifferently. "King Jehan will be down presently."

The words sent Archenomen into a fit of rage. "*King? Jehan!* You'll die! All of you!"

They tossed the former King, sputtering and gurgling in incomprehensible monosyllables, into the cell Kai had occupied, and padlocked him to the floor like the rest of them. Then they turned and left, without a word.

Naitachal favored him with a sardonic smile, and despite the gravity of their situation, he could not resist getting a dig in. "Hard to find good help these days, isn't it, Your Majesty?"

Archenomen ignored him. He raged at the end of his chain like a maddened lion. "Where is Sir Jehan? Where is the traitor? Is he such a coward that he can no longer face the King he claimed he was willing to die for yesterday?"

Naitachal sadly shook his head. *He still doesn't understand, does he?* the elf thought dismally. *Was he so blinded by Jehan that he thinks none of this was planned?*

Down the hallway, he still heard sounds of fighting, although these were a little more subdued now. Apparently the capture of the King had taken some of the strength out of the battle. *How many are still loyal? How many are willing to keep fighting? How loyal are his men?*

How long do we have before we're executed?

Naitachal marveled at the expertise with which his magic-using abilities had been neutralized. Unbelievable. He had never before come across anything, spell or drug, that could have so thorough an effect. Lyam looked frantically from the Dark Elf to his King and back again.

The guards had left them in a hurry, apparently to return to the fighting. If only he could use his magic, or even pick the lock of his chains!

Archenomen sat, dejected, in the center of the cell. "Oh, what a fine mess this is! Lyam, you were right all along. I wouldn't have thought it possible before, but that murdering, oath-breaking blackguard is out for the Crown!"

Lyam squirmed over to the bars, as close to the King as he could manage. "Who does he have? How many? I can't believe my men have fallen in with him."

"*Your* men are the only ones who are staying loyal!" Archenomen said, despondently. "It's the bodyguards, the Swords of the Association, and some of the constables who are trying to take control. The Royal Guard are the only ones standing between Jehan and my throne!"

Were, Naitachal thought dryly. *Now that Jehan's troops have you, Archenomen, there is nothing standing between Jehan and the throne. But you don't seem to have figured that out yet.* "Have they taken prisoners?" Naitachal asked. "We seem to be the only ones in here."

Archenomen looked over at him with a face full of woe, and white as the snow outside the palace. "The only prisoners I've seen have been taken away, to the Association Hall. That seems to be their stronghold. Last I saw the traitors had run the guard out of the palace and cornered them in the guardhouse."

"These aren't the only dungeons," Lyam informed Naitachal, then turned his attention back to the King. "Tell me, Your Majesty, where are they putting the prisoners?"

Archenomen shook his head. "I think they're going to — to the Prison of Souls, if not now, then eventually."

Lyam groaned. "There's a network of catacombs under the hall, designed to confuse anyone who is not familiar with the layout. That is the Prison of Souls, Naitachal. There are also regular prison cells, where they could keep prisoners before actually stealing their souls and putting them in the crystals."

"They would have to be using every last one of their men to keep the Royal Guard at bay," Naitachal observed. "I doubt they have time or peace for any involved spell-casting."

"True. I suspect that when the battle is over then they will start imprisoning the souls of those they hold captive." Lyam shuddered. "All my men . . ."

Archenomen looked around, feverishly, as if suddenly noticing his son was gone. "Kainemonen? Where is he? Have they taken him away?"

"Yes, Your Majesty," Lyam said sadly. "I think I overheard them say they were taking him to the Association Hall."

"No!" Archenomen said. "They can't be thinking to —"

"I'm afraid they are," Naitachal said absently, his mind busy trying to see *some* way out of this. And wondering if there was anything left of his hapless apprentice. *Alaire? What has become of you? Are you even alive?*

The arrival of more guards in the dungeon interrupted his thoughts. Four of them, wielding loaded crossbows, covered four more who opened the cells, entered, and started unlocking the chains from the floor.

"I don't suppose this means were going to dinner?" Naitachal inquired innocently.

"Silence, prisoner!" one of the guards shouted. "No talking! You're needed elsewhere!"

Naitachal already knew where.

The Prison of Souls.

Chapter XIX

Alaire remained crouched on the cold, stone floor, listening for any signs of his captors. He groped for a weapon, but the mages had been thorough; they'd even taken his belt along with his little belt-knife. He listened with every fiber, but heard nothing but his pounding heart and his shallow breathing.

The room was as frigid as the pond in the garden, and his breath fogged before his face in the darkened room. A light source at the entrance cast a dim triangle on the floor; hard to tell what it was; perhaps an oil lamp, or a perhaps a candle. Flickering light made moving shadows all around him, the only movement in the room since he'd awakened.

Well, whatever is going on, they aren't going to come back for me right now, I guess. He relaxed a little, and straightened from his crouch. *Well, is everything intact? Have they hamstrung me, or anything? I wouldn't put it past them.*

But other than bruises and an aching head — and the fact that he was still stiff and cold — everything seemed to be in working order. His clothing was still intact, though he did wish it was black; that would have been useful for lurking in the shadows. The back of his head had a knot on it, his neck had a slight cut on it from the dagger at his throat, and there were some other slight injuries he didn't remember taking that were probably from the fight. If they had done anything else to him, he saw no indications of it.

The spell they had cast to take his soul, however, still fogged his mind. He felt as if he had awakened from a very deep sleep — as if, in fact, he still was not quite awake.

He vaguely recalled that his mother, Grania, had reached across the vast distances separating their kingdoms and had somehow broken the spell that kept his soul locked up in the crystal.

No, he corrected himself. *She didn't break it. She inspired me to break it! Mother, how in the name of heaven did you do that? And where are you now?*

He listened for her soft voice, waited for her gentle touch on his mind, but sensed nothing. She was gone now, as far away from him now as she had ever been. He felt somehow abandoned, and terribly alone.

Naitachal — Kai — Lyam — oh gods. What are they doing to you? Are you dead? Or have they turned you into crystals too? Panic and helplessness overcame him for a moment, bringing him close to tears. But tears would not help his friends, nor would they save him. He could not remain here forever.

First, I need to cover my tracks, he thought, glancing around the dark room, at the rows of shelves containing the coffins. Alaire shuddered at the reminder that a few moments ago he had been in one of them, destined to stay in it indefinitely while his soul was suspended in that strange state of numb notbeing. Far above, on another row of shelves, he saw the crystals, hundreds of them. Each one was about the size of his thumb, each in its own little wooden cubicle, suspended with wire.

The crystal seemed so much larger, when I was in it, he thought. When he took a few steps, his boot crunched on something. The floor was covered with broken crystal.

He took his booted foot and swept the remains of the crystal under one of the shelves. There were still some pieces left, but he had cleaned up enough to fool the casual observer. Next, he pulled his former coffin off the shelf and dragged it to a corner, where he slid it under one of the lower shelves, out of sight.

The next task was not one he looked forward to. He almost decided it wouldn't be necessary, but when he saw the big, gaping space his coffin had once occupied, he knew that if he didn't put something in its place someone would notice.

I must have raised enough magic getting out of that damned thing that I'm surprised nobody's noticed yet. Then again, someone might have, and they might even be on their way down right now.

He paused to listen for approaching footsteps, heard only the distant drip of water somewhere, and went about his task with tightly controlled fear.

These people are not dead, he reminded himself. *They're only sleeping. Under a spell.*

The coffin lids were fortunately not nailed on. He opened the first one on his right and peered in. The man looked like a poor vagrant, passed out from too much to drink. He wasn't breathing, but his skin was a good color, and while it was cool to Alaire's hesitant touch, it was not as icy cold as a corpse would be in this place.

But his soul is gone, he said to himself, and shuddered. *He doesn't look anything like me. Keep going.*

He replaced the lid and began a thorough search for someone who resembled himself. He came upon one poor soul who must have been about seventeen, with blond hair and a set of clothes that were a cut above poverty level. This boy had a much larger nose, and even larger ears, but other than that he looked vaguely like Alaire.

This one will have to do, Alaire decided, and replaced the lid, and then began dragging it towards the vacant space. With a great deal of difficulty he managed to lift the boy's coffin up to his former space and, panting and sweating, pushed it into place.

Now I've got to get out of here and find Kai!

For a dreadful moment he thought that his friend might have also been imprisoned here, before he remembered the Prison of Souls was only for magicians. And Kai was no magician. *He must be somewhere else.*

Alaire found a key ring, with four large keys on it, hanging on the wall beside the door. One of them opened the door to this very room, but he had no idea what the others matched. *They must go to something,* he thought. *Might come in handy.* He wrapped the keys in a scarf, to mute any sounds they might make rattling together, and stuffed them in his pocket. He entered the corridor just outside, and found himself at the juncture of three hallways, each leading off at odd angles. Candles flickered from sconces, providing dim illumination.

Wish I had a decent weapon. Those candleholders might be better than nothing, but not by much. He considered them, then rejected the idea. *No, I couldn't even pry them out of the wall.*

Since he had no idea of which way to go, he picked a corridor at random and headed away from his prison-room. The corridors twisted and turned at odd intervals, not really leading anywhere, and not revealing any new rooms or chambers. It was as if the corridors were an end unto themselves, a labyrinth with no clear entrances or exits. Dust on the floor indicated no foot traffic had come this way for quite a while. The footprints he left behind concerned him briefly, but he could see no other way, short of levitation, of avoiding them.

And Naitachal hasn't bothered to teach me that yet —

The first indication that he had made any progress out of the labyrinth was when he scented the most vile stench he'd had the misfortune to encounter. His first impression was that this was a decomposing corpse, laid to rest down here and forgotten. But there were other odors besides the stench, some of old food and stale wine, some of fresh food, and some he could not even identify.

Dead, yet alive. He was afraid to find out what this thing was, questioned whether or not he really needed to investigate it. *What can this smell possibly have to do with my escape from this place?*

On the other hand — where else could he go? Everything else so far had been a dead end.

As he moved forward, he heard voices from up ahead. The stench worsened, and his stomach churned. The voices became louder, clearer, and he was able to make out a few words among the echoes. And he recognized one of them.

Sir Jehan.

He stopped, tried to determine where exactly the voices were coming from. Finally, he got down on hands and knees and crept closer, peered carefully around the corner, saw that the corridor ended at a large, cavernous room. Candles and an occasional torch illuminated the area.

There were boxes and crates, bags and barrels piled everywhere. Shadow-shrouded shapes hinted at furniture stacked amid the confusion. There were plenty of places for concealment, and he took advantage of that. He found a niche between two large wooden crates, in an area that appeared to be a staging area for supplies, and crawled in, working his way towards the sound of the voices.

Eventually, he found himself peering out between two more crates at a thoroughly bizarre scene taking place in the center of the huge room.

Sir Jehan stood several paces away from — something. Whatever it was, it was not like any creature Alaire had ever seen before; shapeless and bloblike. Jehan's posture was one of deference, and Alaire guessed that Jehan was serving it in some way.

Interesting. He had never see Jehan act this way around the King; if anything, the man had acted as if he were the royal equal of King Archenomen, an attitude the King had never corrected while Alaire was around.

But here, Jehan was clearly the inferior. When he spoke, his voice was pitched much higher than normal, showing not only deference, but fear.

Alaire turned his attention to the creature Jehan was talking to. To call this a human, or even humanoid, would have taken a great leap of the imagination. The large, doughy blob of flesh sat directly on the floor, with a vague outline of legs at the bottom. There were stubby blobs that could have been arms near the top, waving and gesturing as it spoke. A large drapery — or maybe a tent had been hacked up to provide some modest clothing — covered it, more or less, though the drapery still left great flaps of bloated, diseased flesh exposed.

And it looked diseased. Whatever had infected the creature had spread all over it. Great raw pustules covered the body, oozing a thin, clear fluid that dripped down its sides and onto the floor. A pair of wings, distorted and bent, sat on its back, and oddly, they reminded Alaire of fairy's wings. But fairies never looked like *this*.

Could this have been a fairy at one time? Alaire wondered, transfixed by the creature, fascinated in spite of his repulsion. *What could have caused all this to happen?*

The longer he looked at it, the more he began to feel that this probably *had* been a fairy — once. A fairy gone horribly wrong —

The wings were what decided him. They were of that peculiar insectoid shape common among the fairy-folk, who could fly about like mosquitoes with little assistance from magic. Fairies were also shape- and size-changers, and could change their size from a hands-breadth to human height in the blink of an eye.

But whatever had caused this to happen must have made this size, and appearance, permanent. Who, or what, could ever choose to stay this way?

Jehan and his — master — were clearly arguing about something, and the words reached Alaire's ears slightly distorted by echoes, but mostly understandable.

"— would have thought that by now you would have had things under control," the bloated thing said. "After all these years of planning this, I expected it to go smoothly and quickly. But *no.* You're still fighting the King's men, even though you have the King in custody. Why are they resisting? What makes them think they can win? *Answer me.*"

Sir Jehan shifted from foot to foot uneasily, wringing his hands, timidly holding a single finger up as if to silence the creature. "The King, the Ambassador, the Captain of the guard, are all on their way over here as we speak. That twice-damned magician secretary of theirs is in the Prison of Souls now. His companion, the Prince, will soon join him! Prince Kainemonen is chained up in the extra cells on this level, awaiting incarceration in the matrix. These things take time, Queen Carlotta. Soon they will all be in the Prison of Souls, and the magical power there will be twice what it is now!"

The mention of the thing's name took Alaire aback. *Did Sir Jehan call it Carlotta? Where have I heard that name before — I know it's important, but I just can't quite place —*

"If the young magician is incarcerated there now, then why can't I feel *any* increase in power?" the bloated thing hissed. It attempted to fold its arms resolutely, but the clumsy attempt was more comical than regal. It lost its precarious balance and nearly teetered over. "In fact, I felt a *decrease* a moment ago. Are you sure you know what you're doing? Were you certain this was a magician?"

"Certain. And Soren swears he is a Bard, too."

The creature hissed again, turning several different colors with rage. "A Bard? I *hate* Bards! A Bard is responsible for doing *this* to me!"

Then it fell into place. *This is Carlotta, the sister of King Amber! Naitachal was part of the group that thwarted her plan to take the throne from her brother a long time ago, long before King Reynard. Kevin, the bardling, and Naitachal's student, performed the spell that unmade her human form and returned her to her fairy status. But that Unmaking didn't do this to her. There must be more to it than that.*

"Yes, I know," Sir Jehan said solemnly. "There is a surprise I've been saving for you. Perhaps it will please you to know that the Ambassador from Althea is none other than the Necromancer Dark Elf Naitachal! Soon he will be here, and you will be able to do with him what you will."

The blob was silent for several long moments. Then obscene, cackling laughter poured from the thing's mouth. "You jest!" Carlotta said. "Naitachal? Captured? *Here?*"

"Yes, he is," Sir Jehan said quickly. "I knew you'd be pleased."

"Indeed," Carlotta said. "But why didn't you tell me that before! Seven hells bedamned, you've withheld information from me again!"

"Oh, but it was only meant to be a little surprise," Sir Jehan said quickly, in a panic. "Certainly there was no harm."

"Perhaps not," Carlotta said, unable to keep the glee from her voice. "When will they be here? I must know."

"Momentarily," Sir Jehan said. "I sent my men over some time ago."

Carlotta let loose another peal of obscene laughter, and rocked back and forth on the enormous buttocks, waving her hands, cackling, like some kind of disgusting perversion of a nursery toy. Apparently, this substituted for jumping about for joy. The sight made Alaire's stomach churn, but he was too fascinated to look away.

"Ever since his bardling student Kevin un*made* me I've wanted to get even," she said, in a self-satisfied tone. "They turned me back into a fairy and all I could do was flee. They spoiled the very plan that would have made me Queen of Althea centuries ago. And ever since I've had to hide here. I'd almost forgotten Naitachal would still be alive. He would be the only survivor of that pathetic little group. And he's coming here. To see me. How wonderful!"

Sir Jehan was smiling and nodding, nervously glancing around himself as if looking for unseen intruders. Alaire crouched still further into the shadows, praying that he wouldn't be seen.

The blob continued. "You know, your grandfather

was not as stupid as you are. He knew a good deal when he saw it. He had the vision to form the Magicians' Association as soon as I suggested it to him. But perhaps that is only to be expected; he was, after all, a mage, and you have nothing in the way of magical abilities. You don't even know if you've really imprisoned a Bard in the matrix."

Jehan grimaced. "Of course he's a Bard! Soren guaranteed it!"

Carlotta snorted; it was not pretty. "What does that fat magician know about Bards anyway? He's never even *seen* one. Suinomen hasn't seen one since I had your grandfather prohibit them from entering the kingdom. How did this one get in, anyway?"

"He was in disguise, acting as Naitachal's secretary, and careful not to reveal his true nature. Soren has *assured* me he is indeed a Bard." Jehan folded his arms across his chest, and tried to look impressive. He failed.

Carlotta snarled at him. "You should certainly hope so. You and your little dog Soren, too. Mistakes are intolerable. Without my plan, you would be herding dieren, and this entire kingdom would be just the same backward barbarian bastion it was when I arrived."

"And a cunning plan it is, my Queen," Sir Jehan said ingratiatingly. "When Grandfather eliminated all the mages except the ones in the Association, you proved that we could manipulate the throne as we pleased. With your knowledge of drugs, we managed to cloud Archenomen's mind enough to make him turn against his own son. Now, we are only a half-step from gaining his Crown."

"And don't forget what this cunning plan was all about," Carlotta said, interrupting him. "I don't plan on looking like this forever!"

"Soren knows what he's doing," Sire Jehan soothed. "Once we capture the soul of Naitachal, after whatever torture you have in mind, of course, we will incarcerate him, the King, the Captain, and every other prisoner we have taken in the matrix. Even though they are not mages, you will still have a wealth of power to draw from. We can break the Unmaking spell this time, I promise."

Carlotta seemed to swell; she towered over Jehan, and Alaire saw then why Jehan was so terrified of her. She might be hideous, she might be rooted to one place physically, but it was obvious that her *power* could reach any corner of this kingdom. "Well, you had better. If I get any fatter or uglier as a result of these efforts, it will be *your* soul that pays. Each time that Soren cooks up a cure for this condition of mine it backfires! If it backfires *again* — "

"It won't!" Sir Jehan squeaked, cowering before her, clearly frightened out of his wits. "I promise."

"Now where have I heard *that* before!" Carlotta replied sardonically, but she shrank back down to her "normal" size with a sigh. "But now, with all the powers of the Necromancer and Bard, I think even that fraud Soren will be able to break the spell so that I can resume my human form and powers. Secular *and* magical!"

Jehan stroked his beard, nervously. "Only a stepping stone, my dear, only a stepping stone. A war with Althea is all but guaranteed. Now that King Archenomen is out of the way, we can blame his 'disappearance' on Althea's ambassador, Naitachal, and implicate King Reynard. That's all the justification we could ever need for a war. And when we conquer that southern land —"

"I haven't forgotten our deal," Carlotta said slyly. "You will be made King of Althea. Then we will share the spoils. But that's only if all, and I mean *all*, goes according to plan!"

Something about the way she had said that alerted Alaire. *She doesn't mean to keep her bargain*, he thought. *Not surprising. She always was treacherous. . . .*

"Your wish," Sir Jehan replied, bowing flamboyantly. "Is my command."

Alaire remained perfectly still in the shadows as the full implications of what he had just heard came home to him. *This is worse than I could have ever imagined! They're out for Althea, and it doesn't look like they'll stop until they have it.*

Jehan and Carlotta did not seem to be finished with their conversation, but Alaire had heard all he needed to. He carefully withdrew from his hiding place, and crept back to the corridor, in search of Kai.

Kai's got to be somewhere back here, he thought as he made his way down one of the halls. *They said he was on this same level. Where would they put prison cells?*

After a brief search through the labyrinth, Alaire found Kai. The corridor turned into a second-floor balcony overlooking a line of iron-barred prison cells. Kai was chained to the floor of one of these, while four guards stood watch. Two of the guards seemed ready to fall asleep on their feet; even so, the odds weren't very good. Alaire had no weapons, and even with a sword, two of these men would be too many to fight, especially if they trained under Captain Lyam. Looking down on the guards from his shadowy hiding place, Alaire considered ways to distract them.

I've got to get them away from Kai. Maybe one of these keys will let me into his cell. He peered at the chains binding Kai to the floor, saw the sturdy padlock there. *Good. So long as they didn't weld him to the spot, I might be able to free him.*

Kai sat sullenly near the front of the cell, the chains draped around him. He stared at his captors, the hate and anger on his face there for anyone to read. Clearly undefeated. Still in the game, and fighting.

Good. I'm going to need him to get both of us out of there, Alaire thought. *If I could create a diversion to lead some of those guards away, I might be able to get him out.*

Just as he thought that, the noise of fighting erupted down a corridor. Alaire couldn't tell if the echoes were contributing to the ruckus, but sounded as if hundreds of men were clashing down there. The guards started; Kai looked up, snarling.

Two of the guards ran off, heading for the conflict. The other two stayed, but they were clearly distracted. They conferred for a moment, then, before his amazed eyes, one of them opened Kai's cell, while his partner stood nervously outside, watching back in the direction the noise was coming from!

Alaire had no idea what the man thought he was about — perhaps he meant to move Kai to someplace more secure. It didn't matter. Kai was ready to snatch any opportunity, and he wasn't about to let this one pass.

He waited until the guard was within his reach — then leapt!

He flung a loop of his chain around the guard's neck, and pulled it tight. The guard outside had been looking down the corridor for that single vital second; before he could come to his companion's rescue, Alaire had already made his move.

He leapt down from his perch on the balcony, aiming for the guard's back, but knowing he was probably too far out of reach.

He was; he hit the floor far short of the guard, and rolled, coming up in a crouch.

Barehanded, of course. Facing a man with a sword, dagger, and armor.

Still, he had gotten the second guard's attention, all right. That gave Kai a fighting chance with his.

Bluff, fool! He doesn't know you aren't some kind of barehanded assassin!

He stretched his mouth in a rictus-grin that he hoped was frightening, and beckoned to the bewildered guard. "Come on, fool! Come dance with me! I *love* to dance!"

Kai had a good hold on the other guard, and was clinging to his back like a monkey. The guard thrashed about, flailing wildly with his sword, but he was unable to reach Kai, and he couldn't go beyond the chain wrapped around his neck.

The second guard glanced over his shoulder, and Alaire made an abortive movement to get the man's attention back on him. "Come *on*, you lily-livered bastard!" he snarled, gesturing with his hands. "What's the matter? You scared of a little boy?"

He was dancing a fine line, and he knew it; he had to keep his man distracted, but if the guard decided to attack him —

There was a clatter, a sword fell to the floor inside the cell. Alaire had a heartbeat to make a decision, and he opted for the chance to get his hands on a weapon.

He dove past his man, with his hands outstretched, flying just under the startled man's blade. He grabbed for the hilt of the fallen sword; caught it and rolled, then came up against the wall of the cell with a grunt of surprise. A moment later, he was up with the sword in his hands.

Two-on-one was unsportsmanlike, but this was not

a sporting event. As the first guard spun around, finally knocking Kai off his back, Alaire swung —

But not for the chest; he swung for the legs.

The man went down with a scream. Kai leapt on him and grabbed the hilt of the dagger at the guard's belt. Alaire ran for the door of the cell, and was met there by the second guard. Kai would have to deal with his man himself.

This time it was an even match, sword against sword. Even — except that this man was older and stronger than Alaire, and a trained fighter. Even — except that Alaire was not going to fight fair.

He feinted for the eyes, before the man had a chance to settle himself. The guard automatically winced back, and Alaire took a step toward him, clearing the door, swinging again at the man's legs, then feinting up at his eyes again. He gained another step. Now he was completely outside the cell.

Behind him he heard thrashing, but he dared not look back to see how Kai was doing. Kai would have to win or lose his battle on his own.

The second guard made a rush at him, and they closed. They struggled hand-to-hand and blade-to-blade for a moment.

Then Alaire let his legs collapse, and dropped into a back-somersault, catching the guard in the gut with his feet and flipping him over backwards, trying to roll his adversary into the bars and not into the open cell door.

The guard slammed into the bars; Alaire drove both feet into the man's belly, as hard as he could. The guard's eyes bulged out and his cheeks puffed with the impact.

Alaire rolled to the side, and came up on his feet. The guard was still down, but Alaire did not hesitate. He stabbed down, even though, at the back of his mind, a tiny portion of himself was stuffing hands into his mouth, horrified at what he was doing.

As he looked up from his bloody work, he saw that Kai had won his battle as well; the boy was rising from the guard's body, hand and knife dripping blood, face white as snow.

They exchanged a wordless, quick hug; then Alaire bent to the padlock holding Kai's chains to the floor.

The four keys still in Alaire's pocket did not unlock that padlock — and Alaire was forced to rifle the two bodies, looking for more keys. The sounds of fighting came nearer.

Finally, he found the key, carelessly thrust into a pocket. He fumbled with the padlock and the blood-slick key, and finally heard the welcome *click* of the mechanism opening.

He freed Kai of the chains on his ankles and right wrist, but left a single chain dangling from his left. It made a good weapon, and was one that could not be knocked from his hand.

Kai snatched up the dead guard's sword, and the two of them turned toward the sound of the fighting.

They exchanged a questioning glance, and Alaire finally spoke. "Whatever's bad for the Association is probably good for us," he said, and Kai nodded. They started for the entrance to the hallway —

When the sounds of fighting faded, and turned to cheers.

"And whatever's good for the Association is bad for us," Kai replied. "Let's get out of here!"

"Do you know the way out?" Alaire asked. Kai nodded, and pointed glumly towards the hallway.

Alaire cursed, and glanced around. There was a stairway to the balcony he had leapt from, and he grabbed Kai's elbow and dragged him towards it. "Come on!" he hissed. "I know a place to hide, at least!"

Back to Carlotta. Anything that happened would be reported directly to her — and anyone looking for Kai would be looking in the opposite direction of Carlotta's lair. Right now, hiding somewhere near her would probably be the safest place in the prison.

If there is any safe place here . . . for any of us.

Chapter XX

Just before they reached the lair, Alaire took a moment to pull Kai toward him and whisper some cautions into his ear.

"Whatever happens, whatever you see and hear, don't move or make a sound unless I do," he said, casting nervous glances up and down the hall. "We're going to hide out in a special room down here, where the real power behind the Association and Jehan lives. She's pretty awful, but she's kind of — a — a cripple. She can't move much, and even though she's a really nasty mage, she can't do anything to us unless she knows we're there. Got that?"

"I guess so," Kai whispered, his face mirroring his confusion. "Where she is, that's the last place anyone would look for us, right?"

"Right." Alaire took the lead again, half-running, his heart pounding, and expecting at any moment to encounter a guard or one of the Association mages. But they made it to the room without incident, and as Alaire made a quieting motion to Kai, and wormed his way into the maze of boxes, it dawned on him why Carlotta had chosen to live in a storage room —

Because it *wasn't* a storage room at all — it was a room full of the tangible relics of her power. Loot, in other words; valuable things she had probably had confiscated and brought to her. And like a dragon, she had piled up her treasures here, where she could look at them and gloat over them every day. Certainly there was no other way she could enjoy her power, except by having people brought down here to be killed. She could not move from this place, there was only so much food even a gross lump like Carlotta could eat in a day, and as for enjoying the kind of life — and lovers — she had enjoyed before the backlash of her attempts to break her Unmaking spell . . . well, Alaire doubted that there was anything in the universe that could be induced to find Carlotta's hulk tolerable, much less desirable.

Alaire found a place under a low couch where he and Kai could get a good view of the center of the lair without being seen. Kai started a little when he realized that the thing in the middle of the room was alive, and not some kind of grotesque and obscene statue, or a pile of garbage, but he made no sound.

They had not been in place for very long, when noises from another hallway indicated that the guards were bringing in prisoners of some kind. Alaire thought he was prepared for almost anything, but his heart stopped when he realized the three battered individuals being hauled before Carlotta were Naitachal, Lyam and the King.

That was too much for Kai; he gasped, and started to squirm out. Alaire had to grab him and haul him back, covering his mouth with one hand, and whispering urgently that all Kai could do at the moment would be to get himself killed. Finally Kai stopped struggling, and nodded, and Alaire took his hand away. Fortunately, the noise the prisoners and their guards had made more than covered the noises Kai had produced. By the time the two of them had settled once again, the prisoners were all arranged before the obscene bulk of the former half-fairy.

"Well, your Majesty," Carlotta said, her relatively pleasant voice something of a shock, coming out of her hideous body. "How kind of you to finally pay me a visit! I have been looking forward to this for some time. Tell me, how did you enjoy my little gifts to you?"

The King shook his head, puzzled. "G-gifts?" he faltered. "Who are you? What gifts?"

Carlotta's slit of a mouth stretched in what must have been a smile. "Why, my little cordial," she replied pleasantly. "And my little tonic. You remember. The cordial you shared every night with Sir Jehan, and the tonic you drank every morning on the advice of Mage Soren. They were both *so* beneficial to you." She attempted to cock her head to one side, a grotesque reflection of a flirtatious movement she must have used decades ago. "Of course, your son didn't find the results so pleasant, but you became so much more malleable to Jehan and Soren's suggestions. After a while, you wouldn't even listen to anyone else! I found that so *useful*, especially after trying to deal with that tiresome father of yours. He wouldn't accept anything of mine."

She pouted; another expression that must have looked very pretty on the Carlotta of aforetime, and looked so horrible on this monster that Alaire shuddered. The King was turning purple with suppressed anger, and Kai had gone quite white. Lyam only looked resigned, as if he had expected something of the sort. There was no visible effect of this revelation on Naitachal, but then, the Dark Elf had always been difficult to read.

Naitachal had been bound tightly, and gagged; Carlotta was taking no chances on his even *humming* anything, Alaire suspected.

"And Naitachal!" the creature said in a parody of sweetness. "How very pleasant to see you here! I confess, this was a benefit I had not even thought of, much less hoped for! I thought that I would have to seek you and Tich'ki out all by myself — once my conquest of Suinomen and Althea was complete, of course. It is a pity that you two are the last of my enemies still alive — although I suppose I can take a kind of belated revenge on my brother Amber by destroying his descendants. That dratted Kevin died childless, more's the pity. Although, in a way, *you* are both his child and the child of his Master." She regarded him thoughtfully. "So you became a Bard and renounced your former magics. The more fool *you*, Naitachal. You should know that the Dark Powers will always overcome the Light. To give up the greater power for the sake of the lesser is the act of an idiot —" She laughed. "And now I have stopped your lips, and removed your puny Bardic power from you. You are helpless, Naitachal. Think on *that* for a moment!"

But Naitachal didn't give anything up, Alaire thought, puzzled. *He must have told me a hundred times that you can't "give up" Necromancy, you can only stop practicing it. The knowledge and the power stay with you, whether you like it or not —*

But Carlotta had turned her attention to Lyam, ignoring Naitachal for the moment. "And Lyam, good, honest Lyam. You thought your spies were good ones. Did the King know you still kept your network of informers after he made Jehan his Spymaster? No? Why how remiss of you not to tell him!" She laughed. "But your spies never told you about me, did they? So perhaps —"

Alaire never had a chance to find out what that "perhaps" was all about — for at that moment,

Naitachal called upon the powers he had not used in a hundred years — powers that did not require the use of voice or hands.

The guard holding him gasped once.

In a single instant of time, the man's hair faded from black to white, his skin wrinkled and sagged, and he collapsed, falling, even as Alaire watched in numb horror, into ancient dust.

And Naitachal's eldritch eyes blazed, not blue, but red.

The bonds holding him parted with a *crack;* he pulled the gag from his mouth with one hand, and gestured with the other — and a sword suddenly appeared in it. A sword as black as night, that swallowed up all the light — and which, as Naitachal sliced into the torso of the guard behind him, laughed softly when it touched the man's flesh.

Naitachal did not deliver more than a scratch — and yet the guard collapsed in the boneless way of a man struck dead on the spot.

Gods. A Death Sword! Alaire had only that single moment of realization — because all seven hells were breaking loose at once.

Carlotta shrieked, and raised her stubby arms. The rest of the guards recognized the sorcerous origin — and power! — of Naitachal's weapon, and backed away frantically. Lyam and the King took advantage of their fear and confusion; Lyam bent over and butted the nearest of his captors in the stomach with his head, and the King slammed his considerable weight down on *his* jailer's foot, then cracked him in the jaw with a quickly raised knee when he bent over. In moments, they were free and armed, and squaring off against opponents.

Carlotta began lashing the crowd impartially with bolts of power, until Naitachal banished his Death Sword and stepped between her and her intended victims, his own hands upraised, and black energy pouring from them and forming a shield between Carlotta and the rest of her lair.

He's using his Necromantic powers to save us all — Powers Alaire knew Naitachal had hoped never to use again.

Powers that could claim him for their own, and this time, with no turning back. The Powers of Darkness were jealous masters, and both Naitachal and his bardling knew how narrow his escape from them had been. Invoking them now could mean an end to his cherished life as a Bard.

But there was no time to think about that. Kai was already halfway out of their hiding place, trying to get to his father's side to aid him, and Alaire could do nothing else but follow.

With Naitachal involved in holding off Carlotta, and thus effectively out of the fight, the guards had regained their courage and were trying to retake their prisoners. Alaire and Kai arrived none too soon. The King and Lyam fought back-to-back, surrounded on all sides by enemies. Jehan had singled out Lyam for his own target, and was proving to be no mean adversary. Kai fought to get to his father, with a single-minded ferocity that frightened Alaire, and a blood-thirstiness that astounded him.

All Alaire could think to do was to protect Naitachal's back from any of the guards who might think to come at him while his attention was on Carlotta. So he cut his way across the room, and stood defending his Master, doing his best to ignore the flying bolts of power, the dark smokes, and the licking flames of the magic raging between them.

Then, just as he fended off yet another attacker, Carlotta sent a lance of power, not at Naitachal — but at Archenomen.

And in deflecting that unexpected side-attack, Naitachal's own defenses slipped. Quick as a striking snake, Carlotta let off another bolt of power, that penetrated his shields and struck him squarely in the chest.

Naitachal fell without a sound. Alaire then did the bravest thing he had ever done in his life.

He stepped between Carlotta and his fallen Master, heart in his mouth, fear screaming along every nerve, ready to defend the Dark Elf with his life.

Carlotta took one look at him, and laughed.

She made a single brushing motion, as if shooing away a fly. Alaire found himself sailing across the room, slamming into the wall so hard he saw stars, and every bit of breath was driven from his body. He slid down the wall, helpless, gasping for breath, tears of anger and frustration springing from his eyes.

"Oh, Naitachal!" Carlotta laughed, her shrill voice clearly audible over the clash of swords. "You complete *fool*! You have been away from the Dark Powers for too long! I am the Master here! I shall slay you, just as I will slay your friends, just as I slew that cretin, that oh-so-holy, ever-so-noble vapor-brained White Elf Eliathanis —"

Only Alaire saw what happened then. Naitachal *had* been broken, defeated, until the moment Carlotta spoke the name of the White Elf who had been his friend. And in that moment — Naitachal became unrecognizable.

His eyes blazed up again, and went from fiery red, to lightless black. He rose up, his face a mask that Alaire shrunk back from in terror. And before Carlotta could react, he crossed the room in a single bound —

And with a terrible, backhanded blow to her face, knocked her over backwards.

She lay on her back, tiny arms and legs flailing in

the air in what would have been a funny sight, if Naitachal's unhuman expression had not sucked any touch
of humor from the entire situation. And while Carlotta
lay at his feet in stunned and helpless shock, he took a
step backwards —

— and began to sing.

But Alaire knew from the first note that this was no
ordinary working of Bardic Magic. In fact, no other
Bard in the history of the world could have produced
this blood-chilling melody. For this was an unholy
melding of Bardic and Necromantic Magics, a Song of
Unmaking that was so terrible, and so powerful, that
Alaire cringed against the wall and stopped his ears
with his fingers, weeping at the despair and fear it
engendered in him.

Nor was he alone. No one else could stand against
that song. Several of the guards gave up completely,
and fled the scene before they were overcome. Lyam
had just enough time to knock Jehan to the floor,
unconscious, before he too had to back away with his
hands over his ears. Kai and his father clung together,
tears streaming down their cheeks with the pain the
song invoked in them.

And Carlotta began to scream.

Horribly, Naitachal took that scream and incorpo-
rated it into his song.

Alaire hid his face, unable to look, once the screaming began. It sounded as if every pain Carlotta had
ever inflicted was being delivered back to her, three-
fold. He hoped he would never be able to remember
this moment — this eternity. It was worse than the
spell that held his soul in the crystal, infinitely worse.
All he could do was to remember the song that his
mother Grania had sung to him, and the song he had
made of it; he clung to that song while the other went
on and on —

And finally, ceased.

He looked up in the sudden silence. There was no sign of Carlotta, and no sign that she had ever been there, except for the tentlike garment that had covered her, now lying limply on the floor.

Naitachal turned.

He gestured, and the Death Sword was in his hand again. And the inhuman expression on his face had not changed.

He doesn't know us — Alaire thought, fear forcing him to his feet again. *He doesn't remember us! The Dark Powers have taken him for their own again, just as he feared! He's going to kill us all!*

He had thought that stepping between Carlotta and Naitachal was the bravest thing he would ever do in his life. He discovered that there was one thing braver.

He stepped between Naitachal and the rest of the room.

And as the Dark Elf's eyes focused on him, and the hand holding the Death Sword rose, he began to sing.

He started with the song of himself, but this time, he concentrated on all the things that Naitachal had meant to him, how much the elf had taught him. All the moments they had shared, laughter and sadness, defeat and achievement. As Naitachal's Song had been one of Unmaking, this was a Song of Making.

Naitachal paused. His eyes changed, going from black, to a sullen red.

Alaire continued, pouring his soul into the song, now calling on his memory for everything he had ever heard or read of Naitachal's life as a Bard — from Kevin's time, to Gawaine's, to this very moment. Reminding him how important Life and Light were to him — and how trivial Death and Darkness were in the face of Light and Life.

He sang friendship, he sang hope, he sang joy. And

then, greatly daring, he sang of Eliathanis, whose sac-
rifice had saved Naitachal so long ago — whose name
had roused Naitachal to his deadly rage. He sang of all
that the White Elves believed in. And he told Naitachal, with his music, that Eliathanis would have
perished in vain, if Naitachal returned now to the
Dark he had rejected.

Slowly, the man that Alaire knew and respected
came back to Naitachal's face — and the eyes faded
from red to deep and vital blue again.

But as Naitachal blinked, and looked down at the
sword in his hand, his expression turned soul-sick and
filled with repugnance for what he had done. With an
oath, he cast the Death Sword from him, and it disin-
tegrated in mid-air.

Time froze for an instant. Lyam, the King and Kai
stared at the Dark Elf with fear and horror in their
eyes. Those few guards that remained tried to crawl
away.

Alaire did not consciously decide what to do at that
moment. He saw only the agony in his friend's eyes,
and he acted on it, with sure and certain instinct.

He walked across the room to Naitachal, looked up
into his Master's eyes, and placed one hand trustingly
on his arm. "Master," he said, calmly, and simply, "you
yourself have taught me that there is a time for making
and unmaking. There was no other choice."

The fear faded from Lyam's eyes, and Kai's. The
Captain sheathed his sword, the movement drawing
Naitachal's gaze to where he stood.

The Captain nodded, then said, gruffly, "Sometimes the only weapon you have is one you hope you
never have to use. It happens. You move on, and try to
make up for whatever you did, using that weapon."

Naitachal regarded him gravely for a moment, then,
slowly, nodded. "I cannot bring back those I slew," he

said, "but at least *she* will no longer be working her will on the unsuspecting."

He turned to the King, and bowed gravely. "The power that moved against you is no more, Majesty, and the back of the revolt has been broken. What is your will?"

Archenomen blinked, as if astonished that this creature of Power should ask *him* for *his* will. Then he drew himself up to his full height, put one arm around his son, and took on a dignity and power that Alaire had never seen him possess before. And only then did he realize how much of a shell the Archenomen he and Naitachal had seen had been.

"I think," Archenomen said, weighing his words carefully, "that we all must go and rebuild what Jehan and his mistress have tried to destroy."

Naitachal sank down into a chair, feeling bone-weary and sick to his soul. The last of the Association mages had been brought to him for disposition — *him*! As if he was any less guilty than they! They had been only too happy to tell their stories of corruption under Jehan's leadership; the tale of their duplicity was more than enough to finish the Association and all it stood for. There would be no more Association regulating mages in Suinomen, and no Swords to enforce their will.

There had been a single moment of mild amusement, when the King's guards had brought Soren before him. The chief of the King's mages had been blubbering with fear, and *not* because of Naitachal! No, he had been holding the ring he had taken at arms' length, terrified of it, and yet more afraid to put it down. When he had seen Naitachal, he had been incoherent with gratitude, and had pulled free of the grip of his captors to fall at Naitachal's feet.

"Please, *please* take this b-b-blasted ring back!" he had sobbed. "In the name of the gods, *please*! It's — I've —"

Naitachal never did learn what it was that the ring had done to Soren, but the man had practically been incontinent with fear of it. He had plucked it out of Soren's nerveless fingers, while the man babbled gratitude, and pledged to reveal anything Naitachal wanted revealed. . . .

Now he turned the ring over and over in his hands. His father's ring, the ring of a Necromancer.

Like me . . . like me . . .

How could he live with himself, now? More importantly, how could he ever trust himself again? And if he could not trust himself, how could anyone trust *him*?

He stared into the ruby eyes of the skull; they seemed to wink at him with sardonic amusement. *See,* they seemed to say, *your father was right, all along.*

"Naitachal?"

The familiar voice broke into his despondent musings, and he looked up. Alaire stood beside him, harp in hand, Naitachal's harp tucked under his arm.

"Master," the boy said, with grave formality, "would you come with me for a moment? I really need your help with something."

More mages cowering under their bunks, most like, Naitachal thought glumly — but it was something to do, something constructive.

Not destructive.

He followed Alaire, listlessly, out of the Association Hall and back down into the labyrinth below it. *Odd,* he thought, as wooden walls gave way to rock, and the air grew chill. *I thought we'd rooted all the mages out of these tunnels. And there weren't that many down here to begin with —*

But Alaire led him deeper and deeper into the maze, until at last they came to a place where he had not yet been.

Alaire opened a door, and icy air rolled out to greet them. Something else rolled out to greet them — a wave of power the likes of which he had never felt before. He stepped inside, and Naitachal followed, all his senses suddenly on the alert.

The room was lit only by the lantern outside the door — and the dim, white glow of the hexagonal crystals that ringed the upper part of it. Row after row of them, ensconced in little niches. And below the crystals, row after row of — coffins?

He realized at that moment where they were — and what this was.

"The Prison of Souls," he whispered.

These were the stolen souls of all the hapless victims the Association had taken.

"Master," Alaire said softly, "we have all tried to break the spell holding these people prisoner. Everyone from Soren on down — singly and all together. Carlotta was the only one who knew how to break it. I could free myself, because I knew myself, but I can't free them."

He moved so that he could look directly, and challengingly, into Naitachal's eyes. "You are a *Master* Bard," he said forthrightly. "You have all the power and experience that we don't. You will have to help me — and them."

It was not a request — it was a demand. And a rightful demand. He had already pledged this, in a sense; what Carlotta had done, he must take a certain responsibility for.

He opened himself to the power of the room, and sensed the pain of all the imprisoned souls there. But instead of being *excited* by it, as any "good" Necromancer would have been —

— as my father would have been —

— it brought tears, *real* tears to his eyes. All the despair — all the lost hope! The tears he so seldom shed burned down his cheeks, and as Alaire told him quickly and concisely how the boy had freed himself, he listened, then reached eagerly for the harp he had thought he was not worthy to touch again.

Alaire put it into his hands, and he sat down on a stone bench, resting it against his chest like a lover. And it felt right there; not heavy and unnatural, as the Death Sword had felt, but warm and welcoming.

Yes. Yes.

He considered his options, reached for his power — and began a song combining both making — restoring those held prisoner to what they had been — and unmaking — melting away the crystals that held them prisoner.

He lost himself in the song; this time the unmaking blended in a bittersweet harmony with the power of making. He sang until he grew hoarse, and his hands, exhausted, faltered on the strings.

But then a younger, stronger voice joined his, and Alaire's smaller harp took up the melody, supporting the notes of his instrument.

And together, at last, they broke the spell.

The icy crystals melted away, leaving only the bare walls.

He opened his eyes, and saw that while they had been singing here, the room had filled with people, men and women, of all ranks and classes. And as those people ran to the opening coffins, and began to help those who had been imprisoned within the boxes to their feet, he realized that these must be the friends and relatives of all those who had been brought to this terrible place.

They crowded the room, taking a moment to touch

his hand in gratitude, to smile tremulously, or to drop a word of thanks. There was as much joy in this room now as there had been despair —

No. There is more!

The room warmed with it, until it seemed to be no longer a prison, but a pair of warm hands, cupping them all.

The joy filled him, and he closed his eyes again, opening himself to it, letting it wash away his sickness of heart.

Finally, they were alone again. But the joy was not gone; it remained with him still, filling the bleak place where his Necromantic power had lived and festered for so long.

"You see, Master?" Alaire said as he opened his eyes on the empty room. "You aren't what you were. You're more than the old Necromancer now "— then the boy grinned, impudently — "and I even think you're more than Naitachal the Bard, who was afraid to make use of half his power!"

Naitachal had to smile, still suffused with the joy he had found, and he cuffed his former apprentice playfully. "And who made you so wise of a sudden, Bard Alaire?"

"Oh, I just —" Alaire did a double-take that was so comic that Naitachal laughed aloud. "*Bard* Alaire?" he exclaimed, astonishment choking off his voice.

Naitachal clapped him on the shoulder. "Anyone who can face me down in a killing rage and remind me of what *I* am is more than worthy to be called Bard," he said. "And I will say that to anyone's face."

As Alaire beamed in delight, Naitachal looked around, feeling a lightness of spirit that he had not expected ever to have again. "I think we have both been changed profoundly by this place, young friend."

Alaire shrugged, shyly. "You're still a Master, and

still *my* Master, no matter what. But — you know, I would really like to go home now."

Naitachal sighed happily, thinking of his house, his garden, the view of the stars from his little tower. "Yes," he said with content. "Home. What a *good* sound that word has. Musical . . ."

"Musical?" Alaire grinned widely. "Why Naitachal, do I hear a *song* coming on?"

"Another? Dear gods, boy, will you have me play my fingers to the bone?" Naitachal exclaimed, and made to cuff him again. Alaire ducked and laughed.

"I think it can wait, oh noble Master," the boy said, standing up, and taking both their instruments, like the apprentice he was no longer. "But there are a lot of people who would like to thank you properly. *Then* you can make your song. After we *are* home."

"Indeed," Naitachal replied, with serene happiness. "All things in their time. That is a *properly* elven attitude. I think I might have taught you something after all!"

And together they left the Prison, to greet the newly freed mages.

GRAND ADVENTURE
IN GAME-BASED UNIVERSES

With these exciting novels set
in bestselling game universes,
Baen brings you synchronicity at its
best. We believe that familiarity with
either the novel or the game will
intensify enjoyment of the other.
All novels are the only authorized
fiction based on these games and
are published by permission.

THE BARD'S TALE™
Join the Dark Elf Naitachal and his apprentices in
bardic magic as they explore the mysteries of the
world of The Bard's Tale.

Castle of Deception
by Mercedes Lackey & Josepha Sherman
72125-9 * 320 pages * $5.99 _____

Fortress of Frost and Fire
by Mercedes Lackey & Ru Emerson
72162-3 * 304 pages * $5.99 _____

Prison of Souls
by Mercedes Lackey & Mark Shepherd
72193-3 * 352 pages * $5.99 _____

And watch for **Gates of Chaos** by Josepha Sherman
coming in May 1994!

WING COMMANDER™

The computer game which supplies the background world for these novels is a current all-time bestseller. Fly with the best the Confederation of Earth has to offer against the ferocious catlike alien Kilrathi!

Freedom Flight by Mercedes Lackey & Ellen Guon
72145-3 * 304 pages * $4.99 _____

End Run
by Christopher Stasheff & William R. Forstchen
72200-X * 320 pages * $4.99 _____

Fleet Action by William R. Forstchen
72211-5 * 368 pages * $4.99 _____

STARFIRE™

See this strategy game come to explosive life in these grand space adventures!

Insurrection by David Weber & Steve White
72024-4 * 416 pages * $4.99 _____

Crusade by David Weber & Steve White
72111-9 * 432 pages * $4.99 _____

If not available at your local bookstore, fill out this coupon and send a check or money order for the combined cover prices to Baen Books, Dept. BA, P.O. Box 1403, Riverdale, NY 10471.

NAME:_____

ADDRESS: _____

_____

I have enclosed a check or money order in the amount of $_____.

MERCEDES LACKEY:
Hot! Hot! Hot!

Whether it's elves at the racetrack, bards battling evil mages or brainships fighting planet pirates, Mercedes Lackey is always compelling, always fun, always a great read. Complete your collection today!

Urban Fantasies

Knight of Ghost and Shadows (with Ellen Guon),
69885-0, 352 pp., $4.99 ☐

Summoned to Tourney (with Ellen Guon), 72122-4,
304 pp., $4.99 ☐

SERRAted Edge Series

Born to Run (with Larry Dixon), 72110-0, 336 pp., $4.99 ☐

Wheels of Fire (with Mark Shepherd), 72138-0,
384 pp., $4.99 ☐

When the Bough Breaks (with Holly Lisle),
320 pp., $4.99 ☐

High Fantasy

Bardic Voices: The Lark and the Wren, 72099-6,
496 pp., $5.99 ☐

Other Fantasies by Mercedes Lackey

Reap the Whirlwind (with C.J. Cherryh), 69846-X,
288 pp., $4.99 ☐
Part of the Sword of Knowledge series.

Castle of Deception (with Josepha Sherman),
320 pp., $5.99 ☐
Based on the bestselling computer game, *The Bard's Tale.*℠

Science Fiction

The Ship Who Searched (with Anne McCaffrey), 72129-1,
320 pp., $5.99 ☐
The Ship Who Sang is not alone!

Wing Commander: Freedom Flight (with Ellen Guon),
72145-3, 304 pp., $4.99 ☐
Based on the bestselling computer game, *Wing Commander.*℠

Available at your local bookstore. If not, fill out this coupon and send a check or money order for the cover price to Baen Books, Dept. BA, P.O. Box 1403, Riverdale, NY 10471.

Name: _____

Address: _____

I have enclosed a check or money order in the amount of $_____

THE BEST OF THE BEST

For *anyone* who reads science fiction, this is an absolutely indispensable book. Since 1953, the annual Hugo Awards presented at the World Science Fiction Convention have been as coveted by SF writers as is the Oscar in the motion picture field—and SF fans recognize it as a certain indicator of quality in science fiction. Now the members of the World Science Fiction Convention— the people who *award* the Hugos—select the best of the best: *The Super Hugos*! Included in this volume are stories by such SF legends as Arthur C. Clarke, Isaac Asimov, Larry Niven, Clifford D. Simak, Harlan Ellison, Daniel Keyes, Anne McCaffrey and more. Presented and with an introduction by Charles Sheffield. This essential volume also includes a complete listing of all the Hugo winners to date in all categories and breakdowns and analyses of the voting in all categories, including the novel category.

And don't miss *The New Hugo Winners Volume I* (all the Hugo winning stories for the years 1983–1985) and *The New Hugo Winners Volume II* (all the Hugo winning stories for the years 1986–1988), both presented by Isaac Asimov.

"World Science Fiction Convention" and "Hugo Award" are service marks of the World Science Fiction Society, an unicorporated literary society.

The Super Hugos • 72135-6 • 432 pp. • $4.99 ☐
The New Hugo Winners Volume I • 72081-3 • 320 pp. • $4.50 ☐
The New Hugo Winners Volume II • 72103-8 • 384 pp. • $4.99 ☐

Available at your local bookstore. If not, fill out this coupon and send a check or money order for the cover price to Baen Books, Dept. BA, P.O. Box 1403, Riverdale, NY 10471.

NAME: _____

ADDRESS: _____

_____

I have enclosed a check or money order in the amount of $_____

PRAISE FOR
LOIS MCMASTER BUJOLD

What the critics say:

The Warrior's Apprentice: "Now here's a fun romp through the spaceways—not so much a space opera as space ballet.... it has all the 'right stuff.' A lot of thought and thoughtfulness stand behind the all-too-human characters. Enjoy this one, and look forward to the next." —Dean Lambe, *SF Reviews*

"The pace is breathless, the characterization thoughtful and emotionally powerful, and the author's narrative technique and command of language compelling. Highly recommended." —*Booklist*

Brothers in Arms: "... she gives it a geniune depth of character, while reveling in the wild turnings of her tale.... Bujold is as audacious as her favorite hero, and as brilliantly (if sneakily) successful." —*Locus*

"Miles Vorkosigan is such a great character that I'll read anything Lois wants to write about him.... a book to re-read on cold rainy days." —Robert Coulson, *Comics Buyer's Guide*

Borders of Infinity: "Bujold's series hero Miles Vorkosigan may be a lord by birth and an admiral by rank, but a bone disease that has left him hobbled and in frequent pain has sensitized him to the suffering of outcasts in his very hierarchical era.... Playing off Miles's reserve and cleverness, Bujold draws outrageous and outlandish foils to color her high-minded adventures." —*Publishers Weekly*

Falling Free: "In *Falling Free* Lois McMaster Bujold has written her fourth straight superb novel.... How to break down a talent like Bujold's into analyzable components? Best not to try. Best to say 'Read, or you will be missing something extraordinary.'" —Roland Green, *Chicago Sun-Times*

The Vor Game: "The chronicles of Miles Vorkosigan are far too witty to be literary junk food, but they rouse the kind of craving that makes popcorn magically vanish during a double feature." —Faren Miller, *Locus*

MORE PRAISE FOR
LOIS MCMASTER BUJOLD

What the readers say:

"My copy of *Shards of Honor* is falling apart I've reread it so often.... I'll read whatever you write. You've certainly proved yourself a grand storyteller."
—Liesl Kolbe, Colorado Springs, CO

"I experience the stories of Miles Vorkosigan as almost viscerally uplifting.... But certainly, even the weightiest theme would have less impact than a cinder on snow were it not for a rousing good story, and good storytelling with it. This is the second thing I want to thank you for.... I suppose if you boiled down all I've said to its simplest expression, it would be that I immensely enjoy and admire your work. I submit that, as literature, your work raises the overall level of the science fiction genre, and spiritually, your work cannot avoid positively influencing all who read it."
—Glen Stonebraker, Gaithersburg, MD

" 'The Mountains of Mourning' [in *Borders of Infinity*] was one of the best-crafted, and simply best, works I'd ever read. When I finished it, I immediately turned back to the beginning and read it again, and I can't remember the last time I did that."
—Betsy Bizot, Lisle, IL

"I can only hope that you will continue to write, so that I can continue to read (and of course buy) your books, for they make me laugh and cry and think ... rare indeed."
—Steven Knott, Major, USAF

What do you say?

Send me these books!

Shards of Honor • 72087-2 • $4.99 ____
The Warrior's Apprentice • 72066-X • $4.50 ____
Ethan of Athos • 65604-X • $4.99 ____
Falling Free • 65398-9 • $4.99 ____
Brothers in Arms • 69799-4 • $4.99 ____
Borders of Infinity • 69841-9 • $4.99 ____
The Vor Game • 72014-7 • $4.99 ____
Barrayar • 72083-X • $4.99 ____

Lois McMaster Bujold:
Only from Baen Books

If these books are not available at your local bookstore, just check your choices above, fill out this coupon and send a check or money order for the cover price to Baen Books, Dept. BA, P.O. Box 1403, Riverdale, NY 10471.

NAME: _____

ADDRESS: _____

_____

I have enclosed a check or money order in the amount of $ _____.